MAYBE

EUGENE·FRANCIS-WILLIAMS

© **Eugene Francis-Williams, 2019**

Eugene Francis-Williams has asserted his right to be identified as the author of this Work in accordance with the Copyright, Designs and Patents Act 1988.

All rights reserved.

No part of this publication may be reproduced, stored in a retrieval system, or transmitted in any form or by any means, electronic, mechanical, photocopying, recording or otherwise, without the prior permission of the copyright owner.

Email: maybeeugene@yahoo.com

For Dot

Acknowledgements

The author would like to thank the following people for their help in turning the idea into a reality.

Mrs. Burdett, Mrs. Rees, the Doctors Jones, his sons, Mrs. Hatton, Mr. Boyesen, Eleri, Ms. Emerson, Mr. Keegan and a very special thanks to Mr. Wilson.

Table of Contents

Part 1

Chapter 1 1
Chapter 2 9
Chapter 3 15
Chapter 4 19
Chapter 5 29
Chapter 6 33
Chapter 7 39
Chapter 8 41
Chapter 9 45
Chapter 10 57
Chapter 11 61
Chapter 12 69
Chapter 13 73
Chapter 14 79
Chapter 15 83
Chapter 16 87
Chapter 17 91
Chapter 18 97
Chapter 19 105
Chapter 20 115
Chapter 21 119

Chapter 22 123

Chapter 23 129

Chapter 24 133

Chapter 25 137

Chapter 26 143

Chapter 27 149

Chapter 28 155

Part 2

Chapter 1 169

Chapter 2 177

Chapter 3 185

Chapter 4 189

Chapter 5 197

Chapter 6 203

Chapter 7 209

Chapter 8 221

Chapter 9 229

Chapter 10 237

Chapter 11 239

Chapter 12 243

Chapter 13 253

Chapter 14 259

Chapter 15 261

Chapter 16 263

Chapter 17 269

Chapter 18..273
Chapter 19..285
Chapter 20..291
Chapter 21..299
Chapter 22..301
Chapter 23..305
Chapter 24..311
Chapter 25..317
Chapter 26..319
Chapter 27..327
Chapter 28..331

Part 3

Chapter 1..343
Chapter 2..349
Chapter 3..357
Chapter 4..361
Chapter 5..365
Chapter 6..377
Chapter 7..383
Chapter 8..387
Chapter 9..391
Chapter 10..395
Chapter 11..401
Chapter 12..405
Chapter 13..409

Chapter 14 411
Chapter 15 427
Chapter 16 441
Chapter 17 447
Chapter 18 455
Chapter 19 457
Chapter 20 461
Chapter 21 469
Chapter 22 471
Chapter 23 477
Chapter 24 481
Chapter 25 483
Chapter 26 493
Chapter 27 501
Chapter 28 505
Chapter 29 513
Chapter 30 515
Chapter 31 519
Chapter 32 521
Chapter 33 523
Chapter 34 529
Chapter 35 531
Chapter 36 537
Chapter 37 547

Part 1

Chapter 1

They were in the bedroom

I heard the bed there too,

I shouted loudly "FIRE!"

The only thing to do.

Finger came from bottle,

He hurtled to my bed,

Said he, "well where's the fire?"

Said I, "inside my head."

Guessing Angelo's thoughts at age 6. 1950.

Blame is a friend that hasn't got your best interests at heart. An unhealthy procedure for the giver and getter both, curdles your thoughts like sour milk and drives the real reasons for what you do deep and distant. Blame shovels coal onto the boiler of excuses, makes you believe that the false is true. But if you're taught the difference between right and wrong and make that a part of your character then blame never enters your thought processes, it's bypassed because it's unnecessary.

The truth just stares you in the face and you get on and deal with the problem. Stan had this attribute. He didn't blame anyone for what happened to him when those bombs rained down like gigantic shouts, ripping the fabric of his London flat apart in the time that became known as 'The Blitz.'

He was just nineteen, a little mentally challenged - 'tup' was the expression where he came from. He'd moved down from a farming community in the north west to work on the underground railway system, following in his Uncle Theo's footsteps. With the war raging, manpower was short but requirements for getting the job were still stringent, one of which was being able to recite the layout of the entire network, from east to west and north to south, a bit like the 'knowledge' of the taxicab drivers. Stan had found this such an arduous task that he'd almost packed it all in and gone back home, but Uncle Theo had spent long nights with him, turning the station names dotted along the lines into stories and Stan managed to learn it all like that, just by remembering interesting stories.

When he'd completed his training and faultlessly named the stops with that symbolism, the bombing began to intensify. The Blitz, fifty-seven consecutive days of aerial bombardment both day and night, had begun, tearing and burning the infrastructure of the great city. Twenty-one days later, on September 28th, 1940, Stan was making his way home. Yet again, the sirens cranked to a hum and then a wail and he broke into a run, confident he could make it back to his flat, grab the sleeping bag and thin mattress and return to the underground, his place of work by day, shelter by night.

Usually, there was a lifesaving time gap before the bombs began falling but on this particular night the fliers must have been expert at avoiding detection. Stan was a short and chubby individual. As he bounded up the concrete steps, cursing the fact that his flat was one of two at the very top, he was sweating and gasping for breath. Yanking the key out of his pocket he fumbled it into the lock. As the door closed behind him and he hurriedly scooped up his overnight things he heard a sound, like a cotton rag being torn, deep within his ears. A split second later the cold air seemed to be sucked out from every inch of that room only to immediately return with a force and heat that pushed him against the wall. Before he had a chance to cover his ears the explosion erupted, popping and pinging them like a bell.

It was as if the building had been punched by some enormous fist.

Everything freestanding in the room jumped then crashed down in unison, ceiling lights swayed wildly and the eight square panels of the only window shattered. The bones in his legs turned to jelly and he slithered down onto the floor, eyes darting around the room, ridiculously thanking God that he had putty to fix those windows. This absurd thought evaporated when the cloth ripped again and another ear piercing clap of thunder made him howl. Another bomb had detonated. He thrust himself forward, poleaxed by the sudden realisation that he was about to die. Stan lay tight and stiffened. The whole world had become silent and he popped his lips to check if his ears were functioning.

He listened hard then relaxed a little, closed his eyes. They'd gone. He began to breathe quickly and deeply to get some control back. After a short while he lowered his head backwards to the floor, feeling lucky to be alive, but he still had to get out of there. As Stan began to stand he became aware of a distant purring, like some enormous machine was coming to life. The purring turned into a vibrating buzz then an almighty thrum. The bombers had looped after completing their first run and were heading back for a second.

There were no preliminaries this time as the third one slammed in, shaking the building's very foundations, causing it to sway and heave like a beaten boxer. He forced himself off the floor and bolted for the front door, desperate to get out, only to find it solidly wedged from the outside. No matter how much he pushed and pulled, kicked and shoulder barged it, that door could have been nailed shut. He turned and was making a dash for the bedroom as the fourth came in. The oscillation actually twisting him off his feet and once again he hit the floor, winded by the impact. Stan forced his chest up, gulping air, not realising that the acrid odour making him gag was acetone from the bomb's cordite propellant.

He could hear people outside in wild panic, screaming, and frightened children bawling. The grinding drone of the warplanes like a guttural flatness. His heart was hammering and the speed of the blood racing through his head was fogging his vision. Adrenaline pumped and saturated every pore of his body, overloading and leaking out like a squeezed sponge. He was alone, trapped and terrified, convinced that at any second his apartment and the whole building was about to implode and crush the life out of him. Then, panting like a thirsty dog, wild eyed and open mouthed, something very strange and startling occurred. Amidst all the mayhem and pandemonium he quietly became serene.

As a further shockwave broke anything left intact, Stan slowly raised himself onto all fours and cautiously and methodically crawled under the bed. His heartbeat returned to normal, the panting subsided and his vision gradually became clear like objects in an unfolding dawn. Many of those soldiers in the hell hole trenches of the previous war had experienced it, their bodies' defence mechanism taking control of the situation to prevent them literally dying from fright and this was exactly what was happening to Stan; adrenaline, stimulating the production of cortisol, being the downside.

His body was overproducing the chemical at an alarming rate which, in turn, was poisoning and steadily degrading his already simple mind. He lay motionless under that bed and began to melodiously hum an unwritten song as his left thumb found its way into his mouth and right hand tightened firmly around his crotch.

Uncle Theo and Stan had no other living relatives. His uncle had moved down to London two years earlier leaving Stan feeling isolated and alone, yearning for them to be reunited. Minutes after Theo's letter had arrived Stan was on his way to the local town. He purchased a handled packing case on wheels and a one-way train ticket, spending the rest of the long day making his goodbyes and getting excited. The following morning he heard the train a good five minutes before it arrived, the mighty anthracite fed engine pumping steam like some colossal heart. As it pulled into the station Stan felt alive with happiness and on the journey south he read and reread the letter from his uncle. Accommodation had been arranged and he was going to become a train driver on the grand London underground, an apprentice with his very own uncle as the instructor. As Stan disembarked he was beaming, grinning from ear to ear and that was the image that formed in Theo's mind's eye. The image that kept returning to his uncle when Stan didn't arrive for work that morning. He knew that the bombardment the previous night had been particularly destructive and the shift seemed endless as his concern for Stan's safety grew. By the end of it his imagination had converted that concern into a fearful dread and his long trek that evening, through the once varied and engaging streets of the capital, was harrowing and sad.

Ruination was everywhere. A dark, calamitous evil, intent on destruction, was flying in from the continent every night and he, like millions of others, thought it only a matter of time before their mighty city would be transformed into acres of rubble, dust and death.

Entering Stan's borough it was obvious that the area had been subjected to a major assault and he quickened his pace. Once familiar streets were now huge smoking mounds of twisted metal and shattered masonry, making navigation difficult. His sense of direction sharply resurfaced as he turned a corner and recognised the owner of Stan's local shop, sitting on a chair in the middle of the carnage, a brown battered suitcase by her side.

He approached uncertainly.

"Excuse me," he began hesitantly and she slowly looked up at him. "It's Mary, isn't it?" The lady nodded affirmatively, her face black smudged, eyes red from crying, and he knelt in front of her. "What are you doing here, where's the shop?" He immediately regretted the question as she hooked her thumb and pointed at the deconstructed piles of bricks behind her. Uncle Theo's eyes widened with fright as he began to understand. "Oh my God, Mary," he whispered, looking around him, "then where the hell is Stan's building?" He reached out and placed his hands softly on her shoulders then asked again, "Where's my nephew Stan's building?" and he followed her gaze as she turned her head and looked up.

Theo couldn't understand how he had missed it but there, less than fifty yards away, stood a sight that was so extraordinary it caused his jaw to involuntarily drop. The block that Stan lived in had been virtually demolished and all that appeared to be left was a central concrete core. Perched upon it, maybe a hundred feet in the air, was a room. It reminded him of a sinewy arm, jutting vertically out of the ground, with a clenched hand on the end.

Almost thirty years later, Stan would be sitting by an open fire in a farmhouse watching the television as two black American athletes defiantly thrusted their fists skyward on the Olympic podium. That grainy image had stirred a vague, deep memory within him, but nothing, other than that, materialised; the cloudy recollection departing almost as soon as it had appeared.

Due to the blackout, work on erecting the scaffolding couldn't start until first light so Uncle Theo escorted Mary to the nearby Balham tube station, a station that just weeks later would be devastated by a three thousand pound armour piercing bomb. They spent an uncomfortable night on the platform along with hundreds of others. When the scaffolding was completed around noon of the following day, Uncle Theo began to tentatively climb; the men of the volunteer assignment having agreed to his request to be the first to go in. After removing the stone lintel that had prevented Stan's exit, he entered into what remained of the room.

The sight made him almost collapse with sadness.

The ferocity of the bombing had pushed the heavy wooden bed up against the small hand basin which in turn had fractured, the miraculously still functioning, lead water pipe supplying it. Stan was under that bed, lying on his side, with freezing water spraying over him, bending rhythmically at the waist, slowly and deliberately rocking and humming, his mouth sucking on that thumb so hard it was now bleeding and raw. Uncle Theo walked across the room and bent down, placing his hands on Stan's head in an attempt to calm him, but he continued to rock, shivering uncontrollably from the cold water, completely unaware that his relative was beside him.

It was a difficult operation getting him down and they didn't rush; tragedy was part of their everyday lives and the men dealt with the situation kindly and courteously. They were driven out of the city in an ambulance manned by the Voluntary Aid Detachment to an old county general hospital in Kent. His uncle holding him firmly and close for the entire journey, stroking his hair and talking calmly in reassurance; but he could have been talking to himself. Stan's mind had closed and wasn't taking anything in. Theo still held on as they wheeled him in and still held on as he answered their questions and filled in their forms, only letting go when he was told that the last bus was about to leave. Looking back as he left the ward, that previous vision of Stan, alive and energised as he stepped from the train, passed through his head. As he focused on him lying in the bed, still rocking, still oblivious, he rushed out covering his face not wanting anyone to witness his flood of tears.

The first person to write an observation in his case note history was a young, fresh faced auxiliary nurse called George Goodwin who was just two weeks into the job, having been excused military duty. Back then, inexperience was of no concern and any staff member could write a comment about a patient. After watching Stan rocking and humming and holding himself he wrote on the first line of the first page in large black print:

'THIS MAN IS AN IDIOT AND MASTURBATES.'

Those seven words, written by an untrained hand, became the first description that anyone who cared to read Stan's notes, for whatever reason, were confronted with. They would be their introduction to Mr Stan Heart.

Nothing about shellshock, traumatic stress or psychosis due to overwhelming fear. He had been crudely portrayed as an imbecile and on the next day, when he was driven the thirty miles to the mental institution, those notes went with him, along with that sentence ... and everybody knows how important first impressions are.

Chapter 2

The first five years in that institution passed uneventfully for Stan but they turned out to be the lull before the storm.

At the beginning he was placed in seclusion, a misnomer for a padded cell. This was common practice for patients deemed to be 'off their rockers' and a potential danger to both themselves and those around them. The first night he huddled in the corner, his mind rewinding to the fear and panic of that appalling event, his body responding to the explosions he remembered with sudden jerks and spasms; pressing his ears in a futile attempt at lessening the noise. At times he would wail like a mother cradling her dead son then maniacally laugh as the fleeting, lucid thought that he was safe ricocheted through his mind. Occasionally, the metal plated door would be swung open, invading light stinging his eyes. The red-headed, odd male nurse would enter and help him to the toilet next door, give him something to eat and have him drink a sweet syrupy mixture which smelt of apricots and mint.

When all that was finished he`d give him a long hard pinch.

Stan spent three days in that room, ranting and raving and that suited the odd male nurse just fine because any bruising he might inflict could be easily explained away. On the third day the noises in his head and the fear in his heart began to abate and he regained a modicum of awareness. He was allowed out of that soft, womb-like cell and installed in the long stay geriatric ward.

Uncle Theo would visit as often as he could but the cards were stacked against him. He had little spare time as the workforce shrank and the workload grew. The journey out to the hospital was arduous and difficult. Every time he managed to see his nephew a little more of his heart broke. He would always find him in the conservatory sat on the green, urine resistant, leatherette chair, outwardly groomed and tidy, inwardly chaotic and disordered; occasionally humming, sometimes grimacing, neither happy nor sad. During his visits Uncle Theo would pull up a seat and sit in front of him, holding his hand, remembering a young man with slow thoughts but quick to be kind and compassionate. There was another characteristic of Stan's that delighted him - his ability to say something profound; something that could stop him in his tracks because it seemed so incongruous. One long night, soon after Stan's arrival, they had been slaving over a meaningful story for Barons Court station. It was proving difficult. Theo was getting tired, but not wanting to dampen his enthusiasm, had made up a headache as a reason to finish. The man was a bad actor and he got a long, serious, piercing stare for that excuse followed by, "Uncle Theo, a lie is a child that returns to kill its parents!" That one statement and its mature and deliberate delivery galvanised him and he remembered carrying on with ease, far into the night, until the story had been grasped.

During the following years, Stan began to make slow but definite progress. An understanding of his situation began to appear and his bizarre symptoms lessened. He was able to do things for himself and make brief but coherent conversation which tempered his uncle's dismay. The love he felt for his young relative was as strong as ever but the demands of his job coupled with the burdensome journey was meaning a lot less contact and once again, like the padded cell, this situation was very acceptable to the odd male nurse.

Visitors would notice things and get in his way.

When they were alone during his shift he'd often emulate Theo and sit in front of Stan but unlike his uncle he'd maybe squeeze his hand as hard as he could or perhaps stand on his foot as a parting gesture. The nurse was a cruel man who hated those he should be caring for. Stan, along with many other patients, was sick scared of him.

The conservatory was large and bright and ideally situated for the highlight of Stan's day. Each afternoon a steam train would appear at the foot of the distant hills and he could just make out the dull thump of the engine as it heaved coal across the landscape. Funnelled smoke finding form then melting as the train thundered through. All of this activity thrilled him, vaguely reminded him of a magical train journey he'd made in happier times. It was on one such afternoon that William Wilson, teenage paranoid schizophrenic, galloped past Stan and ended up impaled on the railings thirty feet below.

The odd nurse's pleasures weren't only reserved for Stan, and on this particular afternoon, in the privacy of a side room, William's neck was in a headlock and he was having difficulty breathing. Managing to break free from the grip he began to run. Meanwhile Stan, sitting thirty yards away, was becoming exhilarated because he could hear the first low rumblings of the steam train's approach. As he leaned forward in the leatherette chair to glean the best view, young William, crazed and terrified, ran into the conservatory at speed. He leapt onto the chair adjacent to Stan's, bounced, somersaulted in mid-air and hit the front of the structure feet first in a horizontal position. Over the years, the whole front of the framework, having had little maintenance, absorbed a lot of what the weather could throw at it. When William impacted it easily collapsed. He and it cascaded down the front of the facade, William's fall being terminated by the railings; wood and glass showering over him like a final insult. When the odd male nurse arrived on the scene, flustered and out of breath, scared witless as he weighed up the consequences, he noticed Stan standing on the edge of the now open fronted room, looking out across the vista. William, in his desperation, had removed the barrier allowing Stan to hear and smell, for the very first time, the magnificence of that steam train. He stood open mouthed, mesmerised by the turning wheels on the rails, the billowing white circles of steam, the sheer strength of the sight.

A normal human being would wonder why they showed no concern for William but of course neither man was normal. As the odd male nurse pulled himself together and approached his patient he could almost feel Stan's elation as he jumped up and down, laughing and waving at the train. For a brief moment an urge to push him into that drop, an urge he would forever regret not succumbing to, passed through his thoughts; in for a penny in for a pound, but self-preservation prevailed.

"They can't see you, you idiot," he said coldly and grabbed his arm hard to direct him back into the safety of the room.

"It doesn't matter," Stan replied in his childish way and turned to look at his tormentor, the excitement subsiding. "Was William running from you?" he asked matter of factly, his face relaxing as he lost the smile.

"Of course not," he stuttered, momentarily uncertain. He led Stan back into the room and sat him down, regaining his composure in the process, "and you mention that again," he said menacingly, moving his face to within an inch of Stan's, "and your miserable life won't be worth living."

They stood looking at each other and both could hear people rapidly approaching, alerted by the noise of the conservatory front being demolished.

"Don't worry about all of that," Stan whispered reassuringly, a line of a smile appearing, "if anyone asks, I'm going to say I shoved him," and he patted the odd nurse's hand. The running people had almost reached them. "And why would you say that?"

Stan didn't immediately answer but rose to his feet, walked back to the opening and looked out, saddened by the sight of the train disappearing into the distance. As the people arrived, looking around in bewilderment they didn't see him turn nor hear him say in a hushed tone, "because it'll save a lot of trouble if I do."

The name of the odd male nurse was Bill Ernald Sweet and Bill had the opinion that evolution shouldn't be tampered with. His rationale was that compassion and sympathy weakens the human race because it results in keeping the abnormal alive. If Bill's brain had been removed from his head the surgeon would cringe at the appalling repugnancy of the organ, but that mess of a brain didn't make Bill naive or unwise. He knew that thoughts like that had to be locked away in the nether regions of his mind, considering they were akin to the leaders of his nation's recently defeated enemy. Though Bill could silently think those thoughts whenever he liked and he thought them a lot about the patients. However, beyond any doubt, a man with those ideas, working in a hospital for the insane, was a dangerous man, a very dangerous individual indeed and although Bill and Stan never meet again they are unwittingly on a collision course as sure as two of those trains being controlled by a drunken signalman when he pulls the wrong lever and falls asleep.

CHAPTER 3

During the evening of the day that young William Wilson flew to his death, Georgia Spanswick was finishing her make-up with a final layer of crimson lipstick. She lived in a terraced house with her parents, four miles away from the institution, in a village renowned for absolutely nothing other than a weekly dance in the community hall and that was the reason for her efforts. This was her only avenue for meeting men and meeting men was very high on Georgia's 'to do' list.

The war had ended two months previously. Even though rationing was causing hardship due to shortages of all commodities, national morale was high and the privation seemed to engender a perception of togetherness. People had adopted the attitude that everyone was in the same boat and should help those less able to help themselves. However, this altruism didn't chance upon everyone, especially the Spanswick family who had never made, or wanted to make, its acquaintance.

Certain familial traits can pass through the generations, sometimes hair colour or a physical weakness of some sort and often they can skip a line and appear in the next, but heartless and uncaring parents always infect their offspring and Georgia had a bad case of inhumanity; just like her mother and father and they just like theirs. She didn't despise them for being hard hearted and callous, it was more the fact that she had inherited those traits and getting away from them, a desire only understood by similar minds, appealed to her.

She was eighteen years old. Employment as a means to independence didn't appeal to her torpid nature so marriage seemed a promising option. The contrast of her pale skin, jet black hair and cobalt blue eyes turned heads and tonight she had one man pictured in those eyes, one man in her line of fire, one man whose head she wanted to turn. Although Georgia didn't give jack shit about the huge social stigma attached to unmarried parents, she knew her intended victim certainly would.

George Goodwin was a good looking, gentle sort of soul who spent most of his time ambling through life, eagerly trying to avoid any strife or conflict. A year before, when he was twenty-two, he'd got lucky and the small cottage he was left by an aunt he'd never met made it even easier. He worked in the same mental hospital as good old Bill Sweet and Georgia recognised him as the means to achieve her ambition.

The previous week at the hall she had taken her time looking away when their eyes met, smiling as she looked down, then casually rejected his first request for a dance. However, she agreed to other men's invitations, although continuing her long glances whilst doing so. She knew the game and knew how to play it. Eventually, the band struck up the slow tune she had been waiting for and going against the social etiquette of the day, had asked George if he would dance with her. He readily agreed and she danced so close and held him so tight that poor George's knees were trembling.

He thought he'd died and floated off to wonderland.

When she wished him goodnight immediately after that slow number had finished, even though the end of the night was more than an hour away, she knew that the coming week would be the longest of George's life. He might even be the first in next time.

When Georgia was young she'd had a puppy that would salivate and quietly whine at the aroma from the can of dog food being opened. She'd take her time, taunting the poor thing, moving the can close to it then cruelly moving it away, time and again, before scraping the contents into a bowl. As she walked into the dance hall the following week that memory resurfaced as she saw George, dressed up and dandy, standing by the bar. She walked straight past him, aware that in her wake perfume would waft over him; aware that his eyes would zero in on her pert backside in that audacious, skin-tight, pencil skirt. She sat down at an empty table, crossing her legs to show just enough inner thigh and shortly after, puppy George walked over carrying two drinks.

"Hope you don't mind, Georgia, but I thought you might like a drink," he began nervously, offering her one of the glasses, then continued, "Gin and tonic, I noticed you were drinking one last week."

"Oh, George," in mock surprise at seeing him, "that's so kind, but how d'you know I'm not seeing someone tonight?" and a faint aroma of dog food hovered around her nose.

"Well, I'm hoping that you aren't," he said cautiously, still holding the drinks, eager for the answer. She took one.

"I'm only playing with you, Georgie, I'm on my own tonight," and she took a sip. "Sit down and keep me company," and she patted the chair next to her for him to sit.

The can was opened and the contents hit the bowl.

They spent the whole evening together, drinking and flirting, George feeling empowered by the envious looks of other men, jealous of his catch. She occasionally touched him or brushed against him to gauge her impact and everything was good. The lead and the muzzle were on and he was obeying every command. She knew she'd never love him, that was an emotion she didn't possess. She also knew that soon she'd probably loathe him, but first things first, Georgia had a game plan, its focus being a child and so far it was going like clockwork. The band started their customary smoochy last number and, once again, she took his hand and led him onto the dance floor. As they held each other tightly and began to move she pushed her pelvis close to his so no one would see her hand rubbing him. All week he'd been thinking of her and his legs almost buckled from her touch.

She breathed in his ear and whispered, "I'm not wearing any panties, Georgie, I left them off just for you," and she squeezed and felt him growing. "Would you like to put your hands between my legs?" she whispered again, that puppy memory bobbing back to the surface as he whined, unable to speak.

"Take me back to your place, George," she gasped." I'm dying for you."

George hadn't had anyone dying for him in his life and his passion was preventing the question surfacing of how she knew he had a place at all.

He had sex with her three times during the course of that night and early morning. Firstly, up against the inside of the front door moments after they had closed it; secondly in the bath as she had read somewhere that water and heat can aid conception, and lastly in the back of his car whilst parked on a piece of waste ground before dropping her back home. She knew that her parents would be drunkenly asleep and, as she opened the front door, made no attempt at being quiet; awkwardly trying to keep the top of her legs tightly together whilst climbing the stairs.

In her bedroom she undressed and lay carefully on the floor propping her calves on top of the bed. She wrapped a cotton scarf twice around her middle, tying it tight and then attached a bandage to the back of the scarf, pulling it firmly between her legs and tying it off at her midriff. Georgia was determined to keep as much of his sperm inside her as possible and help it on its way by adopting that position. She lay there for a few minutes before falling to sleep, exhausted. Uncomfortable but happy. When she awoke in the morning her legs had come off the bed and the scarf had loosened but she knew she was pregnant. In some instinctive and intuitive way her body was already telling her.

What her body wasn't telling her was that a boy, who was to be called Angelo, had begun to grow inside her. If she'd known that she would have never, absolutely never, even dreamt of going prowling that night.

Chapter 4

Thirty minutes later Stan was still in the same seat.

The conservatory had been taped off and a maintenance crew were busy putting the place back into order, sweeping up the glass and boarding up the panels. They had erected a tent-like structure around William who straddled the pointed railings like some failed escapee, a red pancake of blood beneath him, deciding against moving him until the police had arrived. Dr Tim Richards, superintendent of the hospital, swaggered into the room, ducking under the tape and holding it up for the ward charge nurse and Charlie, the ward staff nurse, to get under. The noise of the crew forcing them to raise their voices in order to be heard.

"I'm not sure whether the men should be tidying all of this up," the charge nurse said, looking around at the activity. "Shouldn't we be waiting for the old bill to get here? I mean, won't they want to examine the scene or whatever it is they do?" He was a long serving employee of the hospital and one of the very few who dared to question the doctor.

"It's an open and shut case," Tim Richards replied loudly. "Young schizophrenic, hears voices, reacts to them," he shook his head as if he was sad, "no, it's an open and shut case." Although he absolutely knew it wasn't and also absolutely knew he didn't want the police nosing around. Their three heads turned in unison as Stan threw up his arms and theatrically declared,

"It's an open and shut case because I did it!"

The noise immediately stopped. His outburst had been heard by all and the crew joined the medical staff in gawping at him. The charge nurse frowned, Charlie raised his eyebrows and the doctor's dropped jaw made his mouth open. Stan began fidgeting in his seat and Charlie, who had had more contact with him than anyone, walked across and looked at him sternly.

"What do you mean, Stan? You did it?" He was genuinely concerned and upset by the farcical admission and felt protective towards him. "He was annoying me, Charlie, going on about he was Jesus and the nails were hurting his hands so I pushed him, hard, I pushed him hard against the glass." Stan was failing to make eye contact and Charlie thought this odd. He looked back at the other two with anguish in his eyes, not knowing what to say next. The doctor quickly intervened.

"Let me have a chat with Mr Heart alone," he began, realising his plan was in danger. "There's more to this than meets the eye, I think he needs a little space."

"But this is now a police matter," the charge nurse interjected abruptly, "surely?"

"Please!" Dr Richards exclaimed, overly loud, getting everyone's attention. "Let me have a few minutes with the patient," and he glared firstly at the charge nurse followed by most of the others, "in private," he added less loudly but somehow more threateningly.

It was at that point that Charlie shivered; a feeling had come over him that the situation had in some way become dangerous. He felt confused by the idea and wasn't happy at leaving Stan on his own, but he noticed his superior start to leave and reluctantly trailed him to the door followed by the maintenance crew who had all been listening intently.

Although Dr Richards was an impatient man he was more than happy for this to take as long as necessary. Bill Sweet being one malignant member of staff in the institution was bad enough but adding in the doctor, well that's double the hit and twice the shit and poor young Stan was going to find himself deeply embedded in it. Like Bill, the doctor had no fondness for his charges and had to force a smile as he approached and sat by his side causing him to clench and tighten as he held his hand.

"There's no need to be afraid, Mr Heart, I'm trying my best to help you here, don't you understand that?" Stan relaxed a little. The doctor felt him loosen and grinned, took a deep breath and continued. "Just over a year ago, when the car went up in flames outside the hospital, do you remember?"

Stan nodded sheepishly.

"Wasn't it you who said you were responsible?" He nodded sheepishly again. "And when we had a little chat about it, privately like now, what did you tell me?"

"Don't know," Stan replied, strangely cute.

"To begin with you told me that it was your fault, didn't you?"

Stan nodded affirmatively.

"And then, after the car had been checked over and it became clear that a leaking petrol pipe had been the cause and it was nothing to do with you whatsoever, you told me you were simply trying to save everyone a lot of trouble, isn't that right?"

Stan remained silent.

"Isn't that right?" he asked again more forcefully.

"Suppose so," Stan replied and tried to pull his hand away but the good doctor wasn't letting go.

"Ok, Mr Heart, ok." He looked up to where William Wilson had obviously left the building.

"Now for a second, look at that exit hole up there," pointing but still looking at Stan. "Now I'm no structural engineer but I would say William was about eight feet in the air when he hit that glass, what would you say?"

"'Bout that," Stan agreed.

"Okay, now then, you're a reasonably fit young man, aren't you?"

"Yep," he beamed, inflating.

"But you're maybe five two and nine-and-a-half stone, right?"

"Maybe," he pouted, deflating.

"So how are you going to throw Mr Wilson eight feet in the air? Now I know you were annoyed and your strength can increase when you're annoyed, but I'm six three and fourteen stone and I can get as mad as the next man, but as sure as you've got a hole in your arse, I couldn't lob him that high. I'd have a job getting him up half that height."

Stan opened his mouth and went to answer then paused as he digested the hole in his arse comment, grimacing at the picture that had formed in his mind. Suddenly, he looked down at the hand holding his and blurted,

"Well I did, I can't remember much of it, only him annoying me and grabbing him by the seat of his pants and chucking him up in the air," and Stan shuffled uncomfortably in his chair.

Dr Richards unclasped his hand and stood up. He was indeed a tall man, impeccably dressed in a Huntsman suit and Canali bow tie. Chamomile blonde hair accentuated his blue green eyes but the one piece of attire that stood out for Stan, almost amazing him, were the shoes, his pristine, mirror-like, dazzling shoes. He was undoubtedly a man to whom appearance was overwhelmingly important. A man who liked to advertise where he was coming from before he got to you.

With manicured hands in expensive pockets, he walked over to the damaged glass panels, lit a cigarette and looked out. A mild wind blew into the open conservatory and he stood there for a while, silent, closing his eyes as the warm air drifted over him. He often needed time during a conversation to reflect and gather his thoughts. Then he opened his eyes slowly and looked down at the shroud of a structure that had been erected around William and sighed at the turn of events; that sigh wasn't of despondency but relief, signifying that a large problem in his life had been resolved. Rubbing his chin he turned around to look at Stan, an individual as diametrically opposed to himself as he could think of.

"Yes, that little chat we had was full of surprises," he continued, "full of surprises if I recall. Can you recall it, Stan, the talk we had?" He'd decided to use his first name, always paid dividends.

"Some of it."

"Well try and recall all of it, Stan, all about the car going up in flames," and the doctor lowered his head and raised his eyes, "and I can remember you telling me about the steam trains going by here and how much you enjoyed seeing the clouds of smoke and the speed of the wheels."

Stan began to nod eagerly like a yes man.

"I did, I mean I do, I does," excitement always jumbled his speech.

Dr Richards returned to his seat and much to Stan's annoyance held his hand again; the little man reminded him of a three-year-old at Christmas.

"There's going to be a lot of pressure on me to get rid of all this glass," he was going in for the kill, "have it replaced by brick or some such thing." Stan sat bolt upright, his face twisting despairingly as the doctor went on. "People are going to say if it happened once it'll happen again; someone else is going to go flying through it and the best thing would be to just brick the whole thing up."

"You mustn't do that," he protested, "no one will be able to see the train!"

"I know," Dr Richards replied, nodding his head in agreement," but my responsibility is with the patients, you can see that, can't you?"

"No!" Stan shouted, jumping to his feet, "you can't do that."

Dr Richards moved back in his seat and gave him a long, serious, eye to eye then said harshly, "Well you get nice and comfortable in that old seat and tell me exactly what happened to William Wilson. This isn't any schoolboy tell-tale crap," and he kept up the gaze, "this is William's life and I want to know what really happened or by God I'll make sure the builders are here tomorrow and you're thrown in the rubber room to make doubly sure you can't see those trains."

There was a lull. Whenever Stan realised that one of his lies had been rumbled he didn't pull any punches, he just told it the way it was with no excuses, as if the lie had never been spoken. Dr Richards had witnessed this behaviour before. When Stan had been told the fuel line had caused the vehicle to explode that time, he immediately capitulated, became almost infantile and owned up to being untruthful, no apologies, no reasons and this trait was re-enacted here.

"It was Bill's fault," he proclaimed, breaking the silence.

"Bill?" Dr Richards questioned, knowing full well who Stan was referring to.

"Bill Sweet," confirmed Stan. "He's a bad nurse here, pinches and squeezes and stamps on everyone."

"What are you saying, Stan, it was this Bill Sweet who threw William through the glass?"

"No, it was Bill Sweet who chased him," Stan corrected, becoming agitated. "He chased him and William was so frightened he ran in here, jumped up on that table and went flying through that glass ... he was scared stiff."

Stan had just confirmed what Dr Richards had thought from the beginning and his plan was beginning to firm up.

"Right, okay," the doctor said, trying to calm him, "I'm beginning to understand." He rubbed his forehead then continued. "Right," he repeated, "I'm going to get rid of this Bill Sweet for good, okay? As from today he's gone."

"That's good that is," Stan whispered like a child.

"But you still want to see the trains, don't you?"

"Yes please," again in a whisper.

"Well if you want to keep seeing the trains and you want to see the bad nurse gone you mustn't say that William was being chased, you must say that William just ran in here and jumped through the glass." He held Stan's chin to get his full attention.

"Do you understand, Stan? It's very important. Never say it was your fault or Bill Sweet's, none of that, you just say William came running in here and launched himself through the glass."

Stan didn't answer and Dr Richards became annoyed.

"Do you understand?" he asked in a raised voice, but it wasn't a case of misunderstanding, he was simply repeating the word 'launched' over and over in his mind, liking the sound of it.

Dr Richards shook Stan's chin. "Are you grasping this? For God's sake, speak to me," now almost shouting.

"I am," he said quietly, "William ran in here and jumped through the glass, that's what I will say, but remember, Doctor," and Stan put his mouth right up to the doctor's ear, "like I told my Uncle Theo a long time ago, a lie is a child that comes back to kill its parents."

They repositioned their heads and looked squarely at each other.

"What?" the doctor asked, with a look of disgusted bemusement.

"Just saying," he replied, nodding as if he were the master of all wisdom.

The moment was exploded by a sudden knock at the door and the inspector and police constable marched in without waiting for a reply.

"Hello, Tim," the inspector called out, approaching Dr Richards with an outstretched hand.

"Henry," he replied, shaking it, "dreadful event."

"Yes, dreadful event," he concurred.

"Have you spoken to anyone yet, Henry?"

The inspector said he hadn't, and thankful, the doctor continued. "Well it's an open and shut case by the looks of it. Young chap by the name of William Wilson, delusional psychotic, responding to voices and decided to launch himself up and out of here onto the railings down there."

They both surveyed the damage.

"You've checked the poor fellow, haven't you?"

"Of course," Dr Richards replied, somewhat indignantly.

"Sorry, Tim, I had to ask," he almost apologised.

"About half an hour ago, died on impact, massive trauma and fatal damage to internal organs," he tutted, "terrible sight."

They were both behind Stan and the inspector pointed at him mouthing 'who's that?'.

"And say hello to Mr Stanley Heart, Henry." Stan looked around, the inspector raising his hand in acknowledgement. "He saw the whole thing; in fact he's just been describing it to me, shocked to the core by it all."

"LAUNCHED!" Stan suddenly blurted out, swinging his arm in the air and the constable, who was stood by the door, was so surprised that he automatically grabbed for his truncheon.

The inspector wrapped his arm around the doctor and moved him away and out of Stan's earshot.

"Won't need to ask him too many questions, Tim, if you know what I mean," and Dr Richards winked at him knowingly. "Perhaps you could have Mr Heart dictate a few lines about what happened, just for the file, you know."

"Consider it done," he affirmed.

"And the glass, could you get it replaced with that toughened stuff, covers both our backsides?"

"Going one better, Henry, the bricklayers start first thing in the morning."

"Even better," confident in the knowledge that his friend would see to everything. Anything for a quiet life.

"Well I think that's all, Tim, we'll leave you in peace," and they once again shook hands. "Obviously you'll deal with the deceased?"

"Undertakers are on the way." He smiled at his friend. "You can leave everything to me, Henry, you needn't worry about a thing."

"Good man, I wish all cases were this straightforward," and the two police officers departed the hospital.

The police constable, being an astute young recruit, couldn't help himself from asking the inspector a question as they drove off.

"Sir, please don't take this the wrong way, but shouldn't we have checked the body or at least questioned Mr Heart?"

"Listen, son," the inspector replied condescendingly, "when you're dealing with integrity and professionalism of the highest order there's no need, it would simply be a waste of everyone's time."

But the constable wasn't completely convinced as they made their way back to the station.

It was many years before Stan saw his next steam train and then it was on the television, not in real life; but Stan didn't mind, the treatment Dr Richards had organised for him saw to that.

Chapter 5

Two months had passed and Georgia decided to announce the pregnancy. Her parents offered no congratulations or words of encouragement. They weren't horrified or ashamed as most would have been in 1946, it was more a case of them not caring very much; they were drinking partners and wrapped up in their own selfish world. However, when they realised that George was the father, young George with his good job and own house on the better side of town, they could see money coming into the family and both began warming to the idea of grandparenthood.

When, on the other hand, George was told, he wriggled and squirmed but Georgia had thought of every escape plan and installed counter measures. During their short relationship he had seen her as a bed mate rather than a soul mate, but quickly understood that to stay living and working in the town, whilst retaining any semblance of respectability, he would now have to marry her, a prospect he found alarming. There was no alternative. She was attractive, stunningly attractive, but George had reached the conclusion that there was something wrong with her and that contradicted her allure. Something cold and heartless seemed to dwell inside her and her callous nature troubled him. Her demands, not on his time but on his wallet, were also becoming a worry.

"Oh, George," she'd gush as they walked arm in arm, window shopping the High Street, "that dress would make me look lovely for you," or "buy me a ring, George, I'll think of you every time I look at it," or the clincher, "buy me that underwear, Georgie, you can feel them on me tonight," and therein lay the problem.

His head had reservations but his loins would win the day. She knew exactly how to play him, knew he wasn't big in the brains or ambition departments but enormously into hip thrusts and using her cute bum and dirty tongue it worked every time. When he'd found out she was pregnant, her physical attributes were the only saving grace and the only piece of good cheer in what he considered a bad news day.

When Angelo was eleven weeks into his development, George and Georgia were pronounced man and wife in a short, registry office ceremony. There was no best man. He was thinking of asking Charlie, a work colleague at the hospital, but he knew his soon to be in-laws would have been outraged at a black man being present so thought better of it. The office was sparsely furnished and smelt damp and the once warm, welcoming manner of the registrar had died with age and he conducted the ceremony in a graceless monotone. The two other people in attendance, her parents, had only just arrived in time, having been waylaid en route by a pub and filled the place with alcoholic fumes and belches.

As the event took its course George couldn't help but think that he had been stitched up like a kipper shortly after it had been caught hook, line and sinker; that he had become a foolhardy fly that had glided at speed into a beautifully constructed web and should he even think of struggling, that gripping thread would surely tense and strengthen. Georgia, however, had found herself constantly staring into space, daydreaming. She imagined standing in the trellised porch of his quaint old cottage, the sun shining on the full bloomed roses, weaving in and around the woodwork above her head; and the pram, the pram bearing the lovely baby boy (oh yes, it was always a boy) fast asleep, no movement and gentle breaths.

She felt released and free in these imaginings, released from a weight that had been confining and preventing. A weight that for so long had crushed any happiness out of her, created by her parent's constant, relentless bickering. Their arguments, their criticism that had warmed her hate and cooled her love. Any expectations she had were ridiculed, any desires stifled. Mistakes she made were exposed, enlarged and mocked; friends were belittled and discouraged. She was never physically abused, although sometimes she thought that pain would have been easier to handle, it was just the perpetual head messing that had turned her into a self-obsessed, pessimistic schemer.

The beauty within blossoms in the face but Georgia was an exception. Her voluptuous features never failed to get her attention, especially male attention, but they masked a tortured personality. Attractiveness gives a person immeasurable advantage and it was those looks alone that had come to her rescue; looks that had bought her the ticket to ride away from her parents and open the door of George's little paradise. As he pressed the ring onto her finger and lightly kissed her lips, the memory of that puppy entered her head once again and she smiled.

Chapter 6

Four hours after William Wilson took off, Bill was panting heavily outside Dr Richard's office. He had been summoned by the head of the hospital and his imagination was getting the better of him. Dismissal, a trial, prison? Had Stan Heart said anything? He knew William had died, everyone in the hospital knew that and he also knew the coppers had come a calling, so what was this meeting all about? Merely the top man going through the motions, checking all the staff's recollections of the event? Or worse, an interview before he was handed over to the authorities.

Bill was holding off knocking as he could barely cope with the suspense and didn't want to go in panting like some parched loon. He had been lying on the bed in his staff quarters since the incident, churning over the possible outcomes of his actions and the one chink in his armour, his Achilles heel, was Stan. If only Stan would keep his mouth shut then he was in the clear. There was no evidence, but the thought of his fate being in the hands of a simple mental patient made him feel hopeless. The death of William Wilson meant nothing to him, it was the life of Bill Sweet that mattered.

He began to breathe more evenly, still through his mouth, then after a while through his nose, and when he felt his heartbeat lessen and his mood more settled he rapped on the door and walked in.

Dr Richards was looking out of the window, one hand in his pocket the other holding a just lit cigarette. He didn't know if the doctor had realised his presence and forced a small cough. Without turning around Tim Richards took a drag.

"Please sit down, Bill," and Bill sat.

His breathing began to quicken again, globules of sweat formed on his forehead while the doctor was still looking out through the window, moving only to smoke. Bill looked around the huge office, framed certificates of academic achievements hung on the walls, bookcases full of all kinds of psychiatric literature, but the one striking feature of the room, which seemed so out of place, was the statue of an old man on a plinth just behind the doctor's swivel chair.

Towering almost eight feet in the air he appeared old and wizened, his face bearing an olive hue and Bill imagined him to be foreign, obviously an elderly medic, with the briefcase in his left hand, walking stick in his right and a stethoscope dangling from his neck. It was so odd and he suddenly realised that when the doctor eventually sat down he would be confronted by two of them, one dead and one alive. Dr Richards knew exactly what he was doing.

Many lunchtimes had been spent with Inspector Henry and after a few loosening drinks he was more than glad to share the latest interviewing techniques with his medical friend. Dr Richards leaned forward and extinguished the cigarette on the outside window ledge.

"Like the statue, Bill?" still without turning around. He was slightly startled by the question and wriggled in his seat.

"Yes, I do, it's ..." immediately his mind went blank, "it's good," and he squirmed at his ridiculous response.

"Any idea who he is?"

"Um," and he strained to focus on the features of the face, "is he maybe a famous surgeon, wartime surgeon, inventor of a medical procedure, something like that?" He was thankful his mind had returned.

"Well done, Bill, you've got it. He is indeed the inventor of a procedure, a psychiatric procedure to be exact. Any idea of nationality?"

"Spanish perhaps?" Bill was feeling easier. He felt things were going better.

"Italian actually. Born on September the twenty-sixth, eighteen seventy-seven in Conegliano; it's in the Veneto region, Bill, did you know that?"

Bill shook his head.

"No, I didn't think you would," and he shrank a little. The doctor continued. "His name is Ugo Cerletti, almost certainly the inventor of electro convulsive therapy."

Bill pursed his lips and nodded his head. He was an ogre with the weak and sycophant with the strong.

"And do you want to know how he did it?" he asked twisting to look at the statue behind him.

Bill pursed his lips and nodded again. "Yes I do," he replied firmly.

"Well Ugo did it by being vigilant. By knowing and being aware of what was going on around him."

Dr Richards turned and stared intently at the frightened form of Bill Sweet sitting two yards in front of him, legs crossed, fingers around chin, desperately trying to seem interested.

He reminded him of a dog, looking up as its owner walks into the room to find a half chewed slipper. Tim Richards sensed he could have asked him to kiss his arse and Bill would have replied, "Which cheek?" He was putty in the doctor's hands and they both knew it.

"You see," he went on, "Ugo happened to notice that the symptoms of epileptics suffering with depression were alleviated following a fit. He didn't know why but the important thing was that the depression lifted after the convulsion." He lit another cigarette, smiled at Bill, then sat down in the chair at the front of the figure. "Now, Doctor Ugo obviously gave this some thought and came up with the idea of inducing a fit in depressives who didn't have the ability of doing it for themselves and he decided to find out if plugging them into the mains would do the trick."

Bill was listening intently and Dr Richards was pleased by that. He took a long draw on his cigarette and continued.

"So he attached a basic electrode to the patients' temples and flicked the switch. There were teething problems, excuse the intentional pun, because apparently the first guinea pigs were biting clean through their tongues. The luckier ones that followed, if you can call them lucky, were given mouth guards to prevent it happening, but out of a sample of a hundred patients, eighty per cent experienced a lessening of their depression."

Bill continued to listen earnestly, he thought it advantageous.

"I don't know how many millions of these treatments have been administered since and how many potential suicides have been prevented but all of this came about by one man being aware of what was going on around him." Dr Richards then stopped talking, moved back in the chair and took the final drag of his cigarette.

This interlude was very awkward for Bill; he wasn't sure if he was expected to respond in some way and was unsure of how to proceed. He looked at the live one glaring across at him and then up at the dead one glaring down at him. At one point he wondered if he should just excuse himself with a "well, thank you very much" and get up and leave. Then just as Bill's anxiety was peaking the silence was abruptly broken.

"Do you think I'm aware of what's going on around me, Bill?" The words shot out through his glare.

"Yes, I think you probably are," he stammered.

"Do you think I'm aware enough of what's going on around me to know how William Wilson died this afternoon, Bill?" He was using the put 'em at ease, distract the mind then pull the trigger technique. Bill was flustered.

"Well yes, sir, I think you probably are," he repeated.

"Are you going to tell me how you think it happened, Bill?" The doctor sat upright, waiting for the answer. Bill copied him by also straightening himself and after clearing his throat explained that the most likely reason was that William's paranoia had caused him to leap to his death or, possibly, one of the other patients had pushed him and in fact Stan Heart was in the room when it all happened.

Dr Richard's opinion of Bill was rock bottom before any of this, but following that contemptible statement it had sunk without trace, though his thoughts couldn't show if his plan was to materialise. He decided to play his ace.

"Ok, Bill," Dr Richards began, smoothing his hair back with both hands then folding them behind his head. "I'm going to be brutally frank with you and I want you to listen very carefully to what I'm about to say."

"Yes, of course, sir," his voice trembling, preparing himself for something terrible. The doctor stood up, walked around and sat on top of the desk in front of Bill, looming over him like a bird of prey hovers over a petrified mouse.

"In five minutes' time, you and I can either be sitting here happy and contented, about to say goodbye, or sitting here waiting for the police to arrive."

Bill gulped, the game had just changed.

"You see, Billy Boy," there was a nastiness in his tone now, "the chap that you just miserably tried to lay the blame on actually told me exactly why Mr Wilson did what he did and also confirmed something that I'd guessed was true for some time."

Bill was looking up at the doctor looking down, his fingers intertwined as if in prayer.

"You're an underhand little bully who gets satisfaction from tormenting those who can't fight back; you're a disgrace to your profession and this time your sickening behaviour has resulted in the death of someone you should've been caring for." His face had turned red and his knuckles, from clenching the edge of the desk, white.

Bill felt a sickening surge emanate from his stomach and did what many revealed bullies do in this situation, he began to cry. Whimpering at first and then bawling like a child in a bike crash, lowering his head into his hands and almost screaming in disbelief and desperation. Terror cut through him at the realisation of being found out. He could almost feel the revulsion that the doctor possessed making it even harder for him to understand why Tim Richards had now knelt before him and was cradling his head as a father would a distraught son. Those strong arms around him reverted the bellowing sobs to whimpering then a further wave of self-pity reignited them and the doctor held him more tightly, Bill's feelings of disgrace turning to bewilderment, unable to comprehend this dramatic show of kindness.

He looked directly at his comforter and it was then that Tim Richards realised he had achieved his aim. Mr Sweet was now one of his and that was what this was all about.

"What's going to happen to me?" Bill whispered pathetically.

Dr Richards pressed his mouth to Bill's ear and continued stroking his hair. "Everything can be sorted out, Bill," he said reassuringly, "everything can be sorted out."

Chapter 7

Bill relaxed. The doctor's harsh words were reverberating through his head, little bouncing hurts, but his sudden change in attitude and soothing touch was a counterbalance and he felt perplexed when the doctor refrained from stroking his head and returned to the window. The embrace had pacified him; he was a child in the company of its caregiver, able and willing to extract him from any trouble. He looked at the figure framed in the window and felt a surge of love.

"Other than you and me, Mr Heart is the only person who knows the truth of what happened," Dr Richards said rhetorically, "so Mr Heart will be prescribed a treatment that will prevent him from ever revealing that truth."

The surge of love heightened.

"But make no mistake, Bill, I'm helping you for a reason and you must play your part in this. I'm going to help you so that you can help me."

The surge of love decreased slightly.

"You're going to leave the hospital today," he continued, "in fact as soon as you can pack. If anyone asks what you're doing you reply that Mr Wilson's death has dreadfully traumatised you and you have been offered an alternative position following an interview with myself, do you understand?"

Bill nodded automatically; he was concentrating on his prayers being answered.

"I can't hear you!"

"Sorry, yes, Doctor. I completely understand what you're saying," he replied softly, the dryness of his mouth making speech difficult. Tim Richards turned and, approaching Bill, placed a sheet of paper in his top pocket.

"All the information you're going to need is there. Accommodation has been arranged within the children's unit and you commence your duties the day after tomorrow," and Tim Richards slowly winked at him, his head rotating forty-five degrees, a gesture designed to promote security and wellbeing in the recipient. "Just report to the nurse's office, everything's in place" and he put his hand gently on the side of Bill's head, "now off you go and good luck, I'll be in touch shortly."

Bill left the office without saying a word. The encounter had left him utterly confused. He inhaled and was relieved and overjoyed, exhaled and was suspicious and worried. As the door closed, Dr Richards resumed sitting on the swivel chair, brought his head back and stared up at the ceiling. This was a dangerous game he was playing but one in which he had participated and won before. He lit the last cigarette in the packet and sucked deeply. A quick intermission.

He had to get back and see Stan, tie up all the loose ends.

Chapter 8

As George ceased kissing, the lethargic registrar pronounced them man and wife. The groom of the following wedding assisted by signing the register as a witness and they began their journey back through the town to the cottage.

Mum and Dad revisited the pub.

It was almost a year since the war had ended and luckily the region had escaped any damage, there being no industry of any significance to bomb. The main employers were the prison and the mental asylum, the former being referred to locally as the 'arse stretch' and the latter 'The Nuthatch'. For two years George had worked in the nut hatch as a nursing auxiliary, a euphemism for a human being who takes care of everything that another human being can't, usually the vomit inducing things.

He had begun his nursing career in a general hospital thirty miles away but found that sort of nursing far too strenuous and opted for the mental institution instead. The two missing small toes on each foot, a birth defect that affected all the males in his family, had excused him from military service although his disfigurement came with benefits. He had no feelings of patriotism and had no desire to be a soldier. Many of his contemporaries had signed up with enthusiasm, some even lying about their ages to get enlisted, but not George; he'd far prefer to be nursing the nutters than being shot at by them.

The walk took them through the small municipal park on the edge of town, the shifting direction of the sharp wind making the leaves swirl in a circular reel, the autumnal sun taking the heat as it sank. Georgia pulled the coat collar tightly around her neck and wished for the time when nylon stockings would become more available. Watered down gravy browning and a painted thin line at the back of each leg, giving the illusion of hosiery, afforded no protection against the cold. As they strolled through the black and gold wrought iron gates and out of the park, George began relating a funny story about a patient, Sid 'Fukum' Smith and his encounter with the visiting lady mayoress.

"George!" she interrupted loudly, pulling her collar even tighter, "you've a week off from that shithole so just forget about the place, I don't care what goes on up there."

"I'm only trying to make conversation, Georgia," he replied meekly.

"Well don't, all right? All I know is that dump is full of retards and whenever you come home you stink of lunatic piss," and she quickened her pace.

"It's my job, Georgia," he complained, "one of us has to work."

"I know that, bonehead, but stop talking to me about it ... I do not want to know!" and they continued their journey in silence, George walking some distance behind her.

When they arrived there were a few embers glowing in the fireplace and George revived it with a handful of kindling and a shovel of coal. Georgia had gone to lie down in the bedroom. He made himself a cup of tea and settled on the large rocker facing the fire. The transistor radio was in touching distance and he switched it on. Some posh chap, they were always posh chaps, was explaining the allies' efforts at creating a new Jewish state in a place called Palestine and he quickly turned it off. He had no interest in current affairs or politics; he had no knowledge of them and didn't want any. Folds of smoke began to curl through the coals, always a good sign. He placed a few more lumps on and sat comfortably back in the chair. His eyes focused on the picture he had drawn when he was very young. A picture of his father, a policeman, who had died far too early just months after the portrait had been completed. Although childish and simplistic it took pride of place above the fireplace, the image warming his thoughts as the fire warmed his body. He remembered his dear old mum saying that he hadn't given his dad a nose. But George had done that for a reason. One of his father's favourite sayings was that there are those who can't see beyond their own noses and he had decided not to give him one so he would never have that problem … funny how some little boys look at the world.

George led a simple life before meeting her. He didn't care much for his work but it became less of an imposition when the cottage had been left to him and his situation became more agreeable. He had money to spend and enjoyed nothing more in his spare time than visiting the pub, drinking a little too much and lurching home to sit and fall asleep in the chair by the fire. He knew he played too much and worked too little but it wasn't a worry. He was happy with no inclination to better himself; he had found his little niche and felt blessed.

George liked the ladies and met them at the local dance, even flirted with the idea of a wife, maybe a family, but he wasn't that concerned about it, and then came Georgia. He knew that, unlike him, she was a fiery type, he also knew she could be selfish and manipulative, but those eyes and that body and the raw energy of their love making made any faults vanish like dew in the sun. But since announcing her pregnancy all of that was beginning to alter, the sun was losing some of its heat.

She had talked him into signing a legal agreement granting her half of the cottage, all of it, should he have the misfortune to die and she had started demanding his salary each week, returning only a small amount for his personal use. Her attitude to him personally was also changing. The dirty talk and naughty touches had all but stopped and wasn't she wearing less make-up? Didn't she have the same dress on for four days? Could he say or do anything that wasn't criticised? Though perhaps more worrying of all, wasn't that alcohol he could smell on her breath when he got home from work?

Suddenly, he sat bolt upright. He thought of her parents sitting in the pub, slowly, gulp by gulp, swallowing their way to drunkenness. Her father desperately hanging on to a scintilla of sobriety in case he said or did something wrong leaving him prey to a barrage of venomous side swipes, a condemnation of his character, chipping away at the bricks of his happiness. He could picture the man right there in front of him, a beaten bootlicker, overpowered by a personality from which he had no means of escape.

He squeezed the arms of the chair, eyes widening as he envisaged his life ten years from now, sharing it with a potential monster who despised him and he shuddered, going cold at the thought.

The bedroom door was open and he could faintly hear her shallow, rhythmic breathing. He looked in and momentarily a wispy chimera of him holding a pillow over her dazzling face found a space and he shuddered again, shaking his head as he returned to the living room, frightened that he could harbour such an idea; because George was maybe an idle and limited being but he would never intentionally harm anybody and certainly never his wife. No, no, at that particular stage of his life, relaxing there enjoying the radiance of the open fire, he would never intentionally harm anybody.

Chapter 9

As Bill Sweet began to pack, Dr Richards was making his way through the dark unwelcoming corridors of the hospital to the long stay geriatric ward. Charlie, the staff nurse, was sitting beside Stan who was getting himself into a bit of a state.

"I'll never see the trains again, Charlie, I know it, I know it."

"Stan, the panels will all be fixed in a few days, believe me."

"I can't believe it, I love the trains, I don't know what I'm going to do, Charlie."

"Come on, Stan, you're getting yourself upset."

"I should never have pushed William, none of this would have happened if I hadn't pushed him."

"Stan, you've got to stop saying that, you had nothing to do with it."

"I can't help it."

"FUKUM!"

They simultaneously looked to the door of the conservatory and Sid 'Fukum' Smith entered.

Sid was one of the oldest residents of the hospital and his day consisted of wandering around shouting out loudly, other times quietly, sometimes once, other times maybe five or six times, the portmanteau word 'fukum.'

He took his rubbery face, thinning straight hair, short legs and big hands to the far corner of the room and sat on the window's ledge, completely ignoring the tape and barriers that had been erected, breaking and crashing through as if they didn't exist. It was an entrance to be proud of complimented by a slight upward movement of his rear end allowing a resounding, rasping fart to escape anally followed by a whispered 'fukum' vocally.

Stan frowned as Charlie grinned.

"Hey, Sid," he called over, "you're a star, there's no denying that," a smile opening up his big face and Sid completely ignoring him.

"I don't think you really care about me, Charlie," Stan said, peeved by the distraction and he looked away.

"Oh, come on," he replied indignantly, "what more d'you want me to say? the glass is going back in tomorrow, the trains are still going to be chugging through, everything's going to be back to normal, you've got to stop worrying about it, man," and then Tim Richards walked in and Charlie jumped up. Nursing staff sitting down and talking to patients was frowned upon by the management. If you were sitting down talking, you weren't somehow doing your job.

One drop of oil can spoil a gallon of beer and the introduction of one wrong individual can bring gloom into the room. As the good doctor rolled in the good cheer rolled out, but as soon as Sid had shouted 'fukum' twice, at the top of his voice, the atmosphere quickly lightened.

"Stan," Dr Richards declared, sitting in Charlie's vacated seat - the sitting down and chatting was perfectly all right for the management. "It's been a difficult day for you, how are you feeling?" Stan was grateful he didn't hold his hand.

"Can't see the trains," he said curtly.

"No, I'm aware of that and the problem is going to be addressed."

Charlie bravely decided to intervene, he felt Stan needed protecting.

"Sir," he began, "I think all of the staff realise Stan was simply making up his involvement in William's death, although he still maintains it was his fault. He's owned up to things he couldn't possibly have done in the past."

Has he now? Keep going, thought the doctor.

"And I think he knows that he should never have said it." Stan nodded almost imperceptibly. "However, he feels that he'll never see the trains again, that the glass panels aren't going to be reinstated and he's pretty much stuck with those ideas."

Dr Richards looked at Charlie.

I just told him they would be put back and I can't remember asking you for your worthless opinion, he thought, though not verbalising it.

Had he had the ability to decapitate Charlie he would have used it right there and then. Instead, he replied, "Okay, nurse," and clenched his fists in an attempt to hold his temper, "if you would leave Mr Heart and I alone now, I'd like to have a chat with him." Charlie felt uncomfortable but knew his station and left. As he walked out of the door Sid let fly with a rather beautiful expression of his one-word vocabulary, a long and extended 'fuk' followed by a quiet and shorter 'um.' He couldn't help but snigger.

Every mental hospital has its characters, patients that stand out for various reasons. Sid 'Fukum' Smith was known to everyone. He was completely institutionalised and allowed to wander the hospital and grounds at will, most staff actually called him by his trademark word. A story went that just before the outbreak of war, for some unknown reason, the lady mayoress had been invited to visit the ward. Much painting, cleaning and deodorising went on and come the day the then charge nurse, Tom Jelly, found it to be his responsibility to guide the visitor around the ward as no one from the management team wished to do so.

Sid approached them as they walked through the day room, the charge nurse stopping and tentatively making the introduction.

"This is Mr Smith, your majesty," he said, not knowing, or having been told, the correct way to address her.

She offered her hand, "Oh hello, Mr Smith. I hope Mr Jelly and his staff are taking good care of you."

Sid responded with five of the finest fukums he'd ever produced to which the mayoress responded, "Good God man they can't be that bad, surely?"

The encounter became one of the many outlandish stories recounted over a few beers at the staff bar. Some were hilarious and some were sad but perhaps the biography of Stan was remembered as the most melancholic.

Tim Richards was still beside him trying to look tired and sad, slowly shaking his head, breathing deeply and loudly. Stan had difficulty interpreting this behaviour so he decided to blow up his cheeks like a croaking toad.

"What are you doing with your face?"

"Don't know."

"You don't know what you're doing with your face?"

He waited a while and answered, "Just," then after a little while longer repeated, "don't know."

"All right Stan," Dr Richards decided not to push it. "I suppose it's your face and you can do what you like with it," and he deftly removed a pack of Players from his trouser pocket and lit one. "You know you've let me down badly, don't you?" he said nonchalantly.

Stan inflated his cheeks again and shook his head in denial.

"Yes, you've let me down; you've again told nurse Charlie that it was you who pushed William through the glass, haven't you?"

He continued shaking his head but the doctor persisted.

"You told Charlie it was you that pushed him after you promised to say nothing."

Stan's mouth popped as he opened it to speak. "I didn't promise," he corrected, "you told me not to say anything but I didn't promise."

All of a sudden, Dr Richards realised that the man he was talking to maybe somewhat odd but had full control of his memory and therein lay the problem.

"I told you I would make sure the glass was replaced and even though many people, including the police, would want me to brick the whole thing up I'd refuse because I know how much you like to see the trains, and as a favour, I asked you to say William ran into the room and before you knew it he was crashing through the glass. However, for some reason, you have once again told Charlie it was your fault."

They were alone, other than the fast asleep Mr Smith.

"But Charlie's my friend," he whined.

"Yes Stan, I know he's your friend but I'd like to think I'm your friend too."

The doctor stopped talking, and stretching his neck, scanned the room to make sure they only had Sid for company, then continued. "That's why I'm not having that damned glass wall bricked up," gesturing toward the boarding with his thumb.

"Well I won't tell anyone else," he conceded.

"I don't know if I can believe you and I don't like having these feelings about a friend," he scanned the room again.

"Well I promise I won't tell anyone."

"Thank you." The doctor smiled at him. "Are you my friend, Stan? I know I'm yours."

"Yes, I am your friend," he replied innocently,

"And would you do anything to help a friend?"

"Yes, I would."

"This request to not tell anyone is very important to me, Stan, it's one of the most important things and it's worrying me very, very much."

"I don't want you to be worried and I won't do it again." He heaved a sigh and returned the smile adding, "I promise."

The doctor was pleased with the progress and pulled a form from his inside pocket. "I knew you would be a good friend to me, Stan, as I am to you by stopping the bricklayers."

Stan nodded, oblivious to the fact that he was a pawn sitting with the king.

"That's why I'm doing you this favour," he continued, "but one good turn deserves another and I want you to do me a favour in return." He removed the middle pen of three sitting in his top pocket.

"I've got this little agreement here, Stan," he placed the form in front of him, "You sign your part promising not to say anyone chased William or you pushed him and I sign the part that states I won't have the wall bricked up; it's like a contract between two mates." The doctor lifted the official form and placed it in Stan's lap.

"It just means," he went on, "that we both, as friends, agree to not letting the other down."

Stan stared down at the form. His reading glasses were somewhere in the rubble of London and had never been replaced, a fact of which the doctor was well aware.

"Friends should trust each other," Stan blurted, "no need to sign contracts," and he suddenly sat bolt upright, the agreement curving on its way to the floor as the storm of lucidity hit him. "If friends have to sign contracts between themselves that tells me they're not really friends."

The doctor had occasionally experienced Stan's unclouded and enlightened statements before, in fact, didn't he mention something about a lie and a child an hour or so ago?

Stan was staring at him defiantly and the doctor decided to change his tactics before his patient's shrewdness became permanent. He began by moving his chair directly in front of him.

"I want you to calm down and relax. Friends shouldn't get upset with each other. Please, just be quiet and relax." Stan didn't object as the doctor held his hands. "Just relax for me, old friend," he continued, "simply relax and be quiet and now close your eyes." Stan closed his eyes.

"Hum along with me, old friend." Dr Richards purred a deep murmuring as he exhaled and Stan joined in, too loud at first but quickly adjusting to the volume.

They continued for some minutes then softly, the doctor whispered, "Be quiet and relax and don't worry." Tim Richards had now lowered his voice to its nadir and was somehow chanting the words. "You have nothing to worry about and I am going to look after you," then repeated, "I am going to look after my friend." He slowly raised Stan's hands and pulled them deliberately towards him, effectively straightening his arms. Stan could feel his brain swaying inside his head and a sensation of well-being starting to flow.

The doctor gently released Stan's hands which surprisingly stayed in position.

"Imagine you have a magnet in each hand and imagine those magnets are pulling them together; they're like friends, like us, they want to be with each other." Stan's hands slowly began drawing nearer.

"Only think of your hands and my voice Stan, nothing else matters, nothing else, the magnets are pulling and pulling, your hands are coming together," and they were and the doctor again looked around to make sure no one else was in the room.

"You're relaxed and calm, my friend. You're quiet and still and warm and you only hear me, my voice, your friend's voice." Stan's hands continued their relentless journey to be with one another. When they were a fraction of an inch apart the doctor quickly forced them together and almost simultaneously Stan's head fell forward. Tim Richards then gently pushed him back into the chair placing a cushion behind his head. "Hello, Stan," now in his normal voice, "you are quiet and relaxed and nothing can harm you. Concentrate on my voice and nothing can harm you. Do you believe me, my friend?"

"I do," Stan whispered.

"What can you hear?"

"You."

"Only me?"

"Only you," he replied quietly and the doctor was pleased that his hypnosis technique hadn't let him down.

"Do you remember we were talking earlier about us being friends, Stan, and how friends should do things for each other?"

Stan affirmed with an 'um' and a slight nod.

"Good, well done, and do you remember I mentioned the contract that I thought would be a good idea ... a contract that we should both sign?"

Stan again affirmed with a mumble and it was then that the doctor saw Charlie out of the corner of his eye, standing at the door. He felt his heart begin to thump and realised he had to think quickly then whispered to Stan to remain still and walked across to the nurse.

"What is it?" he hissed impatiently.

"I'm checking the ward," he replied defensively, "I didn't mean to intrude on—"

"Well you have!" Dr Richards snapped. "Mr Heart is upset and confused by all that's gone on and I'm trying to reassure him."

Charlie craned his neck, looking into the room, attempting to see Stan.

"What do you think you're doing?" the doctor gasped, acting as if he couldn't believe Charlie's action.

"I was just trying to see if I could—"

"How dare you!" the doctor cut him short once again. "Attempting to look at Mr Heart like that! Am I to assume you think something untoward is going on?" he said angrily.

"Please sir," and he stepped back slightly, raising his hands deferentially to reveal his palms, "I didn't think anything of the—"

For the third time, Tim Richards cut him off in mid-sentence. "Well that's how it seems to me, nurse; it seems you don't believe me and you're questioning my integrity."

Charlie couldn't comprehend the situation he was in and couldn't deny a smidgeon of suspicion had crossed his mind, a suspicion that the doctor's reaction was reinforcing. He decided there was no point in replying.

"Very well," he continued, "I think it best that you carry on doing whatever you have to do somewhere else and I'd appreciate it if no one else came in here until I've finished my conversation with him, do you understand?" and Charlie turned around and walked out, closing the door behind him.

Standing in the corridor with his back firmly planted against the wall he heaved a frustrated sigh whilst making a mental note to steer clear of Dr Richards as much as he could. Meanwhile, the doctor returned to Stan making a mental note to cause difficulty in Charlie's life whenever he could.

He sat down as quietly as possible in front of his patient, took a deep breath to compose himself and began. "Hello, Stan, you are still relaxed, calm and quiet; you have no worries and I am here to look after you, you understand that don't you, my friend?"

Stan responded as before.

The doctor again took a deep breath, relieved that Stan hadn't departed the trance. "We were talking about the contract and how important it was to me," he said rhetorically. "And I understand how you felt, and I think it was a good feeling, that's why I consider you a good friend because you think good thoughts, but I also want you to grasp my thoughts. This is so important to me and if you knew how important it was, as a friend you would sign it and that's what I'm asking you to do Stan, I am asking you to sign the contract or we can't be friends anymore." He then deepened and slightly raised his voice.

"I am telling you that when I ask you to wake up you will sign the agreement and you will feel you have no reason, no reason whatsoever, to not sign it." He eased himself forward and once more grasped Stan's hands.

"You will remember nothing of William Wilson's death, you will remember nothing of our conversations about him and you will sign the contract without question, do you understand me?"

There was silence and the doctor realised he was squeezing Stan's hands too hard but Stan wasn't aware of it, he was only aware of the words popping into his head, although unaware they were changing his memory of recent events.

He vaguely comprehended that a reply was necessary and utterly and completely knew that the doctor's reasoning was genuine and correct and it was an unarguable certainty that he would comply with everything being asked of him.

"Yes," he said confidently, "I do understand you."

"Then when I count down from five to one you will immediately awaken, remembering everything I have told you and forgetting everything I have told you to forget and then we shall sign the contract."

Dr Richards made the countdown and as Stan's eyes slowly opened, a broad smile grew from his mouth upwards to his now alert eyes.

"Now, my friend," the little man exclaimed, "show me where to sign this contract and let's be done with it."

Tim Richards fleetingly flirted with the idea that the agreement was no longer necessary. He hadn't planned on the hypnosis, only performing it due to Stan's belligerence and momentarily felt the procedure alone could be adequate in keeping Stan quiet but he decided to belt and brace it and he bent to pick up the form and passed Stan the pen, guiding his hand as he unwittingly signed the consent form for an unspecified amount of electro convulsive therapies. Stan handed the pen and form back to him and sat back in his chair as the doctor placed them securely in his jacket.

"You won't regret this you know, Stan," and he actually believed the words he was saying, "sometimes, forgetting about something is the best thing for you."

"I know," he agreed, although whatever the man said would be agreeable. Stan had no idea what the 'something' referred to in the doctor's sentence, but accepted what he'd said because now, Tim Richards was his very, very, very best friend.

Stan didn't question why he was being given an injection early the next morning and as he slowly lost consciousness they placed him on a trolley and wheeled him away to receive the first treatment. During the next six weeks he was the recipient of another twenty-three. Charlie knew they would be of no benefit and was sickened by it but felt powerless to act. The shell shock had erased the memory of the bombings and the ECT was erasing the truth behind William Wilson's death.

Over the following years Dr Richards paid much attention to Stan, conducting many consultations and a further course of treatment was prescribed whenever he perceived a return of Stan's memories of events. After sixteen years, owing to a sea change in psychiatric thinking, Stan's therapy was stopped. At one hundred and seventeen, records showed that he had received eighty-one more than any other patient in the hospital and sixty-one nationally. No member of staff understood the efficacy of the therapy but such was the authoritarian nature of Dr Richards' personality, no one dared ask.

Stan was forty-two years of age when the treatments stopped. Almost half of his life had been spent in the hospital and the result of his residency was him becoming imbecilic. He hummed a lot, dribbled a bit but always had a smile on his face because he was happy ... he had nothing to be sad about. His day mostly consisted of sitting in one of the pee proof chairs in what was still called the conservatory, although the whole of the front section had been bricked up leaving only the ceiling as glass.

MAYBE

After sixteen years Sid Fukum Smith had become slightly less vocal, though not that you'd notice. For some reason Sid had taken to occasionally tickling Stan, making him laugh like an excited child and that was about the highlight of Stan's day. All of the staff felt sorry for him and Tim Richards was well aware that he was blamed for what they thought to be a gross professional error, but the grip that the abnormal perversion he possessed, the reason behind all of this, was so vice like, so crushingly engulfing, that it made him completely unconcerned about any adverse opinion.

Chapter 10

As Georgia's pregnancy progressed their relationship worsened. She had little time for meal making or housework but plenty of time for smoking, drinking and criticising. In the 1940s the dangers to the unborn child due to inadequate maternal behaviour hadn't been established but George knew instinctively that smoking and drinking in particular could only be harmful. It had become noticeable around the time of their marriage and her consumption had increased ever since. He felt she was becoming a mirror image of her mother; selfish, foul mouthed and obnoxious. As a sop he had applied to the local prison for a warder's job, thinking she was embarrassed by his position at the mental hospital; constantly condemning the place and him for working there, never showing interest in his daily routine or experiences. He didn't really want to change jobs but thought it might lessen her indifference by doing so and make her feel proud of him. He would try to be stoical and roll with the punches but life was becoming difficult to bear, he hadn't the first clue of how to deal with her; he was no angel but this was a different league.

"Georgia, I don't think you should drink so much when you're pregnant," he would say calmly, "it can't be good for you or the baby."

"If you don't like it you can fuck off then! This is my baby and I know best."

"It's our baby," he corrected her, remaining calm, "and with the amount you're drinking lately you might fall, you might hurt it."

"You might fall, you might hurt it," she would repeat mockingly and take another slurp, "well I know one thing matey, if I do fall it'll be your fault because I got lumbered with a useless, lazy shit and it's you who's driving me to drink!" her piercing blue eyes staring out of a reddened face.

"That's not true and you know it. I go to work."

"Work? Is that what you call it? More like glorified turd scraping."

He took a deep breath. "I go to work," he repeated, "then get home and start doing more work around the house. You don't lift a finger and when I do get home you're already drunk. God knows what's going to happen when the baby arrives." He sat and put his head in his hands. "I just don't know what I can do," he moaned pathetically.

"Well I know what you can do, nursey boy," she sneered, "for a start you can go and look at yourself in the mirror. You go to the pub and get pissed; you sit in your wonky fucking rocking chair drinking your beer, so don't try and make me feel guilty with all that bollocks."

He walks over to her, breathes in her gin soaked breath and fetid body sweat, a combination that appals him, then says to her unhurriedly, "But it's not me who's pregnant, is it Georgia? It's not me who's damaging an innocent child." His words hit home but have no beneficial effect. She places her glass on the table and stands directly in front of him, a look of sheer malevolence inhabiting her face.

"I don't know if you've heard the saying 'taken to the cleaners'," she began menacingly, "but you're that pile of shit clothes and I'm the one who's taking you there." She took a long hard drag on her cigarette and blew smoke purposefully and accurately into his face, making him cough and splutter. "When I met you in that dance hall," she went on, "I thought you were okay, you'd fit the bill, nothing special though, just okay."

He recovered his composure and kept listening.

"You see, I saw a way out, George; I saw a way out from the shit house I was living in and the shits I was living with." She sat and took a drink. "I knew I'd never love you, too much like my twat of a father I suppose, but I thought I could pretend and just go through life like that because it would be better than the life I was living, the hell I was in with my excuses for parents and you don't know half of it George, believe me, you don't know the half of it," and as she paused for thought he actually began to feel sorry for her, notwithstanding all the insults he felt an urge to comfort her but it didn't last for long. "But I was wrong," she continued and took another drink, George cringing at the sight of it. "I was wrong because you are such a weak person, doing everything I tell you," she emphasised with a toss of her arms, "saying stupid things you think will make me happy," another arm toss, "never," she shook her head, searching for words, "NEVER BEING IN CHARGE!"

Silence erupted and they found themselves staring at each other.

"I don't respect you," she looked away as she said it, "I don't respect you and I'm beginning to hate the sight of you. I can't help it but there it is and I drink because that hate makes me."

George sat down, a low groan escaping from his mouth and again placed his head in his hands. After a short while he gradually raised his eyes to look up at her and whispered, "I don't know what to say, Georgia, I don't know what to do."

"I know you don't, George," and she emptied the glass with one gulp, "and that's the fucking problem."

Chapter 11

Bill had had a bad day.

His world had fallen apart only to be repaired by the head of the hospital. He hurried back to his quarters, pulled the suitcase out from under the bed and began packing his belongings, amazed by how little he'd accumulated during his three-year stay. Once finished, he closed the case and pressed home the clasps then sat on the bed and retrieved the instructions he'd been given. He thought it peculiar that they were handwritten, expecting a formal, typed letter, but put it down to the short timescale.

He was to become the assistant to the matron of the children's home and was to report to her on arrival. His salary remained the same and accommodation within the home would be provided free of charge, all very acceptable, however there were two unusual items that surprised him. Firstly, a vehicle was to be provided with the post and he was required to pass his driving test within two months of taking up the position. This was an incredible bonus. Car ownership was limited to the few and considered quite a status symbol, although he was daunted by the prospect of having to pass the test within two months. Driving tests had been suspended for the duration of the war, the examiners being deployed to traffic duties and supervision of fuel rationing and had only recently been reinstated, and by all accounts the tests had become considerably more difficult. Secondly, he was to ensure that he was always available whenever Dr Richards requested his presence. He folded the paper and returned it to his pocket then rose and gave his face a quick rinse in the sink. He knew he was in no position to either refuse the job or question any of the instructions. He sat back down and put the case in his lap, sitting like that for some time, exhausted by the day's events. He reread the letter in his mind; a car would be provided? It was simply unheard of for such a job; and always to be at the beck and call of Dr Richards? He shook his head and rubbed the side of his forehead. What had he let himself in for? But truth be told, Bill Sweet didn't really mind. Bill Sweet was just grateful he'd been plucked out of the god awful mess he'd found himself in. Bill Sweet was going to do anything the good doctor wanted him to do because Bill was not only a repulsive and repugnant little weasel with the appropriate thoughts and ideas but also a self-preservationist who would feed his mother to the pigs if it saved his skin. He lifted his case and began the long walk through the hospital and grounds to the bus stop. Nearing the main entrance he noticed a casual acquaintance of his, a nursing auxiliary by the name of George Goodwin coming the other way. He put his head down and determinedly carried on walking but George stopped him, asking how he was.

"Not good," Bill replied, "I've had a bad day. Dr Richards has transferred me out of here; up to the children's home, I'm on my way—" and he suddenly stopped in mid-sentence, taken aback at the features and demeanour of George. Bill noticed he had lost a lot of weight, weight he couldn't afford to lose and his clothes were dowdy and creased. Dark circles surrounded his sunken eyes and his hair was unwashed and uncombed. He knew George was a lazy type but he always took care over his appearance yet this man who stood before him looked like one of those victims of the Nazi concentration camps whose pictures had been spread across the front pages just a couple of years ago. Bill gazed at him, unshaven, unclean and unhappy.

"Are you all right, George, you aren't ill, are you?" Bill couldn't have cared less about George's health but friends can have their uses.

"No, no, I'm fine it's just," and the words trailed off to nothing. "This is my last day too," he restarted, "applied to the prison for a warder's job, had a nod and a wink it's mine," but he hadn't, he was hoping upon hope that he heard something soon having resigned without knowing if his application had been accepted, another mistake for Georgia to rave over. "New start, you know," he continued, "getting a bit pissed off with this place," and it was then that Bill realised George had alcohol on his breath.

"Well best of luck with that," Bill needed to go, "perhaps we could meet up for a pint sometime?"

"Yeah, wet the baby's head." He chuckled.

"Baby? What baby?"

"Well my baby, haven't you heard? Mine and Georgia's." He could sense that Bill wanted to go and began walking off, "Not born yet, but any excuse eh?" He shouted, disappearing into the darkness of the hospital. As Bill walked to the bus stop he decided he would have that drink with George. He figured if Dr Richards, somewhere down the line, was unable to protect him then a friendly screw up in the prison would be invaluable.

George continued through the hospital and arrived for his last shift on the long stay geriatric ward. The two pints he'd had at the Falcon had eventually reached his bladder and he was bursting. As he came out of the toilet, wrestling with his fly, he noticed the charge nurse approaching. Tom Jelly was a large, rotund and ruddy individual who always looked on the bright side but he wasn't looking forward to the task he was about to perform and wore a stern expression.

"Hello, George," he began, "need a few words with you in the office."

Ordinarily he would have sensed something was wrong and been apprehensive but the couple of beers had put pay to that insight and George followed him in without a care. The charge nurse wasn't going to beat around the bush and wanted to get this over with as soon as possible.

"Look son, you were seen drinking in the pub an hour or so ago, by a member of staff who was on his way home; came back specially to tell me."

"I wasn't," he interjected, but the charge nurse ploughed on.

Maybe

"You know the rules about drinking before coming onto duty; it's completely unacceptable, completely unprofessional, George."

"But I—"

"Just listen, son," he paused for a second, then added, "please," and he shifted a little in his chair. "I can smell the alcohol from where I'm sat for Christ's sake so don't make this any harder for me. I like you, George, always have and I know this is your last shift but I can't allow you to work it. I'm going to be brutally honest with you for your own sake," and George braced himself, "you look dreadful, you don't smell so good and you're half drunk."

"I'm not half—" but the charge nurse wouldn't let him get a word in, "and I'm going to have to ask you to remove yourself from this ward and the hospital, I'm sorry, George." He rose to his feet whilst looking at a man who seemed beaten and somehow lost.

"I really am but I've patients to consider and staff morale so I'm going to walk with you to the door now and I'd like you to get yourself home."

But George didn't go home. He went straight back to the pub, sat at the bar and ordered a pint. It was just him and the landlord, a large and friendly character not unlike the charge nurse. During his second drink, George got a lot more talkative and began telling him his troubles and as he got up to leave the landlord grabbed his arm and, feeling sorry for him, offered one piece of advice.

"Can I tell you something, mate, that's stood me in good stead over the years?" George listened up. "Well it's pretty straightforward, if you're in a shit situation there's only two ways of sorting it, you either change it or get out of it," and he left the pub with that suggestion flowing through his thoughts.

Change it or get out of it, change it or get out of it.

He turned the key and opened the door to the cottage with trepidation. It was six weeks ago that Georgia had dropped the bombshell about beginning to hate him and things were getting a whole lot worse. He was dreading her finding out that he'd given up a job before securing another and shivered at the verbal stabbing he was going to get for it. She had recently began adding cider to the gin which was becoming difficult to get hold of and too expensive. His usual first job on getting home was clearing up the brown scrumpy bottles that she'd strewn around the place. On a couple of occasions lately he had found her blacked out, wetting herself the last time, and those sheets took some washing and that mattress was still propped up against the back wall, but his biggest problem was how to handle the worry he had for the baby inside her. He didn't know much about the internal workings of the female body but he wasn't that ignorant to not know that the child was getting everything it needed from her and that particular well was poisonous. He couldn't help thinking that the baby had a permanent hangover and if it could sing, well those songs would be the bar room, bawdy sort.

'Change it or get out of it.'

He closed the door and walked in. He couldn't change it, he knew he couldn't change it. She hated him and trying to get someone to stop hating you is as difficult as turning shit into pearls. He trod on the letter lying flat on the hall carpet, bent down and picked it up, squeezed his finger under the flap and ran it along to tear it open. It was the acceptance from the prison service he'd been craving for. He stood looking at it, wanting to remain stuck forever in that moment of complete relief and exhilaration. Before it arrived he had been at the foot of the mountain, fearful of the climb ahead but here he now was, letter in hand, standing tall and proud at the summit, chest thrust out and feeling he could fly.

"Georgia," he called out, "Georgia, I've been accepted to work at the prison, I've got the letter," and he ran into the living room alive with his first taste of happiness in months.

She sat with her back to him, motionless.

"Georgia," he stood in front of her, looked down at her, "I've got the job in the prison, what d'you think of that?"

She looked at him through half-closed, bloodshot eyes and she could see that he was pleased and delighted. She had convinced herself that this man had ruined her short life, was to blame for her misery and she didn't like what she was seeing, not one teeny weeny bit and she certainly and absolutely didn't want him to be pleased and delighted. She held out her hand and motioned to him to give her the letter which he eagerly did. She carefully and methodically put her cigarette in the ashtray, stood up, grasped the hem and lifted her skirt above her waist.

"What are you doing, Georgia?" he gasped, but she put her finger to her mouth in a gesture for him to be quiet. Slowly, she pushed her cotton knickers down to the floor and stepped out of them then turned her back to him. George thought the impossible. He thought she was going to offer herself as some sort of reward for getting the job until she bent over double, brought the letter up behind her and began wiping her backside with it, back and forth, back and forth.

George's descent of the mountain had just begun.

He couldn't believe what he was witnessing and staggered back into his much maligned rocking chair. Georgia then abruptly stopped the performance, turned around and began squeezing the letter between her hands; squeezing it and compressing it until it resembled a golf ball and seductively moved across to him, naked from the waist down.

"It's a joke, George," she lied. "It's just a joke," and she knelt down in front of him and positioned herself between his legs, "It's wonderful news you've got the job." She was rubbing his inner thigh and when she went a little higher he was right back there, maybe three-quarters of the way back up the mountain.

"Now close your eyes," she urged, "and pucker your lips because I'm going to give my sexy prison officer a big smacker," and he did. He closed his eyes and pursed his lips. This was the old Georgia, all naughty talk and electric touches and he sat there thinking that he wouldn't have to get out of it after all because he had changed it.

He was nearing the summit when she firmly pressed the soiled letter ball hard into his mouth. He gagged to get rid of it but she grasped the back of his head with her left arm, pulling him towards her and pressed the hand that had delivered it strongly against his mouth. It seemed an age before he was able to release her grip and spit it out during which time

Georgia simply laughed and hysterically laughed. He pushed her away and rushed to the small kitchen and cupped his hands under the tap, sloshing water into his mouth, frantically rinsing and gargling, disgusted by the thought and taste of that letter. George gargled as Georgia laughed, an increasingly mad and frenzied laugh, an eerie and frightening laugh that only stopped when George's hand connected with her cheek and her joyous expression suddenly became a scowl.

Georgia heard the term from an American G.I. when she was seventeen. She'd never used it but now seemed a most appropriate time to do so. Teeth bared and eyes glaring, she hissed at him, "You motherfucker! You hit me!" and he visibly quaked.

"I had to," he mouthed it, barely audible, ashamed he'd struck his wife, and then bellowed, "you were SCARING ME!"

She knew she had now won this argument and held the higher ground. She knew that someone suffering from unrequited love always behaved like a bloody idiot. "Well let me tell you something you pathetic, squirming little bastard," and weeks later, when George looked back at this moment, he would swear that he could see horns protruding from her head and she was standing on goat's legs, "you have damned my life and your child's life and I will never forgive you," and she began to walk out of the room, "never," she emphasised and opening the front door the 'never' she again screamed was loud enough to mask its slam.

Georgia made her way through the dark night to her parents' house. She didn't want to but there was nowhere else to go. Meanwhile, George went to bed and lay awake for many hours, worried for his wife and child's safety but knowing deep down where they'd be. He cast his mind back to the landlord and his advice, shit situation, change or get out, change or get out. He thought that landlord didn't know how apt his advice was going to be. The wind whistled outside and he heaved the blankets tighter. As he began to lose himself to sleep a rational voice rose out of nowhere.

"Come on old son, you ain't gonna change this." In his half-sleep he mistakenly thought it sounded like the voice of a patient in the geriatric ward, a man who, although seemingly as daft as the rest, occasionally surprised everyone with his wisdom. George sat upright in the blackness, he was back at base camp but responded confidently, "I know I'm not, Stan, I know I'm not," and it was there and then that he decided there was no choice; he had to get out of it.

CHAPTER 12

Bill Sweet and his worldly belongings made their way to the bus stop which was a further five minutes away and he used the time to consider his situation. He had been the reason for William Wilson's death, no question, and Dr Richards and Stan Heart were the only other people to know. The doctor had assured him that Stan would be silenced and not only that, had arranged a new job for him. The doctor was his saviour but for what reason? They had no relationship with one another, in fact over the years they had had little contact at all. The doctor held him in low regard, which was patently obvious by his behaviour at their meeting. He shivered. The evening was cold but it wasn't the temperature, rather the vulnerability of his situation. The bus arrived and he boarded. The journey was short and before he knew it he was disembarking. He began walking when an idea crossed his mind to just wait for another bus, then catch another and get as far away as possible, find some other job and live anonymously. Then another idea, the idea that, should the police decide to further their investigation, his running away would raise serious suspicions. That thought made his legs work faster and he walked into the children's home out of breath but satisfied he was doing the right thing. The letter had instructed him to report to the matron and after finding her office he gingerly knocked on the door. Expecting a voice command to enter, the door was opened instead by a tall, slim woman offering her hand. He immediately shook it and introduced himself.

"I know who you are, Mr Sweet, please come in and take a seat." The office was clean, neat and tidy and its occupier old, thin and weary. Bill observed her. She seemed poised and self-confident, her lank greying hair framed a gaunt, wrinkled face with lines like lashes surrounding her smoker's mouth. Bill thought she'd had a lot to put up with in her life, then she began to speak.

"You are to be my assistant, Mr Sweet. I have assigned you a small suite of three rooms at the top of the building and, although simply furnished, are more than adequate."

A smile appeared on her face and most of the wrinkles and lines disappeared with that smile and he realised that once she had been beautiful. "I'm sure you're very pleased that an automobile will be put at your disposal," her smile widening as he nodded. "I have arranged a course of lessons with a local company that prides itself on their pupils' high success rate in the driving test, your first lesson is tomorrow at three." This lady is extremely well organised, he thought, and he was quickly warming to her.

"Do you have any questions before I show you to your accommodation?" she asked, opening the desk drawer and removing a set of keys. Bill sat upright and cleared his throat. "I'd like to know what my role will be here." She repositioned herself in the chair and placed the keys on the desk.

"You're going to shadow me for the next twelve months," she began, "and at the end of that period I will retire and all being well you will take over the running of the home," her smile once again flattening the ridges. Bill couldn't believe what he was hearing. He was experiencing doom and boon in the space of twelve hours. He'd had much bad luck in his life but this news was cancelling out a lot of it. He realised the phrase 'all being well' began right here, with this conversation and his manner and speech promptly changed. He leant forward and looked directly into her eyes.

"I will diligently endeavour to be a worthy successor to you ma'am," he said solemnly, "and I thank you for giving me the chance to further my career." As much as he tried he was always thinking of himself.

"Well in reality it's Dr Richards you should be thanking," she advised, amazed at his sudden eloquence, "he feels you're a young man with potential and should be given the chance."

She knew exactly what the doctor's opinion of him was and it certainly wasn't that. Just an hour ago he had explained to the matron at length about the events of the day and Bill's involvement and she was finding it difficult to make those smiles seem genuine.

"Well in that case I think I should include the doctor in my gratitude, he truly is a man I look up to," and it was there and then, right at that precise moment that Bill decided to radically change his persona. He transmogrified into an outwardly affable human being, saying the right things and doing the right things. Being compassionate and considerate to others, showing no ill will and never taking sides. He thought of the car and the prestige of his forthcoming position and vowed that nothing was going to jeopardise this dream. A tidal wave of narcissism had enveloped his ego and he knew without doubt that he had to alter the impression he gave to succeed. But annoyingly, his intended personality change was coincidentally joined by a physical one as if his body was objecting to his strategy. As Bill sat in front of the matron he suddenly felt a small tug to his face, almost imperceptible but definite. He had become the owner of a facial twitch, not a grand neck-wrenching movement, more of a slight half-wink accompanied by a slighter turning of his head. This involuntary movement shocked him for a moment and a look of surprise crossed his face.

"Are you all right, Mr Sweet?" she asked, attempting to look concerned.

"Yes, of course, matron," he lied, trying to make light of it. "It's just a lot to take in," and he felt that tug again which she noticed and ignored.

"Then let's get you in your quarters," and she picked up the keys and led him to the top of the building. As the matron had mentioned the rooms were indeed small but perfectly adequate; much more adequate than the single room and shared kitchen he was used to. She handed him the keys and arranged to meet early the following morning. He thanked her again and gently closed the door as she left. Giving her time to get out of earshot he flung down his case and flopped heavily onto the bed.

"God is good," he half shouted, squeezing his hands into fists and shaking them, "and I'm in line for the old cow's job," he said more loudly but it wasn't only Bill who could hear that statement, the matron, who was standing directly outside with her ear to the door, could also.

She tiptoed her way down the stairs to her office and sat back on the chair. The slightly open window allowed the cold evening to push in a cooling breeze and she was glad of the fresh air which seemed to clear her mind. She wasn't looking forward to the coming twelve months. Dr Richards had told her all about this odious young man, all about his cruel little ways but those with perversions lurking inside them find it easy to judge and detest others of the same ilk and when they met she had immediately regarded Bill Sweet with disdain. Unbeknown to Bill, this well organised and poised lady wasn't the innocent she'd have him believe, not by a long chalk, and she knew that none of those feelings of dislike would ever be allowed to surface during her dealings with Bill Sweet as that would be very dangerous indeed, because Dr Richards had told her to be discreet and of course he was always right. He and only he knew what she liked to do and if anyone else became party to that secret, well, her life just wouldn't be worth living.

Chapter 13

The next day it took George an hour to make the twenty-minute walk to his in-laws. He paused many times and questioned what he was doing; he was about to turn his back on everything he had, but each time he convinced himself it was the right and only thing to do. He arrived at the featureless terraced house, the chrome door knocker glistening from the beam of the streetlamp. He lifted and lowered it three times and after a few seconds a light appeared in the glass above the door. His mother-in-law opened it. She was a short, tense woman, huge breasts counterbalanced by equally huge buttocks. Her crow black hair was pulled tight and tied at the back and the odds on her being in a good mood were much worse than evens.

"Come on in, George," and she put her back to the wall, allowing him to pass and enter the house. When he was a couple of feet beyond her she added venomously, "You little shit!" and hit him hard in the back with both clenched fists. He stumbled into the living room, arms bent up to protect his head and she ran after him continuing the onslaught.

"Get off me, you raving lunatic," he grunted and managed to grab her hands forcing her back onto the settee, pinioning her.

"Stop him, Jim," she shouted and George turned to see his father-in-law walk into the room, "he's killing me, he's a murderer," she wailed and Jim took a pace towards him.

"Stop there," George said compellingly, "I'm not trying to kill her, if anything she's trying to kill me," he shouted, still trying to subdue the wriggling lump of spite. Jim stayed where he was. Possessing only a meagre amount of brain matter he was confused by the two almost simultaneous commands.

His mother- in-law was panting, trying to regain strength for more attempts at escape when George spoke again, eyeing them intently in turn. "Now calm down both of you," he said forcefully. "Where's Georgia?" he asked him, "where's my wife?"

"Your wife?" she said, twisting her face horribly, "your wife?" she repeated, "if she's your wife that would make you a husband and that's something you're not!" She relaxed and he released his grip allowing her to stand, then placing her hands firmly on her hips and stretching her head out towards him, continued. "A husband doesn't kick his innocent wife out of the house!" and she poked him hard in the middle of the chest. George now realised Georgia had been lying to them about him. "A husband doesn't come home drunk with an empty wage packet," then looking at Jim, "although that stupid twat used to and I soon put a stop to that!" Then she resumed poking George in the chest and concluded, "and a husband doesn't try and suffocate his wife - a six months' pregnant wife to boot!"

Had Georgia seen him that time, he thought, looking in at her when she was supposed to be asleep and somehow sensed what he had been thinking? Or was it just coincidence?

She was fuming now like an old battered engine with an oil leak and he pictured Georgia as this woman thirty years hence; he looked across at Jim and saw himself in the same time frame.

He knew there was nothing to be gained from trying to reason with them and asked again, directly, "Where is my wife?"

"Here I am."

He looked in the direction of the voice and saw Georgia standing in the doorway of the kitchen, the baby lump making her appear all the more feminine and voluptuous.

"What do you want, George?" she said resignedly. She had been crying and her eyes were puffy and swollen but he knew they were crocodile tears, designed to make her lies more believable.

"I need to talk to you, Georgia," he began, but was instantly answered by her mother.

"You're not talking to my daughter," she shrieked, "you've hurt her too much, you'll not have another chance to—"

"Shut up, Mum," Georgia interjected, "why don't you just fuck off down the pub," then as an afterthought, "and take him with you?" She motioned her head towards her father who immediately picked his jacket up from the back of the chair.

"Stay where you are. I'm not leaving him alone with my daughter."

He replaced the jacket.

"Oh for Christ's sake," Georgia moaned, "since when have you given a shit about me?" She walked over to her father and picked up his jacket. "Put this on, Dad, and the both of you just piss off down the pub."

"I'm only trying to protect you, love," she complained, "I don't want you to be hurt anymore!"

"Oh yeah," she sneered, "well you should have thought about that years ago. I won't forget the way you dragged me up."

"Georgia," her father suddenly came to life, "don't speak to your mother like that."

"Don't speak to your mother like that?" she echoed, "I'm speaking to the fucking pair of you!" she corrected him. "What makes you think you're any different?"

George was cringing in the crossfire. Her parents walked out of the room, her reluctantly, him thankfully, and seconds later the front door slammed and they were alone.

"What do you want, George?" she repeated and sat down in the chair her father had vacated.

"I need to talk to you, no, I need to say something to you," the revision of words only meaningful to him.

"Well make it quick, I don't want to have to look at you for too long." Her astounding callousness forced a thin, bizarre laugh to escape his lips, infuriating her. Slowly he began shaking his head.

"You do nothing to make people like you, do you, Georgia?" The head shaking stopped. "You're a selfish, self-centred, nasty bitch and I wish I'd never set eyes on you."

"The feeling is mutual so spare me the bollocks. Now tell me what you came here for and fuck off."

Her display of incredible arrogance stunned him again and for a moment he was lost for words. He merely looked down at her and restarted the slow head shake. In unison, she also began to shake her head, sarcastically mocking him.

"What's with the head shaking, George? You'll crick your fucking neck," she said, speaking the words in rhythm with her head movements. He stopped, she stopped, then bolstered by her attitude he began.

"I'm leaving you, Georgia." A wave of self-gratitude rippled through him as he said it. "I'm leaving you, the baby, the cottage, everything. I'm starting again and I want nothing more to do with you. If I see you in the street I won't acknowledge you. You can have the cottage and everything in it, I don't want any of it, I just want to be free of you and everything that comes with you." He paused for breath. "That's what I came to tell you."

George felt overwhelming relief, empowered by the courage he had summoned to use those words. He wasn't sure what would happen next and he readied himself for her reaction. The only item of value in the house rested on the mantelpiece over the unlit fire. The Florian ware Moorcroft vase had resided on that mantelpiece for more than sixty years, originally a present from her now dead grandfather to her now dead grandmother. It was the precious thing of the household. Her mother had carefully dusted and polished it every week for as long as she could remember but blind rage doesn't differentiate between a pot and a pistol and it fitted perfectly in her hand as she jumped from the chair and grabbed it.

George understood what was about to happen and his courage departed as he ran for the exit. The vase was airborne as he reached the doorway and he suddenly felt a knock on the back of his head, not a thundering crunch as he'd expected, followed by a resounding, echoing thud from the wall to his right and in front of him. He hadn't taken the full force of the vase as she'd intended, it had just ricocheted off him and crashed into the wall, shattering into a hundred pieces. He stopped momentarily, his brief encounter with courage now a million miles away, then resumed running up the hallway, through the door and into the road, not stopping until he was safely back in the cottage. Lathered in sweat, he swiftly packed two suitcases afraid that Georgia would appear at any time. As he slammed the door behind him he began to walk quickly in the opposite direction from whence he came. He continued the pace until he reached a park bench and sat in the cold night, his breath like the steam from the trains that passed the hospital, not knowing what to do next. Meanwhile, Georgia was alone in that terraced house, drink in hand, baby in tummy, smile on face. Her mother was going to go crazy when she found out George had hurled that vase at her daughter.

Chapter 14

Stan had been a patient for eleven years in 1951. It was the year Queen Elizabeth the second came to the throne and the year that Stan came into money. Uncle Theo's visits were becoming few and far between. His health was rapidly deteriorating and the trek left him fatigued. Four years previously he had been pensioned from the underground having reached the level of inspector. The adjustment of running in employment to sitting in retirement was difficult for him to make and most activities now needed concentrated effort, most of all, that journey. In the December of that year Stan had received fifty-eight electro convulsive treatments and his memory had worsened to such an extent that he had no recollection of his relative whatsoever. As a child, Uncle Theo had suffered rheumatic fever which weakened his heart muscle and brought on pulmonary oedema, weakening his lungs and, although unrelated, it was two other events that coincided in the winter of 1951, which were to end the life of this lovely man.

Event one was in early December when he visited his nephew for the very last time. Stan's inability to recognise or remember him, his loss of weight and coherence and the realisation that Stan wasn't getting out of there had filled Uncle Theo with sadness. It was with a heavy heart and tearful eyes that he began the long train and bus journey back to his home on the Isle of Dogs.

It was a cold and dank winter and this day was particularly so. When he eventually arrived he immediately set about lighting the coal fire and therein lay the second contribution to his fate. The exceptionally cold winter coupled with the fact that Londoners were burning cheap, rough coal, the quality grades being exported to boost depleted treasury reserves, meant that much more polluting smoke was floating into the atmosphere. Now Theo could never have known, along with millions of others living in the South East of England, that a freak of the weather, called an inversion of an anti-cyclone, had occurred that day trapping the smoke laden air beneath it. As the sun was shrouded the temperature fell even more resulting in existing fires being stoked and refuelled and many more new fires being lit in parts of houses usually left unheated. Thus, on Friday, the 5th of December, 1951, the Great Smog descended on the capital. Drivers abandoned cars, public performances were cancelled and Londoners literally couldn't see their hands in front of their faces. Unfortunately for Uncle Theo and his neighbours, the Isle of Dogs was at the epicentre where visibility was officially recorded as zero. After lighting the fire he eased himself into the chair beside it. A black depression swathed him as he thought of his nephew, alone and bewildered in that faraway place. His nephew who displayed no recognition; his only living relative who he loved so much, thin, shabby and daft. He was uncertain whether the electric treatments were beneficial or not but it was simply not in his nature to question the authority of a doctor.

A movement caught his eye and he looked across at the closed door. A grey cloud of what seemed like smoke was seeping in from under it, floating and creeping towards the fireplace. Sections of that cloud began to follow the fire's smoke up the chimney but other sections remained in the room. Ordinarily he would have reacted in some way, perhaps looking for the cause or maybe sealing the door, but the will to act just wasn't there. Following his soul destroying visit to the hospital a boulder of apathy had landed in his lap and he simply sat there complacently wondering if some part of the house was alight, not concerned if it was. Smog continued to enter the room, the fire's draw sucking and pulling. Pictures on the wall were becoming difficult to see now and his eyes began to sting and weep. The amount of smog going up the chimney decreased as the environment above the house compressed and pushed down. As the tendrils of smoke weaved up his nose and down into his already weakened lungs he began to cough, gently at first, then more vigorously.

Coincidences happen all the time and most have simple explanations but there are some that can't be interpreted and remain forever strange.

Twenty miles away in the hospital that Uncle Theo had visited just hours before, Sid Fukum Smith had tickled his nephew for the second time that day and Stan was gleeful, sitting in his chair chuckling like an amused child. As the arrow of pain dug deeply into Theo's left arm Stan's giggles subsided and a tear appeared in his eye. Uncle Theo wrapped his right arm around the agony, his face screwed up unrecognisably, his neck taut strings of sinews. As the bolt of pain travelled up into his shoulder more tears appeared in Stan's eyes and as his uncle's heart stopped beating and he slumped dead in the chair Stan was wailing and crying uncontrollably. Charlie the staff nurse ran in, alarmed by the noise and rushed to Stan's side to cradle him in his arms. He thought of him now with great fondness and was upset to see him so distraught.

"Fukum!" he shouted angrily over the commotion, turning to look in Sid's direction. "Have you got anything to do with this?"

"Not Fukum," Stan whispered through his sobs, "Not Fukum."

Charlie eventually managed to calm him but remained confused by his unusual behaviour, so much so that he decided to note the episode in Stan's medical history report, shaking his head in disbelief at the first entry he noticed there.

Uncle Theo had been a frugal and penny wise individual. When the state appointed executor had finally sold the house and its contents and reconciled the various savings accounts and fees his estate was worth two hundred and thirty-two thousand pounds - ten pounds for each day of his life. When the Charge Nurse informed him of his uncle's death and the huge amount of money he had inherited Stan simply nodded. The money was deposited with the General Post Office, as were all patient funds and he was given a blue savings book which he was to keep in a safe place.

Stan kept it in his sock both day and night, his addled mind considered this place as good as anywhere.

Chapter 15

George sat on the park bench mulling over his situation, grateful that they hadn't had a further confrontation at the cottage. This was a momentous step to take but he had no alternative. Thankfully, lodgings came with the job but he didn't start for three days and needed somewhere to stay in the interim. A young couple walked past him arm in arm, glanced quickly at him, unsure. He looked up, guessing they were married and wondered how they reacted to one another, probably in a loving and decent way, caring for and respecting one another, planning their future together. How the hell had this disaster happened? It was the strong beating the weak, he mused, the bad beating the not so bad. She'd planned all this, she was just like her mother, the scheming cow, and her bloody father is just like me. His thoughts were jumbled and needed arranging. He began reliving recent events; Tom Jelly escorting him from the ward, the landlord and his advice, bumping into Bill Sweet and being assaulted by his mother-in-law.

"Wait a minute," he said out loud putting his thoughts into reverse, didn't Bill Sweet say he was off to work at the children's home and wasn't that home just a ten minute walk across the park and wasn't he going to live in? Bill would put him up for a few days, of course he would. They weren't what you'd call bosom buddies but George felt he could call him a friend. Some of the staff thought Bill was a cold fish and others thought he didn't have the compassion to be in a caring profession but speak as you find and George never found that to be true. So he picked up his cases and made his way through the deserted park to the home. The building that suddenly loomed in front of him was tall and imposing, warm lights within giving it a welcoming face.

It was run under the authority of the hospital and treated as a ward although they were a couple of miles apart. Twenty-four patients resided there from the ages of ten to twenty-one with varying psychiatric and behavioural problems. He'd never met the matron, who had a reputation for aloofness, but he'd seen her occasionally taking a child for interview to Dr Richards' office, always smartly dressed, walking with a purpose and always firmly holding the patient's hand no matter what their age.

He entered the building, glad to be out of the freezing evening and finding the staff office, knocked on the door. The duty nurse called him in and baulked at the dishevelled man that entered. George recognised her surprise.

"Please don't be alarmed," he said reassuringly, raising his hands as if to say, look, no guns, no knives. "I'm a nurse from the geriatric ward over at the hospital." Well until recently, he thought. " I know it might seem strange turning up here unannounced, looking a bit weather beaten but I need to see a colleague of mine, Bill Sweet, I think he began work here today."

She hesitated for a moment, not remembering seeing him on her visits to the hospital and feeling a little mistrustful.

"Ah, Mr Sweet," she brought his name to mind having been informed of his arrival by the day staff, "yes, I don't think he's actually started work here yet," then she stopped, needing her doubt to be allayed.

"Can I ask you your name?" she said cautiously.

"George Goodwin, good friend of Bill's and in need of a cup of tea," he replied in a friendly manner.

The name of the charge nurse on geriatric and his wife came to her.

"Do you know Tom Jelly?" she asked, fishing.

"Good God yes, Tom's the charge on my ward."

"And his wife ... um?" and she placed her index finger on her cheek, pretending to try and remember.

"Margaret!" he enlightened her, "known her for years." He hadn't but recalled Tom mentioning her a few times. The duty nurse was satisfied that George was who he said he was and visibly relaxed, the little interrogation had cancelled her doubts.

"Sorry if I sounded a bit suspicious, Mr Goodwin, but I can't be too careful, you know how it is," and he shook his head in agreement.

"George, please, and I completely understand."

"Ok, George," she continued, "I'm sure Mr Sweet has been allocated the rooms at the top of the building," and she explained how to get there. He signed and dated the visitors book and followed the route she'd described, struggling with the overfull cases.

Bill opened the door on the third knock. "George!" he said, taken aback, "what the hell are you doing here?"

"It's a long story, Bill. Can I come in, I need you to put me up for a few days I'm pretty desperate?" but Bill remained where he was.

"I'm not sure, George," he muttered anxiously, "I've only been here a few hours, I don't know the rules, maybe I'm not allowed to have guests stay," and he noticed Bill twitch, something he'd never seen him do before.

"Bill, I'm begging you, I've nowhere else to go." He looked at this hapless soul and wished he'd just vanish; in Bill's book a friend in need was best considered an enemy. But wasn't George going to become a prison officer, potentially very helpful, and hadn't he resolved to be an altruistic human being? He moved out of his way.

"Come on in, you look beat." He ushered him to one of only two chairs in the room. "Now tell me what the bloody hell this is all about."

George introduced him to his world and asked again if he could stay for three nights.

"And that's got to be all, George," he said definitely. "I don't want to sound awkward but I've landed myself a great little number here and I don't want to jeopardise it," he said with difficulty, looking into the eyes of his unwanted visitor. "You know what I mean, don't you, George?" he asked almost pleading with him to understand.

"I don't want to cause you any trouble, Bill, I really don't," he said genuinely. "If it comes about that I'm not allowed to be here well I'll just thank you and be on my way."

"You'll have to sleep on the floor."

"Slept in worse places," said George relaxing, grateful to his friend for coming to the rescue.

Chapter 16

It's like sports day for the maladjusted and it's time for the relay race as The Baton relentlessly keeps getting passed.

No one knows how far back in the tree it started and no one knows why, but it continues its inexorable passage from one generation to the next. Usually the parents run with it, nurturing and moulding, topping up the toxicant to deliver to the kids then the nieces and nephews. Everyone who comes into contact with The Baton gets influenced one way or another.

The kids grow up surrounded by the hate it emanates and when they're old enough to breed it's delivered into the hearts of their brood, as fiercely and surely as death and taxes. No one seems to have any remedy for it, no one seems able to pluck it from the blood line and say enough is enough and that's where Georgia found herself, holding that imaginary Baton as she wrote the note and propped it on the mantelpiece. It simply read:

'George threw the vase at me and I'm going home.'

When her parents returned from the pub he was rocking and she was rolling. It was she who trod on the pieces first, crunching and breaking them even more; then Jim bent down and examined a fragment and enlightened her as to its origin. They both sat unsteadily in the living room, the atmosphere a floating bubble ready to pop. Jim was petrified to speak, fearful that his wife was readying to explode but he needn't have

MAYBE

worried. She had no intention of saying anything. An all-consuming loathing of her son-in-law had rendered her speechless. Revenge, that was all she wanted, retribution. But how to go about it?

Jim couldn't help, maybe Georgia? But little did she know it was going to be her prospective grandson, Angelo, who would eventually come up with the goods.

Georgia headed straight up the dog legged stairs of the cottage to check if he'd gone, the missing clothes and suitcases confirming that he had. She retraced her steps and walked into the kitchen positioning a glass on the battered wooden table, the coldness of the place of no concern to her. Holding an unlabelled bottle of rough cider in her right hand and steadying it with her left she poured the brew into a stained pint glass. During the last few weeks she had become tremulous, something she had been going to great lengths to disguise and as the liquid filled her mouth calmness enveloped her and she breathed a sigh of gladness, a gesture of thanks from her craving.

She had recognised the determination in George's face, a look he rarely adopted and knew that he'd meant what he'd said, what she wanted him to say, and her mood lightened further with the second gulp as she lit a cigarette, pleased with the way things had turned out. She was now independent, away from her parents and of course George. A beautiful cottage was going to be hers along with a beautiful child. The joint, soon to be sole, post office account had sufficient funds to see her through for a few years and then she'd get a little job somewhere when the baby was old enough for nursery. Might meet another man, she thought, might be the boss.

She sat on George's old rocker and pushed her jet black hair behind her ears, leaving her left hand behind her neck, then pushed her bottom down into the chair and moved her hips slowly from side to side.

Yes, she thought, the boss, that would be nice, he'd look after us with his strong arms and forceful ways. She felt a sweet tingle and pushed her backside a little farther down, the pressure making that tingle throb. And if there's a wife, well that could be sorted out, oh yes, she was expert at naughty talk and touches, wifey wouldn't stand a chance, Georgia knew all about the spider and the fly.

Extinguishing her cigarette she drank the last of her drink, maintaining downward pressure on the chair then drawing her right leg back and up onto the chairs arm she slid her hand down to her crotch and began caressing that sweet tingle, slowly massaging and rubbing it in a circular motion. Her mouth began to open and eyes began to close as she repositioned herself again to widen her legs. Then she suddenly froze. She'd heard something far away and remote.

Concentrating, the noise, like a vocalised thought, came again.

"Get another drink."

There it was, as clear as crystal, a voice from the back of her head commanding she refill her glass. She shivered a sigh as she stopped and went back to the kitchen, unaware that her dreadful addiction had now become the number one of her desires.

The tremors had lessened and she was able to pour from the bottle using one hand. That night, when she eventually collapsed on the bed, Georgia had drunk six bottles and eaten nothing during the entire day. She lay curled up with her knees almost touching her breasts, the baby cocooned within and if some small aquatic creature had somehow found itself swimming in that womb it would have been deafened by the rhythmic boom of the hiccups of the child, tolling like some gigantic bell in a shipwreck at the bottom of the sea.

For the remainder of her pregnancy Georgia continued in much the same vein, eating little and drinking lots, oblivious to any harm it may be causing. Due to her patient's obstinacy and truculence, the midwife who had been assigned to her, gave up advising on alcohol misuse, relying instead on subtle suggestions but even then she found herself being criticised and verbally abused. However, she did dig her heels in on one particular point and that was where the baby was to be born. She insisted that the child be born in a hospital. Georgia detested hospitals and demanded a home birth but on this the midwife would not be swayed.

Maybe

She knew there was a likelihood of major complications with this birth and stuck to her guns, a stand that was to prove unnecessary.

Chapter 17

The three days of George's stay were very different.

On that first night, the blankets George had rummaged up cushioned the hardness of the floor and made sleeping bearable. When Bill returned the following evening he was full of enthusiasm. After checking it was all right for his guest to stay he'd spent the morning familiarising himself with the children and their conditions using their individual case histories for his research, finding the notes were meticulously maintained and thorough, a testament, he thought, to the lady in charge.

In the afternoon he had his first driving lesson and found it came naturally. It didn't start well due to the cranking handle kicking back and almost dislocating his wrist but the actual driving seemed like second nature, mastering double declutching on the first attempt. George, however, spent a lot of the first day sleeping, drained by the events of the previous day.

When he woke it was mid-afternoon and the rest had sharpened his mind. He was able to get things into some sort of perspective. They were a diseased lot and the loss of his cottage and savings, and especially the prospect of never seeing his child, held him horror struck, but it was a heavy price he considered worth paying to be rid of them.

On the second day, Bill actually met the children and it was during this time that one of them decided to nickname him 'Twitcher'. They had already christened the matron with 'Wrinkle' due to her lined face and when he eventually found out their labels he thought they'd been treated lightly.

Meanwhile, George had taken a bus up to the prison and presented himself, as the letter had requested, for a preliminary induction prior to commencement. He, along with three other new recruits, were given a tour, a uniform and a start time - 9 a.m. the day after tomorrow. George was impressed by what he saw. The staff were his kind of people and he knew he was going to fit in. When Bill entered that evening he caught him trying on his uniform; George didn't know why but he felt embarrassed.

"Snazzy," Bill observed, emphasising the last syllable, making George redden and feel awkward. He looked back in the mirror.

"Fits me anyway, mate," he bantered, pointing at Bill's new, overlarge white jacket. "I might make a shit prison officer but I suppose I'll look the part."

"Oh come on, George," he said reassuringly, "clothes maketh the man or something like that," and for a second his mind flitted back to Dr Richards and his immaculate appearance.

"Yes, I guess you've got to look the part," he agreed sitting on one of the two chairs.

"At least you got the job," he continued, "there's thousands of blokes out there who'd change places with you."

I doubt it, thought George, and this time it was his mind doing the flitting.

"Maybe," he replied without conviction, "tell you what though, Bill, there's some right nutters in there, bigger nutters than those up at the nuthatch." He leant forward and draped his new jacket over the side table.

"I bet there are but they're in the right place, George. At least they're not walking around free are they?"

"Well that's another thing," he replied, "it was the assistant governor who showed me and these three other fellows around today and he reckons that they come in bad and go out just as bad, in some cases even worse." They both mused this over for a while and Bill joined his friend sitting down.

"They should make their time so bad that they never want to go back in there, never want to do anything wrong so they end up in stir again," Bill exclaimed.

"Yeah, perhaps that's the answer," he concurred, "but there's some of them in there who'll never be put off."

"Is there? Who are they then, George?"

"Ah, those bloody nonces."

"Those what?" he asked, sitting up and paying more attention.

"You know, the tot bunnies, blokes who mess with kids. The assistant governor reckons they can never be cured. When they've done their time they've got to let them out knowing for certain they'll do it again," he said, exasperated.

This was something that Bill was well aware of and having his own ideas on the subject said, "Knock 'em all off I say, George. If you can't cure 'em either leave them locked up or knock 'em off like old Adolf did."

"Don't mention that bastard, Bill."

"Well I figure he was right on a lot of things." Quickly, Bill realised he might have spoken out of line, especially when he was now supposed to be Mr Nice, but he was in the driving seat. George had been appalled at the evil deeds the Nazis had committed during the war: details of the atrocities that were carried out were only now being drip fed to the nation and people across the country were being physically assaulted for merely hinting anything favourable about them. But he was in a personal dilemma and had no inclination to censure his host or condemn his opinion. He needed to be pragmatic and not bite the hand, after all, he was relying on his friend's hospitality.

Bill sensed his ambivalence and an awkward silence ensued then he declared, "Look George," and he opened his fingers and spread his hands, "you told me your wife was pregnant right," and George winced at being reminded, "well imagine in a few years' time some pervert messes around with your kid and it comes to light he's just been released from the nick, maybe even living next door, and you found out that there were people who knew he was probably going to do it, perhaps knew it for sure, but had to release him because legally they couldn't keep him locked up."

George was thinking about it.

"They couldn't cure him of it," he continued, "but just because he'd served his time they had to let him out. That's not a system that protects kids, that's a system that positively puts them in danger."

Bill may have been a scheming bully who only recently had instigated William's death but on the subject of child molestation he was genuinely concerned. George was coming around to his host's way of thinking and began to understand why he had mentioned Hitler. Bill stood up.

"No, it's all bloody wrong." He moved to the window, noticing the matron holding a young boy's hand and leading him to her car. George joined him looking out and gently squeezed Bill's shoulders in a friendly and forgiving way. "No, it's all wrong," he reiterated and George noticed him twitch for the first time that evening. "All I'm saying is if they can't be cured either keep them away from everyone or give 'em a big jab of Ethyl Chloride and as they fade away whisper in their ear, 'sorry son but this time you didn't make the grade'." He watched the matron and her charge get in the car and drive away. "You see, I think they've got a mental problem like the good old boys up the hospital so it's not revenge or anything like that I'm after, it's just a straightforward process of damage limitation."

Neither spoke for a while and then George broke the quiet.

"Ethyl Chloride?" he questioned, screwing up his face, "what's Ethyl Chloride?"

Bill didn't think it important but seeing as he'd asked. "It's an anaesthetic, George," he said impatiently, "but that's neither here nor there, it merely fits the bill for killing 'em."

They both realised there wasn't much else to say on the subject and during the evening little conversation passed between them. Bill decided to have an early night and when his friend had left the room George folded his new uniform and hung it on the back of the door.

He sat and began to think ... he had much to think about. He'd noticed that Bill's tic seemed to get worse if he got annoyed or bothered and wondering why he had suddenly acquired it, toyed with the idea of asking him but thought better of it; perhaps Bill didn't even know he had the damned thing.

In the morning he had to sort out gifting the cottage to Georgia, organise the finances, and he needed to set in motion a legal separation or divorce, he didn't know which.

He wondered what his in-laws' reaction had been when they encountered the broken vase, wondered how much Georgia had drunk that day, if he'd ever go back to the dance hall and maybe meet a normal girl, what his first day at the prison would be like, where the matron was taking that little boy; George popped out of his thoughts, surprised at how that one had sneaked in.

He heard Bill gently snoring next door and returned to contemplating. He's not a bad bloke at all really, he mused, don't know why so many people dislike him. Strong opinions certainly but made a lot of sense, made an awful lot of sense. But he might have thought differently had he looked under Bill's bed and found all those books about the Third Reich and all those pamphlets produced for Moseley's black shirts.

He undressed to his underwear and spread two blankets on the floor then lay down and wrapped another tightly over him. Tomorrow was going to be a busy day and he wanted to be on top form.

Chapter 18

In the June of 1954, Stan had received seventy-eight electro convulsive therapies and the bit of his brain controlling memory had thrown in the towel.

Every hospital nurse has a favourite patient, a patient they'll go the extra mile for, but it's seldom admitted to, like a mother who secretly prefers one of her children. In Charlie's case it was Stan. He'd make sure he was getting enough to eat and he was clean and properly dressed and that old Fukum wasn't tickling him too much because wasn't Stan liable to piss dribble when he laughed and if no other member of staff noticed, well, that leak could cause his skin to burn. Charlie was the only black staff member, a fact that strengthened his pride and self-respect but he knew there were some of his colleagues who had difficulty concealing their prejudice and he tended to keep a low profile and stay, as much as possible, under the radar.

But Charlie had a troublesome worry. Stan's continuing treatments were tormenting him. He detested the sight of Stan being wheeled back onto the ward, gowned up and semi-conscious, the plastic airway protruding from his lips like some sprouting growth. Being manhandled onto his bed, bewildered and nauseous, taking weeks to recover and then as time went on, when he began to show signs of perception and self-reliance, wheeled off again for a further swim in the current.

Maybe

He couldn't square the circle, couldn't understand why it was happening. He had been witnessing this routine for eight years and on that wet and windy June morning decided that if he wasn't going to say something then no one would and he took the unusual step of requesting a private meeting with the head of the hospital, ignoring the probability that this would raise his profile immeasurably.

Since his last face to face encounter with the doctor, when Charlie had interrupted his conversation with Stan and been lambasted for it, he had given the man a wide berth. During his visits to the ward Charlie had found something else to do, well away from him to ensure their paths didn't cross, so as he walked into Dr Richards' office he was naturally feeling nervous.

When Bill had walked into the same office all those years ago the doctor had been looking out of the window, a just lit cigarette in his hand and this day he was in exactly the same position, the only difference being that when Bill had walked in Tim Richards was happy but when Charlie walked in Tim Richards was enraged.

"Good afternoon, doctor," he began, his words echoing around the sparsely furnished office, "I'd like to thank you for seeing me."

He remained silent and still with his back to him, looking out through the window, his head silhouetted in the cigarette smoke. Charlie was apprehensive but determined and decided the lack of response wasn't going to deter him.

"I wanted to talk to you about Stan, Stan Heart."

There was no reply.

"I hope you don't mind," he continued and the doctor's anger reduced slightly at this first sign of deference, he liked that, "and I don't like to bother you …"

Much better, the doctor thought, and of course Charlie couldn't see the sly grin.

"... but I simply need to understand why Mr Heart is receiving so many of these treatments?"

The doctor took a long draw on his cigarette, lifted his head backwards and exhaled a stream of smoke toward the ceiling.

"Sit down, nurse," he said casually and Charlie sat down on the visitor's seat, noticing that the chair on the opposite side of the desk was on a plinth effectively raising it a good nine inches above his own. He looked up at the Cerletti statue towering above, a sculpture he'd heard talked of many times and being well aware of its significance, realised that if and when the doctor eventually sat down they would both be towering over him, compatriots in their beliefs. "If I recall," he declared, "you have questioned my professional judgement before."

"That was a misunderstanding," he said defensively but was ignored.

"And oddly enough, regarding the same patient," finally turning to face Charlie. "Do you have some strange fascination with this man, some unhealthy obsession?"

Charlie looked at his face and saw an individual who resented him, bearing an expression he'd witnessed many times on the faces of the racists. But there was more substance here. This wasn't the countenance of a mindless bigot, more the face of someone who was hiding a secret and despising the one trying to unlock it.

Charlie remembered his authoritarian attitude when William Wilson died and he wanted to clear the room to interview Stan; how frightened he had felt by the manner and air of the doctor. But he was older and wiser now and annoyed with himself for beginning to kowtow.

He took a breath to respond.

"I think that's unfair of you, Dr Richards," then tempered it with, "I just need to be reassured that Stan isn't being harmed by these treatments in any way. I don't mean to question your judgement," and he hesitated, searching for the right words, "only he doesn't seem to be benefiting at all, he's always in a state of confusion."

Had Tim Richards been an upstanding, straightforward, decent soul he would have understood Charlie's concerns, warmed to his compassionate nature and calmly discussed the situation. Indeed, had the doctor possessed those qualities there would have been no situation to discuss. He walked around to his side of the desk and sat, the height of his chair cementing his supremacy.

"It's Charlie, isn't it?" he began.

"Yes it is."

"Can I call you Charlie?"

"Yes you can."

"How much training did you have, Charlie?" and he positioned the open fingers of both hands around his cheeks, the two small fingers meeting below his bottom lip, staring intently as if he was interested.

Charlie didn't understand the relevance of the question but nevertheless answered. "I had two years."

"Two years," the doctor echoed, "and how many months of that was at the general hospital?"

"Four months I think," he looked up, trying to remember, "Yes, four months general."

"Ok, so you actually received a year and eight months' psychiatric training?"

He did a quick calculation, "Yes, that's right," he concurred.

"How many days were tutorial?" His fingers still wrapped around his face.

"We had tutorials once a week."

"Once a week?" he repeated rhetorically, "so tutorials represented a fifth of your training, the rest being taken up with general nursing for four months and assisting on various wards; so by my calculations, your actual psychiatric tuition, minus the fifteen days of annual leave and sickness? Did you have any sickness, Charlie?"

"Couple of weeks with my appendix," he was beginning to understand his direction.

"Right, so with all that considered, by my reckoning you've had something like ten weeks actual illumination into all things psychiatric."

"I came here to talk about, Stan," he interjected.

"I know and we'll get to Stan shortly but you want to understand what's happening, if he's being harmed in any way by the treatment," and his voice began to rise, "and if you keep interrupting me," louder still and removing his hands "I won't bother to explain," now shouting, "and you'll leave here without achieving your objective," and he slammed his hands forcefully on the table.

Charlie sat there stunned by the doctor's sudden lack of control. He wanted to stand up and leave but thought of Stan and let the idea go.

"I won't interrupt you again," he said matter of factly.

The doctor visibly calmed; his eyelids lowered, nostrils contracted, the redness left his face and he recovered control of his breathing. The very thought of a nurse entering his domain and questioning his ability was anathema to him and he had been unable to control himself, though it didn't register with him that the rage had come from defending a lie rather than defending his competency. The doctor cleared his throat.

"It took six solid years of training to achieve my degree followed by two years of specialist study of schizophrenia resulting in a PhD. The field of psychiatry is vast, equal in its extent to that of physical illnesses." He was composed now, focused. "And I could sit here and explain to you in detail the reasons for Mr Heart's treatment but there's three reasons why I'm not going to." He looked at Charlie for a response and was slightly annoyed that one wasn't forthcoming. "Firstly, I have no desire to, secondly, someone who has merely scratched the surface wouldn't grasp the concepts and lastly I'm a busy man."

Charlie sighed, realising it was a huge mistake asking to see him. He had come up against the personification of arrogant self-importance and it was a completely futile exercise. Charlie, however, wasn't a quitter and he decided to have one more try, if not to stop the treatments then at least to encourage the doctor to question their efficacy. He stood up, and now, being above the Doctor, had the confidence to proceed.

"For the first three or four days, when Stan Heart returns to the ward following ECT we have to dress him, feed him and attend to his bodily functions. After a couple of weeks he is doing those tasks for himself, with a few mishaps, but he's a mental shell unaware of who he is and who we are."

The doctor took a cigarette, lit it and walked back to the window, facing away from Charlie who bravely continued to talk.

"After maybe four weeks he is beginning to understand what is said to him but doesn't respond, just sits on the chair in the old conservatory staring at the walls."

Dr Richards remains silent, staring out of the window but Charlie is energised and carries on. "After five or six weeks he's beginning to be himself again, not the brightest button in the box but he recognises where he is and the people around him, he participates, but then guess what?"

The doctor remains still and quiet, hoping that Charlie will do or say something he'll regret, something he can use against him.

"Along comes the nurse and the trolley again, he gets a bolt of lightning through his brain box and the whole process begins again."

Excellent, thought the doctor, all going to plan then.

Charlie stops talking, the doctor's ignorant attitude causing anger to well up inside him. He waits for Charlie to make a mistake knowing his silence would be infuriating, hoping that he would lose his temper.

The dead air was full of an almost tangible murk of hatred between them. But Charlie controls himself, something he has become expert at over the years, walks across to his antagonist and quietly says,

"I thank you for your time, sir. I hope you understand that it was something I had to do," and he walked to the door, confident he would never be frightened by this man again.

Charlie pushed the door closed behind him and as the doctor closed his eyes a hint of an emotion passed through him, as imperceptible as a feather to a scales but nevertheless there. It was a feeling of disgust and self-loathing and for a moment he wanted to cry but as a raging fire vaporises a raindrop, that crumb of remorse disappeared and he extinguished his cigarette and returned to the desk.

Opening his journal, he found the page with his calculations and where he'd written in large letters 'ten weeks actual training'. He ripped the sheet then scrunched it and as a cricketer bowls at the batsman, lobbed it into the air, the ball landing perfectly in the centre of the waste bin, not even touching the sides.

"Hey, Ugo," he said loudly, keeping his eyes on the bin, "ever heard this one?" and he cleared his throat. "Queenie, Queenie, who's got the ball?" then he turned and stared at Cerletti's face and whispered, "I have."

Chapter 19

The midwife was justifiably concerned. She was alone and panicking knowing that she was out of her depth and needing assistance. Fifteen minutes previously she had knocked on the door to perform her weekly antenatal visit and getting no response had made her way to the rear of the cottage knowing that the back door was usually left unlocked.

Georgia and the empty cider bottles were lying horizontally on the carpet and as she moved the empties and turned her on her side a surge of energy passed through her hands. She continued repositioning, attempting to make the body self-supportive and instinctively placed her hands on the place where she sensed the pulsation to be emanating from, her abdomen; and there was no mistaking it. The area was tight and firm, she had felt a contraction. Unbuttoning then ripping Georgia's skirt away she peeled the sodden underwear down and over her feet. There was no way of knowing when the waters had broken.

Realising that to prevent a tragedy she had to think straight and work fast, the midwife removed the measuring instrument from her leather bag and inserted it gently into Georgia, gauging her to be three inches dilated and gratefully thinking there was a while to go.

This was a situation that could be beyond her training and knowing there was no phone in the cottage, she wedged cushions behind Georgia's back to prevent any movement and sprinted the forty yards to the nearest neighbour. Fortunately she was in and a telephone had recently been installed. She barged past as the neighbour opened the door.

"I'm sorry," she panted, out of breath, "but I must use your phone, please tell me you have one!"

"Yes," the neighbour replied, shocked by the dramatic intrusion, "it's in the front room, door on the right," and the midwife rushed through the hall and into the room.

"What's happened for goodness sake?" she hollered, following the nurse.

"It's Georgia down in the cottage, her baby's coming prematurely, I have to get help."

She lifted the receiver, a conversation was in in progress and she looked quizzically at the neighbour.

"There's someone talking on the line!"

"Oh God, it's Mary," and she took the instrument and spoke into it. "Mary, we have an emergency, would you mind putting your phone down, love?"

"I'm talking to my mother," she complained.

"Yes I understand but we did agree if one of us had an emergency then that would take priority."

"You're right, I'm sorry ... Mum, I'll have to ring you later." Mary replaced the receiver and the neighbour passed the phone to the exasperated midwife.

"Sorry," she whispered, "she lives down the road, party lines, such a nuisance."

The switchboard operator gave her an assurance that she would immediately inform the duty doctor, and the midwife ran back to be with her patient, asking the neighbour to go with her. As they scrambled through the open front door they stopped momentarily as the scream erupted. The neighbour was fearful and the midwife grabbed her arm and yanked her forward. They entered the room at speed, almost falling over

Georgia, who had awoken from her alcoholic stupor and was crouched on all fours.

The midwife bent down and began pulling her over, endeavouring to lie her flat in order to carry out an examination but Georgia responded with an elbow to the face that sent her reeling backwards, almost knocking her unconscious as her head connected with the fire surround. Then the neighbour uttered a piercing cry that jolted the midwife back into action.

"Sit on her!" commanded the nurse as she returned to the wrestling match. The neighbour gawped and stayed where she was.

"If I can't examine her we could lose them both," she bellowed, "now get here and sit on her, there's no other way."

The neighbour suddenly realised the seriousness of the situation, but rather than sitting on her she decided to lay on her, leaving Georgia's head exposed, all the while being pummelled until she managed to pin her arms.

The midwife was now using all her strength to subdue the flailing legs. She'd encountered a similar problem in the past with a hysterical first-time mother and she managed to position the legs so that the soles of the feet touched each other making them form a diamond and kept them there by kneeling on the calves.

Without warning, a deep guttural sound roared from Georgia's mouth as a shuddering contraction enveloped her. The neighbour turned her head to look at the midwife, an expression of sheer terror on her face, but was met with uncompromising stoicism.

"You've got to keep her still, there's nothing else for it, I've got to see what's happening with the baby!" She punched the open tub of lubricant and leant forward to insert her hand as Georgia recoiled. "Keep still Georgia, I have to do this!" ten seconds of silence was violently shattered.

"Oh my God," the midwife uttered loudly. "Oh my God."

"What is it nurse, what's wrong?"

"It's breach," she groaned, "It's a footing breach!" and she raised her hands to her head and screwed up her face, desperately thinking of what to do next.

Outside the doctor ratcheted up the handbrake, grabbed his bag from the passenger seat and exited the car, hearing the patient before seeing her.

"Get off me, you pair of fucking whores, get off me or I swear I'll breadknife the both of you and don't think I won't do it!"

As he quickened his pace and entered the room he was shockingly faced with a three woman scrum, the like of which he'd never before encountered.

"Oh thank God!" the midwife wailed, "thank God you've arrived," and then she recovered some composure. "I think it's a footling, doctor, I'm not a hundred per cent but all the signs are there." She pushed her knees down on Georgia's legs as she began to kick out again. "And she'll never birth it, her pelvis is too small, she would have had difficulty with a normal presentation," her voice bouncing.

The doctor placed his hands on the neighbour's back. "No time for introductions I'm afraid, just keep holding her and do whatever I say." She nodded, concentrating on restraint. He then took over holding the left leg and told the midwife to focus on the right.

Leaning over the neighbour he stared into Georgia's eyes to check that her pupils were equal. A scraping noise commenced in her throat and a gob of saliva emerged from her lips and flew through the distance between them, making contact with the bridge of his nose. He jerked his head back, grabbing a tissue from the bag, furiously wiping away the spittle.

"And you'll have another one if you come near me again, you fuckwit," Georgia screamed, still squirming wildly to free herself.

They all increased their grips. "I'm assuming this is the alcoholic patient you briefed me about, nurse?" he gasped, still wiping his face. She confirmed that it was and explained how she had found her comatose on her arrival surrounded by empty cider bottles. Patient confidentiality crossed his mind but he wasn't about to ask the neighbour to leave the room whilst they discussed Georgia's medical history.

She began writhing as another contraction slammed out from inside, an enormous lump of agony splitting into ripples and sharply radiating through her.

"Four minutes since the last one," the midwife informed him, maintaining the pressure and the doctor nodded knowingly as he drew the Pethidine into the syringe and injected it into her thigh.

Georgia didn't react, the pain of the contraction being superior to that of the needle.

"Remind me of the patient's name," he asked, storing the syringe back in the bag.

"Georgia," the neighbour barked, "Georgia Goodwin."

"Missus Goodwin," he said loudly and authoritatively, "you must listen to me. It's imperative you calm down; it's life or death, Georgia, you must calm down and let us do our job, if you don't your baby isn't going to survive." They all felt Georgia physically loosen as if she'd partially deflated.

"That's good, Georgia, you must relax. You're going to feel another injection now, don't be alarmed by it."

The doctor had quickly cast his eye over her emaciated body.

"I didn't realise she was in this poor a condition," he whispered to the midwife." Did you notice any tremors or memory loss, excessive sweating or dyspepsia during her pregnancy?"

"All those things," she replied, "and I've noted them time and again in my reports," she said defensively.

He lifted Georgia's hand and noted how swollen her fingertips were, and again looked in her eyes noticing the yellow hue clouding the white. "If we don't take drastic action we could have a situation here where we lose the both of them," he said urgently. "I'm going to have to perform a Csection," and he introduced the Sodium Thiopental. "Have you ever assisted in one?"

"Once."

"We're in the same boat," he almost laughed, flushing the syringe with distilled water. "I've only carried out one."

Georgia's eyes closed as she lapsed into unconsciousness. He then observed the neighbour who was kneeling by Georgia's head.

"May I ask if you're squeamish?" he said quickly and she nodded her head affirmatively.

"Very well," and he began to quickly remove instruments from his bag, laying them out carefully on the towel he'd placed on the floor.

"Are you a relative?"

"No, I live nearby."

"Right, we have a difficult situation here and we couldn't have got this far without you, but I need you to help us even further. Can you get back home and dial 999? An operator will answer and you say that you need the ambulance service, do you understand?" and the neighbour nodded as he continued arranging the medical apparatus.

"The operator will then ask you for the address and a brief description of the problem. Don't worry if this seems long winded, she's already alerted the hospital where the ambulance is coming from." He began to cleanse his hands. "You tell the operator this address, not yours, and explain I am carrying out an emergency Caesarean section on a known alcoholic and need them to attend urgently; have you got all that?"

"Yes, I think so," she affirmed, and standing up began to tidy her hair and straighten her clothes.

"And I need you to spruce yourself up after you've made the call," he demanded, not looking at her.

"I'm sorry," she stuttered and shuffled quickly out of the room.

"That was uncalled for doctor," the midwife admonished, "she's been brilliant."

"I'm well aware of that but she'll get over it, this lady might not," he replied impatiently and removing Georgia's blouse and vest began to disinfect the incision site.

Asking the midwife to fetch an empty bottle he inserted the urinary catheter and drained the bladder. He made a six-inch incision through the lower abdomen, at the top of her pubic hair line and he opened up the layers of muscle and tissue enabling him to reach the womb. Blood was beginning to pool in the cavity and the midwife asked if she should take a blood pressure reading.

"Under normal circumstances, yes," he replied, "but I've got to persevere with this no matter how low it is." He pushed the empty bladder down exposing the lower part of her womb, although he couldn't actually see anything, the blood was obstructing his view and he was working by touch and memory. He reintroduced the scalpel and ensuring the womb was taught by pressing with his outstretched hand, made a small cut, enlarging it with his fingers. Blood stained amniotic fluid poured forth and the doctor cupped his hands and scooped as much of the liquid out as he could onto the floor around them. Realising he was about to extract the child, the midwife leaned forward and exerted pressure onto the top of Georgia's stomach.

"Well done, nurse," the doctor commented and delved his hand into the uterus positioning it around the baby's bottom and feeling for the descending foot. Speed was essential now as his concern deepened over the extent of the blood loss. With both hands he managed to ease the footling leg back in front of the child and eased out the breech, followed smoothly by the child.

The first appearance of a newborn was a miraculous sight for the midwife and as with all the previous births she'd either witnessed or assisted with, a tear formed in her eye which she quickly wiped away, then speedily taking him from the doctor she cut the cord.

MAYBE

"Needs to be next to your skin I'm afraid, nurse, he's cold," the doctor suggested, removing the surgical gloves to thread the needle.

She knew exactly what he meant and after a firm couple of rubs and squeezes the child coughed and heaved in his first breath. She turned away from the medic and unbuttoned her uniform, raised her undergarment and held the baby close, gently pressing him to ensure as much of his skin made contact with her own. Cradling the infant she moved and knelt by Georgia's head, then looking down, noticed a green tinged fluid escaping from the corner of her mouth. The doctor followed her stare.

"All part of the alcohol problem," he said and fished a guedel from his bag and passed it to her, "and regrettably, once you've done that, I must have help to finish the surgery."

Reluctant to take him from her body she wrapped the infant in a towel and placed him face down on another and inserted the airway carefully through Georgia's lips and teeth and down into her throat; then after firmly turning her head as far as possible to the side, knelt opposite the doctor to assist. He needed to quickly close the uterus and the layers of the abdominal wall but, due to the extensive blood loss, still couldn't see enough to be confident of the anatomy. He instructed the midwife in what instruments to use to retract the tissue from the operative field and as she did so the area took form and he began suturing the uterine wall, the midwife cutting them when instructed whilst mopping blood from the cavity.

She was becoming concerned at the lack of sound or movement from the child but realised that without her help the doctor would be unable to perform the surgery. Dextrously, he continued to close the layers of the abdominal wall and as she started to cut the excess from the remaining sutures he took the scissors from her hands.

"I'll finish from now on, you need to check the child," he urged, sharing her concern.

She instantly returned to him and could hear his laboured breathing. She swiftly unwrapped the towel, placed her palm on his back then urgently pulled him towards her, swaddling against her skin as before, recognising that his temperature was dangerously low.

The doctor was meticulously disinfecting the external incision whilst watching her with unease.

"How is he?"

"Cold," she replied flatly. He covered Georgia and approached them, unbuttoning his shirt and held the midwife firmly, his belly up against the baby, offering warmth from the other side. The neighbour stopped in her tracks as she walked in, shocked.

"Don't worry, he hasn't asked me to dance," the midwife remarked and pointed between them, "the child's here, it's a boy, we're warming him up."

"How are they? Can I do anything?"

"Well they're both alive," the doctor said sardonically, "is the ambulance on its way?" and almost on cue the distant warning siren of the rescue vehicle answered his question.

"Could you go into the kitchen and turn the gas stove full on," he continued, "and check the bedroom for hot water bottles." She rushed off to do as he'd asked.

After lighting the four rings she ran up the stairs to find the bedroom in complete disarray but after feverishly searching through the chaos found what she was looking for and returned with two bottles.

The water in the kettle was warm enough as the ambulance men entered with a stretcher and she positioned them behind the infant as the doctor went back to check Georgia. Her breathing was shallow but regular and pulse was slightly above normal. He looked around at the midwife.

"Well if that little fella perks up I think we may have been successful here today," and he helped the crew to carefully roll Georgia onto the stretcher.

"He's getting warmer and he's beginning to breathe more easily," she observed joyfully and asked the neighbour to remove the bottles so she could turn him around, happy that the combination of their heat and hers was doing the trick.

The baby's new position meant that the front of his head was now properly visible for the first time and as the neighbour stepped forward to reinstate the bottles she abruptly froze and they dropped to the floor. Her sudden intake of breath became audible and everyone in the room stopped what they were doing and paid attention. She placed one hand over her mouth in horror and used the other to point, all eyes following its direction.

"Oh Jesus," she moaned. "Dear Mary, mother of God ... What's wrong with its face?"

Chapter 20

Georgia was six months pregnant on the third and last day of George's stay.

The door slamming as Bill left the apartment woke him and he immediately got up. An appointment had been arranged with the solicitors at eleven, clothes and toiletries needed to be bought and on his return everything needed packing in readiness for his start at the prison.

The door was ajar as he passed the staff office and he overheard the matron and Bill in conversation. She was explaining that a child was to be taken across to Dr Richards for evaluation and she needed Bill to accompany them. He knew that returning to the hospital was going to be difficult for his friend and hoped everything went well.

During his meeting he was disappointed to learn of a legal bar on divorce during the first three years of marriage but arrangements were made to transfer the cottage and savings accounts into Georgia's sole name. The clean break was only partially completed but he resigned himself to it although disagreeing with his lawyer's remark that the law makers knew best.

As he passed the Falcon on the way to the tailors he couldn't resist the temptation and although the room was full, every customer had been served so when George stood against the bar the landlord immediately approached.

"Hello, matey," he said jovially, a bar cloth slung over his shoulder, "you were in a few days ago, weren't you?"

"Yes, I was," George replied, removing the wallet from his back pocket.

"I've only got bottles at the moment, son," he went on, "bloody rationing; used up all my barrels yesterday."

"No that's fine, as long as they're cold and alcoholic."

"Not very alcoholic I'm afraid, son, we're getting the weakest beer now since the beginning of the war, something about most of the barley being used for food production," he tutted. "They haven't got their priorities right," he joked, but was disappointed by his customer's lack of reaction. "Anyway, I've got Golden Ale or Goldcrest."

"Goldcrest," George answered and he popped a shilling on the bar towel in front of him. As the landlord was pouring his beer George looked around at the men in the bar. Unemployed ex-servicemen in the main, grateful for a few hours away from the house, only recounting the good memories, the bad ones locked away like prisoners who never get visited.

The landlord brought his full glass and scooped up the coin. George took a long first gulp and waited for his change.

After the war had ended the government had continued to enforce rationing and, looking into his beer, he hoped that everything he needed to buy would be available. The landlord returned with four pennies and placed his elbow on the bar in front of George.

"Don't mean to pry, son," he said cautiously, "but how did everything go the other night?" and he raised his eyebrows, prompting a reply.

"What, with the ... um?" he genuinely didn't know what he meant.

"You know, with the situation you were in. I was a bit worried when you left; thought you might do something daft the way you were talking."

"No, no, it all got sorted thanks," he said somewhat timidly. "I managed to sort it all out in the end," and he took another gulp.

"Good, good," the landlord replied thoughtfully, "which one did you decide on afterwards?"

George was still confused. The last time he visited seemed like months rather than days ago and he was having trouble remembering their conversation, even though the licensee's advice at the time had massively bolstered his resolve.

"Which one?" he questioned.

"Yes, which one of the alternatives, son, the alternatives ... did you change it or get out of it?"

Thankfully his memory returned. "Oh right, sorry, I've had a lot on my mind recently, a lot's been going on," he apologised. "Well, to begin with I tried to change it and when that didn't work I decided to get out of it and that's where I am at the moment." He tilted the glass and drained it in one, not really in the mood for conversation.

"Right choice, son." He gave him a friendly slap on the shoulder. "Changing it never works!"

George left the pub amazed he'd stuck at just the one drink and after finishing his shopping, was equally surprised that he'd managed to acquire all that he needed, including a pack of Alf Cooke playing cards, a present to acknowledge his host's hospitality.

When he returned to the children's home it was late afternoon and on entering the apartment he removed his heavy coat, placed the bags on the floor and sprawled rather than sat down. I wonder how Bill's hospital visit has been, he thought, unwinding from the busy day. But he had no way of knowing that Bill's day had been very different from his, about as different as it could have been.

Bill's heart had sunk when the matron asked him to accompany them to the hospital. The thought of meeting Dr Richards again troubling him. The man might be his saviour but if he knew what Bill had done to cause the death of William Wilson why had he chosen to ignore it and why had he taken all these steps to protect him? It was scary, he was at the man's mercy and the anxiety showed in his expression.

The matron was adept at interpreting facial mannerisms; to her they were like subtitles to the thoughts and noticing Bill's reaction thought it best to reassure him. "Mr Sweet," she started, always his surname, "I completely understand that the hospital holds unhappy memories for you but difficult deeds need to be faced up to. Think of it as you would falling off a bicycle, the quicker you remount the easier it is to resume riding."

He considered what she'd said and falsely replied, "You're right, matron, and very wise," a hint of a smile accompanied his first tic of the day. "The sooner I face it the better." She consciously remained featureless, thinking of him as a fawning, slobbering lap dog.

"We're to take Joseph across to Dr Richards for evaluation," she said and picked up the car key. "If you can go and find him we can make our way over; I'll be waiting in the car." She noticed Bill's friend walk past the office, "and when will that gentleman friend of yours be leaving us, Mr Sweet? I'm a little dismayed he's here at all." Bill assured her he was leaving the following day and they left the office, she turning left and he turning right.

Bill found him sat alone at the far end of the large, oak panelled day room looking frail and nervous. As he approached, Joseph squeezed the side of the chair, his knuckles white from the grip.

"Come on then, boy, we're going to pop you over to the hospital." Bill offered his hand but Joseph stayed where he was. "Come on," Bill said more forcefully, "what's the matter, we'll be back before you know it." He grasped his arm, wanting to clamp it much harder but mindful of his new ways and eased him up from the seat. The young boy winced and slowly stood but was averse to moving forward. "Come on, boy, hurry up," Bill said impatiently, desperately stifling a desire to pinch the youngster's cheek. "We're only going over the hospital, what on earth's the matter?"

But Joseph couldn't and wouldn't reply. The horrific threat he was under saw to that.

Chapter 21

As she turned him around it seemed as if the midwife was protecting the child from the glaring faces but she just needed to see. Holding her breath she gawped at the sight that confronted her.

The doctor walked across and together they visually examined the newborn baby. The size of its head was small and out of proportion to the body and its skin was dry and red blotched. The eyes were mere slits, as if made by a razorblade, with folds in the corners giving it an oriental appearance and set much too far apart. Their gaze dropped to the short, upturned nose, porcine and crude and then the abnormally thin upper lip, like a short length of pink string. It was the doctor who noticed that the child was lacking the ridge that runs below the nose culminating at the top lip and he gently ran his thumb over the area for confirmation.

"No philtrum," he muttered incredulously.

They continued looking, the concerned expressions of the neighbour and ambulance crew reflecting their own and began to understand the reason behind the baby's gaunt countenance. Whereas a newborn's face is usually round and plump, in this case the cheeks were hollow; the chin and neck overly apparent as if stretched, completely lacking in any fatty tissue.

The absence of nails on the small finger of each hand would be discovered later but what would never be seen was the damaged and deformed frontal lobe inside its head. The doctor stroked the underside of each foot with his index finger and sighed in dismay at the lack of a reaction.

"This is entirely the fault of the mother's alcoholism," he again quietly muttered, "the child's liver is one of the last organs to develop and up to that point it has no way of dealing with the poison. "What a mess," he added as an afterthought.

"You mean the child has effectively been drunk along with the mother?" the midwife asked.

"I think that's exactly what's happened," he agreed, "but whereas the mother had options, this child had none; it depended entirely upon her and she let him down." As he finished the sentence another tear appeared in the midwife's eye, but the source of this tear wasn't joy.

"The placenta can't filtrate," he continued, "and the alcohol goes directly into the child."

She gently squeezed the baby back onto her uncovered stomach and started to rock it. "Poor thing," she whispered," cradling him tightly to her, "poor, poor thing" and her tears began flowing freely.

As the ambulance men lifted the stretcher and transported Georgia into the waiting vehicle the doctor collected all of the instruments he'd used and placed them into a towel then put the whole bundle into a plastic bag and sealed it. Depositing the plastic bag into his case, he looked up as the neighbour uttered a small cough and he mentally admonished himself for forgetting she was even there.

"I think you're both wonderful," she gasped, overcome by the experience and visibly shaking. "I can't believe there's people like you in the world … but thank God there are."

He stepped across and grasped her shoulders, then dropping his head slightly and raising his eyes said caringly, "Are you all right? We deal with this sort of thing a lot, get used to it I suppose, but you, well, it must have been very upsetting," he smiled warmly. "But be proud of yourself, the outcome could have been a lot different without your help."

She looked over at the weeping midwife and thought not all medical staff get used to it and fought an urge to comfort her, thinking it best to leave her to cry. "That's kind of you to say, doctor," she reddened slightly, embarrassed by the praise. "I was a land girl in the war, toughens you up a little." She lightly removed his hands, deciding it best to support the midwife after all. Standing by her side she placed one hand over the child's forehead and softly squeezed the nurse's arm with the other. "Come on, young lady, let me have him for a while, I'm sure there's a hundred and one things you need to be getting on with," and she carefully lifted the baby from her arms and hugged him tightly to her.

Swaying gently, she watched as the midwife dried her eyes and began tidying the room, feeling uplifted in the presence of such caring professionalism. She looked down at the infant, any feelings of disgust subdued by her maternal instinct and common sense, a little innocent spoiled from the start. She took a deep breath and slowly shook her head.

"I wonder what the future holds for you, my little sweetheart?"

But had they known, all three would have been in agreement that, had the doctor slipped as his scalpel sliced the womb causing that instrument to deal a fatal wound to the child, it might not necessarily have been a reason for sadness.

Chapter 22

Bill eventually cajoled the boy into following him and they both joined the matron in the car. She covered the journey in less than ten minutes and after parking in the hospital grounds, the three of them marched into the hospital, the matron firmly gripping Joseph's little hand. Bill was puzzled when the doctor locked the door after they'd entered. Couldn't think of any reason for it, but the thought passed as he grasped the doctor's outstretched hand and shook it. Smiling warmly at him he said,

"Good to see you, Bill. How are you settling in at the home," continuing to hold his hand, "and the driving lessons, have they started yet?"

"Yes sir, I'm very happy there thank you. I'm beginning to get acquainted with the children and the lesson went very well, can't wait for the next one."

"Good, good," the doctor replied and loosening his grip looked over at the matron who was standing a couple of yards away with the youngster. He opened his arms to her and she walked to him. "Matron," he said affectionately, his face beaming and he bent slightly and hugged her tightly causing her to seemingly melt in his arms. As they parted he again leant forward and kissed her passionately full on the mouth.

Bill certainly wasn't expecting that and he cringed at the inappropriateness.

They disengaged but the doctor remained looking deeply into her eyes, the matron returning the look admiringly. They remained like that for some time, transfixed with each other, Bill looking on disbelievingly. Then the doctor flipped out of his trance and looked across at the little boy.

"Joseph," he exclaimed, releasing the matron, "young Joseph, I've been looking forward to meeting you again so much," and as the doctor stretched his arm, inviting a handshake, the underside of Joseph's tongue began pumping saliva, his mouth quickly filling. He swallowed rapidly but the saliva kept coming. His stomach now started to cramp and he gulped again and again but he was unable to cope with the volume of fluid being produced and suddenly his stomach contracted, violently tightening as if some huge belt had been fiercely pulled around his middle and the contents of his insides were forcefully spewed from his mouth and over the doctor's highly creased trousers and shiny shoes.

Bill thought the worst, thought he would explode with rage, but when his eyes focused he saw the man was still smiling, his hand still outstretched as if nothing had happened.

"Get a tissue please, matron, there's one on my desk," he said, desperately trying to keep his attitude friendly "and kindly wipe the boy's mouth." She rushed to the desk, removed a few tissues and complied with the order. He breathed in and unbuttoned his trousers, trying to enclose the drool as he carefully folded them down his legs.

Using his feet, he prised the shoes off and stepped out of his soiled trousers and picking up the bundle placed it in the middle of the rug he was standing on. Calmly, he asked Joseph to roll up the rug, roll it up with his things in the middle and place it over by the door; and as the doctor stepped aside they all watched in silence as the boy, starting with the end nearest to him, began turning the rug with his soft hands, his paper white face expressionless, overlapping it away from him until it resembled a cylinder.

"Now put it over by the door," the doctor reiterated and Joseph dragged it across the room and laid it down where instructed.

Tim Richards made no attempt to redress or cover himself, just stood motionless in his underpants and socks, as the smile began to evaporate. Bill felt fearful, his apprehension growing over what would happen next. Continuing to look at Joseph, the doctor abruptly told the matron and Bill to sit.

"And you come over here to me," he commanded the boy, who was cowering by the locked door, but he stayed rooted to the spot, well aware as to what was going to happen next, saliva once again beginning to pool under his tongue.

Tim Richards moved to the matron and whispered in her ear, "I won't go all the way today, need to break in Mr Sweet slowly." He walked around the statue to the far side of the room and removing his jacket, sat on the leather couch. "Did you hear what I said?" he shouted loudly over to Joseph, but there was no response.

"Shall I get Jo—" the matron chirped up, lifting herself from the chair. But he raised his arm to silence her.

"NO!" and he turned to look at Bill, deciding to ignore the lad's insolence for a while.

"I think that perhaps I need to explain a few things to Mr Sweet first," his smile returning, "I need him to gain some insight into the situation."

Bill was wrestling with the absurdity of it all. The head of the hospital in his underwear, the kiss, the cringing child and he stared back at him, eyes wide with alarm.

"Firstly, I need you to know that the matron here knows everything that I know about you, everything about the circumstances surrounding William Wilson's death, about your cruel little ways."

Bill looked over at her and she looked impassively back.

"So there's no secrets here, Bill," he continued, "no secrets at all; you can be yourself and not worry about anything, just relax." Bill performed his first twitch of the day which went unnoticed by the doctor who had flipped open the packet and lit the cigarette he'd placed between his lips.

He took a long drag and pontificated. "I've heard it said that if God had wanted us to smoke he'd have put a chimney in the top of our heads," and he blew a white cloud from his mouth, "well do you know what I call people who say that, Bill, have you got the first clue?"

Bill stuttered. "No sir, I ... I don't know."

"Fucking idiots!" the doctor blurted, "that's what I call them," and the matron tittered like a little girl; a high pitched, completely out of character, titter and Bill realised he was frightened.

"Anyway," Tim Richards resumed, "back to the things Mr Sweet needs to know." He swivelled to put his legs up on the couch, now almost lying there. "Do you have any notion why I chose to ignore your involvement in William's death when I could easily have had you locked up; any idea why I removed you from the situation and arranged another position away from the hospital, a position probably way beyond your ability?" He was staring at the ceiling now and Bill turned back to look at Joseph, wondering how much of this he was taking in. "Don't worry about Joseph, Bill," and Bill mused over how the hell he knew he was worrying about the child.

"Joseph knows full well that if he ever breathed a word about anything that goes on in here he'll be thrown into the rubber room with no light, where only dead people and monsters and demons crawl about, don't you, Joseph?" The child physically squirmed at the idea of this fate, an idea that the doctor had instilled in him many times and the matron reinforced, leaving his own imagination to ferment and nurture it until now it had become the little boy's waking nightmare.

"Answer my question, Bill," the doctor pushed, "why have I been so magnanimous?"

Bill wasn't sure of the words' meaning but guessed it was something like kind.

"I had wondered," he mumbled, his mouth dry, "but I can't think of a reason."

"Well let me enlighten you," he said. The doctor was now lying on his side, a bent elbow providing a prop for his head. Bill thought he looked like some Roman Emperor and wouldn't have been surprised if the matron had begun feeding him grapes. "The matron and I have what you might call a working arrangement," he went on, "you scratch my back and I'll scratch yours, a symbiotic relationship, isn't that right, matron?" and she tittered again, manically, her head thrust forward like some deranged, inquisitive parrot. "But she's retiring before long and I needed a replacement, someone to fill her shoes as it were, someone to take over from where she leaves off." He put out the cigarette and sat up, his face now very serious, eyes piercing. "The matron here thoroughly enjoys what I do, Bill, and realises that should she be so foolhardy to talk about it, then her enjoyment would make her equally as guilty." He paused to think. "So I'm relaxed and happy with our accord, at ease with it, and that happiness had to be there with her successor. However, I'm not so sure if you would enjoy what I do, Bill, even though you are an abhorrent and repulsive individual, so I'm saying to you," and he stood upright and pointed directly at him, "that if you were indiscreet and happened to mention anything about it then the authorities would be immediately informed of your role in Wilson's death, Stan Heart would cease having ECT and begin remembering, the matron would deny all knowledge and your prosecution would be a foregone conclusion. The three Sundays rule would be invoked and you would be hung by your miserable neck until dead."

After standing and pointing at him the doctor hadn't taken a breath and he was now panting with his mouth wide open.

This was like some terrifying dream to Bill. His whole world had suddenly veered into some inexplicable and appalling place. Tim Richards was posturing and threatening but he still didn't understand what on earth was expected of him. The matron's sickening change of personality, the young lad cowering by the door, what did it all mean? He felt completely lost and confused and urgently needed clarification.

He put his head in his hands to compose himself, cleared his throat and resumed looking at the man.

"I don't understand what you're saying," he began slowly, "what do you mean by I wouldn't enjoy what you do?"

The doctor had controlled his breathing and steadied himself. "I suppose actions speak louder than words, Bill," and Tim Richards felt a pulse pleasurably throb in his penis. "Bring Joseph over to me," he said authoritatively and Bill got up and innocently approached the boy. As he reached him the small figure began trembling. This wasn't new to him, he was petrified of what was about to happen, but as Bill offered his hand he resignedly took it, knowing there was no one in the world who could stop this or help him. He delivered him to the doctor.

"Now go and sit down, Bill, and watch."

The boy stood by the couch and Tim Richards put his arm around him, stroking his hair and face while Joseph remained motionless and vacant. Dr Richard's voice was quivering as he instructed Joseph to kneel in front of him. When the boy was in position, Richards lifted his backside off the couch and eased his underpants down, exposing his erection.

Bill was agog with horror, outraged by the sight before him and the impotence of his position. From the corner of his eye he noticed a movement and looked across at the matron. She had lowered herself into the chair and was slowly massaging her breasts, entranced. Bill moaned; all at once he realised what everything meant, the jigsaw pieces dramatically clamped into place.

Richards leant forward toward the cursed youngster. "Joseph," he gasped and as the child's head came forward the doctor's went back and he groaned in perverted ecstasy.

Bill again buried his head in his hands, a feeling of dread deflating his very being as he understood with pure clarity, as clear as a bell, the terrible price he was going to have to pay for the ownership of his warped character.

Chapter 23

Both ambulance men thought the same thing but it went unmentioned; the stretcher they were using was almost heavier than the patient they were transporting. Traffic was light in the mid afternoon and the ambulance, with the doctor's car following, arrived at the hospital without any delay. For the first twenty- four hours Georgia was lapsing in and out of consciousness. On her arrival she had been given an intravenous injection of vitamin B1 and a chloral hydrate suppository for its sedative qualities, but the harm that had resulted from the abuse of her body and the sudden withdrawal of the alcohol was beginning to create a reaction within her that would be as wild and uncontrollable as a gathering storm.

It wasn't until midway into the second day of her admission that the first seizure racked her fragile and emaciated body. She had been lying still and breathing regularly, her mine black hair even more pronounced against the starched white nightdress and bed linen when a spring suddenly uncoiled in her head and her eyelids sprang open as if startled. She woke to a strong and urgent feeling of jamais vu.

As she looked around, the ward she was in became overly familiar to her, as if she had been lying there for years, recognising every nook and cranny of the place. Then at breakneck speed her thoughts took off like unfettered sparks, faces and images began rushing through; her parents arguing, the first meeting with George at the dance floor, cider behind the bleach, the neighbour pinning her to the floor; vanishing then reappearing like a child having fun with a curtain.

Abruptly the brakes were applied and the careering thoughts vacated her head. She perceived a stillness and quietness in her surroundings and realised she was immersed in complete silence. She looked up at the face of a nurse whose lips were forming soundless words, hands making meaningless gestures. She saw flashing lights, miscoloured, creating an aura around the nurse's head and then the taste welled up in her mouth, a dreadful bitter flavour of tar and burnt rubber. The expression on the nurse's face dramatically changed and the questioning lips stopped moving as she realised something was very wrong. Georgia had begun to rapidly blink her eyes and make strong chewing like movements with her mouth, the neck muscles straining, causing her head to lift and hover oddly above the pillow. When Georgia pulled her nightdress up and began to harshly rub away at her recently stitched wound the nurse decided it was time to take action.

She quickly restrained her in a way not dissimilar to the method adopted by the neighbour just days before and screamed for assistance. Georgia's hearing returned and she stopped blinking, opening her eyes wide in reaction to the scream, but it wasn't the medic and two assistants she saw running toward her in freshly laundered white uniforms and clean, polished shoes, it was three skeletal inmates of a concentration camp, their bloodied teeth looking huge in their cadaverous features, eyes wide and lustful. They were lurching mechanically, getting closer and closer and her entire body cramped as the putrid smell of human excrement and infection made her retch, the vomit causing her to gag as it erupted from her mouth.

The nursing staff unnecessarily restrained her as she was now paralysed with fright. The camp victims had sprouted horns and tongues as long as arms, their faces inches away from hers, the smell of old urine pouring out of them, those tongues like wet sandpaper worming their way into her ears and eyes and mouth, the piss stink of their damp breath making her spew and heave all the more. They easily lifted her petrified frame and rushed her into a private side ward in a controlled panic, fellow patients straining their necks to better view the spectacle. As they carried her she was completely rigid, the doctor recalling later that it was like ferrying a showroom dummy.

For three days and nights she needed constant supervision, as the delusions and hallucinations tormented, her body constantly bathed in sweat and her mind in confusion; the massive doses of sedation barely subduing her symptoms as her child, Angelo, lay in a small crib in another ward of the hospital having been passed The Baton in the most cruel of ways, being wet nursed and cared for by staff who were alarmed by his appearance.

On the fourth day 'the rats', as one nurse had described Georgia's delirium tremens, began to subside. Her mind's eye started to understand the shapes in her room for what they really were, her nose was remembering the correct match of odours to objects and substances and her ears were understanding noises pertinent to their cause. The exhaustion brought on by the physical turmoil was overpowering and she was hand fed for her first meal of bread soaked in milk and barley water. Over time, the vitamin injections combined with rest and more nutritious food began to have a beneficial effect and after three weeks of this regime her strength was returning and she was able to walk unassisted and take care of herself. During this time she had refused to see her one visitor, the neighbour and not once enquired over Angelo's well-being, inexplicably never mentioning the young boy at all.

A decision had been made to allow Georgia to come to terms with her situation in her own good time with no prompting or discussion but the doctor in charge of her treatment was becoming increasingly concerned over her maternal deficiency and following a brief meeting with his consultant, the judgement was that the son should be brought to the mother and Georgia's reaction closely gauged. As the nurse offered the child to her and explained who he was she didn't hesitate in taking him, supporting the strengthless head as she nestled him into her lap.

A bolt of insight surged as everything dramatically came back to her.

He was her baby, ripened inside her, she wasn't alone anymore. Tears of joy began flowing as she eased the shawl off his head and stared down at her little boy not noticing the button nose or slanted, hooded eyes; the almost invisible top lip or angular, thin features. All Georgia saw was the most beautiful little angel in all of the world, pristine and flawless and she squeezed him tighter into her, the first experience of true love making her appear to glow.

Chapter 24

No words were spoken in the car as Bill and the matron returned to the home with the little boy, their thoughts individually enclosed by their enormity. As they exited the car she took the boy out of Bill's earshot and reminded him of the horrors within the rubber room and then, after instructing him to return to the day room, asked Bill to join her in the office. He shuffled in and sat to face her. He was desperately trying to place his conflicting emotions in some order. Bill now despised the doctor for carrying out the abuse but was somehow in awe of him, like a mistreated animal regards its owner.

He held no sympathy for Joseph himself, Bill harbouring the delusion that everyone deserved what was coming to them and as for the matron; well he felt she was as much to blame as a snotty nosed kid was for catching a cold. His jumbled thoughts hit the top of a funnel and gelled and as they began jettisoning through the spout they formed a rationale, a hypothesis, that would remain with him for the rest of his life …

Nobody is guilty for the ideas they possess in their heads and the actions they may instigate, but others must be allowed to take preventative measures if those actions are considered abhorrent.

What he failed to understand was that his lack of empathy towards, and the almost blaming of, the child, negated the majority of his hypothesis, but nevertheless, that was his summation and until his heart stopped beating he stuck with it. Her voice snapped his thoughts back to the now.

"You breathe a word of what just happened, Mr Sweet, and you know what will happen to you, don't you?" she said menacingly.

He frowned at her, this old stick insect of a woman, now so prim and proper, a short time ago massaging her chest, seemingly thrilled by the abuse; but hadn't he also felt a smidgeon of arousal watching her and where did that put him in the scheme of things?

She raised her voice. "Can you hear me, Mr Sweet? I asked if you understood the repercussions if you mentioned any of this." She was annoyed by his reticence.

"I've a good idea," he stuttered.

"Well I'll crystallise that idea, shall I?" She had no need for any pretence now and her dislike for him was demonstrated in the harshness of her voice.

"If you ever mention the little arrangement we have here, Dr Richards will ensure that the relevant authorities are made aware of your involvement in the murder of William Wilson. Do you understand the implications of that, Mr Sweet?"

He felt her eyes boring into him. "I didn't murder him," he said defensively.

"No of course not, and you didn't make him so terrified that he thought jumping to his death was favourable to your assaults! Now answer my question, are you fully aware of the implications?"

"I think I've already told you I have a good idea," he said, bravely in the circumstances, then added, "Dr Richards spelt them out less than an hour ago."

"Well a good idea isn't going to be acceptable so let me again crystallise it for you," she said condescendingly.

"Dr Richards is a highly respected professional whose evidence, backed up by my own, would never be questioned, no matter what you might have to say. You would never be believed, Mr Sweet," she was in full flow. "Coupled with the information Mr Heart could supply following the cessation of his treatment and a few staff members testifying that you actually enjoyed physically hurting those in your care," she stopped momentarily for breath, "and the implications for you would be the loss of your life."

He swallowed, the mere mention of it making him cold.

"You would be led to a platform," she continued, "and a noose would be placed around your neck, the trap door under your feet would be opened, you would plunge six feet down and an excruciating agony would galvanise your body as your spinal column snapped."

His look of dread prompted her to further embellish.

"And do you know the worst of it, Mr Sweet, the extra horror? Before you're dropped a further six feet into the burial hole you may have to go through minutes of living hell, dangling from the rope, waiting to die because the fall didn't kill you immediately."

Bill stood up, the tic he performed stronger than any other.

"You needn't say any more," he said quietly and made his way to the door. "I know what I have to do and I'm resigned to doing it."

"That's good, I'm glad you understand," and a small smile alighted on her face. "Just make sure you remember all that I've said, hold it firm up there," and she pointed at her temple, "keep participating in the little arrangement we have here and everything will be all right." Her tone had become genial.

"I understand, matron," he desperately needed to get away from her. "I completely realise the situation I'm in," and he smiled back at her. "Would it be all right if I go now?" pointing out to the corridor.

She nodded affirmatively and he slowly began to open the door.

"Oh, just one more thing, Bill," and he turned back, aware that she had used his forename for the very first time. Her face was now full with a smile. "What you saw today was nothing, simply a starter," her face now beaming as she emitted a high pitched giggle, "wait until you witness the main course!"

CHAPTER 25

When Georgia and her son were reunited the doctor wasn't sure what to expect, but was more than pleased with the outcome, although still bemused by her total lack of interest beforehand. However, the reason was simple and had he asked she would have told him. Georgia didn't know if it was the drink or the trauma of the withdrawal but she had simply forgotten everything about the birth. Up until the time that Angelo had been placed in her arms she had been completely unaware that her son even existed, an unnecessary situation had the medical staff not pursued a hands-off approach.

For the remainder of the rehabilitation Angelo remained with her. Due to her poor health during pregnancy Georgia had been unable to produce milk and he continued to be wet nursed. Although being only five pounds at birth the child began to quickly gain weight and when they were discharged from the hospital, seven weeks after admission, he had a sinewy wiriness about him.

"Your other mother must be very fit and strong," she'd purr, as she bottle fed her son with the donated milk. After almost two months without alcohol her withdrawal symptoms, severe at first and almost life threatening, were abating and apart from mild bouts of confusion and occasional headaches and nausea she felt her recovery from addiction was almost complete.

The ambulance dropped her off at the cottage gate, Angelo in one arm and a bag full of baby paraphernalia in the other. Entering her home the musty and unclean smell of the place hit her and an overpowering desire urged her to begin cleaning.

The carpet on which the birth took place was scrubbed and hung out to dry; the pile of unwashed crockery was rinsed and put away. The piles of soiled clothes were hand washed and placed on the line. Walls were wiped down, surfaces disinfected and every empty or full bottle of cider was gathered and stowed in the front garden ready for collection.

All except one.

She remembered the bottle in the sink cupboard, behind the bleach, but decided to forget about it like a quitting smoker decides to leave that one cigarette in a drawer. Her need to clean was unstoppable and she became obsessively house proud, a state she inhabited for the next four years. During this time she had cut all ties with her parents. Georgia always knew they were bad people and she also knew that one day she would somehow repay them for their callousness and disinterest, but that was for another day. Her change in character and outlook had forced her to decide that disassociation not confrontation was the path to take and whenever they called, she and Angelo would hide until they got fed up and left. After a few months they stopped calling altogether.

The neighbour who had assisted with the birth, on the other hand, was a welcome visitor.

She was a genuine and concerned individual, eager to help the unfortunate young mother. She felt pity for them both, especially the child with whom she was developing a close affinity, a fondness that seemed to grow with each time she called. On one such visit she enquired if Georgia would be interested in doing a couple of days a week cleaning for her. She lived alone. Her stiff joints gave her an excuse to neglect housework although realising deep down it was lack of motivation, rather than any physical pain, that was the real culprit.

"Your cottage is like a new pin, love, I'm sure you'd do a lovely job," and Georgia had agreed, knowing that the extra money would come in handy.

A week before Angelo's third birthday they walked the short distance and arrived at the neighbour's door, ready for a day's cleaning. He always accompanied her and the kindly neighbour had, among other things, bought a small cot for him. As Georgia lowered the tired boy into it the neighbour approached and placing her hand onto her friends shoulder said gently,

"Can I have a word with you, sweetheart, before you start work?" The two women sat down opposite one another, both equally nervous. "Please don't take this the wrong way, love," she began awkwardly, "treat what I say as trying to be constructive, not interfering," she inhaled lightly and smiled, "but I'm beginning to get a little worried about Angelo."

This had come completely out of the blue and momentarily Georgia was shocked and confused.

"Worried about Angelo?" she echoed, "why would you be worried about Angelo?" The initial shock had passed and she knew exactly why her neighbour was concerned.

"Well," and she leant forward, putting her hands between her knees, "I've had children of my own, I've told you about them, haven't I, and I can't help thinking that Angelo," and she hesitated, hoping that what she was about to say wouldn't result in the end of their friendship, "well I can't help thinking that he isn't developing properly. I mean, he's almost three and he's still just managing to crawl, not even trying to walk." She swallowed, unnerved by her friend's unblinking stare, but there was no going back and she knew it was for the best. "He does say a few words I know, but I remember mine being able to almost string a sentence together at that age."

Georgia remained motionless, her still face giving no clue as to what she may be thinking.

"And he's still in a cot and wearing nappies, love," she smiled awkwardly again. "That can't be right, can it? Have you tried to toilet train him, it would make your life so much easier, you know?"

The neighbour had mentioned some of Georgia's own worries and she took a deep breath knowing that there were many more that she hadn't mentioned or been aware of. The absence of any curiosity, his lack of reaction when cuddled or praised, the headaches he had on first awakening that made him roll in agony around the cot, but if all that wasn't bad enough there was one trait he exhibited that was worse than all of them combined ... his temper. A temper so vicious it had resulted in him being excluded from nursery school in his first week until a suitably trained teacher could be found to deal with the situation.

She remembered George, snivelling when he saw only blackness at the end of the tunnel and unwittingly used the words he had used, even though they angered her so much at the time.

"I don't know what to do," she said simply, a tidal wave of relief as at last she was sharing her fears. "I know there's something wrong with him, I've known for a while, but I just don't know what to do," and she rose from the seat and knelt down in front of the neighbour, lowering her head into her warm lap. She began to stroke Georgia's flowing black hair, saddened but glad that all this had come out into the open. "I don't know what to do," she repeated faintly and a long silence ensued, both women groping for an answer. Then the neighbour spoke.

"Your best, love, that's what you do, your best."

They remained like that for some time, the neighbour stroking her hair, stifling a desire to hum and Georgia feeling deeply at peace with her surrogate mother, gaining succour from the warmth of human contact. Eventually she raised her head.

"Would you mind if I didn't work today?" looking at her pleadingly, "I feel drained."

"Of course not, sweetheart," she said kindly, grateful that her intervention had been of some use, "why don't you let me look after the little one for a few hours and you get back and catch up with a bit of sleep."

She thankfully took up her friend's offer and retraced her steps to the cottage; but Georgia didn't go back to bed. Even though she'd been able to loosen the pressure somewhat by allowing herself to share her worries, that pressure now seemed to have magnified as she realised just how insurmountable those worries were. So instead of climbing the stairs and getting some rest she opened the door of the cupboard under the sink, moved to one side the deep red bottle of bleach with the skull and crossbones on the label and revealed the bottle of cider that stood behind. She sat cross legged and bolt upright, peering in at it.

"Go on," the devil within her craftily whispered, "he's going to get worse, you know he is. Go on, you need a helping hand," but she was summoning up all of her newfound willpower to resist that voice, she was recalling all of the reasons why she shouldn't open that bottle but there were a few reasons why she should and she was having trouble ignoring them.

She remained sitting, cross legged, concentrating, her demon pushing and pulling her common sense. Subtle, devious, offering her an easy way out. She slowly raised her hand, the demon smiling, the bottle only an arm's length away when the loud car horn, raucous and abrupt, violently startled her and she quickly pushed the bleach back to its original position and slammed the door. With the back of her hand she wiped the perspiration from her forehead and stood up, her heart trying to escape from her chest.

That was a close thing, she thought, a very close thing, and she walked out of the kitchen.

But the bottle remained behind the bleach.

Chapter 26

Bill Sweet climbed the stairs ignoring the laughing children who barged into him on their descent.

He'd read somewhere that a person experiences fifty thousand thoughts every day and he was beginning to believe it. The monkey that had now grown on his back was thumping the top of his head, each step up accompanied by a fist coming down.

Bill was an only child but he had received enough paternal discipline for a whole brood, though he didn't blame his father for that, didn't feel he'd suffered in any way and remembered the day he died as a black day, one that kept getting blacker. But what the huge helpings of drilling and control had left him with was a sense that only the strong live to tell the tale; the weak, in whatever form that may take, don't even get to hear the story; eventually get thrown by the wayside and there's no harm in helping them on their way.

Following his father's death he grew to become more intolerant, finding any human flaw or deficiency unacceptable, a miserable existence being the inevitable conclusion. But now a bad situation had become a whole lot worse like a mouse struggling in a trap and suddenly noticing a cat coming round the corner. As he plodded upwards the monkey was bursting, ready to pop with anger and guilt, worries and regrets and as it turned out that monkey was to be in residence for quite some time. George was packing as he walked in.

"Hello, Bill," he said jovially, "how was your day?" and forced down the lid of his case with his knee. "I know you had to go over to the hospital, that couldn't have been easy," he observed.

"Something like that," and his head moved a fraction in time with a tiny eye squeeze.

"Can't stand to be in the place," and he closed the door behind him. Bill looked down at his friend kneeling on the floor.

"Listen, George, I'm bushed, it's been a long day, I think I'll hit the sack."

"It's only half past five!" he remarked.

"I know, but I'm tired and not feeling so good ... I'm going to bed."

"Don't fancy a pint in the Falcon?" he asked tentatively.

"Not tonight," Bill said and headed for his room.

"I'm leaving tomorrow," George piped up pathetically and Bill stopped in his tracks.

"Of course you are," and he turned and walked back into the room.

"Listen, I've had a long day, mate, you wouldn't know," and he put out his hand and George shook it. "I'd like to have a pint with you, have a chat about things before you leave but like I said, I'm exhausted." He squeezed him on the arm. "Best of luck tomorrow, George," and he once again began walking to his room, "give my regards to the kiddy kissers," he grumbled cynically and exited the room.

Over the next thirteen years the position that Bill found himself in was taking its toll.

The matron had duly retired twelve months after his arrival and her warning over the level and severity of abuse committed by the doctor wasn't exaggerated. Very quickly the only feelings he held for him were those of repulsion. During this period he only witnessed the doctor sodomise a child once, the sight making him feel hanging would be a welcome release. Thereafter, he refused to be present during the abuse and would only deliver the victim to the doctor's door, picking him or her up exactly an hour later, Tim Richards referring to this time as his sixty-minute special or happy hour.

On the day that Bill passed his driving test the doctor instructed him in the procedure of suturing and he had become adept at sewing up splits and gashes, a talent that was pitifully put to good use. However, all the while, there was something else that Bill had become adept at, something that no one could have foreseen, least of all himself. Bill Sweet, accessory to death, fascist sympathiser and former antagonist of the weak and vulnerable had grown into a master at solving children's problems and curing their ills and the method he adopted to expedite their recovery was the giving of much love and kindness; it was as simple as that, graces that the children had seldom made friends with and when applied had significant beneficial effects. He was passing them a different kind of baton.

His reputation for steering adolescents from the wavy to the straight grew each year and that standing was to ultimately result in him meeting a young person who would commit dastardly deeds on his behalf, in frightening coldness, deeds that Bill couldn't perform himself because he was a good man now, had to keep his nose clean while his thoughts remained dirty. If he'd looked in the mirror and seen the real reflection, the honest image, the proper truth of the matter, he would have had to admit that the actual determinant was his cowardice; he was frightened to commit such deeds, as scared as the person on the wrong end of them.

Though often, when the sweet lord calls with the good news, the devil's right behind with the bad and Bill's double life of providing good corrective therapy to the majority of the children coupled with his complicity in the ruination of the unfortunate selected few was tearing him apart. But not in any moral or principled place was this conflict forged; he was being torn by the possibility of getting found out. The more success he achieved as head of the home meant the more he had to lose should he be discovered assisting the doctor.

The success and resultant prestige meant everything to him. His disciplined upbringing, although never admitted to, had left him feeling worthless and inferior and the encouraging result he was attaining with the children was changing all that.

Steadily his hatred for the doctor, and all men of that depraved ilk, grew and he actually began to warm to those in his care causing those monkey arms and fists to take on gigantic proportions and from that hatred a plan was beginning to develop in Bill`s ersatz mind. A plan that would necessitate those dastardly deeds to be committed in ferocious coldness, but for it to succeed Bill would need an accomplice or maybe two.

Meanwhile George, good old lukewarm, half-empty, never mind, George, had taken to his job at the prison like a duck to water. Occasionally they would meet for a drink in the Falcon and he was always able to sense his friend's mood by the severity of his twitch … big twitch – bad mood, small twitch – good mood. Bill would enquire after his boy but he never had any information, he had ruled Georgia and Angelo out of his life completely.

George would ask him how the running of the children's home was going but Bill was equally as reticent, seemingly unwilling to discuss any aspect of his job. Their main topics of conversation were the paedophiles in the prison and a man by the name of Oswald Moseley, the leader of a British ultra-right wing movement, operational before the war, both subjects always suggested by Bill's instigation. George gradually realised they had become an obsession for his friend who seemed unable to conduct a conversation without mentioning the nonces in one sentence or Moseley in another. Bill appeared to know all there was to know about the man and had the ability to quote large sections of his speeches word for word and sometimes, if the beer had flowed, with the appropriate hand and facial gestures. He was beginning to think that his only role in this relationship was that of a confidante.

He remembered one night when his friend hadn't twitched at all.

It was a summer`s evening in 1953 and Bill was sitting outside in the beer garden when he arrived. There were no 'hellos' or 'how are yous' when he approached, just two words, "she's dead!" Two words that he felt shouldn't have been uttered in that joyful tone. George had been thinking a lot about Georgia during that day. It was her birthday and as much as he tried he couldn't help himself thinking of what she might be doing, a thought that was there as these two words were spoken and on hearing them he just completely and naturally assumed he meant Georgia.

"She's dead?" he enquired, startled, "what about the boy?"

"What about what boy?" Bill replied, confused.

"My boy!" he cried, as if talking to a five year old, "what's going to happen to him?"

"What's it got to do with him?" he said, sipping his drink, still confused.

"He's lost his mother that's what, who'll look after him?" he said urgently, losing patience.

The penny dropped. "I'm talking about the old matron, George, not your wife," and George shut up, feeling the idiot.

But he remembered that Bill didn't twitch once that evening and seemed glad that the old lady had passed away.

Had George been a mind reader he would have realised that Bill was a lot more than glad, he was ecstatic. Three people in the world knew about his dark and sinister secret and one of them had gone and like the carol he had sung at Christmas, wasn't that good 'tidings of comfort and joy, comfort and joy'?

George's faux pas had cast his mind back to years before when the police had paid him a visit at his lodgings near the prison to explain that his wife, they had never divorced, had gone missing and his son, who was now six years old, had been taken into care. He didn't take much notice as they sat taking up most of the space in his pokey front room, desperately trying to ignore the picture of the policeman he had brought from the cottage, hanging on the wall beside them. Though there are none as deaf as those who don't want to hear. The two policemen, conscious of his disinterest, didn't inform him of the bizarre situation leading up to all of this and left with the story untold.

He could also remember a night when Bill couldn't stop twitching.

He stepped out of a cold, cloudless night in early October, 1959, into the warm bar to find Bill beside himself with annoyance because his now

MAYBE

hero, Mr Moseley, had failed in his attempt to become the member of parliament for the Kensington North constituency.

"It's a bloody travesty, George, "he moaned, "it could have been the start of everything getting sorted out." He hadn't touched his pint. "People would have started listening to him again," he continued, peevishly, "realised he was right all along."

Then, Bill had said something that made him sit up and listen.

"And he'd have sorted the kiddy kissing bastards out once and for all, they'd have been the first mutants up against the wall."

George was intrigued. "What d'you mean when you say up against the wall, Bill?" he asked innocently.

"Oh, come on, George, you know what I mean. The bloody firing squad, stick 'em up against the wall with a black circle over their hearts to aim at, do everyone a favour." Then Bill had leant forward conspiratorially and motioned George to follow suit.

"I've been meaning to ask you, mate, you know when they're let out, you know, released from prison."

"Yes," George acknowledged, lowering his voice,

"Well, d'you know where they go, d'you know where they go to live?" he said quietly and George thought for a while.

"I could find out," he whispered, "why would you want to know?" but Bill ignored the question.

"I can't believe there's no record kept, I mean, wouldn't people want to know who's living next door to them?" He sat back in his seat. "Mind you," he leant forward again, "had Oswald got in things would have been different, he'd have got people to understand the nonces are incurable and the best thing to do was put them out of their misery, euthanase them I think the word is," and he twitched and twitched and twitched.

CHAPTER 27

When Angelo reached his fourth birthday a certain amount of progress had been made.

With her neighbour's advice and encouragement Georgia had indeed managed to toilet train him and hadn't that made her life easier. She loathed the terry nappies, so unhygienic, so not fit for purpose and when he had taken his first steps and was able to walk to the lavatory she persevered and put them away forever. Georgia constantly talked to him as if he was an adult and he eagerly responded to her, everyday understanding more of the conversation but as his vocabulary increased so did his clumsiness and antipathy, seeming completely unable to control his now savage temper, a temper made worse as he vocalised with an enlarged word-stock.

It was a few days after his fourth birthday when she rented a black and white television and Angelo was kneeling in front of it, peering in. Since its arrival he had spent many hours positioned like this, mesmerised by the sights and sounds. Georgia worried that this fascination was unhealthy, but muck and m*erde*, couldn't she get some real cleaning done and when he was sat there he couldn't knock anything over and best of all he couldn't lose his rag and scream the house down. When the door knocker was rapped hard against the front door she had been washing the sink for the third time that morning and felt a little put out that she had to stop. She dried her hands and after a furtive look through the curtains saw her neighbour who was knocking again.

"I'm coming!" and she opened the door, wondering why she was so animated.

"Georgia," she gasped looking flustered, and walked into the hallway, "thank God you're in, are you all right?"

"Of course I'm all right, why wouldn't I be?" She continued wiping her hands with the tea cloth.

The neighbour stopped in her tracks and covered her cheeks with her hands. "You haven't heard, have you?"

"Heard what?" she said bewildered.

"Oh God," she uttered, "you poor child, I am so sorry, so sorry." Taking a step toward her, she opened her arms to embrace her friend but Georgia stepped away.

"What are you talking about?" she demanded, "what haven't I heard?"

"We need to go and sit down, I have something to tell you." She turned to walk into the living room but Georgia grabbed the back of her coat.

"I don't need to sit down," she shouted, alarmed, "I need you to tell me what's happened!"

The neighbour hadn't planned for this and she turned back around slowly, buying herself time to think.

Under the impression that Georgia knew what had occurred she'd simply called around to offer her condolences, see if there was anything she could do, not to be the actual bringer of the news. She realised there was no easy way of telling her and recalled the day that she had been told of her husband's death all those years ago; competently, matter of factly and with no procrastination. She knew it was the best and only way.

"It's your mum and dad, Georgia, "she swallowed. "It was a fire, a fire in the house. They've both been found dead. I'm so sorry, I thought you would have known."

Georgia's eyes glazed over and a large bubble of a tear left her eye, falling all the way to the floor and vanishing into the carpet. Georgia failed to understand why that had happened.

The neighbour once again stepped forward in an attempt to comfort her but Georgia motioned for her to stop. She pressed her lips together and squeezed her eyes tightly shut to compose herself then said calmly, "I appreciate you coming over," she opened her eyes, "you've been thrown in at the deep end and it couldn't have been easy."

The neighbour remained still and quiet.

"Does anyone know how it happened?"

Again she was unprepared for this.

Mary had told her that the father was blind drunk and had probably fallen asleep in the chair with a burning cigarette in his hand, in the chair where his burnt remains had been found. But she didn't want to tell Georgia that, not now poor girl. She'd find out somewhere down the line and by then she might have found it easier to cope. No, she decided to tell her something else, pretend she didn't know.

"Could have been anything I suppose, love," she lied, "I don't suppose it matters," and she felt her face flush, not used to deceit.

"No, I don't suppose it does," Georgia agreed, her voice seeming far away.

"The main thing is they're dead," she added.

"Sorry, love?" the neighbour exclaimed, surprised. "I didn't catch that."

"Oh nothing," she mumbled, backtracking, and made her way to the door, opening it for the neighbour to leave. "Thanks again for coming over," and the neighbour recognised her false smile and felt concerned.

"Reckon I'll need to start making plans for the funeral," she mused, hoping the neighbour would take the hint and leave.

"Yes, yes, all that dreadful business is going to need sorting out," and she moved towards the door, but there was something not right. She tried to put her finger on it but it was the impossible, the unthinkable that she needed, but failed, to consider.

Georgia didn't care.

Approaching the door she stopped right beside her. "You're going to be all right, aren't you sweetheart?" she said anxiously, a quizzical look on her face, "you know I'm just up the road if you need me."

But Georgia didn't answer, she hadn't heard the question.

The neighbour left and she closed the door, propped her back up against it and shook her head in disbelief. She heard the television and walked into the living room, looked at Angelo staring into the set, looked at the drabness of the whole place, perceiving a staleness, a dank mildewy smell when in fact the air was fragrant.

"This is it," she thought, "this is me, this is my life."

She heard a creak and ridiculously put it down to the walls moving toward her and began feeling edgy and scared but most of all she felt forsaken, companionless. Georgia had disowned her parents but she knew they were always there just in case something happened; she didn't know quite what but just in case the *merde* really whacked the fan. She again looked across at her son, the boy who only that morning had told her she was ugly, called her a witch, a bad mother.

Why would he say that? What had she done to make him say that? She looked down at her hands, the skin red and thin from the excessive use of dangerously hot water and detergent. The wood framed mirror hung centrally on the wall. She stood in front of it and opened her mouth as wide as she possibly could then closed her eyes tight shut. The sound from the television seemed to be getting louder and louder and as she opened her eyes, peered earnestly into the mirror.

"You're going mad," she whispered to her reflection.

Angelo looked up at her briefly but quickly returned to the picture.

"You're going bloody mad," she repeated and walked over to the rocker and sat, threw her head back and gazed at the ceiling.

"Go on," it said suddenly, that dark manly fancy that occupied her imagination, "go on, just to get you through this, just this once."

Her hands tightened on the sides of the chair as if some agonising pain had entered her. The smallest of flames, a mere hint of a flicker, ignited in her memory. She vaguely remembered that voice from long ago, from a dangerous place.

She strained to recall and her mind was beginning to fill the void. Didn't its owner have horns like a billy goat and … ? Her hands gripped the chair even tighter as if she was stepping onto some terror ride, and, her head began to ache, and its tongue, as long as an arm, didn't this voice belong to that creature, she thought?

Instantly her fancy changed gender, she sensed a bewitching and ravishing siren had arrived in there and she relaxed, completely at ease with this new alter ego, her memory of 'the rats' departing as she arrived.

"Go on, Georgia," the now female collaborator coaxed, beginning where the other had left off, "It'll take you somewhere else for a while, my darling," she persevered, "away from all this mayhem."

She brought her legs up and wrapped her arms around her knees. The seductive voice was silent now, had planted its seed. Again she glimpsed at her hands.

'Who really gives a shit how clean the house is anyway?' and she tossed that thought around, 'I don't.' And Angelo, he doesn't give a rat's arse about anything.' She looked down at him, entranced by the screen. 'Christ, his head is small with a stretched to hell face on the front of it.' She then pictured her neighbour's face, interfering old crone, fucking loved telling me those bastards had snuffed it, she thought.

There was no hint of hesitation as she stood and walked into the kitchen and removed the glass from the overhead cupboard, placing it on the work surface; then hastily opening the sink cupboard she moved the bleach, the bleach that kept the alcohol out of sight but not out of mind. The bottle stood like a glistening diamond and her eyes lit up as the anticipation rose like mercury in the heat. She lifted the cider off the shelf and put it to her stomach, caressing it.

For four years that jewel had been waiting and the threaded stopper was tight. She banged it firmly against the sink and wrapped her hand around the tea towel to get better purchase on it. As the seal gave it produced an audible hiss and she smiled, realising that the contents would be drinkable.

'You deserve it, Georgia, my darling, you deserve it.'

She poured the cider into the glass, the bubbling foam almost breaching the top then quickly subsiding, like an excited child being smacked. Raising it to her nose she breathed in that delicious aroma, that almost forgotten, tart bouquet, her salivary glands cramping at the expectation of the first gulp.

Meanwhile, twenty miles away in a small terraced house, Uncle Theo was also inhaling through his nose but experiencing a totally different sensation. A dull, dreamlike awareness that he was sucking in a damp fog full of lethal, clogging tendrils and simply resigning himself to his fate.

And just two miles away, in the Nut Hatch, Stan's inhalations were juddering and thunderous as he cried inconsolably with no one understanding why, least of all himself.

She lowered the glass to her lips, tilted her hand and head backwards in unison and allowed the liquid to flow. She had now assumed the identity that her doppelganger wished and felt calmness wash over her.

"I know best and fuck everyone else!"

"I am in control and I'll do whatever I fucking well want to!" And she closed her eyes and let the alcohol slip down her throat, any feelings of loneliness or abandonment riding along right with it, her second self inside her celebrating the return of her old friend as she caught the cider shower in outstretched arms and bathed in it.

CHAPTER 28

In less than five minutes Georgia had finished the bottle, the contents of which seemed to clarify her thoughts.

Her parents had died and she'd expected to be relieved but it hadn't worked out like that. They had failed to act appropriately towards her, especially her father who always agreed with his wife no matter how wrong she might be; wrapped up in their own world, too preoccupied to venture into hers, and she had misguidedly evolved, void of supervision or instruction. She'd often imagined a life free of them, often wished for it, maybe the exhausting emotion of hatred might dissipate but when her neighbour, less than an hour ago, had told her the news her initial, overriding reaction was sadness. A bleakness she put down to her feeling of abandonment. She finally concluded that they had deserted her and sought out the only way she knew to ease that particular pain, climb aboard and hoist three sheets to the wind.

For as long as she could remember alcohol and its effects had always mingled with her life, had been a part if it like an uninvited guest, after all it was her parents' favourite pastime. When a child, she would hide behind the sofa, alone and afraid, Mum and Dad drinking the night away at the local pub. Small noises sparking terror in her imagination. The fright churning in her stomach as she sucked her thumb harder and squeezed her teddy bear harder still, yearning for their return. Strangely the alcohol Baton hadn't been passed to her whilst living at home and on the rare occasions when she socialised drink was never necessary. It was when she began noticing her father's traits surfacing in George that the club was thrust violently into her hands.

She wanted to adore not be adored and his fawning adulation sickened her.

Georgia needed the method of marriage to divorce her from her parents and she needed a weak man to marry her, a man who would bend under the pressure of society's norms of shunning unwed parents, unreservedly, if she became pregnant. She had conceived a plan as well as a child but hadn't bargained for the backlash of being stuck with a sycophant for the rest of her life. Both of them had reacted differently to an intolerable situation although completely in character. George had simply run away, taken the easy way out, content to forego everything for a new start in a quiet life. She, however, still needed him to support her financially and provide a roof over her head so by using a totally contrary method resolved it by hurtful criticism, but mainly alcohol. When she visited oblivion nothing really mattered; and anyway, alcohol wasn't that much of a vice now, was it? Most people had a tipple, helped them get through their difficult lives and indeed her method had paid big dividends and been a great success.

Hadn't she managed to get rid of George whilst holding onto his house and money? Undeniably a first rate accomplishment. Of course, the excess drinking had continued after his departure and that was a conundrum, an inconsistency she couldn't quite fathom and it had taken the rats and the birth of her son to steer her back onto the straight and narrow, hadn't it?

But now she'd raised the glass again and doubts began to interfere with certainties.

Looking at the empty bottle in front of her she racked her brain for a good reason not to get a replacement and her thoughts returned to her parents for the excuse and she began to understand why she needed a crutch; they had died without suffering enough, they hadn't confessed their sins. They hadn't got what should have been coming to them and she felt uncompensated, alone with her increasingly odd son and a festering awareness that she had been robbed of any chance of revenge.

The urge to get more bottles grew. All memories of her near fatal dance with drink having vanished. Her eyes darted to the clock, it was one-thirty. The off licence attached to the pub would be closing in half an hour and remain so until seven.

She stepped into the living room and seeing her son transfixed by the television and knowing that to get him dressed and contend with his fearsome objections would prevent her from getting there in time, decided to leave her four year old alone and she quietly slipped out of the house. Securing the cider her only concern on the outward journey and drinking it the sole desire on her return.

Labouring under the weight, she opened the door then slammed it behind her. Angelo hadn't moved except that his face was perhaps slightly nearer the screen. The beat of the beast was speeding up and she felt no relief that the boy had remained unharmed, it didn't allow such emotions, there was only the desire to pour the drink. As she unscrewed the cap she lowered her head to sniff the fumes, eyes closing as the perfume wafted through her head like a warm, comforting panacea. Glass filled she sat on the floor behind her son, propping her back with the chair. The programme was a government sponsored documentary on the recent introduction of zebra crossings.

He'll watch fucking anything, she thought, thank Christ, she thought again, and set about making her delicious date with nirvana.

Over the following months Georgia became reclusive, only leaving the house in darkness to obtain further supplies of cider and small amounts of food. The neighbour would make vain attempts at contacting her, sometimes banging the door in frustration but she and an angry Angelo would hide prompting him to ask if his grandparents were outside.

"They're dead, you idiot, and don't talk to me about them!" she would hiss. "They're the cause of all our bloody problems, them and your excuse for a father." So he would shut up, unaware of who was banging the door and why, only really aggrieved that the intrusion was taking him away from the precious television.

After nine months of Georgia's relapse into alcoholism, lack of money was becoming an issue. During her sober moments she had thought long and hard about the problem and came to realise that she would have to reacquaint herself with her neighbour, get back into her good books. Georgia had no experience of work and no training for any occupation but there was something that came naturally to her, as natural as breathing in and out, the art of seduction. But that art is best performed at night and would necessitate her leaving the cottage on her own and whereas she didn't mind the risk of leaving Angelo for an hour or so, a whole evening was fraught with danger. If she was caught, prosecution and imprisonment were inevitable, sadly the beast had prevented her considering the possible consequences for her son.

So it was with trepidation that a year after the death of her parents, Georgia, with Angelo in hand, knocked on the door of her neighbour who was taken aback at the sight that confronted her. The little boy's hair, coal black like his mother's, had grown down to his shoulders, something she had never seen before in a male child and she wondered how he could see out of his eyes that had become mere slits, accentuated by thick eyebrows.

His face was gaunt, even thinner than before, his body wisp like and he appeared to be dressed in clothes that were far too big for him. As she peered down he stood facing forward, offering her no acknowledgement, but the most startling change had occurred with his mother. Her once long and flowing hair had become matted and bedraggled. Tiny, spider like capillaries were forming on her cheeks, one crossing over her nose. Her eyes were bloodshot and the skin on her face puffy and bright red. She was quietly trembling like a timid mouse. Although the evening was warm and still the neighbour had the notion that she was shivering. She looked back and forth at the pair then focused on Georgia.

"You've started drinking again, haven't you?" she said matter of factly, her raised eyebrows urging a reply; though Georgia didn't say a word, a small nod confirming the neighbour's assumption. "Come on in," she said despondently, "I'll put the kettle on."

The last thing Georgia wanted to do was join her neighbour for a cup of tea but she was desperate and knew she had no option. They entered and Georgia sat her son on her lap as the neighbour disappeared into the kitchen.

"I'm sorry I haven't been over to do the cleaning," she apologised nervously, raising her voice to be heard, "but things have been a bit chaotic lately, what with one thing and another."

The neighbour re-joined them leaving the kettle to come to the boil. "I've been so worried," she said, sitting down.

"No need to be worried, we've been fine haven't we, darling?" She stroked her son's hair making him flinch angrily.

"He's not very affectionate you know, are you Angelo? He's not a very loving child," and she quickly stopped the caress.

The neighbour observed them, disheartened by their unkempt state. "I came over many times Georgia to see if everything was all right, to see if I could help out in any way."

"We must have been out," she replied nonchalantly but the neighbour not only knew it was a lie she also knew that Georgia didn't care either way, she was in some kind of nether place, making it up as she went along.

"Anyway," not wanting to question the lie, "you're both here now and I don't want to know the whys and wherefores. What is it I can do for you?"

Angelo's bony arse was beginning to numb her leg and she raised him to her other one causing the boy to lift his hand as if to strike her.

"Angelo!" the neighbour shrieked, "don't you dare," and she raised her finger at him threateningly, amazed at the little boy's reaction.

"Please don't shout," Georgia said half-heartedly, "he's got a short fuse," and she pushed his hand into his lap, "you'd never hit mummy, would you Angelo?" she muttered feebly, cringing at the memory of him striking her that very morning.

The kettle began to whistle and the neighbour went into the kitchen, returning with the teapot and cups.

Maybe

"Have you come to see about cleaning again, the place used to be immaculate when—"

"No, not really," she interrupted, "it's more a case of needing you to work for me."

"That's interesting," the neighbour remarked and Georgia smiled.

"I've got myself a job at that new sweet factory, three shifts a week, but they're evening shifts, you know, six till two and I'm going to need someone to look after this little one," and she squeezed his shoulders resulting in another hostile flinch.

"Well that's great news," the neighbour piped up, genuinely thrilled, "I'm really pleased for you," she added, pouring the tea, "a new start with a new job," and she handed Georgia a cup. "Of course I'll babysit for you, truth be known, love, I've missed you both, you're like the daughter I've never had, it'll be like old—" but she stopped in mid-sentence, astonished by the effort Georgia was having to make to keep her cup still.

"Sweetheart," she said knowingly, "things aren't good with you, are they? You've got to do something about this drinking, if not for you for him," and she leant over in an attempt to take the tea away but as her hand touched the saucer a smaller hand grabbed it.

"You need to mind your business, missus!" he growled, the nostrils of his button nose flaring and eyes widening like an opening pea pod.

"I beg your pardon?" she declared, taken aback. "Let go of my arm, Angelo, let go of it now," but he maintained the grip, glaring at her through his gash eyes.

"Do as she says, you horror," Georgia interjected, her guard slipping, "she was only trying to stop my tea from spilling," and he loosened his grip, defiantly continuing to stare.

The neighbour pulled her arm away, instinctively rubbing where she'd been held, shocked and disgusted by the little boy's aggression.

"Georgia," her voice quivering, "you can't let him get away with that, he's not even six years old, is he?" she carried on not waiting for the answer.

"That wasn't a child who just did that, it was …" but she decided not to finish the sentence because he really was a child and you didn't say words like 'monster' in front of children, now did you?

Through the hangover haze Georgia became aware that things were going wrong and she removed a liquorice stick, his favourite, from her pocket and dangled it in front of his face.

"Now apologise, Angelo," she demanded, "apologise and you can have this."

His gaze moved from the sweet, to her face, then back to the sweet. There was a tension in the air as the two women waited for his response; eventually,

"Sorry," he complied, his eyes not veering from the sweet.

"How sorry?" she pressed.

"Very," he replied.

"Good," she said, relieved and he grabbed the treat.

Georgia looked at her neighbour, hoping the boy's apology would make amends but she couldn't catch her eye. The neighbour was focused entirely on Angelo, her concern now morphing into something like grief because to her they seemed to have completely lost each other.

If maternal instinct were a sound it would deafen the world, an impulse that outshines all others and the neighbour had it in spades. When, two days later, they again appeared at the door, the previous events had melted and lost their sting and she greeted them both with open arms. Angelo was to stay with her that night whilst Georgia worked the first shift of her non-existent job, picking him up the following morning.

The neighbour noticed the effort she had made in preparing herself for the new start and was glad that her hair had been washed and plaited, make-up applied meticulously, masking the redness and veining. What she didn't know was that it had taken Georgia the whole afternoon, instead of a couple of hours, to make herself presentable and that underneath her drab gabardine trench coat she was wearing a tight fitting pair of stirrup pants, an equally tight fitting polo neck jumper and in her bag was a beret and high heels. Everything was black, purchased only a week before in a fraught and rushed trip to the city, her son once again left alone.

The beatnik craze had blown in from America and she managed to source everything in one recently opened boutique simply called 'Kerouac' in Carnaby Street. After dropping off her son she had time to kill and walked into the lounge bar of the Falcon, unfazed by the suspicious glances of the customers. She ordered a pint of cider, unheard of for a woman, and sat in the corner, lazily sipping to waste time. After a while she made her way to the ladies and began the business of serious make-up. She used a lighter foundation over that already applied giving her an ethereal, greyish skin tone followed by dark eye shadow, black eyeliner and mascara. To finish the look she carefully coated her mouth in ruby red lipstick, giving them a full and pouting appearance.

Before leaving she slipped on her heels and beret and took one last look in the mirror. It wasn't the Georgia of six years ago but it would certainly do. She checked her purse and barely had enough for the entrance fee. This had to work, she thought, as she exited the pub and stepped out into the busy street.

The place was hot, smoky and loud. After leaving her trench coat in the cloak room she made her way into the dance hall attracting envious glances from the females and admiring ones from the males. She stood out like a black angel, her figure hugging clothes succeeding in highlighting her lithe body.

Noticing a small, unoccupied cubicle at the far end, she moved slowly through the jivers and twisters and sat down. The band was good, playing all the latest American and home grown rock and roll but Georgia didn't take to the floor, not until the very end. As she sat her gaze fell on likely candidates and when their eyes met she gave them a beckoning wink. When they came over to her, and they all did, she flirted and told them to ask her for the last dance.

Time went on and the moment arrived for the band's slow last number and as the lights dimmed five young men were stood awkwardly by her. She gracefully rose and pulling him by the hand, steered one of the admirers, a white suited and dark skinned fellow, onto the floor, deeming him to be the most prosperous. After a minute of slow gyrating she looked into his eyes then whispered in his ear,

"I'm all yours for a fiver, sweetheart. I'll let you do anything you want to me."

He loosened his grip and gently pushed her away from him. "You must be kidding, love," he said earnestly, "I'm not paying for it," and he walked towards the exit, disgusted.

Disheartened she stood watching him for a few moments then rushed back to the cubicle. There was just one of the men still hanging around and she slowed up and approached him casually, knowing this was her last chance.

"Come with me," and she put out her hand, "let's finish the night in style," and they walked to the far end of the room, eased their bodies together and began to move. The band were already halfway through the ballad and she needed to act fast. Her hand moved down to his buttocks and she gently squeezed. His reaction was to hold her tighter, just what she'd hoped for. Then, just as she had with George all those years ago, she moved her right arm around and to his front, tenderly cupping his shaft and feeling him growing in her hand, filling up in her grip and whispered the same words as she had to his rival. He also pushed her away but instead of objecting and walking off he held her hand and guided her through the swaying bodies and out into the night.

"Where?" he said urgently.

"Anywhere you like," she responded and he led her to a dark alleyway behind a fish and chip shop that was just closing, turned her around so her back was facing him, peeled down her tight trousers and pants and forcefully pushed his cock into her. She leant forward as far as she could allowing him to plunge deeper and he came in a spasm of delight, groaning as he gave one final thrust.

MAYBE

He pulled away and zipped up his fly, slid out his wallet and removed a five pound note. Georgia straightened her clothes and placed it in the small side pocket of her trousers. A cloud moved from under the full moon and the alleyway was suddenly lit from above. He had a handsome face, his features emphasised by the moonlight. She put her left arm around the back of his head, pulled him towards her and deftly squeezed her right hand down the front of his trousers. He was still pulsating and he sighed as she caressed the full length of him.

"Fancy sleeping with me?" she breathed playfully, continuing to massage.

"How much?" panting, he could barely speak.

"Same again," she replied as she curled her hand around the top of it and fifteen minutes later she was opening the front door, allowing the first of many men up and into the bedroom of her ill-gotten cottage.

There were many different dance halls open on varying nights and she set up a basic rota system, not wanting to visit the same one more than once a month. The only real problem was having to portray an air of sobriety when she dropped off her son. Her plan was working well and needed the arrangement to continue; she'd have to get a bigger box for all the cash before long and she made every effort to hide the effect of the drinking when she handed him over. Though whereas the neighbour had been fooled into thinking Georgia had a bona fide job she certainly wasn't deceived by her attempts at controlling her swaying posture and slurring voice.

"You don't operate any machinery at the factory do you, Georgia?" she'd ask?"

"Nah, just pack 'em and stack 'em," she'd reply.

Her alcohol intake was on the up and it was all she could do to cope with her own life let alone be a mother.

Recently, on picking him up from the neighbour, she'd noticed he had been calmer, more settled, but it wasn't long before his mood swung to spiteful and by mid-morning had reverted to a mean and aggressive rube.

The first glass of cider made it less intimidating and by the second she couldn't really care less. It was then that he'd find solace in the television set and they'd sit in the same room, inches away from each other though miles apart.

He was six-and-a-half when he first asked about his father. What was he like? How did he look? And when the reason for his leaving was raised Georgia made a huge mistake that was to culminate in the termination of her underhanded plan.

All the old hatred of George resurfaced and she decided to make it her goal, her personal mission, to turn Angelo against his father by informing him that George was the very worst type of human being to walk on the face of the earth. A selfish, violent and lazy man. An uncaring, miserly, pig of a man. She never let up, the alcohol assisting her venom. He was an idle, lackadaisical follower who couldn't think for himself or make any kind of decision. Spoke falsely to gain acceptance and should be locked up in the prison not work in it. But worst of all he was gutless, a yellow streak curling through him like a snake from the back of his arse to his neck. She could spend hours venting her bad blood onto this six-and-a-half year-old boy until eventually, using his damaged, immature brain, he concocted a scheme of his own.

What she had failed to understand was that Angelo simply craved her love. None was given when she used to be cleaning the house maniacally and none was given when she drunk that sparkling liquid. During the day, prior to him being babysat, she hardly drank resulting in a state of almost uncontrollable stress and remoteness and all the other days she just drank and slept making her similarly unreceptive. So he would vilify her when reachable or find consolation in the television set when not.

Two days after his uncelebrated seventh birthday and two minutes before they left for the neighbours, Angelo slipped a kitchen knife between his belt and trousers concealing it under his jumper. Later that evening, when he heard the neighbour close the door of the bedroom next to his, Angelo waited until he was confident she was asleep then noiselessly stepped out of his room, crept down the stairs, opened the front door and began making his way to where he thought the prison might be.

The core of his hopelessly unfeasible plan was to leave his sleeping babysitter, kill his father, dispose of the knife and return before she awoke. Funny how some little boys look at the world. He'd seen similar scenarios played out many times in the black and white films and his limited mind could see all the advantages. Mum hates Dad, Angelo kills Dad, Mum loves Angelo.

Holding the knife he felt omnipotent.

The black and silent night held no fears for him and he marched with stern determination, but when he passed the same Belisha beacon for the third time a picture of circles entered his head. It was three hours and three miles later that the neighbour, escorted by two policemen, found him shivering in the doorway of the grocer's, wearing only a pair of pyjama trousers and when they forced entry into the cottage, to find his mother and a man naked and completely incapable on the living room mat, the decision was made to involve social welfare and that resulted in Angelo's first taste of the nation's children's home system.

The bud of resentment that was already within him began to grow and flourish from the nourishment it received, from its diet of cold hearted, brutal austerity but when one Bill Ernald Sweet, nine years later, told him he was special, that he loved him, this new fare transformed that bud and it flowered in a glorious profusion as he realised he had found his saviour, his muse, and readily became the one half of their *folie à deux*.

PART 2

Chapter 1

Mirror, mirror on the wall,

Who is the real me of them all?

Guessing Georgia's thoughts at age 34.

The Baton is to blame for the majority of the children who find themselves in a home.

Inadequate parents inevitably fail their children and the state has to find a way to pick up the pieces. Containment was deemed to be the answer in the 1960s but for many of the youngsters it was a case of out of the frying pan and into the fire.

Beautiful minds combined can feed off each other and produce astounding ideas and innovation, unfortunately feral minds combined can feed off each other and produce enhanced moral bankruptcy. Over the years, Bill Sweet had come to understand that allowing two human beings the right to have offspring, and as many as they want, was the most absurd expression of a free society. He had seen too many children blighted by their upbringing, and subsequently blighting the lives of others, to realise that freedom to procreate should be earned and not simply given. For Bill, it beggared belief that a social order would give those who were patently ill equipped to raise children the right do so and, as a consequence, have to create a huge machine within the infrastructure to deal with the error.

However, not all of the children who resided in these establishments had been passed The Baton; some of them were the recipients of tough luck and tragedy and Akan Dotse fell securely into this category. In 1963, Akan was thirteen and fascinating. She was dark, and always draped her athletic frame in white. Her mermaid braid, a technique taught by her mother, fell sculpturally between her shoulder blades giving an air of sophistication, and the permanent gold tragus earrings blended richly with her clay skin colour, a shade that afforded her the luxury of never having to acquaint herself with make-up. Energised by a bright and enquiring mind, her sparkling eyes and effervescent personality entranced those in her company; but the standout feature of this extraordinary young girl's singularity, a trait that left those in her presence deeply impressed, occurred when she spoke. Not only did she converse maturely and eloquently but she did so using a low, almost mesmeric tone, the husky pitch making her words impossible to ignore. As much as others revered her it was nothing compared to the adoration she had for her father, Kufuo, named this way by his Ghanaian Fante mother. During the pregnancy her husband had worried so much that she felt he had shared the pains of birth and had decided to name her son 'Kufuo' to reflect this.

Kuffy, as he was affectionately referred to by those closest to him, stood out from the crowd like the only twinkling star in an otherwise black sky. It wasn't only his height and poise and stylish dress sense but his confidence and self-composure that made him so conspicuous. He seemed to move like smooth oil, his demeanour spellbinding to the opposite sex but now there was only one female who had his heart and her name was Akan. Unlike Georgia and Angelo, Kuffy and Akan were inseparable: a situation made easier by his profession enabling him to work exclusively from home.

When alive, Kuffy's parents were academics and he benefitted greatly from the emphasis both they and the Ghanaian Government placed on universal education and at the age of eighteen, he won a scholarship to study architecture at University College London.

Whilst there, he met and fell in love with Esme, a fellow student on his course from the remote island of Rhum off the west coast of Scotland. Their upbringing couldn't have been more different but their outlook upon life was very similar, both being passionate and adventurous. They were attracted to one another from the beginning. They flew high amongst their contemporaries and when they married, three months after graduating, they were in high demand, their names always at the top of any invitation list.

A year later, on a sunny Friday afternoon following an uncomplicated pregnancy, Esme gave birth to Akan. Kuffy explained to Esme that the name was that of a Ghanaian river he loved to play and swim and fish in when a boy, which was true, but he failed to tell her that it also meant 'father's joy' in Ghanaian Ashanti, not wanting his self-indulgence to upset her. Over the following twelve years, through hard work and endeavour, the small family prospered and grew ever closer. Their daughter bringing them much happiness as she blossomed into a young woman.

On the eve of Akan's thirteenth birthday Esme was oiling her skin after a shower when her stomach cramped and coiled as she felt something hard and solid in her left breast. On further examination she thought it felt more like a small piece of dough. Esme looked more closely into the mirror and noticed a scaly rash on the underside and moving further toward the reflection saw that the nipple on that breast had inverted, turned in on itself. She never mentioned any of this to Kuffy, not wanting to alarm him unnecessarily, but when the positive results came back she tenderly held her husband's head as they lay on the bed, silent and despairing, he wondering how they could live without her, she wondering how her death would leave her without them. It was an aggressive and pernicious cancer. Four days after receiving the results a secondary lump appeared accompanied by a smaller one in her armpit. Four weeks after Akan's thirteenth birthday her mother died. On the night of her unbearable funeral, Akan lay with her father on the same bed, curled up like a fern, each trying to comfort the other in their impossible sea of grief. Time is a great healer but in their case it only seemed to teach them how to conceal their agony, the pain always floating just below the surface. This was apparent some months later when they were preparing to attend a party being thrown by an important client. Akan entered his room after she'd finished dressing, her dark skin seeming to shimmer against the white clothing and Kuffy stared at her in amazement.

"You could be your mama standing there, Oburoni," and he lifted her up in his powerful arms and squeezed her to him.

"I love you so much my baby and I miss her so much," he whispered.

"I miss her too, Dada," and she wrapped her arms around his neck and buried her head in his shirt, not wanting her father to see her tears and not wanting to see his.

As they entered, the party was in full swing; the sight of the young lady surprising none of the guests as they had become accustomed to her presence on such occasions.

Esme and Kuffy had always included her whenever and wherever they socialised. She experienced the opinionated and indifferent, the polite and the coarse, the genteel and unrefined: had heard bad language and ardent oration, witnessed social charm and social ineptness, but her parents were well aware of her immaturity and following any exposure to adult company, would take great care in explaining the correct way of interpreting anything they considered could be harmful to her. However, there are occasions when no matter how conscientious or protective a parent may be they are still unable to safeguard their child and this was one such occasion.

Unknown to Kuffy, their host, although outwardly appearing an exemplary member of society was in fact a huge fan of cocaine and had recently had a fall out with his street pharmacist. He knew he didn't owe him any money and the dealer knew that he did and the dealer also knew that if he let it go, then people would find out and that would be bad for business, very bad indeed. So as he sat in the back of the taxi, the sheathed machete strapped to his left leg, making the journey a tad uncomfortable, he was chomping at the bit, eager to sort this dispute out.

As he settled with the driver and began to ascend the stairs, Kuffy was sipping his first Mateus Rose, the smooth voice of Ray Charles pleading for the chains to be taken from his heart. After kicking the door the dealer burst into the room, the ferociousness about him causing the nearby guests to recoil in horror. The party fell silent other than Mr. Charles still pleading for the chain release. As he walked determinedly toward the host, people parted, some dropping their drinks, unnerved by his savage appearance and as he bent and withdrew the machete, men instinctively grabbed their partners, suddenly aware of a great danger.

Kuffy, who was at the far end of the room, abruptly realised something was wrong and he put his daughter behind him and strained to look across at what was happening. He could see the man standing menacingly in front of his client, the long blade high above his head.

"You owe me money, man," his voice shrill and piercing, "you owe me money and I want it now, d'you hear? I want it right now or I'll chop you, man." He moved closer to the host who cringed and covered his head with his arms.

Kuffy immediately realised the seriousness of the situation and knew he had to act fast to prevent a catastrophe. As the adrenaline pumped, every muscle in his body clenched and in seconds he had weaved through the frightened crowd and clenched the arm holding the machete in a vice like grip. His speed was almost superhuman, matched only by that of Akan who had disastrously followed her father across the room. As the dealer swung around Kuffy hit him a thunderous blow on the right side of the temple but as he fell the machete flew from his hand like a guillotine and struck the face of Akan and a crimson furrow immediately appeared from her chin to her forehead.

For a second Kuffy couldn't move, the turn in events had overpowered his senses and it was the host who bent down and forced his hand over the incision in a desperate attempt to stem the blood flow. A fellow guest rushed up with a handkerchief and placed it under his hand then others followed, desperate to offer assistance. Kuffy suddenly gathered himself and grabbed his daughter, squeezing the now bloody handkerchiefs and reapplying them to her face. People began to panic, a calmer one picked up the phone, another stooped down to the motionless dealer and pushed her thumb firmly into the soft flesh beneath his chin, swiftly moving it an inch to the right then left. When she failed to find a pulse she repositioned her thumb to his wrist and pushed down. Again she felt nothing. People jostled to either help or gawp and a shout came from afar.

"The ambulance is on its way!"

The woman who had been checking for signs of life stood and shouted back at the voice, "Ring back and get the police here, I think the man's dead!"

Kuffy ignored the audible gasp from those around, his mind focused entirely on the wellbeing of his daughter. The handkerchiefs were again becoming sodden and he cried for more. Akan was limp in his arms as women began ripping strips from their dresses and men yanked off their shirts to use as replacement mops. The cumulative relief was almost tangible as the incoming wail of the siren grew in intensity. A minute later three crew members walked quickly and confidently into the scene and after a quick assessment of the child, two of them gently removed her from her father's arms and moved her carefully into the kitchen to cleanse the wound and gauge its severity whilst the other appraised the dealer. Unable to find any signs of life, he asked the person nearest to him what had happened and as he was about to ask if the police had been informed the two tone blare of the black maria answered the question.

In the kitchen Kuffy was distraught, standing behind the emergency team as they delicately parted the incision to determine the depth. When the police entered they were immediately informed of the fatality by the ambulance man and they ordered everyone to remove themselves to another room and await further instructions, no one was to leave. Meanwhile, the two medics had finished their examination.

"Its depth unknown," one said to the other, "and I'm not sure about the eye," and he placed a large gauze swab over the wound, wrapping tape completely around the head to keep it in position.

Kuffy was frantic with worry. "What do you mean, depth unknown and what's wrong with her eye? *Ao me nyame!* (Oh my God)" he bellowed, unable to take it all in and reverting to his native tongue. "*Me pa wok yew* (please) Akan, *me doe*, (I love you!)"

"It means we have to get to the hospital as rapidly as possible, sir," and, carrying the young teenager, they began to quickly walk out of the kitchen. "You can stay with your daughter in the ambulance, but stick with us, speed is essential."

"Oh no he can't," boomed the officer who had suddenly appeared before them. "I'm afraid you're coming with us," and he approached Kuffy who jerked back and held out his arms, pleadingly.

"Please, I beg you, my daughter is seriously hurt, I must be with her."

"She will be taken care of, sir," and he was joined by another officer who let the medics out and then stood at his colleague's side, barring the door.

"There is a man dead in there and we've been told you're responsible, now please come quietly to the station, we need to find out what happened."

Kuffy stood panting, shaking, the front of him covered in his daughter's blood.

The officers began to move forward and he thought of escape, to escape and find where they were taking her but he heard a second siren and a third, looked at the policemen looming down on him and realised it was hopeless, there was nothing he could do and he crumpled to his knees and they quickly got to him.

His arms were extended and they deftly clamped the thick, heavy handcuffs on, then effortlessly lifted him up and walked him out. As they descended the stairs and walked into the street the other police vehicles arrived, the road and buildings seemingly in motion from the revolving lights. He looked across to the ambulance, its rear doors open, blinding light inside: two people, a man and a woman working quickly, applying more bandages to the small, prostrate figure. Then another person appeared and closed the doors, ran speedily to the driver's compartment and set the vehicle in motion, lights flashing, siren wailing.

"Akan," he roared, "my darling, my darling!" and the policemen tightened their grips, marched him to the black maria and forced him in.

CHAPTER 2

It was 23 years since Stan had first been admitted and 10 days since his last electro convulsive therapy.

He sat motionless in the conservatory, staring ahead as he used to all those years ago, waiting for the appearance of the steam train, but he couldn't remember any of that; couldn't remember his Uncle Theo and certainly couldn't remember William Wilson launching himself, like a frightened gazelle through the glass that was once there. Fukum Smith was the only other patient present, asleep in the corner, head back, mouth open, gently snoring; his nicotine-stained right hand dangling over the side of the chair. Over time, he had become a little slower and podgier but the most apparent change for Fukum wasn't physical; it was in the respect afforded him. Although he was uncommunicative other than the use of one expletive he was completely independent, unlike a lot of the old timers who needed virtually everything doing for them. It had earned him the admiration of most of the hospital staff who treated him with great affection and fondness.

Stan's mind was empty and unthinking. It was too soon after the treatment for his perception to have returned. Thoughts lay jumbled in his head, cut in half and at right angles to one another; but unbeknown to Stan, events were occurring that would change the course of his miserable existence. Charlie's long gone attempts at stopping the treatments had been fruitless,

MAYBE

but recently another had begun to question their efficacy, a person more senior and worldly wise.

A Mr John Turvey was beginning to take more interest. Occasionally, Charlie would still voice his objections and his new superior had started to take notice, observing the routine, and now he'd become completely at one with Charlie's view and had decided to do something about it. Being aware of the doctor's bullying nature he resolved to summon fictional help, to gather the troops, and when he entered the doctor's office he wasn't alone, he had many non-existent allies with him.

Dr Richards knew he had to be careful with the man. This was a senior and respected long standing member of the team, an individual he knew would be difficult to intimidate and the smile he offered was a nervous one as the charge nurse sat opposite him.

"Hello John," Tim Richards began and tapped a cigarette out of the packet, "will you have one?" but the nurse raised his hand and declined.

"Gave up years ago when they hit a shilling for twenty."

"Those were the days, eh John?" they were on first name terms. "They're more than twice that now, still, we've all got our little vices," and the doctor uttered a muffled laugh. "Anyway, you haven't come here to discuss the price of fags, what is it I can do for you?"

"Well, I've come as a spokesman really, Tim," he lied and the doctor lit his cigarette and sat more upright.

"As you know, the charge nurses all get together once a month to have a chinwag over a couple of pints in the hospital bar," and Tim Richards nodded, trying to conceal his contempt for these meetings, "and one patient's name has been cropping up a lot lately and I thought it best to bring it to your attention, to make you aware of it."

"Well that's good of you, John, who is it?"

"Stan Heart, he's on the geriatric ward."

The doctor clenched his teeth. Moreover it wasn't only John Turvey who was coming to the rescue.

A sea change in psychiatric care was beginning to develop, a theory that was to prove disastrous and cause not only homelessness but also many innocent people to lose their lives. Enlightened thought was put forward as the reason but the reality was that it saved money. Nursing in the community was being touted as a huge leap forward in the management of the mentally ill and the hospital, one of only two chosen nationally, was being used as a test bed. Dr Richards found himself under increasing pressure to get the job done.

John Turvey had no way of knowing but, prior to the meeting, the doctor had actively been considering Stan Heart for discharge; it fitted neatly into his plan. He recognised the undercurrent of concern over the treatment he was receiving, although not to the extent portrayed by the charge nurse, and he was beginning to think that if Stan were removed from the scene of William Wilson's death he would be less likely to remember it. The doctor contemplated John Turvey's determination and quickly came to the decision to listen with consideration to the man and go along with what was obviously his reason for being there; the cessation of Stan Heart's treatment.

He nodded sagely as he listened to the carefully thought through case for the ECT to end. Agreed with much of John Turvey's rationale and said that he understood the staff's apprehension, although neither man voiced the opinion that the treatment had been incorrectly instituted, and finally the doctor explained that, following a satisfactory consultation with Stan, he would be more than happy to reconsider the use of convulsive therapy in the future.

The charge nurse rose from his seat and thanked the doctor for his time, quietly astounded by his success. As he began to leave the room the small brown teddy bear, lying behind the three tray file on the desk, caught his eye.

"I didn't know you had a liking for teddy bears, Tim, perhaps you do have a soft side after all," and he grinned boyishly.

"Puts the kids at ease when they come over for interview," and he picked the thing up and looked at its face. "You're a great help, aren't you,

Bertie?" and he stroked the top of its head. "They hold you ever so tight don't they, Bertie? You take their minds off things," and an abnormal expression appeared on the doctor's face, a bizarre, deviant countenance that unsettled the charge nurse, frightened him a little and he turned and left the office, pleased to be out of his presence.

It was three weeks later that Stan now occupied the same seat. The delay was necessary as the doctor wanted to allow recovery time from the ECT and he was also waiting, unsuccessfully as it turned out, for a delivery of scopolamine.

The Cerletti statue loomed large behind the doctor and it was this that Stan was focusing on, not the man sat opposite. Whereas John Turvey was large and tall and overwhelmed the chair, Stan was small and tubby and fitted like an egg in its cup. The old and frayed gingham shirt and buttoned up, woollen cardigan hid his slight pot belly and the hospital issue corduroy dungarees, turned up to expose his open heel slippers, were just ample enough to conceal his chunky, butterball legs.

The doctor, conversely, was dressed immaculately, as usual, in a double breasted light grey suit, white shirt and matching grey tie, the hazy blue leather brogues polished and gleaming like sunlit chrome. He looked at Stan with a mixture of disdain and disbelief. How could this person, this rotund and scruffy simpleton, have caused him so much trouble? Getting in the way like a guest who's outstayed their welcome. Made him instigate a treatment that had possibly alienated him from the staff who were now questioning his authority and integrity.

But it was his deviance and conceit that prevented him from understanding it was completely self-inflicted and his self-denial that was making him pass the buck.

He looked at the little man who was obviously fascinated by Cerletti and his enmity grew, but what he didn't know was despite the fact that he could afford to dress expensively and impeccably and inside his shoes could be found Llama wool socks, inside Stan's tattered right slipper could be found a post office savings book, confirming that he possessed more money than the doctor had earned in his entire life; although this had little relevance for Stan. He wasn't even in charge of his everyday circumstances let alone his own destiny. Unwittingly witnessing a murder had seen to that.

The doctor observed Stan's eyes moving, roaming around the memorial behind him.

"Find that interesting, do you?"

Stan had recovered enough from the treatment to understand the question and respond to it. He nodded his head, "Yep, it's big."

"Imposing, isn't it?" the doctor remarked.

"It's huge," Stan replied, "like something huge watching over us," his eyes continuing their investigation.

"I'm impressed by your use of words, Stan. He is indeed watching over us. He's a doctor you see and all doctors look after their patients, don't they? Do the best for them, don't you think?"

"Suppose so," and his eyes dropped to Tim Richards.

"I've been looking after you for many years, Stan," he said, satisfied that he now had his patient's full attention, "always looking out for you, doing my best for you, do you agree with me, Stan?"

"Yes I do," he replied.

The doctor swallowed and leaned forward slightly. "You've never had an uncle, have you, Stan?"

"No."

"And what was his name?"

"I've never had one."

"Ever been on a train, Stan?"

"Don't know."

"Has your uncle?"

MAYBE

"Don't have an uncle."

"If you did, what would you call him?"

Stan thought for a moment. "Just Uncle, I think."

"What d'you like doing best of all, Stan? I mean, if I said you could do anything you like, what would it be?"

Stan inflated his cheeks and gently exhaled. "Just sitting down and watching."

"If I gave you the most comfy chair in the world, one you could lie back in and watch everyone and even lie down in and go to sleep, would you like that?"

"Yes, I would," he replied, smiling slightly at the thought.

"And what would you like to eat, Stan, when you're sitting comfortably on that chair, if you could have anything in the world?"

"A corned beef and pickle sandwich," he answered immediately as if it were a ridiculous question.

"And would you be happy sat in the comfortable chair eating the corned beef sandwich, watching everybody?"

"I would," he responded, "Very happy," he added.

"What sounds like Leo, Stan?"

"Leo?" he questioned.

"Yes, quick, Stan, what's a word that sounds like Leo?"

"Um," and he pressed his middle finger into his cheek. "Trio," he answered, "that sounds like Leo, doesn't it?" and the doctor nodded in agreement.

"What colour hair does your uncle have, Stan?"

"I don't have an uncle, why d'you keep asking?"

"What colour hair did he have?"

"Don't know, never had one," he replied, somewhat annoyed.

"Who set the car on fire?" the doctor asked immediately.

"What car?" he replied, frowning.

The doctor sat back in his chair.

"Don't worry, Stan, it's just a small test to see if you're getting better, that's all," and as Stan saw him grin he decided to grin back.

"How would you like to leave the hospital, Stan, leave this place and live outside?" and as his grin vanished a frown appeared.

"I think I'd be a bit frightened," he whispered.

"You'd have lots of help, you know, we wouldn't simply throw you out."

Stan thought about this for a while. "Could I have somebody with me, Fukum maybe?" and he looked at his tormentor wide-eyed.

A sneering chuckle escaped from the doctor's mouth as he considered the possibility.

"If you were to leave the hospital would you honestly want him for a companion?"

Stan thought again. "Better than no one, I suppose."

"All right, we'll leave it there. Go on back to the ward, Stan, that's enough for today," and Tim Richards rose to his feet. "I'll see you again in about four weeks, see how you're getting along then, all right?" and Stan nodded and walked towards the door, but as he grabbed the handle, abruptly stopped and turned.

"Wait a minute," he blurted, "I've remembered!" and the doctor's jaw momentarily dropped in dismay.

"Remembered? Remembered what?" he asked cautiously.

"Zero!" Stan exclaimed.

"Zero?"

"Yep, that rhymes with Leo doesn't it? You know, Leo zero, Leo zero, they sound a bit the same," and the grin returned to his face as he set off down the corridor.

Tim Richards heaved a sigh of relief as he resumed sitting at the desk. He was reasonably pleased with the outcome of his little test but, without the scopolamine, had purposely avoided mentioning the death of William Wilson, fearing that it might cause a spark of recall. However, he knew that during their next meeting that problem would have to be addressed.

The stakes were too high for it not to be.

Chapter 3

The driver's twin priorities of getting her there quickly and keeping her still in the process was a difficult juggling act as he swerved around stationary vehicles, occasionally having to mount the pavement. A doctor and three nurses were waiting anxiously as the emergency vehicle eventually drew up. The male medic gathered Akan in his arms and carried her out of the ambulance and they rushed her into a nearby room equipped for such emergencies.

Realising the blood loss had been extensive, a transfusion was commenced using O Negative serum as they couldn't wait to determine her type and the doctor began to clean and sterilize the wound, which ran from the left side of her neck, over the cheek, across the bridge of her nose and right eye and ended at the scalp line. The lesion was closed with thirty-six catgut sutures and then he examined the eye. There was a surface incision to the sclera which he thought may affect her vision, though to what extent would have to be determined in time. The left side of her head was then bandaged in its entirety and two nurses remained to monitor her vital signs.

As this was happening, her father was sitting between two officers in the rear of the black maria, his mind in turmoil. All he could think about was little Akan, his precious Akan. Was she still alive? Where was she? What damage had the blade caused? The urge to escape, to fight his way out from the clutches of his captors rose in waves, but his common sense prevailed and he sat, racked with frustration and worry.

The interview room was stark and unwelcoming with four chairs and a table being the only furniture. His repeated requests for information about his daughter were ignored and he informed the investigators that he would not cooperate with them until he was advised of her situation. He sat forlornly in his now dry clothes, Akan's blood stiffening them, and held his head in his hands. Seated to his left was a duty solicitor advising him to explain his reason for attacking the man, or the police would form their own opinions; but Kuffy refused, continuing with his stance of non-cooperation until he was told of his child's condition.

One of the two police officers sat facing him, the one wearing the tie, informed him that witnesses had said that his attack was unprovoked, that he had pounced on the man from behind. The other police officer, the one without the tie, informed him that drugs had been found at the flat and the victim was a known drug dealer. The officer wearing the tie asked him if he thought taking a thirteen-year-old child to a party like that was a good thing, or was this the sort of parental behaviour that was exercised in the country he came from. That racial slur dug deep but be still refused to participate, feeling this to be his only option if he were to remain with some control of the situation. The officer with the tie then told him that only guilty people refused to give their version of events, followed by the one without the tie suggesting that when a person is in someone else's country they should adhere to their laws and practices and not behave like an uncivilised savage.

Kuffy knew that this personal attack came from their frustration but he stuck to his guns, convinced that defiance was the only course of action to ascertain his daughter's wellbeing, but unfortunately they were sticking to theirs, equally convinced that refusal to release any information was the key to finding out the truth.

The solicitor left at 5 o'clock the following morning and Kuffy, in his blood caked clothes, was taken to an adjacent room and fingerprinted. With the ink still damp on his fingertips he was escorted to a single cell and ordered to remove his belt and shoelaces along with any other loose personal effects. The officers placed them all in a large plastic bag, sealed it and took it with them as they pulled the heavy, reinforced metal door behind them. The leaded thud brought home the stark reality of his situation: his daughter had received a terrible injury, possibly life changing or even life threatening and because he took her to the party he was being blamed.

They were also suggesting that he had murdered a man in an unprovoked attack, maybe some sort of drug feud, but he cast those thoughts out, his mind quickly returning to his baby who looked so much like her mother, the daughter who missed her mama just like he missed her. Kuffy cared little about the police accusations, his thinking now centred squarely on the welfare of his child; his craving to be with her heightened by the fact that he was her only parent. Spiritlessly, he looked around at the graffiti scrawled on the walls and door of his tiny cell, stretched out his arms and was almost able to touch both opposite sides.

Suddenly overwhelmed by the terrible and desperate situation, his knees buckled and he slowly sank to the floor.

"*Boa me, Boa me,* (help me, help me)" he moaned and looked up for some sort of unearthly intervention and then Kuffy felt a dreadful sickening emerge in the pit of his stomach as an appalling reality enveloped him. He had become forsaken and no longer able to influence events. If no one turned the key to open the lock this is where he would stay forever. A surge of fatherly protection erupted within him, but his inability to provide it seemed to drain his life force and he sank, his body now prone on the cold floor.

Kuffy was going insane.

"*Akan,*" he groaned, "*me dor wo,*" (I love you).

This once elegant, sophisticated and refined man, this loving and caring single father, had been horribly reduced to a whimpering wreck simply because he had selflessly tried to defend someone. He slowly lifted himself off the floor and began pounding the door with both fists.

"Let me out," he bellowed, "let me out, I must see my daughter, my Akan, let me out!"

His pleas reached the ears of the duty officers but they didn't react, they'd heard it all before. The drunks shouting obscenities, the thieves screaming their innocence. A sweeping urge to be with his daughter, put his arms around her, overwhelmed him and he again fell to his knees, helpless in his impotence.

She'll be calling for her mama, he thought, calling her to come and help her; then she'll realise that that was impossible because she only had her dada now. He was the only one who could help her, the only one who could protect her. But he had abandoned her, got himself locked up in a concrete box with a metal door and he couldn't get to her. He abruptly realised he couldn't stand the anguish any longer and his mind became crippled.

Rising to his feet he placed his back against the wall opposite the door. He neither spoke nor thought any other words, just took two deep breaths and charged, his head colliding with the cell door, his skull going the way of an Easter egg in the hands of a destructive child with a hammer.

And Akan was now alone.

Chapter 4

When the conservatory was bricked up it was necessary to construct two windows, one on the right and one on the left of the building to provide adequate ventilation. The left hand window overlooked a small, gated circular driveway that serviced the hospital's acute admission block and if Stan decided to look he was able to observe all of the comings and goings of that particular place. The hospital was situated centrally in ten acres of grounds, a result of the Victorians adopting an out of sight out of mind approach to the problem of the mentally ill, but even though the institution was mostly invisible to the public it hadn't prevented the architect designing a grand and impressive structure full of interest and detail.

However, the acute admission block couldn't have been more different. The building had been added around the time of Stan's admission and was square, flat roofed and saddened the soul.

It was a few days after Stan's interview with Tim Richards. Spring had sprung and he could hear excited birdsong beyond the partially open window on the left. He approached it, breathing in the fragrant fresh air and looked down at the admission block's entrance, something he had done many times before. In the past few months he had seen downcast people arrive with what appeared to be relatives or friends, others in ambulances, some in police cars and he would occasionally catch a glimpse of those very same people leaving, usually a month or so later and seemingly cheerful, but there were a few who didn't leave. There were a few who needed more intensive treatment and there were some who were deemed unsafe, a threat to society and these people went to the locked ward and never left.

Stan had seen Barry arrive almost two weeks ago. It was a wet and cold day that accompanied the end of a long winter when the taxi pulled up outside the reception door and Barry emerged and stood by its side, simply staring down at the tarmac. The driver walked around and handed him his small leather case then, without a word, returned to the vehicle and drove off, leaving him there like a lost tourist. A few minutes elapsed before a nurse walked out of the unit and ushered him inside and that was the last Stan saw of him until that morning when Barry, holding his small leather case as if he'd never let it go, ambled into the geriatric ward with a nurse holding his case notes. They disappeared into the office and a few minutes later the nurse reappeared and left followed by Charlie and his new patient. They walked into the dormitory, depositing the meagre contents of his case in the bedside locker, and after explaining the geography of the ward Charlie escorted him to the conservatory and asked him to sit.

The day had an uplifting feel. A low sun, lighting up dust specks, made visible beams in the room. Outside, leaves were beginning to unfurl, colour returning and brightening the gardens but when Stan looked across at the new entrant sitting opposite him his mood altered. He saw a poor man, a sad man, someone in need of help and plenty of it. He looked so utterly lost and somehow bewildered, like those little children rendered parentless in some evil and pitiful African war.

Charlie came back into the room with a cup of tea and placed it on the side table next to Barry.

"There you go, Mr Stone, a nice sweet cup of Rosie Lee," he said, upbeat. "Dr Richards will be here shortly for a chat and I'll come and get you when he arrives, is that OK?"

But Barry didn't answer.

"Wouldn't harm you to say thank you now, would it, Mr Stone?" he commented, a little peeved. But still he remained silent and Charlie left, although had he known the full story of what had happened to this unfortunate fellow he would never have felt irritated by his lack of gratitude.

"He's a nice man that Charlie," Stan remarked casually after minutes of silence, "he's a nice sort of happy kind of man."

Barry languidly looked up and saw, sitting a few feet in front of him, a youthful middle-aged man, plump and pale with a huge smile stretched across the whole of his face.

"Why are you grinning at me like that?" he asked tonelessly.

"Well I didn't know how to look at you, I didn't know whether to smile or just not really look at you at all." He paused, becoming a little flustered. "You look so sad, so tired and I usually smile at everyone and I thought not to smile at you would be sort of wrong."

Barry continued staring disconcertingly at Stan, his face showing no expression or emotion. They remained focusing on each other like this for an awkwardly long time then Barry suddenly broke the silence.

"I don't want you to think I'm being rude," he began, his words slow as if he were practicing them, "but you're right in what you just said, about me being sad anyway, and I don't know if you've been very, very sad in your life but right now that's how I'm feeling so conversation at the moment is out of the question," and he lowered his head and resumed looking at the floor, "I'm sorry," he added as an afterthought.

Stan wasn't upset or intrigued by what he had just heard, in fact he didn't have an opinion one way or the other. The man was sad, indeed very, very sad and he didn't want to talk and that was OK. It was a simple statement of fact and Stan unthinkingly took it on board, eased his head onto the back of his chair and relaxed for a long look at the elaborately decorated ceiling. Almost a half hour had passed when Charlie returned.

 Nothing had changed. Stan was still looking up and Barry still looking down.

"Mr Stone," Charlie questioned placing a caring hand on his shoulder, "are you all right there?"

"Not really, but there you go," he replied, solemnly.

"Only Dr Richards is here and would like to see you."

Seemingly exhausted, Barry got off his chair and stood up almost knocking the untouched tea as he allowed Charlie to lead him away by the arm. Stan, meanwhile, was unaware of any of this; he was captivated by the intricacy of the ceiling.

The salubrious figure of Tim Richards dominated the small office; the social worker, sitting by his side, bland by comparison. As Barry Stone shuffled in and sat down, the doctor upended the bundle of papers in front of him and tapped them on the table to give them some order.

"Mr Stone," he began, offering a hand that Barry didn't shake, "Mr Stone," he repeated, "my name is Dr Tim Richards, I'll be in charge of your care and this is Mr John Hayes, a social worker colleague of mine, who will be sitting in today as long as that's acceptable to you of course."

John Hayes didn't offer a handshake, realising it to be pointless and Barry Stone neither said nor did anything, also realising it was pointless. The doctor cleared his throat, as if it might help in correcting a bad start, and carried on.

"I would straightaway like to offer you my condolences. You have suffered a great loss, one that anyone, even myself, would have difficulty in coming to terms with."

John Hayes balked at the 'even myself' comment but he was used to the doctor's self-admiration.

"However," he continued, "come to terms with it you must and I am here to help you achieve that. Now reading your notes I see you have been receiving psychotherapy in conjunction with anti-depressant medication and it appears that these treatments have had little beneficial effect. Would you agree, Mr Stone?"

He nodded, although not sure what he was agreeing with.

"All right, let me be straight with you," and he lit a cigarette, sat back in his chair and unbuttoned the jacket of his cream suit. His associate coughed slightly as the fumes hit him but the doctor ignored it and carried on. "Let me attempt to crystallise this situation," he said voluminously taking a long drag. "You have suffered a terrible tragedy and your reaction has been to withdraw. I know you're not eating adequately, your weight loss proves that, and it says here in your history that you are awake for most of the night and without meaning to sound harsh, you have become virtually reclusive."

Barry didn't react; he quietly sat and looked ahead, staring at the space between them.

"Please don't be alarmed," Tim Richards went on, "these are well documented, classic symptoms of reactive depression," and then he stopped briefly, and readjusted himself in the seat feeling a little perplexed that his patient wasn't looking at either of them directly.

"Now as I was saying, initial treatments … " and then he abruptly stopped. "Mr Stone," he said loudly, "would you be so kind as to look at me when I'm talking? It's most off putting to have someone concentrating on a spot three inches to the side of my head when I'm attempting to converse!"

The room fell silent and an anxious anticipation ensued. The pause allowed Barry to catch up on what was being said and after a long while he arrived at the doctor's request and all at once he flicked his gaze to that of Tim Richards.

"Thank you," they said, ridiculously in unison, causing John Hayes to move his chair a little further away from the doctor's.

"Initial treatments," and the doctor threw an irritated expression at his colleague, "have proved unsuccessful and what I would now like to try is a short course of electro convulsive therapy. For years we've had tremendous results with this procedure and I'm sure there will be no exception in your case."

"What is it?" Barry said softly.

"I'm sorry, Mr Stone," he said, leaning forward, "I didn't catch that."

"What is it?" he said, more loudly.

"Well, following a general anaesthetic, an electric current is passed through your head via electrodes attached to your temples and—"

"How could that possibly help me?" he said in a monotone.

The doctor firmly stubbed out his cigarette in the ashtray. "It was observed many years ago that epileptics with depression experienced a positive mood swing following a seizure and we are simply reproducing the effect by inducing one. It is my professional opinion that a brief course of possibly six treatments would be of benefit. I understand that you may have reservations, to some it may be looked upon as a radical measure, but the alternative is months, probably years, of debilitating depression and you need to bear this in mind when you consider giving your consent."

He didn't reply immediately. He quietly sat there with his face firmly in the palm of his hands pondering over the position he was in. His whole world had collapsed and here he was, in front of two men, one vocal one silent, explaining that the only way to get to the light at the end of the tunnel was to allow himself to be knocked out and plugged into the mains.

"Look," he said, talking through his hands, "can I think about this or do you want an answer here and now, only …" and he abruptly fell silent before a juddering, haunting, half-laugh half-sob emanated from his mouth, "only, to be truthful, I don't think there's any treatment that could help me at the moment," and he sighed fitfully, trying to keep his composure. "To be truthful," he repeated, "I'm not sure if I want to be helped at all."

John Hayes looked at the doctor but his gaze went unnoticed.

"Again," Tim Richards resumed, emphasising the word with outstretched arms, "the way you feel at the moment is indicative of a reaction to a tragedy."

Then John Hayes reverted his gaze to the patient and spoke for the first time. "We can't just sit back and do nothing, Mr Stone. You have been admitted to this hospital to be made well and we have a duty to ensure that happens—"

"And frankly," the doctor interrupted, "electro convulsive therapy, in my genuine opinion, is our best course of action." The room became soundless and the doctor used the hush to gather his thoughts. "As far as having time to think about it," he carried on, "of course you can have time, but please be aware that the quicker we commence therapy the sooner your depression will be lifted and you can begin to piece your life back together."

Barry continued to sit with his head in his hands only half listening. He knew he'd go along with them; it was just that his head was full of remembering. Remembering, like poor Kuffy, the day his daughter had been born and how wonderful he had felt and how now he could never imagine ever smiling or laughing again. He removed his hands to reveal puffed and swollen eyes, the pressure from the fingers on his cheeks leaving wet indents. He stood up from the chair and looked at them individually and John Hayes thought he'd never seen anyone so full of sorrow in all of his life.

"I'll let you know tomorrow, if that's all right?" and he shivered, then after retrieving a handkerchief from his pocket, blew his nose.

"Tomorrow would be fine," John Hayes answered and he fought back a desire to put his arms around him to console him. Dr Richards pressed a button under the table that rang a bell in the ward informing Charlie he was needed, and moments later he entered the room and led Barry away. As the door closed Dr Richards walked around the table and lit another cigarette.

"What's the situation at home with this man?" he asked.

"Not good," and the social worker opened a file. "Before the accident the chap was behind on his mortgage payments and it appears that the building society have repossessed the family home."

The doctor shook his head in an attempt at disbelief.

"His job seems to have gone; it was a small company and they've had to employ a replacement out of necessity," he turned the page. "He's an only child, his mother is still alive though living in a care home and I'm not sure at the moment of the position with the in-laws. I think there's a degree of malevolence over the accident. I think they're blaming him for what happened, so on the face of it Mr Stone appears to have just about lost the lot."

"OK," said Dr Richards urgently, "we need to get him on ECT pronto. This is the main priority now, we could have a self-harmer or even suicide risk on our hands here. I'll see him again tomorrow, increase the pressure, and then we'll have another get together in say a week, is that good for you?"

"Yes, that's fine," he replied, opening his diary, "in the meantime I'll find out bed availability with the community houses, I presume that's where he'll be going after the treatment?"

"Yes, you presume correctly, this poor fella needs help in and out of the hospital," but to the doctor he was a number. An individual who increased the size of the hospital's population which was contrary to everything he was trying to achieve.

Chapter 5

Bill Sweet had moved out of his rooms at the home four years after taking charge, having bought himself a small bungalow at the edge of town. It was a reassuringly warm May morning, the memory of the worst winter in living memory still vivid in everyone's minds. He drove into the home's car park, pulled up the handbrake, picked up the briefcase from the passenger seat and walked up the steps. It was exactly 8 a.m., the time he always arrived and all of the children, all sixteen of them, were having breakfast just like they always were. He opened the canteen door.

"Morning, you lot."

"Morning, Mr Sweet," they replied almost as one.

"Everyone had a good night?" he asked, his left hand still holding the door handle.

"When I got his armour off!" shouted Ruby, the eldest resident at fifteen and much too advanced for her years.

"Ruby," he said reproachfully.

"Sorry Mr Sweet," she said half-heartedly, "couldn't resist it," but not many laughed, most didn't understand.

"Well, I'll see you all later," and he closed the door of the canteen behind him and made his way to the office at the far end of the building, cruelly fantasising over Ruby lying on the operating table, clamps holding open the incision, the surgeon slicing out her ovaries and dropping them in the shiny kidney dish.

The home was old and rambling, not exactly purpose built, but he'd developed a liking for the place and he felt at ease there. The park entrance that George had once traversed was a few yards across the road and many a time he had sat on one of the benches and looked up at the building, feeling amazed that he was the one in charge, though the delight in his good fortune was counteracted by the monstrous reason for it.

He walked into the office. As always, two bleary eyed night staff would be there, sipping their last cup of tea and today was no exception.

"Good morning, ladies," and he put his briefcase on the fabric covered desk.

"Good morning, Mr Sweet," said one.

"Good morning Mr Sweet," said the other.

"All quiet last night?" He walked over to the small wooden trolley and switched on the kettle.

"Yes, no problems, even Ruby got to bed early," said one and she drank the last of her tea.

"Ah, that explains her exuberance this morning," and he dropped six lumps of sugar and two heaped teaspoons of dried coffee into the cup. He liked it strong and sweet.

"Has there been any news on the new admission at all?"

"Oh yes," said the other, standing and slipping her coat over her shoulders, "we had a phone call about fifteen minutes ago, they'll be arriving about ten."

Bill's facial tic appeared for the first time that day as he became annoyed that he had to prompt that information.

"Perfect," and he poured the boiled water into the cup, "that'll give me time to sort a few things out." He took a sip of coffee. "I've no idea what to expect actually," and he blew on the surface, the drink was way too hot, "normally the child's case notes would be sent to me days before their arrival but I've received nothing at all on this one."

"A real mystery then, Bill?"

"Indeed," he concurred. "Anyway, all will be revealed at ten. Now you ladies get yourselves home and thank you very much for your efforts, truly appreciated." He always thanked them and they always respected him for the gesture and they walked out of the office, their spirits lifted a little by the presence of this lovely man.

Max Lewis was a child psychologist attached to the children's unit that Angelo was now leaving. It was his first post after graduating two years previously. He was gregarious, good humoured and completely honest and professional, but he couldn't help admitting there was a tinge of relief that he was transferring this particular young man to another establishment. Max could normally forge a working relationship with anyone, regardless of their age or sex or beliefs but his time spent with Angelo had caused him frustration, disappointment and on occasions to be fearful for his safety.

At the beginning, Angelo had been aggressive, threatening violence if he wasn't left alone. He had used every aspect of his training to get through to the boy, to try to understand the reasons for his dangerous and anti-social behaviour, but all to no avail. Other members of staff considered the home the wrong place for him to be. They felt the supervision he required could not be adequately provided and opined that at any moment Angelo was capable of carrying out a serious assault to themselves or fellow residents and the anxious atmosphere he created was not conducive to delivering a calm regimen. In the last three months of his stay Angelo had decided to withdraw from any conversation and became completely uncivil. If communication was attempted it was met with a steely stare until the person looked away. Max had hit a brick wall and being a realist determined that some new strategy had to be tried, some different sort of treatment that perhaps he was unaware, or incapable, of providing. He had achieved nothing with this sullen youth and for his own sake he needed to be somewhere else.

Max had heard a lot of good things about the children's home run by a man called Bill Sweet; how respected he was, the success he was having with the most difficult of cases so he had hesitantly applied for Angelo to take the sideways step to this new place. Bill had agreed to the transfer but with uncharacteristic lack of ethics, Max decided against forwarding his case notes in order to avoid Mr Sweet having second thoughts; a decision that Max Lewis was not proud of but one he felt wholly justified in making.

As the journey commenced Max tried to make small talk, telling him he'd be missed, hoping that everything went well in this new community, but it was difficult to have a dialogue when he was the only participant.

They arrived at the home just before ten and as the car came to a halt so did Angelo's train of thought. He had certainly heard Max Lewis saying those inane things at the beginning of the journey all right. 'Are you looking forward to your new home, Angelo? I'm sure everything's going to go well, Angelo.' He'd heard every single word but there was no point in answering. In his eyes, Max was a simple idiot. He didn't particularly like or dislike him and he didn't care what he had to say. He had no desire to engage in any conversation because he had no interest in what was being said. Should this man suddenly stop the car, grab his left shoulder as the pain dug deep and suffer a fatal heart attack, Angelo would simply open his door, leave the car and make his own way to the new home without looking back. It would be an inconvenience but the death wouldn't concern him and neither would getting to his destination. Angelo had been infected by a parental virus and no one, especially Max Lewis, got it.

No, Angelo positively did not want to converse, didn't want to waste his breath, so he just sat stock still in that car and fantasised. He pictured the living room of the old cottage with the television, then went back a little more, saw himself as a very young boy, maybe a year old, laying in his mother's protective arms as she petted him adoringly. He tried to imagine how wonderful it would feel to breathe his mother's fragrance as her hand tenderly stroked his head and body. The sensation of calm and security and the powerful ache of mutual love; and then came the image of her baring a plump and soft breast for him to suckle on, he had never known that he was wet nursed, and he started to suck and her milk, sweet and rich, began to flow. He sucked harder and her nipple then breast entered his mouth. He looked up ardently at her face that seemed to emit a sparkling luminescence. He sucked now with all of his might and his mother began to change shape, to somehow elongate as she slid into him. The little boy was now lying on the chair all alone. His mother had lost all of her size and all of her was inside him. Angelo smiled now but Max was too busy driving the car to notice. He was smiling because Mummy couldn't go missing anymore, Mummy couldn't leave him anymore because she was inside him and could never escape, though perhaps the most important reason for the big grin was of course his daddy couldn't get near her, couldn't spoil everything again and he would have been with her now not sitting in this car with Saint Max the Dope being taken to yet another institution full of deranged kids and equally deranged adults.

Realising the vehicle had come to a stop he replaced that unusual smile with his usual ancient scowl. As he turned off the car, Max tilted his head to look at him. He saw a youth with something rotten in him, where something had gone horribly wrong, an adolescent with an unfathomable plight and he didn't relish poor old Bill Sweet's forthcoming task, not one little bit. He just hoped that this man would be able to give him some purpose, some new direction to take, but had Max been privy to what that path was going to be he would never have driven that car, never have walked into that office: he would have tried a lot harder himself.

Chapter 6

Four months before Max and Angelo walked up the steps and into the home, the doctor checked Akan's haemoglobin level and determined the blood transfusion had been successfully administered. There were no signs of fluid overload or any type of allergic reaction and her lungs were clear. She was moved into the critical care unit for three days where she regained consciousness and stabilised and then into a side room to convalesce. She received no visitors and nobody contacted the hospital to enquire about her. A week later a police officer and social worker visited and met with the doctor. The circumstances leading to her injury were fully explained along with her personal situation. Following their meeting they made their way to the side room and interviewed Akan, disclosing that her father had taken his own life whilst in custody and she would be admitted into a local authority home when discharged. She took the news calmly and impassively showing no sign of emotion, explaining that she had suffered the loss of her mother and thus felt able to deal with the loss of her father.

They left full of admiration for this dignified and courageous young lady and full of despondency over her injury and the circumstances she now found herself in. Her resolute demeanour quickly vanished following their exit and she buried herself under the blankets and cried the tears of the saddest kind, the lonely tears that go unseen by those you love. She lay like that for many hours. A kindly nurse tried to comfort her but without success and she decided to leave her, allow her to weep away her sorrow. It was beginning to get dark when her lament began to subside. Something her father had told her shortly after her mother's death kept repeating in her head, blocking out the anguish.

"Physical strength is measured by what we carry – inner strength is measured by what we can bear."

That sentence began to give her fortitude, began to expand the deflated balloon. She started to realise that this was how her papa would want her to react, with spirit and tenacity and the next time the nurse came in to check she was sat up in bed and acknowledged her with a soft smile.

"I thank you for your kindness," she said to the nurse, the depth of her voice making it purr and she held out her hand. "I'm feeling better now. When you follow in the path of your father you learn to walk like him."

The phrase baffled her slightly but she was overjoyed that Akan seemed positive and she sat on the bed and held her hand tightly. She saw in this child's face a maturity and understanding far beyond her years.

"You are a wonderful child," she said tenderly, "it's very easy to be kind to you and I will always remember this moment."

The social worker returned a few days later to pick up her charge and when she walked into the room Akan had her back to her. She was dressed entirely in white, her tight braid intertwining like honeysuckle. As she turned around she had to stop herself from gasping. The bandage had been removed and the wound was now clearly visible; it was a raised furrow, the suture marks making it resemble an oared long boat sailing across her face. She quickly steadied herself and explained that she was there to escort her to the new home and Akan gathered her few belongings and followed her to the car, saying goodbye to the staff as she went. It was a short ride to the home although quite treacherous. The hardest winter in years had only recently begun to release its grip and the roads were still difficult to navigate, the need for the social worker to concentrate denying much conversation.

They walked up the steps that Max and Angelo were to ascend four months later. Bill was waiting for them, her scant case notes, delivered two days previously, lay on the desk in front of him. He had studied them, knew all about the disfigurement but it still came as a shock. She made no attempt to conceal the scar and he was having difficulty in preventing himself from staring. It seemed to split her face in half, bisect it as if he could squeeze his fingers in and open the front of her head, take a look inside. They sat and while the social worker made the introductions, Bill made the coffee, the whole time hardly acknowledging Akan's presence. He didn't like darkies; they should live in their own countries.

They concluded their business and she bade Akan farewell, reassuring her that it was a lovely place and that Mr Sweet was just that, just like his name. Bill chuckled, feigning embarrassment, and the social worker left confident in the knowledge that she was leaving her patient in a place of warmth and care.

The door closed and he kept looking at it, waited a while, then he looked at her, coldly and seriously and his face jerked momentarily. He thought she resembled a slashed portrait, vandalised and ripped apart by one of the nutters over at the hospital.

He scanned the notes in front of him. "Drugs was it?" he said abruptly, "they were all taking drugs, were they?"

She held his stare. "What do you mean?" she whispered, the hoarseness in her voice giving it a menacing tone.

"At this party: it says here that some drug dealer attacked you at a party you were at with your father."

His persona of nice had slipped but he couldn't help it. The child represented virtually everything he found abhorrent, a personification of all that was wrong with the world; drugs, improper integration of cultures, unethical parenting. She made him sick to his stomach and his loathing was beginning to show.

"The notes are wrong! My father knew nothing of drugs," she growled. "He prevented a man harming another and this was caused because my father forced the weapon from his hand," and she sat radiating malevolence as she pointed at the scar.

"But it was his fault for making you look like that," he responded callously.

"My father was a brave man, a courageous man!" and she fiercely removed the single tear that had formed in her eye, believing it a weakness, then ran her fingers lightly over the disfigurement.

"And a pretty face and fine clothes do not make character," she recited, again remembering a saying of his.

Bill stared at Akan without saying a word. He was an opinionated bigot with a chip so big it lowered his shoulder; but he had no right to be. He was a man so tainted that begging for everyone's forgiveness would only scratch the surface. He had been a party to exploitation for years and even though it gnawed away at him every day, undermining what he thought were his high principles, he still did it, still acted as an accomplice in child abuse, still lived an irreconcilable life; his duplicity in the abuse rocking the foundation of what he thought to be right. Bill Sweet was just a someone who acted immorally to save his own skin.

But as a veil seemed to lift from his closed mind he suddenly honed in on what she had said, 'a pretty face and fine clothes do not make character,' and he thought of the doctor and empathised with that, realised the depth within it.

"I hope you're not going to give me any trouble," he said quietly, "I'm in charge here and what I say goes, d'you understand?"

She remained silent, studying him with an expression that made him feel she could see into his soul.

"A large chair does not make a king, Mr Sweet," her expression remaining.

He thought about this for a moment and an emotion welled up inside him as he recognised her insight, a sentiment that he rarely made contact with.

He had begun to pity her.

As he looked beyond the scar he allowed himself a new perception. He saw a young woman who had lost both her parents but still maintained an air of self-reliance, a determination to defend herself, holding a command of her appalling misfortune associated with someone far beyond her years. As they sat pondering one another his feeling of pity abated being replaced by a further sentiment he knew little of; respect. His original feeling of contempt had now softened and fled. This female was beginning to have a profound effect on him.

"No, Akan, I don't suppose it does."

"I'm sorry?" she said with a quizzical expression.

"A big chair," he replied, a friendly aspect replacing the glower, "I don't suppose it does make a king."

Akan's refinement and rationalism had a big impact on all of those both residing and working in the children's home but Bill was impressed the most. Her courage greatly influenced him, making him reflect on his own shortcomings. He began waking happy in anticipation of seeing her, looking forward to being in her company. He saw in this girl everything he lacked and gained a certain solace when in her presence. However, it was the week before Angelo arrived that the bolt hit him squarely between the eyes. Just before dawn the nightmare made his back arch and eyes pop, unconsciously, wide open.

In the dream he was leading Akan up the dark corridor to Dr Richards' office, pulling her slightly. After knocking and walking in he had passed the child to him, gave him her hand, and she glanced across forlornly as if to say, 'how could you be doing this?'. The doctor snorted like a pig and grinned at her, the grin of a heartless maniac and he whispered in her ear, "Welcome my darling, welcome to happy hour," and he pushed Bill back out into the corridor, the slam of the door returning him instantly to wakefulness.

Night was becoming day as he splashed the cold water over his face and head as if to erase the dreadful images. He looked ahead into the bathroom mirror, making no attempt to dry the dripping water, panting, the panic still within him.

MAYBE

"You can't let that bastard set eyes on her," he said loudly to his reflection. "You mustn't let him find out she's here!"

CHAPTER 7

Charlie escorted Barry Stone out of the meeting and returned him to his seat in the conservatory. Stan, by this time, had fallen asleep, a shallow snore emanating from his head that was flopped way back in the chair. As Charlie left, the memory of the crash flooded into Barry's thoughts. Everything was still vivid making the five weeks seem like five hours. The lorry driver's look of astonished horror seconds before the collision, then the sounds, that resounding clap of his wife's head crashing into the fascia and his young daughter, the scream as her small body was lifted and thrust forward, shattering the windscreen into a thousand small squares.

He didn't know exactly how they had died, he didn't know how he had walked away completely unscathed, but none of that mattered anymore. What mattered was them not being with him and his loneliness, the hopeless loneliness. His whole being craved to touch and hug his family again; to tuck his daughter into bed, tell her stories, kisses goodnight. And his wife, all those money worries but never any criticism, never any bitterness or arguing. She loved him and he loved her and problems, large or small, would never affect or alter their love. But something had - spectacularly, horrendously, and for ever. They got caught and he got away and right at that moment Barry Stone felt he had the worst deal. He was drained and exhausted, unable to see how he could ever lose this sense of guilt. He knew he was blameless but nevertheless it had caused him to endlessly question himself, those questions always prefixed by 'what if?', 'if only' or 'I should have'.

He began to cry, softly and pathetically and Stan continued to snore, lightly and quietly. Wiping his eyes and composing himself, he looked across at Stan and rising to his feet, slowly walked over to the sleeping figure. Barry was a compassionate individual and his fragile state made the shame he felt for his earlier behaviour acutely real. He gently patted Stan's face waking him with a start.

"It was me, it was me!" he cried out, confused, still cradled in sleep, "I did it!"

"Slow down," Barry urged. "I'm sorry, I didn't mean to frighten you, I just wanted to apologise," he paused, "for being ignorant earlier on, that was all."

Stan gathered his senses, the sleep leeching out of him like a squeezed sponge and he looked up at the man curiously, the memory of their conversation returning.

"Ignorant? I didn't think you were ignorant, just very sad that's all; I can understand that."

"You can?" he enquired,

"Yes, I can, I was sad once but I'm fine now."

Barry returned to his seat and sat back down. "My name is Barry, Barry Stone," he announced, all of a sudden.

"And I'm Stan," he replied, "smiling Stan I think they call me in here, but—"

"No, I'll just call you Stan," Barry interjected, "and you just call me Barry." Stan nodded. "Tell me," he continued, "have you been here long? I don't mean to pry, I'm interested that's all."

"Yes, a long time, but the doctor's thinking of sending me out, away from here, said it's the best thing for me but I said I couldn't go out on my own, wouldn't know what to do," he said matter of factly.

"Well I'm sure they know what's best."

"Yes, I'm sure they do, I mean they cured me, didn't they?"

Barry was beginning to warm to this man, suddenly feeling that their conversation was actually taking his mind off things even though he thought Stan a little simple.

"Excuse me asking, Stan," he said tentatively, "but why were you admitted to this place?"

"Well," and he leant forward putting his elbows on his knees, "I used to be very unhappy and blame myself when bad things happened. Mind you, I always owned up to save any trouble, but after I had the electric treatment those thoughts about doing bad things have gone; well more or less and I'm happy now and when Fukum tickles me I feel happier still."

"Fukum?" Barry questioned, frowning.

"You'll meet him, always around here somewhere," he replied, reassuringly.

Barry took a few seconds to observe Stan and go over what he'd said and concluded that he wasn't quite as cured as perhaps he thought he was, but he was happy, a state with which Barry was eager to reacquaint himself and Stan's reference to the electric treatment had intrigued him.

"This electric treatment," he enquired, "d'you think that's what it was that cured you because that's what they want me to have."

"Well, do you want to forget things, Barry?"

"Do I want to forget things?" he echoed.

"Yes, you know, are there things, frightening things that you don't want to remember?"

Barry raised his hands to his face and with his middle finger and thumb squeezed his eyes together, thought for a moment then answered. "I suppose we could all say yes to that one."

"Yes, I know that but there's some that could say yes a lot louder than others," and Stan smiled, proud of his reply.

Barry continued looking at him, captivated by this perception and it was at that precise moment that he knew he had to proceed with the treatment as quickly as possible.

"Where's the nurse at the moment?" he asked, getting to his feet. Stan strained to look at the large white wall clock behind him with its sweeping second hand endlessly rotating.

"He'll be in the office now I expect, why? Are you going to tell on me? Tell him I've been doing bad things?" and his smile quickly vanished.

"What d'you mean, Stan? Of course I'm not," he replied incredulously.

"You know," he said sheepishly, "you know what I mean."

"Listen," and as Barry stepped closer Stan flinched.

"I'm not going to hurt you, Stan, for God's sake," and the little man's smile reappeared and Barry couldn't help but be charmed.

"Listen," he repeated, "neither of us want to be in here, now do we?" and Stan nodded affirmatively. "Right then. Now I know we've only just met but I'm a good judge of character and if you think that electric treatment sorted you out then I'm willing to give it a try." He could feel his mood lifting, not only at the thought of the treatment's possible success but also, oddly, by being in this man's company. "My life has taken a big turn for the worse; I know that sounds a bit melodramatic but that's the way it is," he paused then went on, "I've got to find some way of stopping this misery so I'm going to see the nurse."

"Charlie," Stan enlightened him.

"Charlie," Barry confirmed. "I'm going to see Charlie about having this treatment to sort me out. Nothing to do with telling tales or anything else, okay?" and he set off, a man on a mission.

"OK," Stan concurred, his smile widening as the idea that he had done this man a favour delighted him. As he was about to walk through the door the sound of his name being shouted stopped him in his tracks causing him to spin around. Stan stood up, excitedly moving from one foot to the other.

"Barry," he repeated, "will you be my friend?"

He considered the face of this man, this plump, smiling man looking over at him like an expectant puppy, like a child that didn't know which way to go and he had an inkling that this man was going to be his friend for the rest of his life. He returned his smile.

"Of course I'll be your friend," and Stan giggled as his new friend walked off to the office.

Charlie was sitting at his desk filling in the following day's menu rota and it didn't take long to get the ball rolling once he was informed of Barry's decision. When the doctor received his call he silently punched the air and scheduled the first therapy for the next day. The consent form was signed and filed and it was then that Barry began to cry again. Charlie moved his chair around and sat by his side putting a comforting hand on his shoulder.

"Mr Stone," he began, "I've been reading about what happened to you and your family, I'm so sorry." He said sympathetically, "I can't imagine what you're going through but I'm pleased that you've decided to do something positive about it."

Barry sighed; he knew he had little option. "Life has to go on, I suppose," and he wiped his eyes and got up from the chair. "Tell me nurse, did this electric treatment make old Stan in there any better?"

Charlie almost choked, but stoically keeping his composure, responded, "It's not the done thing to discuss other patients, however, I can say that Stan was admitted when psychiatric hospitals weren't exclusively for psychiatrically ill people. They were a bit of a dumping ground where anyone, even remotely showing signs of abnormal behaviour, ended up."

"Yes, I can understand that, but he wasn't given the treatment for nothing was he? So did they benefit him?" he pressed.

Charlie contemplated this for a second and looked up at him, unwilling to discuss the matter any further.

"Has Stan told you it did?"

"Yes," he replied.

"Then it was successful."

Barry pondered this momentarily and decided to let it drop, then asked if it would be all right to take a walk in the grounds. A few minutes later, as he took his first lungful of morning fresh air and stepped out onto the just cut grass, he wondered when the alarm clock was going to go off and wake him from this wretched nightmare but the alarm clock had been involved in the crash, it was the very first casualty.

Later that afternoon Tim Richards walked onto the ward. It had been over a month since his last happy hour and he was beginning to relish another, the old tingling had returned, but for now he had to concentrate on this arranged meeting, had to get it right or happy hours would be a pleasure of the past.

Stan was already in the office waiting for him. His last electro convulsive therapy was seven weeks ago and he was feeling reasonably alert, the post treatment fug almost dissipated.

"Hello Stan," he exclaimed as he walked in sounding almost friendly, "this is just a quick meeting to see how you're getting on, nothing to worry about," and he sat down and loosened his tie.

"How have things been since I last saw you?" he asked.

"I've made a new friend," he beamed.

"Oh really, who's that?"

"Barry Stone, he's my new best friend."

"Ah, Mr Stone, it didn't take long for the both of you to get to know each other, he only came on the ward this morning."

"Yes, I know," but Stan didn't elaborate.

The doctor reached under the desk and pressed the call button and a few moments later Charlie walked in. He stood motionless and looked at Tim Richards without speaking, their degraded relationship demanding the least interaction possible.

"Would you bring four glasses of orange squash, please nurse," and Charlie turned to leave, "and a spoon?" he added.

They had had many such meetings over the years, mainly to enable the doctor to ascertain whether Stan needed 'plugging in' and Charlie had been on the ward during most of them, but as far as he could remember, never before had he been asked to provide four glasses of squash.

He returned a couple of minutes later with the drinks and spoon and left.

The doctor had been administering scopolamine to the happy hour kids for well over a decade. A gram sprinkled into the child's favourite drink at midday rendered them incapable of resisting any of his demands by five past. They would willingly and without resistance participate in their debasement.

Another astonishing effect of the drug was that following the abuse they remembered nothing of it, as though it had never happened. The only downside being that the child was incapacitated for some hours afterwards but Tim Richards had good old Bill Sweet to sort out that little problem. Bill would bring the wheelchair and if anyone asked, which they didn't, well, they were asleep, simple as that and then a quick car journey back to his bungalow where, after the ordeal, they were attended to and allowed to recover and back to the home; no questions asked. It worked beautifully every time. But as far as this meeting with Stan was concerned, this most important of all meetings, it was the final effect that the drug provided that was of most interest to him. Scopolamine was indeed a wondrous substance for not only was it an incapacitant and amnesiac but combined with sodium pentothal it became a truth inducer and on this day that was what the meeting would be all about; but the recovery time still posed him a huge problem. Using the drugs was imperative to confirm that Stan had no memory of Bill's involvement in William Wilson's death but this recovery time, when Stan would be in a zombie like state, was going to be difficult to explain away, especially to that black nosey parker, Charlie.

The doctor took the sachet from his pocket and out of Stan's view placed it on his lap.

"Your uncle rang me today, Stan, asked how you were," the doctor lied, casting him a baited hook.

"My uncle?" Stan questioned. "Didn't know I had one, don't have anybody."

"You do, think hard, close your eyes and try and remember," and he did as he was told and the doctor slipped the sachet contents into one of the glasses.

After a few seconds he reopened his eyes. "Nope, can't remember having an uncle," he confirmed innocently, "can't remember having anyone."

The doctor pushed the laced glass over to him. "It's a hot day, Stan, have a drink," and he lifted his own glass and took a mouthful, prompting Stan to do the same. He lifted the glass and took a tentative sip and, enjoying the flavour, drank the lot and the doctor grinned. "Well done, old boy, you must have been thirsty," but Stan didn't respond, he was beginning to feel odd.

Tim Richards lit a cigarette and began to watch him. He'd given him two grams of the medication, which was double that given to the children, an adjustment he thought necessary due to his size but with psychedelic drugs size doesn't always determine dose, a fact of which he was acutely aware.

Stan put his hand to his throat.

"Still thirsty, old boy?" he asked, well aware of this side effect. Sometimes the victims would drink pints during happy hour.

"Yes, thirsty," he replied, "can't swallow." The doctor pushed across another glass and he drank half.

"Feeling drowsy, Stan?"

"I'm all right, a bit tired that's all," he responded and Tim Richards leaned right across the desk. The pupils of his patient were enormous, the whites hardly visible. When this happened with the children he would begin to unbutton their clothing; with Stan he could begin asking the questions.

"So you don't have an uncle?"

"No, I don't have an uncle."

"Who is your best friend?"

"Barry Stone."

"Did you used to watch the trains?"

"Never seen trains." He was responding quickly with no hesitation.

"Do you know Bill Sweet?"

"No."

"Do you know who I am?"

"Dr Richards."

"Who was William Wilson?"

"Never heard of him."

"Do you know who Sid Smith is?"

"Yes, he's Fukum."

"How did William Wilson die?"

"Don't know."

The doctor was firing questions at him, questions designed to trip him up, their speed and urgency negating any thinking time, but he needed to get it over with, unsure as to how long it would be before the drug started to wear off, begin tugging at his consciousness.

"Who's Charlie, Stan?"

"The nurse, my friend."

"Did Bill Sweet ever hurt you?"

"Don't know who he is," and Stan took another gulp of squash.

"Why did Bill Sweet chase William Wilson?" he was getting to the nub of it now and his voice becoming more intense.

"Don't know what you're talking about."

"Why did William Wilson jump through the glass?"

"I don't know!"

Tim Richards jumped to his feet and swiftly walked to Stan's side. With a deranged sneer on his face he grabbed the hair on the back of Stan's head and pulled him up close and whispered harshly, "Do you remember Bill Sweet chasing William Wilson and the man launching himself through the conservatory glass and impaling himself on the railings below?"

Stan's mouth was dry as if full of dust, bright pins of light were beginning to form in the extremities of his vision. He was mouthing the word 'launched' but failing to verbalise it then the doctor bellowed,

"Do you remember it for Christ's sake?!" and he knew he had to answer. He was full of the drugs and he had to tell the truth or something terrible would happen.

"No!," he shouted, matching the volume of the doctor, "I don't remember!" and the doctor felt him relax. "I don't remember," he repeated quietly and reached out for the glass but Tim Richards had heard enough. He knew the truth was irresistible under the influence of the cocktail and he was satisfied that its job was done. He bent his legs and squatted, ready to action the last piece of his plan. He was positioning himself to execute the maximum impact and as he forcefully straightened his legs to rise up he took Stan's head with him, forcing it as high as possible then brutally thrust down, his head crashing onto the desk's surface, the sound blunt and dreadful, immediately rendering him unconscious. The doctor had solved his problem and he roughly manhandled him onto the floor, reached under the desk for the bell and knelt down by the crumpled body and placed both his hands around Stan's head.

Charlie entered, a look of horror appearing on his face as he saw the scene.

"He took one hell of a fall, nurse," Tim Richards said worriedly, looking over his shoulder at Charlie. "Dropped like a stone. We need to get him somewhere where I can examine him."

Charlie called for help and Stan was carried to the dormitory, carefully undressed and laid on his bed. When the doctor, who was almost achieving a look of concern, had finished checking thoroughly he announced that everything appeared to be normal and the reason for the fall was a mystery. He pulled the arms of the stethoscope from his ears.

"But he'll need ten minute observations until he comes around and that could be some time, it was a big bump."

Tim Richards walked away from them and back to his office with a spring in his step, elated with the proof that the ECT had been successful and that any threat from this man had at last been eliminated.

Opening the door he was the cat with the cream and he swaggered into the office and sat opposite the statue. "You would be proud of me, Ugo," he announced, looking up at the face, "everything is good with the world and it's all down to me." His gaze reverted to the black Bakelite phone and his thoughts to the children's home. He reached across, his hand hovering over the receiver, his intention being to give Bill a ring and arrange a delivery, then the hand became a fist and he decided against it. A visit would be better. Just drive on over there unannounced. Maybe some new blood had arrived.

CHAPTER 8

When Max Lewis and Angelo approached Bill Sweet's door, Akan was sitting with Ruby at the far end of the canteen. For almost a week they had enacted this routine instigated by Ruby's desire to discuss her problems. She had perceived Akan to be someone different, someone out of the ordinary, important and the first time she revealed her worries was astonished by her maturity and sound advice. This young woman was like a mother she'd never had; wise, caring and most importantly sympathetic to her and in Ruby's estimation Akan was the most beautiful person she had ever met.

Bill was finishing his second cup of coffee, musing over what piece of flotsam was about to land in his lap, when he heard the knock. Life for Bill was very much about drinking strong coffee and thinking about the human flotsam that inhabited the world. He opened the door and in front of him stood a light one and a dark one and the dark one appeared interesting, very interesting indeed.

Angelo's warped face had, if anything, become more unsightly with age. His jet black, swept back hair hid none of his unlovely features. The flat, squashed nose, cleft eyes, thin stringy lips all seemingly pressed onto his face like a gruesome mould, on the front of a head too small for its body, seemed repulsive - but not to Bill Sweet. Bill wasn't repulsed, he was fascinated.

Max Lewis put out his hand and introduced himself and then introduced Angelo and as Bill looked at the youth he felt a wrench to the side of his face as if some invisible hand was heaving a plant, roots and all, from out of it and henceforth, Bill Sweet never ever twitched again.

"Coffee?" he asked and gestured for them both to sit down.

"Love one," replied Max.

"How about you, Angelo?" Bill enquired, but the boy didn't even acknowledge the question.

Bill and Max exchanged glances and the latter shrugged his shoulders.

"Angelo," Bill said loudly, demanding his attention, "did you hear me?" but Angelo stared forward, impassively. "Okay, that's fine," he said in a relaxed manner. "Now I want you to get off of that chair, get out of my office and stand against the wall outside the door."

The atmosphere in the room suddenly became tense, volatile, then Bill continued. "And don't move until I tell you to because if you do, I will punish you and I mean what I say."

Max Lewis squirmed in his seat as he watched Angelo meet the gaze of his tormentor then decided he needed to somehow intervene, take the heat out of the situation.

"I think you should do what Mr Sweet says, Angelo," and he looked at Bill for approval, a look that went unseen as his eyes were fixed firmly on the boy.

Angelo simply ignored the annoyance that was Max Lewis, sitting by his side.

Bill glared at Angelo and Angelo glared back. He had encountered defiance many times before but there was something more here. Something that was going to be helpful. Bill's policy with the children was to be the leader of the pack, the alpha wolf demanding respect and he knew he had to stand his ground when Angelo, in a low voice, spoke for the first time in months.

"You will punish me?" maintaining the glare, "you will punish me?" he repeated, "how do you think you can punish me?"

"Look boy," and Bill approached him with his arm raised.

Max tensed, fearful that he was about to strike him then loosened a little as Bill placed his raised hand on the top of Angelo's head.

"Look boy," he restated, "if you don't get out of this office now, you'll understand how I'll punish you." And he squeezed his fingers strongly around the boy's scalp.

Angelo forced his head away from the grip. He was wearing a loose fitting pair of jogging bottoms making it easy for him to insert his hand into the back. He stretched his left arm out in front of Bill to prevent any advance and cupped his right hand under his anus to collect the impending turd. He compressed his stomach muscles and pressed down and it flopped gracefully into his palm where he grasped it gently. Swiftly he removed the hand and held it in front of him then spread his fingers revealing the ejecta within, staring at it as a young boy would a fledgling. He stroked it with his other hand and the two men's faces screwed up in revulsion.

"Who wants this?" he asked, raising only his eyes as they flashed from one to the other.

"I don't!" stammered Max Lewis who reared his head away and stepped one pace back but Bill Sweet stepped one pace forward and whispered ever so quietly into Angelo's ear,

"That was fucking genius, son," he said softly, "I truly mean it, fucking genius," he repeated. "Now shut up and just go along with me," and he pulled away and once again put his hand on Angelo's head.

"Directly opposite this office is a lavatory," he said, "I want you to go in there, put the shit down the toilet, flush it and wash your hands maybe ten times or however long it takes to get them clean; then come back out and stand against the wall like I said before."

Angelo had never been called a fucking genius before and he was quietly delighted. This man was different and remarkably he decided to do as instructed. He moved towards the door but just before he reached it turned and jerked his arm at Max Lewis, as if to toss the turd, causing the man to retreat further until his back was planted firmly against the wall. Bill couldn't conceal the snigger which thankfully went unheard by the preoccupied Max.

They both watched as he exited and heard the toilet door open then close.

Max heaved a sigh of relief.

"That was close," peeling his back off the wall and sitting down.

"Close?" Bill replied. "What d'you mean, close?" and he looked deep into Max's eyes.

"Well, there was almost a combustible situation there, you know," he said awkwardly.

"A combustible situation?"

"Sort of," replied Max, not understanding why he felt somewhat embarrassed.

"Would you have caved in Mr Lewis, this early in a relationship with an extremely aggressive youth? Would you have let him get the better of you?"

"I don't see it in those terms, I think there has to be mutual respect for us to be able to do our job and help these kids."

"You don't think he respects me?" still eyeballing him.

"Maybe not after that," he replied tentatively, trying not to be offensive.

"Mr Lewis, this boy is too far down the road to be responsive to these wishy washy ideas." He sat down. "It's like an iron bar riddled with rust, there's no pure metal left there, you just have to work with what's left."

Max rubbed his forehead and exhaled as if exhausted then Bill continued.

"With kids like this you have to act as the leader, the leader of the gang, speak their language and make sure they fall into line like members of that gang. That's the way you get their respect."

"Well it's a different approach but one I can't say I agree with."

"Why don't you agree?" he said sharply, beginning to become frustrated and then he suddenly realised that ordinarily his face would have been mobile with spasms in such a situation but his attention went back to Max.

"I just don't agree that anyone is beyond help which you're alluding to with the iron bar comment. I think the most dehumanised of us still retain a spark of humanity that can be reached with mutual respect and patience," he replied, making Bill, once again, sigh with annoyance.

"So why's the boy here, Mr Lewis?" he said seriously. "Did you run out of mutual respect and patience?" a sarcastic tone creeping through his words.

Max decided to ignore this jibe, rise above it.

"You have a combative attitude, Mr Sweet. I didn't expect this and I don't think Angelo did either." Max was trying for the moral high ground and Bill was getting angry. "We're on the same team, you know," he continued, "we both only want the best for Angelo don't we? Surely, he's our main—"

"Why didn't I get the boy's case notes in advance?" he said curtly, stopping Max in mid-sentence.

"His case notes?" he replied, stutteringly.

"Yes, his case notes," Bill echoed, "why didn't I have them before you arrived, it's standard procedure?"

Max thought quickly. "Clerical error," he said, haltingly.

"It was no clerical error, was it Mr Lewis? You kept them from me because you were worried I wouldn't agree to the transfer if I'd read them." Max's silence confirmed Bill's suspicion and he raised his arm and pointed at him. "I think you have failed with this boy. I think that he was too much for you to handle," continuing to point. "I think that maybe Angelo should be in a secure unit, but your wishy washy views won't let you believe in the concept of secure units so I've got him instead."

Bill looked at him squirming. He now had complete charge of the situation. How dare this 'wet behind the ears' liberal try and lecture me, he thought, but abruptly he felt uneasy. The real Bill was putting his head above the trench and that wouldn't do at all, not one little bit. He calmed himself down.

"Look," and he ceased pointing, resting his hands on the desk, "let me handle the boy my way, Mr Lewis. You've tried and failed, I'm going to succeed," and he smiled, "with a bit of luck," he added and walked over to the kettle. "Although on that performance it'll be a lot of luck," he added further and switched it on.

"How do you like your coffee?" but Max decided against it and stood up not wanting to spend any more time in the man's company,

"I'll give it a miss I think. Need to get back, lots to do," but as he lifted his briefcase his professionalism bubbled to the surface and he replaced it.

"I need you to understand, Mr Sweet, that I only want what's best for Angelo. I was willing to go off message, bend the rules if you like, to get him transferred here and I apologise for that but at the forefront of my mind was always his well-being and I'm not apologetic for that." He took a deep breath. "But there's something that worries me and I feel I need to warn you. I have only had two years actual hands on experience in the profession but I have colleagues with ten times that amount even more and they are all of the opinion that Angelo could be dangerous, it's all in the case notes. Latterly he's become completely introverted. Today is the first time I've heard him say anything for almost three months; he has become unreachable," he hesitated, "and I know this might sound naïve, but," and he paused again as if were searching for the right words, "sometimes and it's not only me who feels this way, sometimes I feel as if he's evil."

Max readied himself for more sarcasm but was surprised when Bill replied, almost in a kind, fatherly way that when you can't understand something you tend to pin all sorts of labels on it.

"So you've tried your best and now it's my turn. Perhaps in the future, if I'm having no joy with one of my lot I can send them over to you … different techniques, different results, eh?" and he grinned, thinking it advantageous that this young man leave with a smile not a frown.

Bill followed him out of the office and Max said goodbye to Angelo who surprisingly to him was standing by the wall as instructed. He expected no response and received none and Max walked out of the home exactly twenty-five minutes after entering. He descended the steps and walked across the parking area, sat in his car and looked up at the imposing façade of the place, glad to be from there. He pondered over the short handover, a procedure that would normally take much longer. Wondered why he hadn't been asked about the patient or his treatment, about his history or any unusual features. There again, he reassured himself as he reversed the vehicle and pulled out into the moving traffic, Bill Sweet was hugely successful with the most difficult of cases and what was it he'd said, 'different techniques, different results'?

He was getting up to speed when the smell began to waft up from his hands. Keeping his eyes on the road he lifted his right hand off the steering wheel and put it in front of his face noticing what appeared to be brown streaks and flecks. He replayed his memory of the meeting then instantly realised what the smell was. He had opened the door to exit the office using the wooden handle, the wooden handle that Angelo had used before him. He began to shake his head; this had indeed been the shittiest of days.

Chapter 9

On the morning of his first ECT Barry was sitting at Stan's bedside dismayed at his new friend`s evolving black eyes and the huge bump, like a protruding and rotting peach, that had surfaced on his forehead. He had spent most of the night watching over him, holding his hand, the grateful night nurse keeping him supplied with tea. It was an opportunity to consider, long and hard, the treatment he was about to receive and when the first light of dawn crept into the room he had eventually cast any remaining doubts from his mind. Since arriving on the ward his feelings of hopelessness had been replaced by a growing desire for his life to return to some sort of normality and he was regarding the therapy as a shortcut to achieving that. Up to the time that he had supposedly fallen during his interview with the doctor, Barry had spent the previous day almost exclusively with Stan. They were building a strong affinity, an understanding and he wished, more than anything, that Stan's consciousness would soon return and he could speak once again with his new buddy. As he looked down at his battered face he thought back to the odd statements he had made, his interesting and unorthodox view on things.

"But I miss them all so much, Stan, it still seems like yesterday that it happened."

"Maybe it will always be that way so when you meet them in heaven, Barry, they'll only have been gone for a day."

All the psychotherapy, the twilight hour chats with the night staff and the group sessions he'd attended seemed meaningless now. He knew that the staff meant well and perhaps it was all too soon but he hadn't really been listening and certainly not fully participating; he had been too empty. But now he had the treatment to look forward to and the company of Stan, the odd plump man, and things were looking up. That wave of grief that had engulfed him was beginning to flatten out and he was starting to see a pinprick of light at the end of the tunnel. Possibly the match had been struck to relight the candle.

He was feeling optimistic as Charlie approached with the pre-med injection.

"Hello, Barry," they were on first name terms now.

"Hi, Charlie," he replied.

"No change?" he asked, looking concernedly at Stan.

"Still the same, no sign of him coming around yet; is that the jab you were telling me about?" and he craned his neck to see inside the stainless steel dish.

"It is," he confirmed, "and don't worry, you won't feel a thing."

Barry gave him his arm and looked away. He'd avoided needles for as long as he could remember.

"All done," he announced, swabbing the injection site.

"I honestly didn't feel a thing," he said, aghast.

"Plenty of practice," Charlie replied matter of factly, pleased with himself. "How are you feeling? I know you've been up most of the night."

"Least I can do for the old bugger. Don't want him to peg it yet, not before he tells me a few more of his crazy sayings," and as he shook the little man's hand Charlie felt encouraged that he seemed to be departing from his previous languid behaviour.

"How's your mood at the moment, Barry, you seem a lot brighter even though you've been up most of the night?" he commented, adroitly placing the plastic safety cover on the syringe.

"A little less worried about things to be honest with you Charlie. It seems so much quieter here compared to the acute ward, more laid back. Most of the patients went to that operational therapy this morn—"

"Occupational therapy," he corrected.

"Sorry, occupational therapy this morning and as you know I had some long chats with Stan and actually had a bit to eat, d'you know I've lost over two stone?"

"Yes, I know."

"Your job, right?"

"Sort of thing."

Barry smiled. "You're a good man, Charlie, you must be, old Stan here thinks the world of you."

"Well now there's a compliment, coming from such a wise white man," he said half-jokingly.

"D'you know," Barry said somewhat seriously, "I've only known him for a short time but he's a hell of a character and I've got to like him. He's helped me quite a bit you know."

"I can understand that," Charlie observed, placing the dish and its contents on the bedside table, "I think he's just very easy to talk to, you get what you see with him and his quirky look on things makes him appealing," and he motioned to Barry to stand up.

"You're right," Barry concurred, "and he shouldn't be in here, at least I don't think he should," and he stepped into his slippers.

"Tell me something, Charlie, why doesn't he go to this occupational therapy?"

"It's not compulsory, you know," Charlie replied and he began to straighten the sheets around Stan in an attempt to make him more comfortable.

"I thought not, but during the day there seems to be only him and that bloke Fukum, I think they call him that."

"We do," Charlie confirmed.

"Right, and me now of course. Tell me if I'm wrong but if it's beneficial, which it must be, then why doesn't Stan go?" he said, struggling with the dressing gown supplied by the hospital which was way too small.

"Do you know what occupational therapy is?" he asked, carefully easing Stan's head forward and puffing up the pillows.

"Not really."

"Well it consists of sitting at a long communal table and assembling biro pens. The patients have three boxes in front of them; one contains a plastic outer case, one the ink tube and roller and the other a black cap affair that goes on the top. The patient puts all of these components together and that's what we affectionately refer to as OT. However," and he lifted his index finger, "occasionally it gets a little more interesting."

"Yeah, how's that?"

"They get to make red pens," and Charlie wasn't joking.

"You obviously don't approve."

"Stan here certainly doesn't. it's just pin money for fags."

"Right," Barry nodded knowingly, "but all the poor bloke does is sit in that conservatory all day, that can't be much good for him? And another thing. Charlie, it's nothing like a conservatory."

"It's a long story, Barry," and there was a silence until Charlie had completed tidying the bed.

It was obvious that Barry was genuinely concerned for Stan and there being a few minutes before it was necessary for them to leave he decided to elaborate.

"You remember I mentioned to you before that in the past these places were not exclusively for psychiatrically ill people?"

"Yes, I do."

"Well I think Stan fits into that category. There's lots of people in here who should be out and there's lots out who should be in," then he paused to consider how much should be revealed. Sitting down on the bottom of the bed he raised his eyes to look at Barry.

"Something happened to Stan a long time ago during the war and he was admitted because he was acting strangely. There was nowhere else for him to go back then if indeed he needed to go anywhere."

Barry was listening intently and Charlie continued.

"A few years after being here and I was just a young student back then, he witnessed a fellow patient commit suicide, a man by the name of William Wilson. He jumped through the glass that covered this room and killed himself and that's why the whole front was bricked up and why we still call it the conservatory even though it isn't one anymore."

Barry nodded, now understanding.

"Anyway, Stan was really affected by this and Dr Richards decided to prescribe ECT, in fact it only stopped a few weeks ago."

"Hold on a minute," Barry gasped," blimey, that must have been years!"

"It was and it upset me, some other people too, seeing him having all of those treatments. A short course is ..." and he stopped to give himself time to think, "more acceptable," he quickly corrected himself, "no, more appropriate to the problem."

"I'll only be having six though, won't I, Charlie?" he said nervously.

"Without a doubt, Barry," he confirmed, realising that he was beginning to fret.

"And Stan, he won't be having any more?"

"No," he said decisively, recognising that he'd already said too much and wanting to change the subject, "I think you're his new treatment now, you've had a real effect on him. I've never heard him talk or laugh so much, I'm really pleased, pleased for the both of you," and Charlie's smile sparked one in Barry. "And," he went on, determined to get as far away from Stan's past as possible, "it looks as if he will be finally leaving us. He's next in line to go into a sort of halfway house, a place where he can be assessed and helped back into the big wide world. I just hope this fall doesn't get in the way of all that."

"Why d'you think he fell, Charlie?"

"He doesn't do a lot of walking, his legs aren't that strong; got up from the chair and they suddenly gave way maybe. Dr Richards didn't really say how he thought it had happened."

"Hope it wasn't a stroke or something like that," he said forlornly,

"No, the doctor checked him for all of that …" then Charlie stopped abruptly, their conversation interrupted by a groaning noise and Stan opened his eyes.

"He's coming round," Barry whispered and Charlie leant over him.

"Stan," he said urgently. "Stan, it's Charlie, how are you feeling?"

"Head hurts," he moaned through dry lips as he put his hand to his forehead. "Real bad, have I had treatment?"

"No, you haven't, let me get something for your head," and after asking Barry to watch him, rushed out of the room reappearing in seconds with another nurse who was carrying a small cup and some water.

"Stan," Charlie said quietly, "Barry and I have got to go but the nurse here has some tablets I want you to take, they'll sort out your headache."

With a helping hand, Stan eased himself up in the bed and took the medication.

"I'll be back as soon as I can, you'll begin to feel better when those pills kick in," and noticing that Barry was now holding Stan's hand, gently released it and they headed out of the dormitory, through the main entrance of the ward, down the long straight corridor until they arrived at a grey door. The sign above read 'Do not enter when red light is on'.

It was off and they entered.

Chapter 10

As Max Lewis was desperately washing his stinking hands in the equally stinking public convenience, Akan was sitting cross legged on the bed in her small room. An opened notebook lay in front of her, a black topped OT biro in her right hand. Kuffy, her father, had always advised her to write down whatever might be upsetting her followed by as many possible remedies that she could think of. Even though Akan had many troubles of her own she was carrying out this exercise on behalf of her friend Ruby. She had listened intently to her describing what had happened in the past, events that had culminated in her admittance to the home and had decided to list these problems along with as many useful resolutions as she possibly could. Her idea being that her friend could read these in the solitude of her own room, consider them and hopefully formulate a course of action.

She felt it was the least she could do for a person in need.

Chapter 11

Bill Sweet watched Max Lewis leave the home then turned to Angelo who was stood against the wall, head down, hands in pockets. He saw a wounded sixteen-year-old youth; malicious, abusive, scary in appearance and possibly beyond change. A youth who, due to his upbringing, had received The Baton and was now living a chaotic life, dealing with it by hiding within himself and using extreme anti-social behaviour. But this all boded well for Bill because within this directionless piece of flotsam, this pathetic individual made of clay he recognised someone he could mould; mould and meddle with. When he first laid eyes on him he liked what he saw, especially his anger. Now that could be moulded and meddled with all right.

He purposefully moved directly in front of Angelo who remained motionless and as before, placed his hand on his head though this time he didn't push down but pulled, pulled him forward and when they were together he began to cuddle him, right there in the passageway. The boy stayed rigid although not resisting, this was strangely comforting to him. After holding him like this for more than a minute Bill finally whispered,

"Angelo, I'm going to save you. I know why you feel like you do, why you behave like you do and I'm going to do something about it. I don't know what other people have said or done in the other places you've been but here is different, I'm different and I'm going to give you a reason for getting up in the morning. I'm going to show you how to be happy, show you a way to get all your anger out. Would you like that? Do you want that?"

The boy continued to be unresponsive, motionless.

"You must tell me, Angelo," he said pleadingly. "You must tell me or you're going to end up somewhere bad, really bad and I don't want that for you, I refuse to let that happen."

He squeezed him more tightly.

"I know you can be the best at anything, Angelo, you can beat anyone, you're as good as anyone, look at me, son," but still he stood as if set in stone. Putting his hand under the boy's chin he raised his head to face him. "What are you thinking, eh?" he asked. "What are you thinking right now? I've heard all this before? Bill Sweet is some kind of do-gooder who doesn't really care, a waste of time. Is that the sort of thing you're thinking right now?"

But Angelo was thinking much different thoughts; he wasn't even in the moment. He was reliving the times in the cottage with his mother he loved and hated and the confusion and mistrust that those two emotions caused him.

Bill gripped his chin more firmly and Angelo floated away from the cottage and into the corridor, saw the man looking earnestly at him and now focused on what was being said.

"Come on, son, if you help me I'll help you. I need to know how you're feeling, why you're so angry."

Unlike his interrogator Angelo was calm and controlled. Through the partial gap in his eyelids he stared back at the frustrated face just inches away and stayed silent.

"I know hardly anything about you," he continued, "but I do know I like you, I like you a lot." Bill was beginning to perspire, unsure of when he would get a reaction, if at all, but he remained perfectly fixated on what he was saying. "Are you thinking of what happened in the other homes, perhaps things happened there you didn't like?"

This question ignited his mind. "I'm not thinking any of that," Angelo finally replied in a slow, cold monotone, "none of it," he added.

Relieved at the response, Bill smiled and exhaled. "Well please, Angelo, tell me what you're thinking, we have to start somewhere, I've got to have something to help me, to help me understand you, to help me save you."

Bill didn't shift his gaze and he looked into Angelo's eyes expectantly, hoping the boy would give him some leverage. He lowered his head and nodded in encouragement and eventually he spoke again.

"Bad things about bad times."

"Bad things about bad times?" Bill echoed questioningly.

"Yeah," confirmed Angelo and Bill released his chin and the boy's head dropped once again.

"Okay," Bill started, talking to the top of Angelo's head. "Okay," he repeated, "that's a start in my book. You've had bad times and you think bad things about them. That's good because I'm going to be your Dutch uncle, Angelo. I'm going to be your teacher and helper and I'm going to advise and guide you and make you stop thinking bad things," and he lifted his head up again, "do you want me to?"

Angelo shrugged his shoulders.

"I don't know," and he paused for a long time.

"Maybe."

That was what Bill was waiting for. In the many ways the youth could have replied, the many words or sentences he could have used, that one word would do extremely adequately - maybe. That 'maybe' was the first spore of commitment that would be nurtured and developed to grow slowly and surely, bit by delicious bit, until its progress was unstoppable and complete. The boy had at last given him a positive sign and he was very thankful for it.

"All right," said Bill, blowing deeply, "let me tell you something. Courage is about doing something that you're scared of, could be picking up a spider or climbing a cliff. Most people would have no problem saying that word you just used, maybe, but I reckon it took every ounce of courage you own to say it," and this time, when Bill removed his hand, Angelo kept looking at him and Bill grinned at the boy but it was a cold and insincere expression.

"Now I want you to walk on up this passageway until you find a door with the number three on it. It's green and it'll be on your right. This will be your room for as long as you stay here with us. It's clean and comfortable and all yours. I'd like you to lie on the bed and think of what I've said because believe me, son, I am going to sort you out; I like you, you're special and I'm going to make sure you get happy," and Angelo nodded vaguely and began to walk away.

"Just one more thing before you go," and he came to a halt, "I need to tell you a little story, a tale about a rooster and a road," and the boy returned to Bill and listened.

CHAPTER 12

The self-closing mechanism worked beautifully as the door glided to a soft stop behind them. As they entered the brightly lit ante room the three people inside turned to look at them. Barry's first thought was that the place smelt oddly of almonds and the illumination level was way too high making the three faces seem somehow unreal. He immediately recognised Tim Richards, had no recollection of the man by his side and after a few moments of backtracking remembered the third person as the young male nurse who, two days previously, had escorted him from the acute admission wing.

The doctor, who appeared completely out of place in an immaculate grey suit, approached him with an outstretched hand.

"Good morning, good to see you again," and he shook his hand, "so glad you decided to go ahead, you won't regret it."

"I hope not," he replied nervously.

"You can leave Mr Stone with us now, nurse," he said to Charlie, coldly, and without responding to the doctor assured Barry he would see him later and made his way back to the ward.

Having been previously instructed, the young nurse now asked him to remove the dressing gown and he wheeled a black, plastic upholstered, trolley to his side and motioned for him to lie on it. As his head rested on the hard surface he stared up at the ceiling, the four overhead lights pumping out a brightness that made him wince. The unknown man and the doctor seemed to be whispering furtively in the corner of the room looking at, what he presumed, were his medical notes and the young nurse was standing ready to push him through the double doors and into the treatment room. Barry could suddenly feel his heartbeat and he raised his head to look around him. The room and its occupants seemed utterly artificial. An awful idea dawned on him that none of them knew what they were about, that he was some kind of guinea pig. The two in the corner were conspiring together, plotting to cause him harm; and the young nurse ... what was he doing there? The very same one who had brought him from acute admission. That was strange, wasn't it? And then he felt the straps attached to the side of the trolley. He hadn't seen those before.

"What the hell is going on here?" he announced loudly and abruptly and he sat bolt upright, his eyes wide with fright.

"Everything isn't quite right, is it?" and he began to dismount the trolley.

The young nurse grabbed his feet in a panic and the other two rushed to assist.

"Mr Stone!" the doctor half shouted, forcefulness to his voice. "Please don't upset yourself, nothing is wrong, we're simply checking the anaesthetic," and he grasped his shoulders strongly, repositioning him on the trolley.

"It's a formality that's all, you need to compose yourself, concentrate on the benefits," and out of Barry's eyeline Tim Richards flicked his head in the direction of the syringe, urging the anaesthetist to get it.

Barry relaxed slightly and laid back as he was told, not feeling the tip of the needle as it punctured his skin. As the ketamine began to flow through his veins the last image he saw was on the face of the man who was unknown to him, a worried and concerned expression as he looked down from above. As Barry slumped into unconsciousness, Dr Richards instructed the nurse to wheel the trolley through the doors but was stopped by the anaesthetist's intervention.

"Hold on, I need to draw up the Succinylcholine."

"The what?" Dr Richards exclaimed.

"The Succinylcholine, the muscle relaxant, it needs to be given separately."

"Forget that," he said dismissively, "it was only a couple of years ago we were doing this with no medication whatsoever, a few hospitals still don't now," and he again told the nurse to push the trolley ignoring his colleague's look of disbelief.

"Let's get on with it," and he waved his hand at the nurse to move, "let's just get it over with."

But they were all now on edge.

In the equally as bright adjoining room the patient was positioned centrally and the physicians began to work almost robotically. The patient's pyjama top was removed and the doctor placed one hand under the chin, the other behind the neck and forced the head severely back and up to allow easy insertion of the airway. The leather straps, which had almost been responsible for a panic attack, were stretched tightly by the anaesthetist and fastened across the arms, legs and midriff and he then took a handful of conductive gel and spread it liberally on either side of the patient's forehead. Meanwhile, the doctor linked up a pulse monitor and positioned the screen next to the Ectron machine which was dull grey and had three extension ports. A power cable extended from the first and he pushed the plug into a wall socket. Leads from the remaining two culminated in electrodes housed in cups, resembling headphones, which he attached to the slippery sides of the patient's temples. The anaesthetist passed the nurse a steel vomit bowl and asked him to prepare for this possible reaction from the patient and he then began to studiously concentrate on the information provided by the monitor.

Tim Richards stood by the Ectron and asked if everyone was ready. They nodded confirmation and after taking a deep breath he pressed his thumb down hard on the red, rubber covered lever.

"One," he said loudly.

The patient's back arched violently as if the shock had been administered to his backside rather than his brain; straps stretching simultaneously as the body strained against them. Both hands clenched into fists, feet jerked down like a tiptoeing ballerina. His head, trembling, jolted forward; the chin digging into the chest and teeth clamped, vice like, onto the plastic insert.

"Two."

The patient gasped now like a drowning man. A dreadful sound, resembling a stifled scream, emanated from below the airway as his nostrils flared and eyes suddenly flashed wide open. His head was now bouncing, the chin slapping against the bare chest, but his gaze seemed to be stationary and firmly fixed on the young nurse who, in response, was unable to prevent himself from jumping back in sheer fright, dropping the bowl as he did, the thing clanging and somersaulting on the tiled floor.

"Three."

The patient's knees cramped fiercely and bent his limbs upwards causing the straps to fall forward leaving them unshackled. Now unhindered, his legs began to kick out every which way and the trolley began to rock precariously.

"You should have let me use the relaxant!" the anaesthetist called out reproachfully as Dr Richards lunged forward, thrusting his entire weight down upon the flailing limbs.

"Nurse!" he almost screamed, their bodies cavorting as if in some absurd combat "switch off the machine!" but the nurse was mesmerised, welded to the spot, transfixed by the patient's continuing stare.

"For God's sake," he now bellowed, using all of his strength to contain the patient on the trolley. "Turn the fucking thing off!" but it was Ted Beddoes, the anaesthetist, who had the coolest head and he quickly reacted, reaching over the doctor to raise the Ectron lever, powering it down.

Barry's body instantly became limp. With a thump his back fell flat against the plastic: his eyes closed, fists unfurled, legs straightened and the tension fell away from his grimacing, stricken face. The doctor stood back and glanced over at his colleague, heaved an exhausted sigh and thanked him while the anaesthetist, in response, resentfully shook his head as if repulsed. Tim Richards ignored the gesture and instead turned to the nurse.

"I know this isn't a pretty procedure," he said between deep breaths, "but by God, when I tell you to do something will you, in future, do it immediately," the volume of his voice beginning to increase, "and not just stand there like some poleaxed dummy?!" Now completely unable to disguise his anger, the volume continuing to escalate, "If it wasn't for Mr Beddoes' presence of mind this whole session could have been a complete disaster!"

The nurse lowered his head like a found out child. Only the doctor's breathing, laboured from his physical effort, could be heard in the room. The nurse was cowed, the anaesthetist bemused and the doctor furious. Then Ted Beddoes said knowingly,

"This is the first time you've assisted with ECT, isn't it?"

The nurse lifted his head and looked directly at him.

"Yes, it is," he replied meekly and the anaesthetist glared at Tim Richards accusingly and the doctor got the message.

"Look," he said, backtracking, "I wasn't aware of that," the doctor continued, trying to fix the situation, but the nurse's head dropped once again and Ted Beddoes turned to the patient and began to skilfully retract the airway and release the heavy straps, ignoring what his colleague had said.

Tim Richards felt a rarely experienced pang of regret. "Go and have a cup of tea or something, nurse," he said half-heartedly, "have an hour to yourself before you go back on duty," and the nurse made for the door. "And I'm sorry I shouted," he said, but it was without conviction, meant only for his colleague's ears and the nurse left the room silently.

"I had no idea that was his first assist, Ted," but the anaesthetist continued to remove the straps without speaking. He had made his point and further words were unnecessary.

Together they wheeled Barry back into the small ante room and turned him over into the recovery position.

"You know, Tim," he began, breaking his silence, "when we get a performance like that I think the whole rationale behind this treatment was thought up by a patient, not a bloody professor, and a pretty psychotic patient at that."

"I can't believe you said that," the doctor replied incredulously, "It's the only remedy for this man; he was depressed to the point of suicide, lost all of his family for Christ's sake. No other treatments were having an effect."

The anaesthetist walked over to the sink and began to wash his hands. "Time itself is a great healer, Tim."

"Time is something we haven't got," and he joined him at the sink.

"You only come over from the general maybe once a month and then only for a couple of hours so you wouldn't know, but the pressure is on to lessen the time patients stay admitted. It's all about looking after them in the community now and ECT could reduce this man's stay by ... months."

"Could is a good word, Tim. This treatment's hit and miss," and he began drying himself.

"How long have you been thinking like this, Ted?" he asked seriously, shaking the water from his hands.

"I think it really came home when I managed to press the lever in there just now," and he passed the towel to the doctor and went over to check on Barry.

"I know things didn't go to plan in there, Ted, but it was exceptional, the strap wasn't positioned correctly, it should have been much higher."

"Don't try and defend it, Tim," and he pressed the nurse call buzzer, "the facts are we didn't strap the man down properly, unknown to us the nurse was completely inexperienced and the poor patient was subjected to, let's face it, possible physical danger and you know about the Bolam principle as well as I do. God forbid, but if he'd have injured himself in there we could be facing a charge of negligence." He remembered his finger was still pressing the buzzer and he pulled away as if it were hot. "Let's face it, Tim, no one really knows what damage might be occurring by firing 240 volts through someone's brain. The whole thing is, oh I don't know, somehow amateurish and neither of us trained to be amateurish," and he placed his chin in his palms and shook his head.

Tim Richards was becoming impatient with his colleague. He wanted to clasp his hands tightly together and bring them down, like a club, on the back of his head; but he had become adept at hiding his emotions, keeping them in check, so he continued to listen with mock concern then the anaesthetist dropped his hands and looked at him.

"I've been doing a bit of research on this lately, Tim."

I bet you have, he thought, but "Have you?" he said.

"Yes, d'you know that it wasn't very long ago that psychiatrists injected depressives with a soup made from the brain of a recently electrocuted pig to see what the effects would be?"

"Yes, I was aware of that."

"And lobotomies," he continued, "slicing the prefrontal cortex with no understanding of what damage was being caused."

"Look, Ted, general nursing is more black and white. The body malfunctions and you operate or medicate. Psychiatry isn't like that." He threw the towel into the laundry basket. "It was a bad session, things went unexpectedly wrong, perhaps we've become a little complacent about it. The strap won't slip again and I'll personally ensure that nurses are suitably briefed in future."

"You don't have to make excuses for me, Tim. The strap was my fault and mine alone. Those sort of things happen in hospitals every day, simple human error, no, it's the treatment itself, it's just," and he hesitated fractionally, "as insane as some of those it's trying to cure."

"You haven't witnessed the results, Ted," he said defensively.

"Maybe not, I've heard about them though, confusion, memory loss …" but the knock on the door stopped him continuing. He walked across and opened it and the sister from acute admission stood there.

"Hello, Ted," she said engagingly, "you rang for someone?" and she entered the room.

"Hello, sister," Dr Richards greeted her, smiling.

"Dr Richards," she replied, indifferently, having little time for the man. Then Ted piped up.

"We wondered if someone could come along and tend the patient; I'm afraid the nurse you allocated is otherwise engaged for an hour or so."

"Oh really, why's that?"

"Became upset during the procedure, needs a little recovery time like Mr Stone here."

She didn't enquire any further. "That's a problem, no spare staff as usual," and she put her forefinger to her chin and thought for a second.

"Problem solved!" she suddenly exclaimed, removing the finger and pointing it upward. "I'll take him with me to the ward and keep an eye back there," and she began to push the trolley out of the room.

"But sister," the anaesthetist interjected, "shouldn't he really be in the recovery room. If there's a problem all the necessary equipment's here."

"Doctor, that will tie up a member of staff for hours, anyway, nothing will go wrong," she said, reassuringly, "and if by chance it does, well we'll only be a hundred yards away, won't we?" and she pushed Barry away hurriedly to her ward.

They both watched the grey door slowly glide to a close.

"A classic example, Tim," he said as they continued observing the door.

"What of? Lack of staff?"

"Amateurish behaviour," he corrected and began to prepare for his return to the general.

"Oh, by the way," he said, placing the instruments he'd used into the bag, "meant to ask you, how's that little lad from the home, the one we operated on last week, is he back there now?"

Tim Richards couldn't stop the swallow. "Yes, he's back over the home, doing very well thanks."

"Nasty that, Tim, million to one injury; what was it? Jumping up and trying to pull the light fitting down in the broom cupboard and landed on one of them?"

"Yes, apparently so, still, these things happen, eh?" desperate to change the subject but the anaesthetist persisted.

"Only seen an injury like that once before, you know."

"Really? Well that door's padlocked now."

"Yes," he continued. "A teenager, some years ago, if my memory serves me correctly," and he pressed the halves of the bag together and flicked the clasp, "came to light he'd been anally raped by his older nephew for God's sake, can you believe it?"

"Beyond dreadful, Ted, beyond dreadful."

"Isn't it?" he agreed.

"Is that Bill Sweet chap still running the show over there?"

"Yes, excellent fellow, why d'you ask?" and they made their way to the grey door.

"No reason, Tim, just wondered," he said casually and the doctor watched the anaesthetist depart along the long corridor, perversely uplifted that a hint of suspicion had been attached to his partner in crime.

Chapter 13

Bill made himself another cup of coffee and sat down in the small office to read Angelo's case history. As he opened the hard back binder there was a firm knock on the door and he shook his head, frustrated by the intrusion. She stood there, dressed completely in white, even the ring on her finger held a white quartz stone within it. Her hands were clasped in front of her and she looked up at him with wide, penetrating eyes.

His annoyance quickly evaporated. The child enchanted him and he was always pleased at the sight of her.

"Akan," he said, smiling warmly, "what can I do for you?" He gestured her in.

She had inherited her father's graceful bearing and she seemed to glide into the chair. He sat opposite.

"Thank you, Mr Sweet," she began, the huskiness in her voice lending it stature. "I just wanted to speak with you for a short while."

"I have plenty of time, Akan," he replied, "what's on your mind?"

"Can what we say to each other today remain only with us?" she asked. "Not to be repeated to anyone?"

"Of course," he said, intrigued, "I am actually very good at keeping things to myself," he said ruefully.

"Why does speaking that sentence make you sad?" she said, frowning slightly.

"No, it doesn't, it doesn't," he said forcefully, her perception startling him, "please tell me what it is you'd like to say."

She moved closer to him. "Have you heard the expression, by crawling a child learns to stand, Mr Sweet?"

"Umh, no," he said, raising his bottom lip, "I don't think I have but it makes sense."

"Well there is such a child here in the home who has begun to crawl though needs more help to achieve walking; help I cannot give her."

"I think I understand," he replied. "Could you tell me the name of the child?"

"These things stay between us?"

"Please don't ask me that again, Akan. I have told you I am a man of my word," he said, somewhat hurt by her distrust.

"I'm sorry, I didn't mean to question your honour, Mr Sweet, it won't happen again," and she understood by his expression that he had already forgiven her.

"It's Ruby. We have been having conversations and I think she is becoming happier, but now she needs someone wiser."

"Really, please go on."

"Before I do, can I show you something she wrote some time ago when at home. I think it might explain perhaps why she is here?" and she removed an A4 sheet of paper from her white tote bag and passed it to him. He put on the glasses that had been lying on Angelo's case history and began to read the cursive handwriting on the page.

They lay, jerking together, then stiff,

Him pleading with her to shout sex words,

Her responding.

Eugene Francis-Williams

His beer breath condensing on her neck,

Her thighs wriggling,

Helping her depths to become fucked.

Skin underneath nails

Human gulleys underneath him.

And child entered without knocking.

Child's father was stabbing her,

Child's father had his hands around her throat and all her

Glands were being squashed.

Child's father

Was stopping air to her lungs

And at the same time

Injecting her with poison from the syringe between his legs.

Child's entrance went unnoticed by them,

Until

Child's fist crashed upon father's forehead.

"Leave her, she's my mummy."

"Leave her, she's my mummy."

Child's small body smashed against the wardrobe,

Propelled by father's lumpy arm.

Father was going to kill child as well

Child thought.

But mother was not dead

For her mouth opened and said

As if her Adam's apple

Was being tapped with each word.

"And stay there, brat!"

He passed the sheet of paper back to her and removed his glasses.

"Is this just a made up thing or did it actually happen?"

"I have asked her that question and it happened."

Bill Sweet stared intently at Akan. As much as her appearance and confident attitude gave the impression of someone much older she was only thirteen and he decided to answer her with that in mind.

"I think you have to understand that, present company excluded, most of the boys and girls in the home are here because they have bad parents, people who have had a terrible effect on them."

"I can completely see that, Mr Sweet," she replied, assuredly, "but there are bad parents and very bad parents and Ruby has very bad parents." She suddenly closed her eyes and began to gently rub the top part of her scar where it crossed the hairline.

"Does it hurt very much?" he asked sincerely.

"Not hurt that much, itches, especially on my forehead," and she continued to rub. "But that is of no matter," she announced and abruptly stopped and when her eyes opened they were fiercely serious. "Ruby needs to be with someone with more knowledge of how to deal with her problems, the things that are upsetting her. She has told me that no one knows of her past and why she can be so disruptive but she now feels able to discuss these problems and that is why I have come to see you."

He was in admiration of her compassion. She had suffered the most horrendous trauma but somehow she was finding it within herself to show concern and offer assistance to another unfortunate. However, as he had explained, the majority of the kids resided there because of The Baton, hurt by the inadequacies of their parents and Ruby was simply one of many to experience shocking behaviour.

"Akan, I understand what you're saying and I respect you for trying to help Ruby but I can't make her a special case. As I said, most of the kids are here because of their bad parents," and he smiled, almost apologetically, "and our main priority is to keep them out of harm's way."

Her eyes remained trained on him, unblinking, there was no reciprocal smile: then she said as a teacher to a pupil.

"Mr Sweet, you remember me saying there are bad parents and very bad parents," and he felt as if he were being talked to by a mother not a girl, by someone who was more knowledgeable than himself and he replied submissively.

"Yes I do."

She again passed him the sheet of paper with the cursive writing. "Please read the last line again, Mr Sweet," and he focused on the sentence, 'and stay there, brat'. Four words representing a threat, he thought, not particularly significant.

He looked up at her vacantly.

"Does that seem odd to you?" she asked, her stare unwavering.

"I can't see what you're getting at," he muttered, reading them again.

"Wouldn't, 'get out, brat!' fit better?" she said, and as the mask of ignorance began to lift from his face Akan stood up, placed her hands palm down on the desk and leant forward towards him.

"They used to make her watch, Mr Sweet."

"They used to make her watch!"

Chapter 14

The sister wheeled Barry into a vacant room, checking on him periodically whilst carrying out her usual duties. Above all she was a pragmatist. She was well aware that, as Ted Beddoes had remarked, Barry should have remained in the recovery room with a nurse in constant attendance but she was also well aware of how many staff she had at her disposal and by bringing him back to the ward had chosen the best option in a difficult situation. On her fifth check she noticed that one of his legs had straightened and she now stayed with him knowing that any movement of limbs meant the anaesthetic was loosening its grip. Before long he had raised his hand to his throat, a typical post ECT action due to the airway intrusion and she singlehandedly manoeuvred Barry from the trolley onto the adjacent bed. Within minutes he was regaining consciousness, quietly moaning as his head swayed, desperately trying to open his eyes.

"Mr Stone," she said assertively, "please relax, do you know where you are?" and she held his hand to reassure him.

"Aargh," he groaned.

"Your convulsive therapy was successful and you're now back on the ward."

"Back on the ward," he painfully imitated, the anaesthetic reluctant to leave.

"Yes, back on the ward, my love. How are you feeling? Is there any pain, sweetheart?"

She had adopted that strange, familiar parlance that many in her profession thought comforting.

"Yes," he drawled, his eyes remaining stubbornly shut. "My head," which was rolling as if unsupported, "my head is killing me, terrible ache," and he lifted his other hand jerkily and placed it on the side of his forehead.

"I know, my love, I'm afraid your head will ache for a while, I'll give you some medication shortly. Do you feel sick at all?"

She had nursed people recovering from ECT many times and was well aware of the aftereffects.

"No, no," he uttered through still lips, "my throat," and he screwed up his face tightly as the agony accompanied the swallow, "feels raw," and his eyes began to open, "feels like I've been in an accident."

"Well, Mr Stone, you've nothing to worry about on that score, rest assured you haven't been in an accident," and she released his hand and began straightening the pillows behind his head.

"I know," he said hoarsely and weakly cleared his throat. "I've never been in an accident."

CHAPTER 15

Bill Sweet agreed that, if this were true, Ruby had certainly experienced horrific deeds and he would do all he could to arrange specialist support for her. Satisfied, the young lady slipped out of her chair and was by his side in a seemingly single movement.

She held out her right hand and as he took it she snapped her middle finger against his, a Fante blessing.

"*Me daase,* (thank you) Mr Sweet, you are a good man," and seconds later the door was closing behind her.

He looked down at his hands. A black girl, using a foreign tongue and foreign gestures in his country, in his place of work, in his very own office should have been anathema to him, but not anymore. She had caused the meagre amount of humanity within him to blossom and his mood was elevated and soaring. He pressed them together, palm to palm and clicked his middle fingers. He glanced at the door she had just closed and wished she had remained, stayed and mesmerised him a little longer then dramatically he wrenched his hands apart as the ice cold dagger of dread entered his heart and the contentment on his face became a grimace.

His secret world had entered his comprehension and that nightmare of him passing her over made him recoil. At all costs he had to ensure that Tim Richards never found out she was a resident. The child had to remain

Maybe

unknown to him and he quickly reattached his glasses and opened Angelo's case history.

Maybe there was a solution.

Chapter 16

Charlie looked up at the clock. Three hours had elapsed and there was no sign of Barry. He decided to look in on Stan before returning to the therapy room to see why there was a delay. Lining the dormitory were twenty-four beds in two equidistant rows, each one having a locker on its right hand side. It was laundry day and an assistant was changing the very last bed, a huge pile of sheets and counterpanes in the central aisle. Charlie acknowledged him with a wave and approached Stan who had fallen back into sleep. The swelling on his forehead had matured into a lump of purple blue and two dark shapes, like commas, had appeared from the corner of his eyes, spreading around the top of his cheeks and lower lids. Charlie gently grasped his wrist and checked his pulse which was steady and normal. Satisfied with his condition he let the assistant know he would be off ward for ten minutes and walked briskly out and along the deserted corridor. He arrived at the grey door and, after checking the red light was inactive, walked into an empty recovery room. Bewildered, he quickly made his way to the nearest ward, acute admission and was relieved to find Barry sat in the day room drinking his second cup of tea.

"You're being looked after then," he observed.

"Yes," he replied, looking at him with an empty expression, "it's soothing my throat," which he slowly began to rub.

"Are you ready to come back to the ward?"

"Which ward?" Barry questioned, surprised.

Charlie recognised the signs of confusion associated with ECT.

"It's all right, Barry; you can get a bit forgetful after this treatment. We're just going to walk back to our ward, you know, where your friend Stan is."

"Stan?" he asked, putting his cup and saucer down and getting to his feet. "Oh Stan," he seemed to remember. "How is he?" but he wasn't enquiring after his recovery following the fall, merely making a statement he felt to be appropriate.

"He's fine, Barry," and he picked up the crockery, "fast asleep at the moment," but Barry ignored this and they walked out of the room.

The kitchen door was open and he was surprised to see the sister washing dishes at the sink.

"I'm taking Mr Stone back to geriatric if that's okay, sister," and he placed the cup and saucer on one of the steel surfaces.

"No problem," she answered, "how is he now?"

"Confused, forgetful, you know the usual stuff. Why was he brought back here, I assumed he'd be in the recovery room?"

She picked up the crockery and transported it to the sink.

"Well, apparently the assisting nurse found it all too much and didn't see it through to the end so I had to bring him back here. Bloody nightmare! I'm a man down now and having to wash my own bloody dishes," she moaned, half smiling. The sister finished at the sink and began to dry her hands with a tea cloth.

"The doctor told him to go to the canteen and have a cuppa, get his head together," then she paused, "come to think of it he should have been back hours ago," and she looked at the watch that was pinned to her uniform.

"Anyway, ma'am, I'll get Mr Stone back to the ward."

"Yes, all right, Charlie," she said, almost automatically, still wondering where the missing nurse could be, "I'll see you soon," and she walked out in front of him into the passageway where Barry was patiently waiting.

"Goodbye, Mr Stone, Charlie will take good care of you now," and his eyes narrowed.

"Charlie?" he said questioningly and the man suddenly appeared behind her. "Oh, that Charlie," but no one was convinced.

As they started to walk the phone began to ring in the kitchen and Barry abruptly stopped and turned around.

"That'll be for me," he said with conviction.

"No, no," and Charlie pulled his arm to keep him going, "I can absolutely assure you it isn't."

They were passing the grey door when the sister eventually picked it up and found herself speaking to the tutor of the assisting nurse. He informed her that the young man, a second year student, had instead of going to the canteen for a cup of tea, gone to see him for a cup of coffee and he was ringing her to explain why he had arranged to give the student leave of absence.

"But we're severely understaffed as it is," she complained, her annoyance exacerbated by her not being consulted.

"I'm fully aware of the staffing situation, sister, but the fellow was traumatised, made to feel unprofessional, useless, and that's why I've decided to give him leave, time to get over it."

During the long pause that ensued, the sister's irritation, along with her blood pressure, began to rise. Eventually she managed to speak. "Good God, man, these students have got to be told that psychiatric nursing isn't a cushy number, it's bloody hard and sometimes it can get rough."

"Hold on a minute," he said angrily, his blood pressure now rising, "this nurse had no idea of what to expect when he assisted this morning and Dr Richards shouted at him …" He stopped, not wanting to say anything he might regret and gathering his thoughts. "Cast your mind back to the first time you witnessed this procedure, sister," his tone more conciliatory, "it can cause you as much of a shock as the one wearing the electrodes, it can be seriously frightening and this student not only hadn't assisted before but he also had to watch as the patient almost fell on the floor because the straps came loose: he's actually considering giving up nursing altogether. Now he's a second year student, that's a lot of training down the drain and I felt it important he take a break and that's what he's going to have."

Her eyes were closed as she listened to all of this. She was old school; no matter what happens you simply put your head down and get on with it.

The tutor waited for her reply but there was silence and he began to think the line may have gone dead.

"Can you hear me?" he enquired. "Are you still there?" he asked in a louder voice.

"Tell me something," she eventually began trying to maintain her composure, "why was it that this nurse didn't know what to expect during ECT?"

"I've no idea," he replied indignantly.

"You've no idea? You're supposed to be his tutor."

"I didn't know he was going to be there," he said defensively.

"Your students should all be briefed on what to expect if they're participating or not."

"He was under your supervision, you should—"

"Wait a minute," she interrupted, "are you trying to shift the blame for this onto me?"

"I'm not blaming anyone," he fired back.

But the student nurse was.

Now sat in the bedroom of his small flat, he was blaming the entire discipline of psychiatry for two wasted years. He was blaming those who, among other things, thought it a good idea to callously blast a patient with electricity in the vain hope it might produce some beneficial effect. He put his head back against the chair and something he'd read in the past flickered into his mind.

'Human beings will always be mad and those who think they can cure them are the maddest of all.'

He had always wanted to join the nursing profession, had always wanted to help those in need, but he knew right there and then that he'd never go back. He knew he had to stay away before it was him who needed the help.

Chapter 17

During Charlie's absence Stan had woken up and feeling a little better, and not wanting to lie in bed, had asked if he could be allowed up. Not seeing a problem, the assistant had helped him out of bed and supporting firmly, walked with him to his usual chair. Although the majority of the patients were at OT, the conservatory was alive with the sound of the ward maid battling to clean the wooden floor, grunting as she wrestled with the heavy rotating brush of the polishing machine, using brute force to keep it under control. When Charlie and Barry arrived back Stan was grinning from the mental image he'd conjured up of her having lost the battle and being spun around the ward horizontally whilst still holding on for dear life, but the grin quickly disappeared when he saw the alarmed look on Charlie's face.

"What are you doing up, Stan? You should be resting in bed." He sat Barry down opposite him.

"Couldn't stay in there, Charlie, I was bored, the other nurse helped me in."

"Did he now, we'll see about that." He made for the door.

"Please, Charlie," he blurted, "it was my fault, I made him, I said my back was aching from lying there." He looked at him pleadingly. "It'll save a lot of trouble if you don't say anything," and Charlie relented, not realising that he was reverting to type, taking the blame.

"Well, I don't suppose sitting here for a while will cause you any harm," and he visibly calmed down, "but I'll be keeping an eye on you, Stan, you've had a nasty fall, a real nasty fall," and he once again made for the door.

Peace arrived when the cleaner switched off the machine. Exhausted, she stored it away and breathing heavily made for the kitchen and the teapot.

Barry sat silently, his face expressionless and Stan watched him for a few minutes. He was having difficulty remembering how he had felt after the treatments, though unknown to him, when he used to lie on that trolley, the doctor had kept his thumb on that lever for way more than a count of three.

He cleared his throat. "Remember me, Barry?" he said sharply.

Barry looked up, surprised. "Do I remember you?" he retorted and Stan shook his head affirmatively. "Of course I remember you," and he laughed gently.

"What's my name then?" he said as if excited, "go on tell me, tell me my name."

Barry thought for a moment. "Your name's Charlie."

"No, it's not, it's Stan."

"Stan," he said forcefully, "that's what I meant to say, sorry, your name's Stan."

"Who's Charlie then, Barry?"

"Charlie?" he echoed hesitantly. "Charlie's someone else," and he looked down at the floor, confused by his lack of clarity.

"You've had your treatment then?"

"Yes," he replied sheepishly, still looking down.

"I've been trying to remember how I felt after it. I think I felt like they'd hit me with a sledgehammer, knocked all the meaning out of my head. I can remember once looking in the mirror and not knowing who was the real me."

The door suddenly opened and the assistant walked through the conservatory heading for the laundry, clutching a huge bundle of linen to his chest. In his wake, marching behind him was Sid Fukum Smith holding a dreg of a rollie close to his mouth, his other hand squeezed into an unnatural position by the left side of his face as if he was holding an invisible phone. He peeled away and with his usual aloofness walked straight past them on his way to his chair at the very front of the room. As he sat, he removed the stub of the cigarette that was now in his mouth, thrust his head back and almost sang Fuk-Hum at the highest point of his range. It was only recently that he had added the letter 'H' to his two syllable repertoire and it had, oddly, given the words a certain sophistication.

Stan restarted the conversation, not allowing the interruption to upset his train of thought.

"But it did me good, made me forget like you're forgetting."

He looked to his left and through the window saw the high clouds, trees swaying in the breeze and more memories returned.

"Got a headache?"

"Yes, I've got a headache," his eyes rising to meet Stan's, "and a throat ache or whatever it's called," and he wiggled his Adam's apple.

"Yep, that's right; I had one of those, a throat ache. That's where they clamp you down to stop you jerking off the table; that's what someone told me, anyway."

They looked across in unison as Fuk in the note of A followed by Hum in F melodiously wafted around the room as if some Alpine goat herder had kidnapped Sid Smith's very being. They returned to each other and that dulcet reverberation seemed to have triggered Barry's awareness and he recognised who it was talking to him.

It was Stan the smiling man but I'll just call you Stan. It was Stan the cuddly nutcase and he was sitting there opposite the smiling man because his entire family had died in a horrendous crash and he was completely devastated. But the recollection of that, the understanding of how he felt about that, was blurred. It was as if his emotions had lost their edge and although the memory of the event was still there, the severity of his reaction to it had lessened, in fact, was almost non-existent. The ECT had stopped the wine fermenting, had taken the polish off and he refocused on Stan, perched there like a Cheshire cat with a huge plum pudding inside itself and realised what he had meant by some wanted to forget things louder than others. He meant there were those that needed help more than others and he was one of them.

It was all coming back now and he didn't want to return to how he was. He wanted to remember the tragedy, of course, but not with the ferocity that had instigated his admittance and Barry persevered with the treatments having a further five over the following three weeks and the routine more or less continued. Charlie bringing him back to the ward, sitting him down in the conservatory and Stan remembering as he forgot.

Chapter 18

Although the subject was only sixteen his case history was disproportionately thick.

Bill opened the file and began to read.

June 19th. 1953.

Angelo Goodwin, male, Caucasian. Police admission 11.47 pm.
Dishevelled. All vital signs normal. Facial disfigurement and
Cranial abnormality. Underdeveloped, exhausted and
Anxious.
10 ml. oral chlorpromazine syrup administered. Half hourly
Nurse attendance. Placed in side ward.

June 24th. 1953.

Angelo is a young boy with an alcoholic mother and father
Unknown. In, via constabulary. Mother currently in custody -

Hence admission.
Difficulty with communication. No contact with welfare as
Yet. Confined to room.

July 7th. 1953.

Welfare now engaged. Facial abnormality, small skull size and
Stunted physique probably caused at foetal stage due to
Mother's alcoholism. Supervised. Mother in custody and awaiting
Trial, father's whereabouts unknown.
Possible transfer to Springfield home.

August 10th. 1953. Springfield Young Persons Home.

Admission at 10.30 am. From general.
10 ml. oral largactyl twice daily. Supervision necessary. A
hostile and contrary child.

August 13th. 1953.

Not mixing with other residents and antagonistic towards
staff. People intimidated and on edge around him. Views
residents and staff from corner of eyes.

August 21st. 1953.

Eugene Francis-Williams

Displaying gross behavioural dysfunction. Crudely informed pregnant
member of staff that should she unplug the television set
a kick administered by himself would deny the live birth of
her child. Largactyl increased to thrice daily. Confined to room.

August 23rd. 1953.

Following request, visit from known neighbour, though contact
refused. Verbal aggression and threats should she attempt to
revisit. Possible brain abnormality? Echolalia now being presented –
whether symptomatic or sarcastic difficult to tell.

September 1st. 1953.

Transfer to Somerton secure home. Assault on cleaner following
argument over noise, preventing his televisual enjoyment.

September 1st. 1953.

A difficult character indeed. Admitted 11 am. from Springfield.
Repeating everything he hears including clock chimes and birdsong.
Unable to make eye contact.
Mr Loveluck Jones assigned for one on one.

October 1st. 1953.

One month assessment condensed from Mr. Loveluck Jones daily notes. Persistent echolalia although signs of reducing. educationally impoverished and lacking social decorum and skills. Private tuition and interplay essential. Resorts to breathing loudly through mouth when frustrated due to shape of nose. Minimal contact with fellow residents.

October 14th. 1953.

Nocturnal enuresis. Penile binding prescribed. Echolalia diminishing.

October 20th. 1953.

Penile binding unsuccessful. Soiled pyjamas to be retained and soiled bedding re used.

October 23rd. 1953.

Ward informed by welfare that mother sentenced to six and half years for child negligence and prostitution. Patient unaware.

November 1st. 1953.

2 month assessment condensed from Mr. Loveluck Jones daily notes. Free of echolalia although continuing to use neologisms, sometimes whole sentences composed of completely spurious words. Low tolerance for frustration. Strict private tuition and interplay necessary.

November 20th. 1953.

Admonished for excessive swearing and inappropriate sexual references during supper. Television watching denied. Inconsolable, dangerous. Removed to padded room.

December 1st. 1953.

3 month assessment, synopsis of Mr. Loveluck Jones daily notes. Angelo has begun thumb sucking and biting his nails excessively. He has also developed an annoying habit of constantly tapping his fingers on any surface they happen to find themselves. However, educational progress is being made and advancement with anti-social behaviour is occurring although any interruptions will be completely counterproductive hence the absolute necessity for strictly private tuition and interplay.

MAYBE

Bill violently slammed the folder down on the desk and in his rush to get to the sash window, knocked over the chair causing it to crash backwards. He heaved it open, stuck his head into the fresh air and inhaled deeply.

'Mr Loveluck fucking Jones, you bastard,' his brain screamed, 'you were abusing him!'

For him to suddenly start bed wetting, a classic sign, then making sexual references? A boy of that age? And the finger tapping and the nail biting and the thumb sucking: he'd witnessed all these habits arise in the happy hour kids. Continuing to breathe deeply he shook his head in dismay and tried to understand what life must have been like for this young boy but failed miserably, instead concentrating on the reasons.

Angelo was never given a chance. Cast into a world of corrupted adults who had succeeded, through their selfish and debauched deeds, in turning an already damaged newborn into a misguided, anti-social monster.

As the breeze blew, removing the dampness from his skin, it also began to remove these acrid thoughts as a new insight began to emerge, that these corrupt adults had of course once been innocent children themselves and those supposedly providing their care had instilled these abhorrent skills and where did it all stop! What was the answer to preventing the milk of human kindness turning sour?

And then, inevitably, his thoughts released all of this and reverted, as they always did, to himself.

Gradually Bill began to forgive, to consider Loveluck Jones and all those like him as victims of their circumstances. In his mind's eye the man became born again, remodelled out of a stinking, Fagin-like degenerate into a blameless, crimeless character who had actually proffered on him a big favour, a favour that would hopefully suck the sludge of years of worry and self-loathing right out of his very core.

He closed the window and righted the chair, reopened the file and started to scan rather than read every word, his eyes now focusing on only the most pertinent information.

June 1st. 1954.

Nine month assessment, synopsis of Mr. Loveluck Jones daily notes. Good progress in reading and writing though from a low point and pitifully poor compared to contemporaries. Doodling aggressive pictures a concern and oddly, has become easily moved to tears. Vehemently refuses to have his hair cut which is now halfway down his back. Private tuition essential.

May 9th. 1955.

Following Mr. Loveluck Jones' retirement, this boy has confided to a member of staff that the aforementioned was mistreating him. An outrageous attempt to put a blot on this outstanding man's reputation. This is indicative of the manipulative little individual we have in our midst and his accusation has been thrown in the proverbial dustbin where it belongs.

May 10th. 1955.

Small fire in storeroom which was extinguished by cleaner. All residents interviewed but none volunteering information other than one child who saw Angelo Goodwin playing with matches some hours before.

May 15th. 1955.

Incredible accusations once again made against Mr. Jones. Strategic decision made to place in rumble room with hourly observations. Second Ob. found him bloodied from incessant head scratching. Room cleaned and patient restrained in straitjacket. Opportunity taken to cut patient's hair.

December 16th. 1955.

Rumble room – making obscene threats.

August 1st. 1956.

Rumble room – possession of knife.

January 25th. 1957.

Rumble room – obscene behaviour.

October 19th. 1957.

Rumble room – aggressive threat to kill.

October 20th. 1957.

Transferred to Moorings mental hospital, juvenile wing.

October 22nd. 1957.

Angelo Goodwin, 10 years 3 weeks. Transferee from Somerton secure home. Placed in seclusion awaiting Assessment.

October 22nd. 1957.
Assessed as suffering from conduct disorder. Observation, discipline when necessary.
Largactyl 50 ml. orally, 3 times per day.

April 22nd. 1957.

6 month assessment. 10 years 6 months. Quiet and controlled. Medication reduction to 40 ml. Largactyl syrup orally, 3 times Per day.

October 22nd. 1957.

Twelve month assessment. 11 years old. Quiet and subdued. Medication reduction to 40 ml. Largactyl syrup twice per day.

January 3rd. 1958.

Complaint of anal discomfort. Examined. Lack of anal dilation and No resistance shown by sphincter. Allocated single room.

Bill Sweet again shook his head.

They've got to him again, he thought. He turned the page and a comment halfway down immediately caught his eye. Amidst the ubiquitous 6 month assessments detailing the amounts of sedation it took to render Angelo zombielike was an observation dated simply April, '60.

Unknown woman. Conversed with patient. Left distressed.

Who was that, Bill wondered, that neighbour who was mentioned before? He began to look at the dates, working back and then he realised. Had his mother served her full term with no remission for good behaviour she would have been released sometime in April, 1960.

Surely it must have been her. He continued to scan, but all there was left to see was the sparse information on his wasted years at the mental hospital and the entries of Max Lewis when Angelo had been moved to his care home. No further mention was made of a female visitor, in fact it appeared that other than the abortive attempt made by the neighbour and the actual visit by the mystery woman, no one had visited him in the ten years of his incarceration. It also dawned on him that Angelo had been without any medication from the time he had left the other home.

He picked up the phone. "Hello, is that Max Lewis?"

"Speaking."

"It's Bill Sweet."

"Hello Mr Sweet, I've only just arrived back."

"What took you so long? It's been hours since you left."

"Something cropped up," and the smell re-entered his nostrils causing him to gag.

"Are you all right?" Bill asked.

"Sorry, I'm fine," he stuttered, "What was it you wanted?"

"Angelo's medication, I don't seem to have the details."

"It's on a separate sheet, should be in the notes," he replied.

Bill lifted the folder but nothing fell out. "Not here, Mr Lewis, what's he on?"

"Thorazine," he said forcefully, cringing that the subject of his notes had resurfaced.

"Forty milligram capsule, three a day." He looked up at the wall clock facing him. "He was due one four hours ago."

"I'm on it," Bill replied, aware of the urgency and slammed the phone down without another word. He unlocked the med trolley and pocketed a bottle of the required anti-psychotic and was about to leave.

But someone walked in.

Chapter 19

Tim Richards had a spring in his step as he walked across the tarmac to his car. Inexplicably, the doctor had become infatuated with a new pop group from Liverpool and as he drove off to the children's home he was whistling one of their songs. He was still whistling 'I wanna hold your hand' as the engine died and he got out. As he locked the door he gasped at her reflection and when he turned around his eyes widened in delight. There, sitting on the low wall at the top of the entrance steps was Akan, imperious and pure, like a young queen on her throne. He thought she was beautiful and his heart began to pound. His eyes never strayed as he crossed the car park and ascended the steps and as he approached she looked at him curiously. He was smiling at her but it wasn't an open, unguarded expression, more of a covetous look, avaricious even and a cold shiver passed through her as he walked into the building and out of sight.

Entering the office without knocking he almost collided with Bill who was on the other side of the door.

"Dr Richards," he exclaimed, startled by his abrupt appearance, "I wasn't expecting you; I was about to deliver some medication, you normally ring ahead."

"Don't you like surprises, Bill?"

MAYBE

Bill certainly didn't like this kind of surprise and his thoughts immediately leapt to Akan and her whereabouts.

"You're welcome anytime, Dr Richards, you know that," he said half-heartedly. "Coffee?"

"No time, I've a meeting with that John Hayes in half an hour, d'you know him?"

"Met him once or twice, long ago."

"Bloody idiot!" the doctor spouted. "Owner of a rubber spine if you know what I mean."

"Sort of," Bill replied.

They both sat down and the doctor lifted his legs and placed his feet squarely on the desk, a manoeuvre Bill found utterly disdainful; then ignoring the 'no smoking' sign, pulled a pack of twenty out and lit one up.

"Couple of things," he began, "Mr Stan Heart."

He now had Bill Sweet's full attention. "Yes, what about him?" he asked, hesitantly.

"I've had to stop the ECT."

"Stop it? What the hell for, it's been keeping him—"

"Whoa Bill," raising his hand, "I've got it all sorted."

"I can't believe this, it was shutting him up, why have you—?"

"Because I had no option, all right?" he again interjected. "The staff were getting restless, questioning its use."

"Jesus Christ, that's never worried you before," and he began to shake his head in disbelief, the news so worrying it overcame his usual deference. "He's going to start remembering what happened, it'll start coming back to him."

Tim Richards took a long drag on the cigarette, pursed his lips and puffed out a perfect ring of smoke that hovered in the air like a floating halo.

"Don't shit your pants, Bill," he said, sneering, admiring his drifting creation, "Mr Heart and I have had two very long interviews; helped him along in the second one with a cocktail of drugs so potent it would have made your mother tell you who your real father was." He couldn't help the disrespect, especially when he felt he was being disrespected.

"He doesn't remember a thing, believe me, and now I'm going to discharge him."

This was a lot for Bill to take in and almost a minute went by before he responded. "But if he's discharged how are you going to keep an eye on him, make sure he doesn't start remembering?"

"I've already told you," he said, becoming impatient, "he doesn't remember a thing and isn't going to and if you give your peanut sized brain time to think about it, discharging the little shit is a master stroke on my behalf; it's getting him away from the scene of the crime where all those memories are."

Ignoring this other insult, he indeed gave his brain time to think about it. "All right," he said, reluctantly, "I just wish you hadn't stopped the treatment, that's all."

The doctor sighed. "I've just told you I had no choice and I've come up with an alternative so `thank you` might be more of an appropriate response," and he looked at him expectantly.

The last thing Bill wanted to do was thank him but, knowing that any further discussion on the matter would probably push him into a rage, he reluctantly did.

"Well done, Bill, well done," he replied condescendingly, dropping his cigarette into Bill's empty coffee cup.

"Now the second reason for my visit," and he clapped his hands and gleefully began rubbing them together, "you've been hiding someone from me, haven't you?"

Bill looked at him questioningly, worried by his comment.

"Do you have any idea what I'm talking about?"

"None at all," he replied defensively.

Tim Richards stared at him silently; he liked to see Bill squirm.

"That delicious creature sat out by the steps."

The Rectus Abdominis is a paired muscle running vertically on either side of the human abdomen, also shared by some of the earth's other mammals. Bill was ignorant of this but he was very aware that they had suddenly cramped and he let out a slight gasp as one of his worst fears had been realised. This brute had spotted Akan. Bill composed himself.

"Male or female?" he asked quietly.

"Oh female Bill, definitely female. Bloody big scar across her face but I find that rather intriguing. Dark olive skin, exquisitely braided hair, dressed completely in white, without a doubt definitely female wouldn't you say?" He lit another one and took a drag. "A young lady who's acquaintance I'm looking forward to make."

His heart was racing as an array of excuses flooded into him. She's a visitor, she's about to be discharged, he had no idea who she was but he knew they were all a waste of time. He knew this man thoroughly and somehow he always got what he wanted.

"Her name is Akan," he pronounced forlornly. "She's had a tragic history, I don't think it would be appropriate—"

"Quit the shit, Bill," he said flatly, " just bring her over," a seriousness in his voice now. "I'll be a couple of hours maximum with Hayes and I'll interview her then."

Bill's mind went into overdrive, his thoughts tumbling around like a rock fall. He couldn't let this happen to her, he had to come up with something.

"Today is impossible," he half shouted as a believable reason came to him, "she's waiting for her social worker, they're going away on some outward bound scheme."

The doctor eyed him suspiciously.

"Really?" he said, getting to his feet. "Well let's go and have a chat with her Bill, see if we can postpone this little trip," and Tim Richards made for the home's entrance with his panicking lackey in tow.

As well as being ignorant of the names of his stomach muscles, Bill was also blind to the fairy tale that Horace Walpole referred to in a letter he wrote in 1754 to his friend Horace Mann. The tale was entitled 'The Three Princes of Serendip' and it was Walpole who coined the word serendipity, something that Bill was about to gratefully experience.

As they arrived at the steps, Bill's sense of relief was almost paralysing. Not only was she not there but Ruby and her newly appointed child psychologist were driving away from them. As they glimpsed the rear of her head, Ruby's decision to emulate Akan's braid proved a godsend.

The adrenaline forced Bill's mind to respond as quick as a flash. "There they go," he declared and began to wave.

"Fuck it!" the doctor exclaimed and turned to Bill, his face brimming with disappointment. He looked around to make sure they were alone.

"Bring another one over then," his countenance reshaping, becoming devious and crafty. "I'm away on secondment for a month from tomorrow, need to get this itch scratched before I go," and he looked at him knowingly, "but that new girl, Bill," and he began to descend the steps, "make sure she's available when I get back. You don't discharge her and you don't transfer her, got it?" and Bill nodded realising he now had a deadline.

He put his hands in his pockets as he made his way wearily back to the office.

"Bollocks!" he thought out loud, breaking into a trot as he felt the medication bottle and Bill bypassed the office and headed directly for room 3.

Chapter 20

Sitting in the office with John Hayes the look of disappointment was still on his face but his mood lifted as he began to lay the foundations of his plan.

"Tell me, John, the community house, how much room do we have there?"

"Three, possibly four beds at the moment," he answered.

"Any twin rooms?"

"There's one I believe."

"Right then, I think we should take a calculated gamble," he said, pretending it was a spur of the moment idea." Mr Heart has already indicated his reluctance to leave alone so I think we should discharge both him and Mr Stone in, let's say, a week's time, to the community house sharing the same room," and he peered closely at John Hayes for his reaction.

"I feel it's like the blind leading the blind with the two of them," he replied.

"I understand what you mean," the doctor stated cautiously, "but you must agree a lot of progress has been made. They have a mutually beneficial relationship. Mr Stone has become a mental stimulus for Stan who conversely, has become a prop for Mr Stone. I can't see what can go wrong."

"This fall that Stan had."

The doctor's ears pricked. "What about it?"

"Did it have a medical basis?"

"He tripped!" the doctor said irritably. "I was in this room with him when it happened, he tripped over the chair that you're actually sitting on."

"Okay, Tim," he stuttered, put out by the doctor's quick temper. "I was only trying to establish whether or not Stan had a medical problem."

The doctor sighed.

"He doesn't, John, all right? It was a simple trip and nothing more," and a silence ensued.

The two men had an unspoken dislike for one another. The doctor disapproved of his liberalism and the social worker disapproved of his intolerance and they both dwelt on these feelings for a while.

"We've never tried two at the same time," John Hayes declared, invigorating the dead air. "I think the community nurse has enough on her plate with one patient let alone two, what with the reintegration period and—"

"I know that John," he interrupted, "but I think this way could actually save her time and effort; let me explain," and Tim Richards sat more upright, he was becoming excited.

"Barry Stone has only had a brief time out of society."

"Well I can tell you—" and he began referring to his notes.

"Six weeks," the doctor saved him the trouble. "His treatment is working, in fact, bolstered by his friendship with Stan he's recovering well and I envisage that friendship growing on the outside. Stan on the other hand is, of course, going to need a more in depth reintroduction but Barry Stone will give him that by simple association, so the nurse's role will in fact be diminished."

"Well yes, I can see what you're saying," he replied with little enthusiasm, "but can we really rely on Mr Stone to provide for Stan's needs?"

"No, not entirely," the doctor concurred, happy that his colleague was becoming compliant. "A degree of supervision would be needed but consider the positives; the responsibility he would need to adopt could be extremely beneficial to him, take his mind off his own situation, increase his self-worth etcetera."

"Okay," he said guardedly, "that could work." Then John Hayes abruptly had an encounter with realism. This was Hobson's choice and his opinion held very little weight, if indeed any. Once Tim Richards had decided on something there was nothing anyone could do to deter him. "I still think the community nurse will need some extra help," he said tentatively, "but perhaps I could sort something—"

"Good, well make arrangements for their discharge in a week from today, John," and satisfied, he stood up and straightened his tie, mindful that shortly he had a much more enjoyable meeting in his own office.

"Shall we call the staff nurse in, keep him in the loop?" but Dr Richards was already ringing the bell to summon Charlie before his colleague had time to reply.

Charlie entered.

"Ah, nurse," he declared, unusually upbeat, he was getting rid of two and happy hour was fast approaching after all.

"We have made the decision to discharge Messrs. Stone and Heart together, in a week's time in fact. If you could begin doing the necessary this end I'd appreciate it. In the meantime I've a meeting to attend," and he made to leave but Charlie's expression stopped him in his tracks.

"Sorry, nurse, by the look on your face there's something wrong, care to enlighten us?"

"It's just," he said languidly, buying a bit of thinking time, "I think it's wonderful news for Stan, I mean the man has been here for so long, been through so much," unable to prevent the tiny dig at the doctor for prescribing such protracted ECT. "But in a week," he grimaced, "shouldn't he be going through reintegration before he leaves?"

"He'll be having that after discharge," the doctor said brusquely.

"Seems the wrong way around to me but you're the experts." Charlie was riding his luck with that comment and quickly went on. "Anyhow, in Barry's, um, Mr Stone's case," he corrected himself, "I don't think he'll be sufficiently recovered from his treatment in a week. Outwardly he might seem fine but his memory loss is very apparent, to me anyway and he's still moderately disorientated."

The doctor viewed him disdainfully. Moderately disorientated? he repeated in his mind, big words for a small intellect.

"Is he, in what way?" he said whilst checking his watch, needing to be on his way.

"Well it's showing in all sorts of ways," said Charlie sensing the doctor's eagerness to leave and deciding not to rush, mainly because he couldn't bear the arrogant bastard.

"Forgetting names, forgetting what he's supposed to be doing, staring aimlessly into space, asking for the same information over and over again, unsure of the date or time. It seems to be worse in the morning."

"Oh, really," said the doctor half-heartedly, Charlie was beginning to spoil the show.

"Yes really," he confirmed. "I mean, just this morning he didn't show up for breakfast and when I eventually found him he was sitting on the toilet and he looked up at me and said, 'what do I do next?' He came around after a while but you can see what I'm getting at?"

This was all going wrong for the doctor. Neither of them knew the real reasons behind all of this; the possible information lurking within Stan's head, the pressure he was under on ward closures and he didn't want to appear excessively dogmatic, give them cause for suspicion.

"I can see what you're getting at," he said in a measured way.

Tim Richards now realised he had to be careful. He knew all about repercussions and consequences and he had to cover his arse, he also knew that the best way to achieve this was for these two fine fellows to be in agreement with him. He didn't want any 'I told you so's' somewhere down the line. Charlie had temporarily scuppered his plans so he backtracked.

"All right, nurse, I've always been open minded and willing to listen to suggestions," and the furtive glance that passed between Charlie and the social worker embodied incredulity. "But I genuinely believe," he went on, "that the community is now, from a therapeutic point of view, the best place for them both to be."

Dr Richards had no qualms over this new direction that mental health was taking because it didn't matter one way or the other. A long time ago he had recognised that psychiatry was an art not a science, an art primarily designed to subdue, that there was little could be done to help neurotics and virtually nothing for psychotics. Reactive depression could be alleviated to a degree but it was mostly the time it took to administer the treatment that delivered the benefit. He compared psychiatry to the mother of a two-year-old's coping mechanisms, at her wits' end, frantically trying anything to get some peace. This doesn't work so we'll try that; that doesn't work so we'll try this and you've got to keep experimenting because the mother doesn't know why the child is crying and the psychiatrist doesn't know why the patient is mentally ill.

"However, a fortnight or even longer for Mr Stone to recover from treatment and Mr Heart to gain some insight into the outside world is probably a good idea, in fact, thinking about it, as from tomorrow I'm on secondment for a month so let's evaluate the situation on my return," and they both gestured agreement.

He left, repeating that he had a further meeting and John Hayes, after gathering his notes, went the same way, leaving Charlie alone and scratching his head, bemused by how Tim Richards, the head of the hospital no less, had apparently been swayed by the reservations of a mere nurse. But Charlie was gazing the wrong way through the telescope for it was the doctor who could clearly see the stars.

A few minutes later Charlie also left the office and walked out through the day room. Patients were beginning to return from OT and the smell of a meal being cooked wafted from the kitchen. He looked through the glass panelled door that linked the room with the conservatory and as he'd come to expect, in their usual chairs were Stan and Barry, in deep conversation like two brothers who had been separated when young and bursting to make up for wasted time. He toyed with the idea of telling them they were going to be discharged together but he knew it wasn't his place to do that and the idea quickly drifted away. Charlie was a good nurse, a professional who worked at the hospital for all the right reasons and as he observed the two men, he felt proud of himself for saying what he had to the doctor. He'd said what he thought to be right and the idea of bowing to the man's authority never once entered his head. Unlike many of the hospital's employees Tim Richards held no fear for him. Since his unsuccessful attempt at stopping Stan's treatment he recognised the man as a simple bully, nothing more nothing less and if he stood firm the ground beneath his feet would rise and that beneath the doctor's fall. He refocused on the pair and marvelled at their transformation.

From the beginning he knew Barry would pull through, he recognised a strong spirit within the wreck but Stan was the real revelation. For years, little fat Stan the smiling man, with the deep grin lines like rivulets running down his face had been a piece of the ward`s furniture. During his years of treatment when the negative effects of the ECT began to wane he could look after himself, get by, but would only reply monosyllabically when spoken to, only do something when he was told to but now, with the combination of Barry's arrival and the cessation of the treatment, something miraculous had happened, Stan wasn't virtually invisible anymore. He had acquired a personality, laughing, joking, communicating though as encouraging as this was Charlie knew it was too soon for him to be discharged. Stan had been away on a few ward trips to the seaside during his time but he was accompanied, staff were there to look over him. For years he hadn't cooked, shopped, crossed roads, experienced all of the new developments of modern life and although he understood the doctor's rationale of Barry being there to support him, Charlie suspected it could be the other way round.

ECT is a sparking baseball bat smacking you on the back of the head, splattering all the memory bits into space and whereas the short term change in the person can be dramatic, what happens when the memory wants to come back to Mama? Because that's when Barry relapses and that's when Stan's grin lines may start to fade.

Chapter 21

The room was indeed clean and the bed looked comfortable but this was of no importance to him. He noticed the mirror over the hand basin in the corner of the room and approached it, scraped his throat and spat, the glob immediately sliding its way reluctantly downwards.

Angelo didn't like mirrors, didn't like what he saw in them.

He lay on the bed fully clothed, arms straight at his sides, playing with a desire that was new and unfamiliar to him. It was a craving, a need to see Bill Sweet again. He didn't understand this urge so he thought a little harder, plumbed a little deeper and concluded it was down to Bill being different to the other figures of authority he'd had to endure; he was more of a friend than a foe. Angelo raised his head and looked around the room but not in an attempt to discover the easiest means of escape, his usual first act in similar situations, just out of simple curiosity. He liked it here and felt like a chick finding itself free from the confines of the egg, glorious and uplifted.

He lowered his head and lay motionless, the anticipation of Bill walking through the door creating an excitement within him, making him feel safe and wanted, making him feel the way he yearned for his mother to.

But she ignored and criticised him, didn't she? Mocked and shouted at him with her red sweating face and acrid, alcohol breath. Though it was all that man's fault, wasn't it? Good Mr Sweet was nothing like he imagined his absentee father to be, the man he wrongly believed had broken his mother's spirit and goodness; turning her into an uncaring, washed up drunk void of any maternal love. Of any love at all.

As Angelo stared at the ceiling he brought his legs up to his stomach and wrapped his arms tightly around his knees, squeezing his chin so firmly into the top of his chest he could hardly breathe. And then the tears came, pushing out between his narrow eyelids, compressed by their closeness. There was no other physical signs of crying, no noise or facial expression, only tears and if tears could sing, the tune would have been unbearably sad.

Chapter 22

During the first week of Dr Richards' secondment to another hospital Stan's face began to repair and at the end of the second week the bruising had all but gone. At the beginning of the third week a curious incident occurred that strengthened Charlie's opinion that Stan was unready for discharge.

Much to Charlie's surprise Barry had decided to give occupational therapy a try and he, along with all the other patients, had left the ward two hours previously; except two.

Sid Fukum Smith was slumped, fast asleep, in his regular chair. A grunt as he sucked, a sigh as he blew. Meanwhile Stan was at the table where the old valve radio had resided for as long as he could remember. He was intently listening as the newsreader at the end of the bulletin, announced that the first president of Togo, an obscure country in the west of Africa, had been assassinated during an attempted coup whilst seeking refuge in the American Embassy, his death causing much dismay and sadness in the small population. A brief interview with a friend of Sylvanus Olympio, the murdered man, was broadcast in which he stated that only when the killer had been apprehended could the nation properly mourn the great leader.

Stan pulled out the pen that he always carried with him and even though his eyesight was poor, managed to scrawl the president's name on the back of his hand and then he made his way to the office. He knocked on the door, waited long enough to satisfy himself that no one was going to open it and entered. The shiny black phone was perched at the far end of the only table and he picked it up and held it to the side of his head. He was unsure of which end to speak into but was well aware of what number he needed to ring. He dialled nine three times and waited. Almost immediately he could hear a voice in the distance and quickly realised the phone was the wrong way round. After remedying the mistake he heard the voice urgently asking if anyone was there.

"Sorry, yes, I'm here," he stuttered.

"You have rang emergency, what service do you require?"

"Is it the police for a murder?" he enquired.

"A murder!" she gasped, her first in over seven years in the job.

"Yes, I've done a murder, the police need to come," he demanded.

"Hold the line," and he heard a noise like two long, far away, car horn beeps then another voice.

"Police emergency, please state your name."

He told him his name.

"And where are you calling from?"

He told him that too.

"And what is the reason for your call?"

"I've done a murder and I need to speak to a policeman."

"You've committed a murder," he repeated incredulously, "are you on your own at the moment?"

He told him he was.

"Stay exactly where you are, we're on our way."

And it was then that Charlie walked in.

"Stan!" he exclaimed, surprised by his presence. "What are you doing in here, you know you're not supposed to be in here," then he noticed the phone in Stan's hand, "and what are you doing with that? Who have you been ringing, man?" and he took it from him and placed it back on the receiver.

"It was the police, Charlie, don't be annoyed, I had to ring the police."

"The police?" Charlie echoed with alarm in his voice. "Why, what's happened?"

"I've done a murder, Charlie, and I've had to own up to it because it'll save a lot of trouble if I do."

Stan was looking up at him now with wide eyes, then the smile lines appeared and he asked Charlie to sit down which he did automatically, stunned by this revelation.

"I know you're shocked, Charlie, but if you've killed someone you have to own up."

"Who is this person you're supposed to have killed for God's sake, a patient?"

"No, no, I wouldn't do that," and he raised his hand and swivelled so it could be read, "it was this man," and Charlie leant forward to view it more easily.

"Sylvanus Ol something," he guessed, having difficulty with the pronunciation. "Olympic?" he moved even further forward, "Olympio?" he said finally.

"That's it, Charlie, you've got it," and Stan lowered his hand.

Charlie was still sat down and he decided to stay there.

"Let me go over this for a second, Stan," he said hesitantly, "you're telling me that you've killed a man called Sylvanus Olympic or Olympio or something and you've rang the police and told them as well?"

"Had to," he replied frankly.

"Jesus Christ, Stan," he said, holding his head, "I can't believe you've done that, who is this fella you've apparently killed anyway?"

"First president of Togo."

All that was needed was the time it took the six CID officers to drink their tea for Charlie to explain to them that Stan had a history of this sort of thing and apologise for wasting their time. They left, but not before cautioning Charlie that abuse of the emergency telephone service was a serious matter and had the office been locked then perhaps their time would not have been wasted.

Charlie felt suitably reprimanded and seconds after they departed he looked at Stan and began shaking his head in disbelief.

"What on earth made you do it?"

But Stan didn't reply.

"I cannot believe what has just happened."

He stayed silent.

"You're supposed to be leaving the hospital in a few weeks, man, you can't be doing this sort of thing."

And then he spoke.

"No one understands, Charlie, but I know it would have saved a lot of trouble if those police had just arrested me and taken me away, locked me up for it." Charlie remembered Stan having the very same sentiment after William Wilson jumped to his death and at that moment realised that this trait was rooted right down, as deep as it could go, a place where even a hundred and seventeen lightning bolts couldn't reach.

Chapter 23

When Bill arrived at room 3 he was out of breath and before walking in took a minute to calm down. Angelo was fast asleep and he quietly closed the door behind him, not immediately realising what was strange until he moved further into the room and stood adjacent to him. Bill had witnessed children adopt this attitude before but never when asleep. Angelo's torso and limbs were resting perfectly flat but his head was raised some six inches above the bed, his neck muscles taught and stretched under the load. It had been a hard day but before he could end it contented he had to know the boy was on side, that he had his allegiance and he shook out two tablets and placed the medication bottle on the low table next to the bed and stared down at the unnatural features on the raised head. He cast his mind back to the case notes, 'facial abnormality probably caused at foetal stage due to mother's alcoholism' and shook his head disbelievingly. Bill's most iniquitous task, taking a child across for interview, was still in front of him and he needed to get on with it, needed to wake him up.

Now sitting on the side of the bed he gently shook Angelo's arm. He awoke, not with a start or in fright, his eyelids simply parted ever so slightly, departing one dream and entering another.

"I'll be leaving soon," Bill said in a low voice, "I just wanted to see if you were all right and bring your pills," and he handed the two capsules to him and he dry swallowed them.

MAYBE

Although Angelo had fallen asleep yearning for this moment, wakefulness had brought caution. He had only that day made this man's acquaintance and there was a long way to go, had to find out how the land lay. He interlocked his hands behind him and lowered his head, easing the tension from his neck.

"Are you hungry, son?" he said softly. "You've missed your lunch," but Angelo adopted his recent behaviour and lay still on the bed looking up, purposefully ignoring the man by his side.

Intensified by his lack of sedation, mixed emotions were bouncing through his head. He wanted him there yet wanted him away; wanted to be held though squirmed at the very idea. Hadn't lots of men and it was always men, offered him succour then demanded a price, betrayed his trust? This new man appeared different, unorthodox, but he had to wait, had to be on his guard.

Bill, on the other hand, had no such thoughts. His sole aim was to tuck this young man firmly under his wing, have him completely under control and he knew he couldn't leave without some proof of that.

He decided to ask a few uncomfortable questions to hopefully elicit a response.

"Tell me, Angelo, do all men remind you of your father?"

He continued looking up.

"Do you ever have bad thoughts, son, like you want to hurt people?"

No movement, no sound.

Bill took a deep, frustrated breath. "We need to talk to each other or things aren't going to work out." He paused then said earnestly, "I want to be your friend."

This series of words he had heard many times before. They all wanted to be my friend, he thought and his anger rose like the bubbling spring at the source of a mighty river then his next sentence turned that spring into a geyser.

"Would you like to see your mother again, son, it was her who came to see you, wasn't it?"

Angelo slowly and deliberately turned his head and glared at Bill with piercing intensity. He had created a mental wall between his mother and himself, a wall that couldn't be climbed, a structure designed to protect his dubious sanity and now he didn't like this stranger straying into his affairs, didn't like his involvement one bit. Bill had no idea of the depth of this young man's rage against the world but he was about to find out. The intensity of his gaze dissipated and a twisted sneer appeared on his face, his voice deep and trembling with emotion.

"Why don't you get off this bed, walk over to the door, get out and die!"

Bill stared at him, alarmed at the fury he saw through the slits of the boy's eyes. Then Bill did indeed get off the bed and did indeed begin walking to the door but suddenly turned and in one movement raised his right arm, clenched his fist and thrust it down onto Angelo's unprotected stomach. A muted gasp escaped his mouth and he arched with the pain. Bill raised his arm to deliver another blow but he rolled off the bed and twisted onto his feet and before Bill could react Angelo had knelt and positioned himself in front of the multi paned window.

He wanted to like this man, he wanted his help but another door had been slammed in his face.

Bill saw the boy jerk his elbows back simultaneously and lurched across the bed in a vain attempt to stop what he knew was about to happen but Angelo's neck muscles strained prominently and he reversed the action and propelled his fists forcefully through the two bottom panes though it was what happened next that caused Bill to scream.

Angelo began rotating his arms against the jagged edges of the remaining glass, carving and slicing into his skin to the tissue below; blood surging from the wounds and splashing everywhere like crimson rain. Bill stumbled over the bed and grabbed him in a bear hug, heaving him with all his might away from the window and onto the floor using his knees to keep him pinned.

Angelo fell limp as Bill felt the panic surge. What was he to do? Blood continued to pour from the open gashes; he would surely bleed to death if he didn't do something fast and he couldn't let that happen. He had plans, big plans and he needed the boy to enact them. He knew he must staunch the haemorrhaging and get him to a hospital because, whatever happened, these rips were going to need a lot of stitches and a long time to heal. He stood up and Angelo remained lying, slumped in a bloody puddle.

Bill clasped his hands to his head in confusion, desperately trying to figure out what to do next. Should he get him to the hospital before he had a chance to explain the punch? Would Angelo divulge his actions were in response to an assault? Maybe just let him bleed to death; somehow find a substitute cohort for what he had planned?

Whatever action Bill was frantically deliberating suddenly didn't matter as the nursing assistant, alerted by the commotion, burst into the room. As her mind processed the scene she uttered a high pitched screech and mouthed, 'Oh my God' silently.

Bill came to his senses.

"Get the sheet off the bed and pass it to me please," he said calmly as he knelt beside the boy. She did as asked and he gripped it tightly between his fingers and began tearing strips. The nurse looked on aghast as he wound the strips around the slashes, finally wrapping the last two tight around the top of his arms to act as a tourniquet. Angelo lay there letting it all happen, his eyes open watching Bill's every move, then he turned to the nurse, who was stood seemingly rooted to the spot and coolly ordered her to get to a phone and call for an ambulance. It took her a second but it finally registered what Bill had said and she about turned and ran down the corridor to the office.

A cool draught allowed in by the smashed windowpanes blew across Bill's face as he continued to kneel. He found himself too high to be able to support the boy's head so he shuffled onto his backside and almost lay beside him enabling him to cradle Angelo in his arms. This truly was the human being he'd been looking for, waiting for, and he began to speak quietly and deliberately, as he was choosing his words with great care.

"I think I've got a good idea of what's been happening to you over the years, son, in the other homes you've stayed in, with some of the men who worked in those homes." Ever so slightly he clenched the arm that was holding his head, a reassuring gesture. "And I want you to know that nothing bad is going to happen to you here, you have my word and when I said I wanted to be your friend I meant just that. Some men might have said that to you before but they weren't telling the truth, they wanted something more from you didn't they, Angelo?"

But the young man didn't reply, didn't move a muscle, sections of the bandaging blooming red as the blood continued to flow underneath.

"And I also guess," Bill continued, "that lots of people have let you get away with bad behaviour in the past and I'm sure you've taken full advantage of that fact in one way or another, but if you want me to turn things around for you, make you happy instead of sad I can't let you speak to me the way you did and I certainly can't allow you to harm yourself like this."

Bill again clenched the arm that was supporting Angelo's head and persevered, not unduly concerned now by his muteness.

"I hit you, son, and I'm not ashamed of doing it, because I knew that was the right thing to do. You might not believe that, you might hate me for it and that might be the reason you've cut your arms, but I don't think so. I think you did that because you suddenly thought I was just like one of those lying shits in those other places who would try anything and say anything so long as they got to play with your private parts."

Bill held his breath. He realised he was getting through as a single tear emerged in the corner of Angelo's right eye; but he still hadn't spoken and he needed him to say something, anything.

"I'm nothing like them, son, nothing like them. I'm a proper man, Angelo, and I can be hurt but I didn't hit you because I was hurt by what you said to me, I hit you because I couldn't let you get away with saying it. You would have had no respect for me and how can I help you if you have no respect for me?"

Bill heard the office door slam and realised the nurse was on her way back. Time was running out to secure the boy's loyalty and he didn't know what else to say, other than, "I hope you'll soon understand that what I'm saying to you is true. I'm asking you to give me a chance, Angelo, I want to right the wrongs of your parents and all the others, son," but his mouth remained closed as the nurse hurriedly re-entered the room.

However, the need for Angelo to open his mouth suddenly passed. While the nurse announced that the ambulance was on its way his hand spoke a thousand words as it found Bill's and squeezed it gently.

Chapter 24

The Nuthatch had a twenty-bed medical annexe acting primarily as a training unit but was also used for the physical care of patients and the crew decided to take him there due to its proximity and the need for urgent treatment. As luck would have it, a fully qualified medic was in attendance who was able to quickly assess the damage. After cleaning and irrigation a total of fifty-nine sutures were needed, a procedure that took more than two hours to complete, during which time he neither spoke nor moved. Throughout his eleven day residency the entire nursing, administration and cleaning staff were on tenterhooks. Word had got around that this particular individual should be handled with the utmost care and that's exactly what the staff did. When someone has punched holes in foot square windowpanes and rotated their arms for maximum effect then that someone gets utmost space and plenty of it. Angelo's reticence, along with his history and facial disfigurement, made him the source of much fascination, suspicion and fear. His injuries had been considerable and damaging and for the rest of his life he would have minimal feeling in his left hand and virtually no movement in the small and ring finger of his right.

Listening to music or reading, usual pastimes for bored patients was a road he'd never trod, so he simply laid there, trying to come to terms with the anomaly of liking a man who had assaulted him and after only just meeting wanted to be not only his very best friend but also change the course of his life. How many times in the past had his mother dangled him like a puppet, then finally let him drop to become bait for all the predatory fish in that huge ocean and those fish had eagerly reeled him in and taken advantage of their status and his body? But somewhere deep in his fractured mind was a reassuring voice saying,

'Listen to him, Angelo, he means what he says, thinks you're special and has plans for you.'

On a simple level he began to understand why he had been punched. Bill Sweet had big ideas and Bill had to be in charge because they were his ideas after all. As the days went by his respect for the man was growing, as sure as the hair on his small head and that was why a sly smirk arrived on his face when the petite ward sister informed him, one afternoon, that he was going to be discharged and re-admitted to the home where the shocking incident had happened and good old Mr Sweet would be waiting for him in the reception area in an hours' time.

"I think Mr Sweet wants to walk back with you to the children's home, Angelo, maybe have a chat about things," she said, standing by his side.

Angelo was his usual mute self and she continued to look down at him. She placed her hands on her cheeks and inserted her two little fingers slightly inside her top lip; after a few seconds she brought her hands together as if praying then lowered her head to look directly into his eyes. She was a woman with a big heart and Angelo was causing her a big problem.

"Eleven days you've been with us," she said cautiously, "not a smile, not a complaint, even though I know how painful it can be to have dressings changed. Not a sound, not an acknowledgement nor a thank you," she paused, then allaying her apprehension continued. "I've thought about you long and hard. I've tried to understand what might have happened in a young man's life to make him do what you did. Why you don't wish to communicate, why you want to be apart and I just hope that when you leave us this afternoon and return to Mr Sweet and the home, he can get to the bottom of all this and that your life becomes easier for you to bear," and she leant down to touch his arm.

Angelo found words of kindness unimaginably difficult to cope with and met them with aggression. The one person in the world who should have spoken them never did and this interloper had no right nor reason to do so. He immediately moved his arm away, sat upright on the bed and stared at her. The nurse unconsciously stepped back and he could sense her alarm. He suddenly had power over this woman. He knew it and so did she and for the first time in eleven days he broke his silence.

"Can I ask you something?" he said almost innocently, his voice husky as if the vocal cords were unhappy at their abrupt re-use.

The nurse, although perturbed by his movement, was gladdened she had provoked speech and nodded positively.

After inhaling deeply, pushing his head back as far as possible then to the right and left as if trying to click some bone back into place, he said, "Why did the chicken cross the road?"

There was a few seconds silence then she echoed his question.

"Why did the chicken cross the road?"

"That's the question, Florence fuckin' Nightingale," he replied, a repulsive scowl heightening the unloveliness of his face, "why did the chicken cross the road?"

A further few seconds elapsed and again she clasped her hands together, the Florence remark flitting rapidly out of her mind, then exclaimed awkwardly, "I have no idea why the chicken crossed the road."

Angelo slowly closed his crevice like eyes and tensed his entire frame. The nurse had no idea what this was leading to but was about to be fully enlightened. In what appeared as one effortless movement he left the bed and was beside her, instantly wrapping his bandaged right arm around both of hers making it impossible for her to move. He now had not only emotional power over her but physical power too. Angelo put his mouth uncomfortably close to her ear and began to whisper.

"Some say that chicken was trying to get away from someone and others say it was trying to find something but Angelo says that chicken wasn't coming to or going from, no, no, no," and he wiggled the index finger of his other hand in rhythm. "Because that chicken was just being a chicken; just behaving like it had been taught or learnt; it was just behaving in the way that all its experiences had drilled into it," he squeezed her even harder, "and I'm the same," he said bitterly. "So leave out your tender words or I'll put a fist in your mouth to make you!" He released her and as quickly as he had got up he had laid back down and resumed looking at the ceiling.

The nurse stood trembling, her breath coming in short gasps. She was dazed by the speed in which he'd moved, felt defiled by his arm holding her so tightly, frightened by the menacing way he had whispered those words so close to her face. She continued panting but gradually, as her breathing slowed her thoughts slowly returned to the pity she had for him; how he must have been severely traumatised somewhere in his past and her fear abated, believing him to be the victim now not her. She gained control of herself and became calmer, nevertheless, she philosophised, his behaviour could not be ignored and words had to be said. She cleared her throat and bravely moved a little closer to him.

"If it wasn't for the fact that you are leaving us today I would have called security and my head of department to let them deal with you. To manhandle me in such a manner, especially when I was only trying to be of some help to you, is totally unacceptable." His failure to reply made her feel impotent but she continued. "However, I will be contacting Mr Sweet to inform him of your behaviour and I'm sure he will deal with you appropriately," and she turned to leave but as she was about to go through the door she stopped, turned and said finally. "I'm sure you've been hurt very badly somewhere in your past and that hurt is the reason behind you acting like this but taking it out on other people will achieve nothing and believe me Mr Goodwin, there are many people who would genuinely want to help you. A problem shared can be a problem halved."

She stood waiting to see if he would answer but he remained statue-like and she walked away with a dreadful feeling of melancholy. He got up from the bed and went to the sink, purposely ignoring the mirror on the wall in front of him. The water was ice cold and he cupped his hands under the flow and rinsed his face and neck.

"She'll tell Bill Sweet," he said mockingly under his breath, "she'll tell him to deal with me appropriately," he sniggered at that one. "He'll deal with me appropriately all right, give me a slap on the back for remembering the chicken rooster thing almost word for word," and Bill had only told him the story once!

Chapter 25

He dried himself and after throwing the towel on the mess of a bed and easing on his coat he left the ward, unconcerned that no one was aware of his departure. He went slowly, the reception was a five minute walk through the hospital and there was no rush, he would simply amble to kill some time. He turned the corner onto the long corridor, along which Barry had been pushed for his ECT treatment. It was deserted and dimly lit. Angelo was feeling good, he would shortly be seeing Bill Sweet and that was truly a joyful thought and the urge came over him to whistle. He pursed his lips in readiness but his happiness was short lived as he remembered the shape of them made it impossible.

He ran his fingers around his mouth and experienced a mixture of sadness and resentment; raised them up over his pygmy nose to his eyes, parting the upper and lower lids so they resembled those of other people, normal people then allowed them to drop back, to become ugly slits once again. He hated his appearance, hated himself and hated those who allowed all of this to happen. A cloud of rancour descended, dripping with malice and his hostility grew uncontrollably. In the distance he could see a hunched figure, hear soft shouts echoing up the hallway. He looked behind and there was no one, the only occupants of this gloomy space was this hunched outline and himself. As they came closer to each other the distant shape became a man and the soft shout became a word and that word was recognisable to Angelo, but his now dark mood made the word taunting and insulting and made the man a despoiler and violator. As they approached each other Angelo once again checked for people behind him, it was deserted and Sid 'Fukum' Smith didn't know who or what hit him as Angelo's fist smashed into the side of his face. The force of the punch sent him crashing against the wall and as he bounced back and began to drop, Angelo savagely lifted his knee up and into the descending head, a grating, snapping sound coming from within as two cervical vertebrae fractured and separated. Angelo stood over him, the murderous cloud evaporating allowing rays of light to shine and rid him of his frenzied anger. A calmness dawned and the good feeling began to return. The assault had sucked out his fury and left him peaceful and serene. He walked quickly along the remainder of the passageway, through the double doors and with his head down, into the reception area, his bandaged arms concealed by the black Crombie.

The few people present paid him little attention but he knew he couldn't wait there and he walked straight through and made for the home hoping he'd see Bill coming the other way.

The first person to come across Fukum was a visitor carrying a bag of grapes. As she dropped them in shock, a few splattered and oozed their contents in a similar way to Sid Smith's head when it had hit the floor. As far as the duty doctor was concerned it was a straightforward accident and a week later the coroner agreed; accidental death due to a fall resulting in a catastrophic cervical fracture.

All of the staff and many of the patients were saddened by the awful event. He had become an unlikely darling of the hospital and was sadly missed, Stan being particularly upset by the news, but Sid Fukum Smith, unbeknown to everyone, had become something else.

The first of Angelo Goodwin's victims.

Chapter 26

Bill sweet awoke on the morning of Fukum's last day alive refreshed from a good night's sleep. He was due to pick Angelo up from the hospital following a meeting with Akan and he was in a good mood. After washing and dressing he bound down the stairs and entered the kitchen needing to prepare a casserole that he would leave on a low heat and be ready on his return that evening.

He picked out two beautifully clean King Edward potatoes from the vegetable rack, stood at the sink and began to peel, placing them both on the draining board when he'd finished. Bill was about to prepare more vegetables when he noticed a brown hole in one of them. Moving it onto a chopping board he cut through the flesh and found a burrow going through its entire length. He held one half up in front of his face and pondered over that ruination, tilting it this way and that and it triggered a change in his mood, cast a shadow over it. Still holding the potato half he walked over to the wall mirror and stared deeply into it, inspecting his image as he had the potato. It was just a mask, he thought, like the reflective surface of a pond that hides all the murderous activities beneath. He squeezed the potato tightly.

"I think my brain has been burrowed into, a brain with a stain," he said out loud and sat at the kitchen table, closing his eyes.

He knew full well what that stain represented and it had been there all his life. It was cowardice and it manifested itself in many different ways, sometimes very obliquely but nevertheless, it was his cowardice that was the driving force behind most of his actions; his ill treatment of the patients when he worked at the hospital, his daily conscious effort to conceal his true personality, his contemptible participation in the abuse of the children to save his own skin. He loathed himself because he knew he couldn't change but this insight allowed him to understand the nature of those immoral kiddy kissers and he had prepared a plan, but it demanded an accomplice because the stain prevented him from being the perpetrator. However, he knew this plan had to be put on hold because something much more urgent needed to be resolved, something that would have to take precedence.

Bill Sweet was angry about many of the world's ways but at the epicentre of his disenchantment was society's treatment of the men who messed with children in a sexual way. Those men that gave in to their overwhelming desires who, despite knowing their actions to be horribly wrong, carried on regardless to commit their selfish and depraved deeds and perhaps more significantly his belief that these men could not be fixed; they had an incurable disease. To begin with he felt a boiling revulsion but over the years Bill had responded to this hatred with a reasoned answer. He had lost the initial antipathy and now looked upon paedophilia as he would a physical illness. He had intellectualised that the root cause of their behaviour was so all encompassing that they lacked the inner strength to overcome it, they simply couldn't resist doing what they knew to be wrong.

Furthermore, he had also concluded that there were illnesses which, due to their devastating effect on others, could only be cured by the mercy killing of those afflicted. He wanted neither revenge nor punishment; they were simply the unfortunate owners of an incurable illness. Prison, psychotherapy, aversion treatment, none of it worked, nothing made it go away. He knew the only remedy was euthanasia, a quick painless death. Yet, as he sat quietly at that kitchen table thinking these thoughts he knew the authorities would never act. Too many liberal minded individuals held the power now in all walks of life, in particular the penal services, the one part of the legal system that they believed reflected their attempts at civilising the nation, a barometer of their progress in enlightenment and things were going in a direction that Bill didn't like. The criminal being the actual victim was the latest thinking. He got the concept but it crashed into his philosophy, like that lorry had smashed into Barry's car. For a so called civilised society to allow an incurable child molester parole, knowing he will surely re-offend made Bill feel so frustrated he wanted to reach down through his mouth and yank out his stomach, upper and lower intestine, balls, penis and all in a repulsive attempt to protest at this wretched state of affairs and his inability to rectify it.

But now Angelo had arrived and a small smile crossed his face as he sat in the dark behind his closed eyes. He knew he was the one the moment they met. No words needed to be spoken, no gestures needed to be made. It was his demeanour, his looks, his style, his very presence that screamed at him.

"I'm your boy, Bill, treat me right and I'm your boy!" and Bill was excited beyond belief. He wanted to get on with the job, get on straightaway with treating the boy right but that Max Lewis was there and his impatience had made him drop his guard and for the first time in a long time he had dropped the nice and picked up the nasty and that was a mistake because when there are dirty deeds to perform you don't want to give any cause for suspicion.

The smile then dropped off as his thoughts honed in on the girl he was meeting that morning. Akan had mesmerised him, brought to life that long hidden morsel of goodness and he knew he had to do something about the doctor. This had gone on for way too long and it was his admiration for this girl's dignity that had brought it to a head, but the stain was ingrained and he knew he couldn't do it alone, no, he had to treat this boy right and leave it all to him.

Opening his eyes he observed his world with a new clarity, knowing precisely what had to be done and he placed the rotten potato in his mouth and began to chew with determination and conviction, a symbolic act that he gained satisfaction from. As Bill stood up he dismissed the casserole

MAYBE

idea, picked up his briefcase and left the bungalow; Akan needed him and he wasn't going to let her down.

Bill entered the home and bade the children good morning, his usual first job and after a quick scan of their faces noticed that Akan was missing. Concerned, he made his way to the office where his anxiety disappeared as she came into view, standing by the door. She raised her hand as she saw him approaching and he responded with a wave. His day at the home had begun in the most excellent of ways.

"Didn't see you in the canteen, I wondered where you were," he said, opening the door and ushering her in.

She sat and he filled the kettle.

"I wanted to be on time for our appointment, Mr Sweet," she responded, flattening the creases on her white dress. He flicked the switch and loaded a cup with instant coffee and six teaspoons of sugar. Akan looked on in horror as the last spoonful went in.

"You obviously don't like the taste of the coffee," she remarked and he uttered a small laugh.

"My only vice, Akan, my sweet tooth," and her expression made him feel he was forgiven.

"Would you like something to drink?" he asked.

"I had juice with my breakfast, thank you," she replied. The kettle boiled and he brought the drink with him as he sat opposite her, placing it upon the desktop.

Her appearance was extraordinary, her bearing was singular and to him, completely alluring. The savage scar crossing her face, a physical tragedy she never tried to conceal, only added to her enigmatic air.

"You wanted to see me, Akan, what is it I can do for you?" but she ignored his question, leant forward and picked up the cup.

"May I take a sip?" she asked in her low, melodious tone and he gestured her to do so. Her eyes closed as the syrupy liquid entered her mouth and she replaced the cup on the desk. Her eyes opened. "The old woman looks after the child to grow its teeth and the young one in turn looks after the old woman when she loses hers." She flicked the cup with her finger. "If the old woman drank that, the young one would be a nurse before her time."

Bill shook his head, amazed by her intuition.

"I hold my hands up, my sweet tooth is my enemy, I just can't help myself," and the scar rose on her face as her nose wrinkled from the joyful grin that appeared.

Following their very first meeting Akan thought of him as a man whose heart was in the right place but whose head may not be and her maternal instinct came into play whenever they were together. He defiantly picked up the cup and drank from it.

"Anyway, let's leave my teeth out of this, what is it you wanted to see me about?," he asked again.

"I wanted to thank you for what you are doing for Ruby," she began, "and I asked for a private meeting because I didn't want either of us to be embarrassed when I gave you this," and from the pocket within her dress she removed a package. He looked on with interest as she removed the greaseproof paper and placed a small cake by the side of his cup.

"I actually know all about your sweet tooth, you know," and she pushed the cake a little nearer to him, her grin becoming furtive, "but I felt I had to reward your goodness." She pointed into her mouth and then at the cake, urging him to eat and he did so, feeling moved by her kindness.

As Bill bit into it he realised this was the first time he had received a gift from anyone for as long as he could remember.

"You're very good for me, Akan," he said seriously, then breathed out as if dismayed. "I'm not the kind man you think I am you know," but he left his admission there, she was a young girl after all and a patient.

She eyed him curiously. "You were very kind to find Ruby special help as quickly as you did."

He took a deep breath. He didn't want to reveal his inner feelings but she was different, she liked him, had thought of him when she made the cake and he somehow trusted her. "I did it because you asked me to do it," and the word he emphasised was 'you'.

She was somewhat taken aback by this confession, then after taking a second to think said, "No matter what the reason, a child is a child of everyone and you proved that saying to be true."

"You have a wonderful way with words, Akan, and you think very maturely for your years." He picked up the remaining cake and, conscious that he was allowing this girl to see too much of his personality, remarked "and a wonderful talent for baking!" popping the cake into his mouth.

She picked up the paper wrapping, folded it precisely and placed it back in her pocket.

"Thank you for your time, Mr Sweet, and for helping Ruby," and she began to stand up.

"Akan," Bill suddenly blurted and she resumed sitting," there was something I needed to speak to you about actually, something that's quite important." Her face adopted a puzzled expression as she saw the difficulty he was having explaining himself.

"Please continue, Mr Sweet, I am listening."

"Well," he started awkwardly, "things aren't always what they seem, Akan, the world can be a dangerous place and no matter how streetwise or careful a person is," and he shuffled in his chair aware that he was dragging his feet, "what I mean to say is that I don't want you to leave the home with anyone and I mean anyone, unless I know about it. It's very important, you are not to leave the home without my knowledge or permission," he reiterated determinedly.

"I understand," she replied, "but you make me feel a little frightened."

"I'm sorry, I didn't mean to, please don't feel that way, it's just …" and he stopped and sighed, "I worry about the children in my care and I want to protect them in every way possible, so you must tell me if anyone asks you to go with them for whatever reason, do you understand?" and she nodded her head affirmatively, stood up and began to cry.

Dismayed, he walked around the desk, sat on her seat and positioned her on his lap. As he wrapped his arms around her small frame the tears dropped from her cheeks and he cradled her like a newborn, comforting her with the movement of his body. Her sobs lessened and he could feel her relax in his arms.

"Why are you crying, Akan? What has upset you?" he whispered. She was shivering with emotion but his tenderness soothed her and she was able to speak.

"It's your kindness, Mr Sweet. You sounded just like my papa when you said you wanted to protect me. He was like that and I am filled with sorrow when I am reminded he is no longer with me," and as her sobs returned he squeezed her more tightly and vowed to himself that he would stop at nothing, absolutely nothing, to prevent the doctor from getting to her.

Chapter 27

The doctor's month-long secondment was over and he was sitting in the office within the geriatric ward busily ignoring Charlie. He had been made aware of Fukum's demise and his first and only thought was celebratory as his goal of a ward closure loomed nearer.

Charlie was toying with the idea of telling him he was prepared to do a little extra curricular should the two men be discharged, maybe visit them a couple of days a week in his own time, but the doctor was becoming annoyed by the social worker's lateness and his sudden outburst cast the thought from his mind.

"Punctuality and honesty, two traits I admire in a person," he boomed, "if a man is punctual means he's on the ball, ahead of the game," and he plucked a cigarette from the open packet and lit up.

Charlie gave the statement the miniscule amount of head space he felt necessary and had no desire to make any sort of comment. He sat placidly waiting as the doctor became more irritated, tapping the arm of his chair and, knowing the temper of his undesired companion, did his best to ignore him.

The new policy of nursing in the community was about to go national and during his month away at a large teaching hospital in the Midlands, he, along with a carefully chosen group of consultants, had been thoroughly briefed in all aspects of this new approach. However, a decision to not go public immediately had been taken as staff redundancy packages were, as yet, unresolved. Suitably motivated he had returned to the hospital with a blinkered mindset; as long as he deemed them reasonably harmless then sign 'em off and get 'em out, all would be fine and dandy and as the doctor had forced himself to believe, it was all for their own good hence his eagerness to railroad this meeting and get it wrapped up.

Although, during his absence, Barry and Stan had both gone through the reintroduction process, he was completely aware that it may still be too soon for discharge but when the pressure's on, people deal with things in different ways and right now Tim Richards' way was to wipe his arse first and shit later.

Seventeen minutes after the meeting was due to start, John Hayes rushed into the room. Staff nurse Charlie greeted him, Tim Richards glared at him.

"Yes, hello Charlie," and he hurriedly placed his notes on the desk. "Tim, apologies," he said to the top of the doctor's head, "problem over at the day centre, last minute arrival, have you started or—"

"No," Dr Richards interjected, still looking down, "we've been waiting for you," suddenly looking up.

"I'm sorry but as I said, we had this last minute—"

"Yes, yes, I heard you the first time," again cutting him short, "now for God's sake let's get on with it, I've a hundred and one things to do and," looking at Charlie, "I'm sure you have as well."

"No, in fact—"

"Whatever!" the doctor stopped him dead and he eased his chin into his hands, eyed them both individually and began.

"During my absence I've given this a lot of thought," (he hadn't) "and I'm completely comfortable in releasing them to the halfway house. No matter how you look at it, it's for the best," and he repositioned his hands into a praying position, placing the tips of two fingers into his mouth.

Charlie looked at John Hayes who was about to speak.

"I have also given them a lot of thought," (he had) "and I still feel that possibly it's too soon," and he inwardly cringed expecting a tongue lashing but when it didn't materialise he continued, somewhat emboldened. "Whereas Mr Stone has responded positively in the sessions Stanley really hasn't done that well. We have to realise that the last time he left the hospital grounds was three years ago, a day trip to the seaside I think it was and it appeared he stayed on the bus with the driver when they got there and only left once to use the public toilet."

Tim Richards gave the impression he was listening but it wouldn't have mattered if the social worker had declared that Stan had grown a second head and he was scaring everyone witless; they were going to be discharged and that was that.

The doctor now splayed his hands, reinserted his index fingers into his mouth but this time placed his middle fingers under his nose, raising it slightly. Charlie thought he might be about to make that owl hoot like his father had taught him years ago but Charlie suffered from that sort of thing, getting humorous thoughts in the most serious of situations.

"Look John," the doctor said moderately and placed both hands palm up in front of him, (observe … no knife, no guns). "You know I have the final decision on this one but I want you on my side, I honestly don't think you're seeing the bigger picture," and he flashed him that throwaway smile, the one that lasts a second maximum and comes from without, not within.

"Nurse?" and as he looked across at him his upturned hands moved in concert with his head, "The man on the ground as it were, what's your view?"

"Well, I think Stan—"

"Not Stan, do you think Mr Hayes is showing too much caution?"

"It's not my place to comment," he said pragmatically and then his idea returned, "but if you do decide today to send them to the halfway house then I'd be prepared to visit them in my own time, at least to start with anyway," and he noticed John Hayes raise his forehead, lines appearing as his eyes widened.

Dr Richards entwined his fingers and put his hands behind his head, he was liking the sound of this.

"There won't be any need for that, Charlie," John Hayes advised, "my department will deal with it, that's what we specialise in."

"But I don't mind, really I—."

It was the social worker's turn to rudely interrupt. "No, Charlie, on discharge my department will provide the support; it's good of you but that's the way it has to be."

Meanwhile the doctor was responding by giving Charlie a mental hug, having saved him a thousand words and hundreds of minutes. Unknowingly, the nurse had managed to deflect the opposition by tapping into John Hayes' professional pride and egotism.

Calmly and satisfyingly he placed his hands down on the desk, one on top of the other and with an open grin suggested that, in the words of a ship's captain, they should prepare them for voyage.

But ships are only safe in port, the danger lies in the open seas.

Chapter 28

Their discharge day proved to be eventful.

Charlie was sick and absent from work, a situation which was unfortunate for everyone. Barry sat with his small leather case containing a few clothes, some books and a wash pack whereas Stan sat with a larger and much older bag that housed a three inch high wooden donkey with 'welcome to Dublin' inscribed on its base, a gift given by a friendly nurse from years ago, an overcoat and two OT pens: after twenty years at The Nuthatch a paltry accumulation indeed.

The day room was a large and light place and although together both were alone with their thoughts.

"You look tired," Stan said caringly and his friend breathed out heavily.

"Not tired, Stan," he replied, "confused, bewildered, worried maybe, but not tired," and they returned to silence, waiting for someone to tell them what to do.

Seconds later the unoiled hinges of the ward's main door squealed as John Hayes pushed it open.

"I wish Charlie was here," Stan murmured solemnly.

"We'll see him soon, he said he'd visit us," and weak smiles appeared on their faces as John Hayes neared.

"Good morning, gentlemen."

"Good morning," they replied as one.

"I hope you're both looking forward to today? The taxi shouldn't be long but before you leave I'd like to go over a few things," and he drew up a chair and sat beside them. "Now I know you've both participated in the 'inside the outside' programme which I hope you both enjoyed but I want to put your minds at rest over a few other things. You need have no worries as far as bills are concerned, electricity, gas and the like because the halfway house is classed as part of the hospital and therefore funded by the state; although you'd have no problem paying any bills, Stan, that's for sure," and he widened his eyes, gave a little snigger and winked at him knowingly. "All medication, clothing, food and transportation are also provided," he continued, "meals being prepared on site and some nursing staff are resident and available to you whenever needed. The sole aim of this step is to gently ease you back into society in a measured way."

"Can I ask a question?" Stan butted in, holding his hand in the air like a school child.

"Yes, of course you can, Stan."

"You just said about bills and me having no problem paying them?"

"I did," the social worker replied.

"Well we didn't do that in the outside programme thing and I can't remember ever paying a bill in my life, I won't know what to do, will I?" he said feebly, looking at Barry for support, his hand still pointing up.

"Well you will learn how to pay bills, Stan, don't worry yourself about that: we're not in the game of pushing people out ill prepared, absolutely not, although I was really inferring that bills wouldn't pose a problem for you financially. I mean if you had to find the money to sort out any kind of bill you'd be able to very easily."

Stan continued looking at Barry as John Hayes spoke and when his eyebrows lifted his arm dropped and he turned to look squarely at the man.

"Could I?" he whispered.

"Of course, surely you know your worth, Stan?"

"No."

"You have the post office book you were issued with, don't you?"

"Yes."

"Have you looked in it?"

"No."

"Ah," John sighed and looked at Barry who was staring intently at him.

"Certain things have been overlooked by the seems of it. Do you know where the book is?"

"It's in my shoe," Stan replied, matter of factly, as if everyone kept proof of their savings in their footwear.

"What, the one you have on now?" Barry chirped up, taking over the interrogation.

"Yes Barry, the one I have on now," he answered, sounding mildly irritated.

"Why d'you keep it there?" Barry persevered.

"Well," and Stan drew in a deep breath that seemed to suck the two men closer to him but it was his anticipated answer that was doing that. "A long time ago, when I first came here, a nurse or doctor, I can't remember who, gave me a post office book and said he would look after it or I could look after it but anyhow, one of us had to and whoever it was had to keep it very safe. Well I didn't trust many people back then," he scratched his chin and paused momentarily. "I can't remember why I didn't trust many people back then but anyway, I decided to keep it. I put it in my shoe in the day and at night, when I took my shoes off, I put it in my sock because I always go to sleep with them on."

Barry and John Hayes gawped at him, transfixed.

"It made be walk with a limp to begin with but I got used to it after a while and now it's like I don't even know it's there."

The two men continued staring at him as if spellbound then John Hayes seemed to rouse himself and said,

"Right, I can tell you, Stan, that a record of all long term patients' finances are kept here in the hospital, in the main office and in my capacity of senior social worker I have access to these records. I mean, for instance, are you aware that you were the sole heir to your late uncle's estate?" He reached into his folder and extracted the file. "Who passed away in the Isle of Dogs almost twenty years ago and that money has been earning interest for all that time?"

"No," he replied, "never had an uncle."

John Hayes ignored the remark and continued to quote from the file.

"And a premium bond that you also inherited from him, won a considerable amount of money eight years ago and interest has also been accruing on that amount?"

"No," Stan again repeated.

The social worker returned the file to the folder.

"Do you mind me speaking about this in front of Mr Stone?" he asked and then turning to Barry, "It's a question I have to ask, you understand, I hope you don't feel offended?" he said apologetically and Barry nodded his understanding.

"No, Barry is my best friend, I don't have any secrets," and Stan glanced at him hoping he wasn't hurt.

"Ok, Stan, did any member of staff ever ask you for the book, for it to be sent away, to be updated?"

"Yes, a few times I think."

"Did they mention your inheritance or premium bond win, the amount of money you had?"

"Well once someone, maybe a charge nurse, said well done to me when they gave it back and I think another time one of them told me it was wonderful news and patted me on the shoulder," he replied rubbing his forehead,

"Did you wonder what they were referring to?" he quizzed.

"I just thought they were happy that I was keeping it so safe!"

"And you never bothered looking in it when they gave it you back?"

A vacant expression alighted on Stan's face as if his thought process demanded his total attention. An insightful moment had occurred and he leaned forward in his seat and lowering his voice said,

"Mr Hayes, we are in a mental hospital, money has no value if you can't spend it. I can sail a big yacht in my dreams but not around the corridors of this place," and Barry could see in John Hayes's expression that he'd got the point.

"That is very true," the social worker replied nodding appreciatively, "I understand that in here money has little relevance, but the fact is that you will be leaving this hospital today and you will be dealing with situations that you haven't experienced for many years, maybe never experienced and this in itself will be a daunting task. But somehow I think that to suddenly realise you possess a small fortune might be the most difficult of all those tasks, do you perhaps feel that way?"

"No," Stan answered immediately. "No," he repeated shaking his head and a large smile arose like a sun beam emerging from behind a cloud, spreading its light over the landscape of his plump face. "I don't think it would be difficult, not one little bit," but then the cloud reappeared accompanied by a serious expression.

"Though what I can make of it is, when you've got loads of money, you get loads of bad friends and the more money you get the more of those friends you get and they go worse and worse. I always thought if I had a lot of money I'd do something good with it and quick, before any of those bad friends turned up and now I have, that's what I'm going to do, as soon as I can."

John Hayes didn't like the way this was panning out; the way Stan seemed to be saying that he could easily squander the money, and realising he needed to consult the doctor, used the excuse of checking the taxi's whereabouts to leave. He headed out of the day room in search of the nearest internal phone and rang the doctor's private line being mightily relieved when he answered.

"Dr Richards, is that you?" he enquired urgently.

"Yes, who is this?"

"It's John Hayes, I'm sorry to bother you,"

"Oh John," he responded vaguely, "that's quite all right, just finishing off some reports," he said, putting down that day's newspaper, "what can I do for you?"

"I've a bit of a problem with the two patients going to community rehab today."

The doctor had no desire to hear this and didn't answer straightaway. His short fuse had just been lit and he had a sudden urge to slam the phone down and scream … instead he cleared his throat and composed himself.

"What sort of a problem would that be, John?" and he clenched his teeth, expecting the worst.

"Perhaps you weren't aware, doctor, but Stanley Heart, the long stay patient, has accrued a considerable amount of money during his many years with us and it's just come to light that he has no knowledge whatsoever of exactly how much; and there's an added complication," and he paused, waiting for him to say something but there was silence on the line as Dr Richards felt he was dreaming of pushing and pushing whilst being pulled and pulled.

Finally he spoke.

"What's that?" he said flatly, waiting for the killer blow.

"Mr Heart is being discharged with another patient."

"Barry Stone, I know."

"Yes, Barry Stone and he is aware of the situation and I can't be sure he won't take advantage."

The doctor placed his hand over the mouthpiece and exhaled loudly. This wasn't the huge problem that John Hayes was trying to portray after all and wasn't he failing to achieve his ward closure target as the competing hospital consistently hit theirs? Weren't Stan's memory prompts always loitering within the walls of the long stay geriatric ward? But he still had to play safe and be wary. The speed of their discharge and the reasons on which it was being based weren't obviously beneficial and he was mindful of the consequences a wrong decision could bring.

He considered Barry Stone a straightforward kind of chap, didn't strike him as a crook or someone who would mistreat others. His relationship with Stan seemed to be based on mutual respect and genuine accord and Barry was, at the end of the day, ignorant of Stan's wealth during their developing friendship. He had no history of wrongdoing whatsoever but Tim Richards had to be careful, oh so careful. His colleagues had voiced concern and he had to be seen to be doing all the right things.

"Give me five minutes, John," he began, "I just want to refer to the notes." That sounded good, he thought. "Stay by the phone I'll be right back," and he hung up.

For the next five minutes Tim Richards, the man who had long ago sold his soul to the devil and more recently the health board, worked hard on the cryptic crossword. He was a superstitious being and had decided that if he could complete three clues in that time, Stan and Barry would go there and then; if not, he would keep them back for a week and put them through some sort of financial awareness programme to placate John Hayes. He solved three in two minutes and had completed seven when the five minutes elapsed. He rang John Hayes back.

"Yes Dr Richards," he said breathlessly after one ring.

"Hello John, well I've examined both their notes and I can't see the problem. I understand your reservations but I can't say I share them. I think extra vigilance is going to be necessary but we have to remember the reasoning behind all of this" and he remembered the mantra of the briefing. "Living in the community is of great benefit to the patients, a spur and a push toward their eventual recovery."

"Indeed it is, Tim," he said with a hint of frustration, "it's just this situation has never occurred before, I mean we're talking three quarters of a million."

"Three quarters of a million?" Dr Richards spurted, his voice rising an octave.

"Yes, that's right," he replied, "and that sort of money can affect the soundest of characters, be it the recipient or their friends."

There was a pause and then suddenly, "Three quarters of a million," the doctor again repeated, "how the hell has he accumulated three quarters of a million?"

"Inheritance, premium bond win, interest."

Tim Richards needed to think fast. "Right," and he said this word slowly and precisely as if he had only just come across it and was practicing the pronunciation, "as far as I'm concerned, Mr Heart has lawfully gained this money; he is a fortunate man who is going to need sound financial advice which can be given as part of his rehabilitation at the halfway house and that's about all we can do."

"The thing is, Tim, we're talking about a man who an hour ago didn't even know he had this wealth and we're about to let him loose in a world he has no real awareness of, with a companion who could potentially take him to the cleaners! He keeps the post office book in his shoes and at night in his sock for God's sake and up until now has never once bothered to look at it."

Dr Richards began to feel the tendrils of dislike for John Hayes burrowing up from beneath and decided to throw caution to the wind. This conversation had gone on long enough and it was time to put his foot down.

"Listen, John, if a patient wants to keep his post office book up his jacksey it's a matter for him not the authorities. Good God, it's just another plus point for him being discharged into an environment that will teach him independence and self-reliance and as far as Mr Stone is concerned, I think you're apportioning blame before the crime has been committed."

John Hayes made a few curious grunts of protestation but the doctor ploughed on.

"No, I think you've no need to concern yourself. Advice and guidance is all that's going to be necessary," and he iced the cake with, "and you're the man for the job."

Exactly twenty minutes later Barry and Stan were sitting quietly in the back of a taxi being driven down the tree edged road from the hospital. This was the first time Barry had been in a car since the tragedy but he had no feelings of panic or anxiety. The ECT had done its job like a wretched hangover masks the excesses of the night before.

Stan, meanwhile, was marvelling at the sights; the road signs and the moving scenery and the vehicle's splendid dashboard, although primarily his thoughts were on the money and what he could do with it. As they slowed at the T Junction, he leant forward and knocked on the glass separating them from the driver who slid open the panel slightly enabling him to hear.

"Excuse me sir," Stan exclaimed, "could you tell me if three quarters of a million pounds would buy this car?"

"Three quarters of a million?" he asked rhetorically. "Let me think," and after a while replied, "aye for sure and another thousand like it," and Stan wiggled his toes to make sure that book was good and safe.

Roadworks had slowed everything to a crawl and it was some time before a gap emerged that allowed the taxi to join the main road traffic. Barry was sitting directly behind the driver and as he looked ahead, past his shoulder, he could just make out a tall figure in the distance, ambling along in what appeared to be an oversized black coat. They were in a queue and for some reason Barry was becoming nervous as the figure slowly neared and became more obvious. He could see it was a young man but the flowing Crombie almost touched the floor and the collar was buttoned to the top concealing his body and the majority of his face. He noticed other travellers gawping at the strange figure and then no sooner had the taxi driver began to edge forward that he had cause to suddenly brake as a car from the opposite direction cut in front of them, blocking their path. Now stationary, Barry watched anxiously as a person in a white coat, that he vaguely recognised as a staff nurse from the hospital, exited the vehicle and ran to the figure. After a brief conversation the staff nurse walked the youth to the car and opened the door for him to get in. The large black coat was still masking his features but then the taxi driver decided to blast his horn and shake his fist in protest at the dangerous manoeuvre, making the passenger look up indignantly. Barry caught a glimpse of Angelo Goodwin for the first time and he emitted an audible gasp, a sound packed with alarm and sudden fear, because when Barry's eyes sent that image for processing, his brain tensed and screamed DANGER!

As Stan, preoccupied, peered out in the opposite direction Barry was recoiling. Angelo's eyes had met his and for a brief moment he felt cold and shuddered, straining to stop the panic from taking hold.

The taxi driver swerved around the car and accelerated away, the momentum helping Barry to flop his head back on the seat stunned by the malevolence he'd seen in that face. They once again came to a halt behind a line of cars and Barry took the opportunity to lean forward and knock on the glass partition to get the driver's attention.

"Did you see that bloke's face who got in the car back there?" he asked, unable to rid his mind of the image.

"'Fraid not, only watch the road when I'm driving," he replied.

Barry breathed out heavily and shook his head.

"Well you're the lucky one, I just hope I never see it again," and he once again flopped back into the seat completely oblivious to the fact that he had experienced a portent, a foreshadowing and his wish to never see that face again was to be tragically never granted.

PART 3

Chapter 1

It was a cold day.

When the phone rang Bill had been putting on his coat in readiness for his walk to the hospital. The caller informed him that Angelo had gone missing and staff were conducting a search; but he wasn't unduly worried. Bill knew he would be making his way to the home, had no doubts and he proceeded to make himself another sugar infused coffee, his third of the day. As the kettle boiled he pondered over what state of mind the young man would be in and the best way of welcoming him. He could adopt either a strict or lenient approach, but the youth was so volatile and capricious, either could easily fail. He was certain that Angelo had kept quiet about the assault, the hand squeeze had reassured him of that, though he had decided against visiting him in hospital; he wanted to let sleeping dogs lie, wait until he was safely back in the home when he could evaluate and determine the best way to treat him, adopt, adapt and play it by ear.

Bill knew where all this was leading and realised that as long as he kept the end result in the forefront of his mind, then any twist and turn on the journey of their reconciliation could be straightened out.

As he poured the boiling water there were three knocks on the door. He waited then called whoever it was to come in. Angelo and the staff nurse entered. He'd read that in less than three seconds the mood of an individual could be gauged and Bill quickly perceived Angelo to be calm and in control. The coat was still concealing most of him, his thin eyes just visible above the collar.

"Hello, son," he began cautiously, "how are you? How're the arms?"

Angelo had been waiting for this moment, had given it a lot of thought whilst lying on that hospital bed. The fact was that he was yearning to see Bill again and he suddenly lurched his spindly frame forward and did something quite the opposite of calm and in control. He opened his arms wide and embraced him, hugging so tightly that Bill could hardly breathe. The staff nurse stepped forward, unsure that this wasn't an aggressive act, but Bill managed to wave him away. This was as good as it got and as he closed his eyes he positively did not want it to end. The boy was his and any doubts he may have had melted like an ice cube in the sun.

"Angelo," he mumbled, the strength of the enfolding arms distorting his words, "you're obviously glad to be back," and he felt the grip being released and the youth stepped backwards looking inept and embarrassed, not acknowledging Bill's words, deciding instead to sit in the corner and stare at the floor. Bill was delighted by this blundering show of emotion. He had witnessed these awkward displays of feelings by young people starved of love and tenderness many times and he was disappointed that it had come to an end. The staff nurse was looking on, bewildered by Angelo's change of character, trying to understand why this previously sullen youth should suddenly act in such a way. Bill flicked him a sideways glance, could see his shocked expression and knew he had to get rid of him.

"I'm sorry, I don't know your name," though Bill had reverted to staring at Angelo when he made the statement.

The nurse's mind returned to the moment.

"It's James, Mr Sweet," he replied, "James Stamp."

"Thank you, James, for bringing Angelo back safe and well," continuing to stare at the youth, "do you have the notes?" and Bill put his arm out without looking at him.

"Yes, of course," and he produced a folder from his briefcase and placed it in the waiting hand.

"Thank you," and after finally averting his gaze, opened the drawer of his desk and placed it inside. He needed James to leave as soon as possible and looked at him with feigned sincerity.

"I'm sure you're aware of the circumstances leading up to Angelo's admission to your clinic, James."

"I am, Mr Sweet," he said succinctly.

"Well you can imagine that he and I have much to discuss, to sort out."

James Stamp didn't need further prompting. "Absolutely, I completely understand," and he bent to pick up his briefcase.

"I need to be getting back anyway," and Bill nodded knowingly.

"However, there is something that I think you need to hear before I go, Mr Sweet. Would you mind if we went into the corridor for a second?" and Bill, with little enthusiasm, followed him through the door, closing it behind him.

"Angelo was mute for virtually all of his stay with us," he said in a hushed tone, "and only talked this morning when he …" and James hesitated to ensure what he was about to say couldn't be misconstrued, "when he said some very strange things in an extremely menacing way to the ward sister. It was very upsetting for her as you'll see when you read her report."

"Thank you, James," he sympathised, "I am well aware of Angelo's capabilities," and he rubbed his chin and thought for a moment.

"That sort of behaviour is quite common in this establishment, perhaps less so in a general hospital."

"I understand that," James agreed, somewhat agitated that Bill wasn't fully appreciating his unease, "but I think when you read the report, which I urge you to do sooner than later, even you will agree that what happened was pretty scary."

"Perhaps," he replied grabbing the door handle, "and all the more reason why I should get back in that room and get on with doing what I'm paid to do."

James felt it was mission accomplished and after shaking Bill's hand began to walk back to his car. He abruptly stopped and turned to look back into the building. He'd forgotten to specifically mention the warning Angelo had given the sister, that if she didn't shut up he would resort to violence, a punch in the mouth and he toyed with the idea of returning to relay this important information; but Bill had been keen to see him depart and anyway, he would read the report soon enough he reasoned, was probably going through it as he stood there and he turned back around and made for his car, pushing the real reason for his negligence, his desire to never see Angelo Goodwin again, to the back of his mind.

He threw his briefcase onto the passenger seat, sat in and inched forward, lifting his head up to look at the imposing façade through the windscreen. A shiver rippled up from his toes to his top, marched through him like a million dancing ants and he started the car and quickly drove off, realising that the shiver was nothing to do with it being a cold day.

As James Stamp roared out of the car park Bill Sweet had already dismissed their conversation. Like Angelo, he had also given his return much thought but that open display of unrestrained emotion had evaporated any fears he'd had of this meeting being a difficult one.

He sat on the edge of his desk, folded his arms across his chest and looked down at him. As he scrutinised Angelo's features he imagined an invisible someone behind the youth, a someone who had firmly grabbed his ears and was pulling back mightily, knee in his back, stretching the components of his face into an unnatural blur and he knew that Angelo would always have to wear a hood to conceal his face when on an assignment; only a blind man would fail to recognise him.

"It's good to see you, son," he began and Angelo nodded his head slightly in agreement. "You gave a nurse a bit of a hard time I hear?" he asked and again he nodded his head. "Anything that needs to be sorted?" Bill enquired, almost gangster-like.

"Nah, just squeezed her, told her that chicken thing you told me."

"Did she know it was me who told you that?"

"Nah."

"Did you tell her I'd punched you?"

"What punch?" he asked, intimating that it had never happened.

"How did she like the story?"

"Well, I think she was flummoxed."

Bill found himself picturing the scene in his mind's eye. This poor nurse scared cockamamie by this deformed, psychopathic young man, finding herself a minnow trying to overcome a tidal wave and that word he had used to describe her reaction, flummoxed.

Without warning his head suddenly jerked backwards, and as if in a vice, his stomach muscles clenched and that's how the bubble of the laugh was formed. As it welled up through his chest and into his throat it had gained size and momentum and when it exploded through his mouth the force of it caused Angelo to look up at him in awe. The first booming shriek was followed by many more interspersed with interludes of frantic air sucking. Angelo was quickly infected and a tittering sound emerged from him, an uncontrolled tittering, that rose and fell like a whistling kettle whose heat source was being interrupted by the wind.

"Flummoxed!" shouted Bill and he arched his back downwards placing his hands on his knees as if he was about to receive a suppository.

The change in position altered the tone of his laughter, which now reverted to a hooting rather than a howling although Angelo's tittering remained steadfastly flat, he wasn't that familiar with mirth. The imagined event kept replaying itself in Bill's head like a spark plug igniting the fuel of his amusement but it wasn't a wholesome scene and if one of the characters in the picture on the wall could speak that character would have said it was akin to two greedy thugs celebrating the haul from the old lady they'd just robbed, rather than two friends sharing a joke.

Bill's imagery subsided and as he wiped his eyes he felt the wonderful glow that hard and unfettered laughter can produce. Whereas Angelo's tittering had stopped sometime before, not truly understanding why it had started.

Bill composed himself with a final wipe of his eyes, a few coughs and a sniff. He needed to tell Angelo what he required of him and the moment seemed perfect as he knelt down and clutched his elbows.

"I have to speak to you about something that's very important," he said earnestly, all traces of laughter erased. "I've been thinking of almost nothing else since you've been away," and Bill got back to his feet, walked around to the front of his desk and sat down. With his face void of any expression Angelo now watched him eagerly.

"I'd like to talk to you about it now if that's all right?"

Angelo nodded affirmatively and Bill braced himself for an answer to his dreams or the continued acceptance of his nightmare.

Chapter 2

The taxi pulled up outside a four storey, brick built building in the heart of the town. The street was busy and alive and cars started to queue behind them almost immediately.

"'Afraid I'm going to have to ask you lads to speed up," the driver exclaimed, looking at them via his rear view mirror and Stan and Barry quickly stepped out into the world with a shared apprehension. The taxi abruptly pulled off and Barry, ignorant to the fact that it was contracted hospital transport, stood amazed thinking that he hadn't even waited to be paid. Clutching their meagre belongings, both men approached the varnished white door and it was Barry who noticed the illuminated bell push screwed into the frame. He turned to his friend.

"You all right there, Stan, coping so far?" he enquired, stretching his arm toward the bell when Stan, out of the blue, reached up and grasped it, causing Barry, who was still a bit shaky from the encounter with Angelo, to step back in surprise.

"No, I don't want to go in yet, I want to buy a motorbike!"

"You want to buy a what?"

"A motorbike. I've got an idea and we're going to need a motorbike," and the usual smile appeared as he gazed innocently up at him.

"Right," Barry said quietly and gave Stan his hand back, "right," he repeated, "be that as it may, but first of all we've got to press this bell and go inside this house, they're expecting us. We just can't go off and buy a bloody motorbike, Stan, that would be …" and he searched his vocabulary for a word and found, "crazy."

Stan continued to stare and smile. "Tomorrow then," he said undeterred, "or maybe even tonight, but we've got to get one."

"One thing at a time, old son, like I said, first of all we have to get inside and get ourselves settled in," and Barry once again went to press the bell and Stan once again prevented him.

They stood there. Cars hurtling by, people hurrying past and Barry observed his friend dolefully.

"What is it now, Stan?"

"It's a big commotion here isn't it, Barry, and we're slap bang in the middle of it?"

"Then let me ring this bell and we can get some quiet," and his arm extended and his finger finally made contact. Third time lucky.

The door was opened almost immediately by a tall, middle-aged lady in jeans and a T-shirt; her hair pulled fiercely back in a ponytail.

"Hi guys, I've been expecting you, I'm Cressida," she beamed, "but everyone calls me Cressy, come on in," and she opened the door wide and they all walked into a warm, well-lit reception area furnished with sofas and low tables, gentle music flowing from concealed ceiling speakers. The place was deserted and with a gesture of her hand she urged them to sit down.

"Please make yourselves at home and I'll get us all a drink, d'you like coffee?" and they both nodded.

"Good, I won't be long," and she seemed to skip away from them, high on happiness.

They both sat, Stan stiffly and upright with his hands on his knees, Barry more relaxed, his arms folded over his stomach.

"I don't like that street," Stan whispered, "all that noise and rush and all that screaming."

"There wasn't anyone screaming, Stan, don't say there was screaming."

"Well it sounded like screaming to me," he said indignantly and sat even further upright.

"I wouldn't say that to the lady, Stan, in fact, thinking about it, let me do all the talking or before we know it we'll be in the back of that taxi going the other way!"

Cressida returned with a tray of coffee and sat down opposite them, her heady perfume wafting over them.

"Lovely," and she passed them their drinks and positioned the milk and sugar centrally. "Now Barry and Stan, just to repeat, my name is Cressida but you can call me Cressy," and a little chuckle fluttered from her lips, "and I'd like to offer you both a very warm welcome," and she took a sip of her unsweetened, black coffee. "Now I know it seems quiet here at the moment but at this time of day most of the staff and residents are out and about doing various things, but this evening, when everyone's here, the place will feel a lot more lived in," and she took another sip.

Barry leaned forward and added sugar and milk to both their cups and began to stir.

"Oops! You're being mummy I see," and she gave him a huge grin that caused him to redden.

"Let me reassure you," she continued "that I'm fully aware of both of your circumstances, I've been very thorough with my homework," and that chuckle resurfaced, "and perhaps you're feeling a little nervous about things, but I want you both to have confidence that we have everything in place, right here in this house, to make your step from the hospital back into society a successful one," and she took a pack of cigarettes from the bag beside her and offered them one. They both declined and she lit up, then taking an overly large drag, continued. "It's rather unusual to have two guests join us at the same time, actually, it's never happened before as far as I can remember. However, I'm feeling very positive about this and indeed Dr Richards is considering making this hospital policy in the future so you're something of a test case for us," and the chuckle returned as Barry smiled at her and Stan frowned.

"But anyway," she went on, "I'm sure that all you want to do now is unpack and get the lay of the land as it were, so follow me and I'll show you to your room."

"Can I bring my drink?" Stan exclaimed, far too loudly.

"Certainly you can, Barry."

"No, I'm Stan," he corrected her.

"I'm so sorry," and she really was, "of course you can bring your coffee, Stan," and Barry thought that maybe this lady hadn't been quite as thorough with her homework as she'd made out.

After climbing two flights of stairs they walked into a sparsely furnished room that was intentionally austere, as patients remaining in their rooms, other than to sleep, was frowned upon. They dropped their cases on the floor and set their much spilled coffees down on the single table.

"Lovely, well I'll leave you both to finish your drinks and get sorted out and perhaps in an hour or so you could both pop back down to reception and I'll go over the arrangements for tomorrow, is that ok?"

"That's fine," Barry said softly, eyeing his surroundings.

"Yes, that's fine, miss," Stan echoed.

"Please Barry, call me Cressy."

"I will if you call me, Stan," he said rudely and Barry scowled at him.

"I've done it again, haven't I?" and embarrassed, she slapped her own wrist.

"Don't worry," Barry interjected, trying to make amends, "we only have to remember your name, you have to remember everyone's," and he raised his eyebrows at Stan in annoyance.

"That's very kind of you to make excuses for me, Barry," and she left the room abashed by her double name failure.

They briefly sat in silence and then Stan suddenly declared truculently,

"I don't like it here, it stinks!"

Barry was still irked by his previous discourtesy and didn't say anything.

"I don't know what we're doing here," he carried on, "it's like one of those concentration camps."

"We've only just arrived for God's sake," Barry said impatiently, "give it a chance why don't you?" and he thought they were about to have their first argument.

"I don't know what time I've got to go to bed, what time they bring the tablets, if I can sit on my bed even," and his faced screwed up as if he was about to cry. "Don't know where to get fresh clothes from or when it's lights out," then through an enormous sigh, "I feel like a little duckling that's been chucked into a big ocean," and he began to visibly tremble as he walked to the window, "and look at all those cars, all different colours about to smash into each other, all those moving shoes and swaying bags, people walking and standing and running and shouting and screaming," and his breathing suddenly increased and he stopped talking, unable to carry on as the gasps turned into gulps and he felt himself starting to choke. Barry jumped up and placed a firm hand on his shoulder and slapped his back then held him tightly and Stan managed to slow himself, drop his breathing down a gear.

"Deep firm breaths, Stan, deep firm breaths. Come on, let yourself go loose," and he did as he was told and began to regain control.

"Listen to me, Stan, we've been here for half an hour. I know it's going to be hard for you but we don't want to spend the rest of our lives up in that Nuthatch now do we?"

The small man was looking out at the street below concentrating on keeping his breathing level.

"Do we?" Barry repeated, but Stan just continued to stare out of the window and didn't reply.

An hour or so later they were carrying the coffee cups back down the stairs on their way to the reception. Stan had got over his panic but it was Barry's turn to feel agitated. The drama in the room had opened his eyes to the way Dr Richards' new strategy was going to affect him and he wasn't relishing the prospect of taking responsibility for the both of them. The value he put on their friendship was unquestioned, his ability to cope was the worry. The therapy had appeared to imprison his emotions, turned him almost into a bystander witnessing his life not living it and right now, walking down those stairs, he felt he was in the 'to be helped' rather than 'to give help' category.

The large space was still empty and they returned to the same chairs they had used earlier. Stan closed his eyes and was asleep in a minute; Barry closed his eyes and found himself reliving an agony.

Isabelle Beckett was given that forename by her mother and she did indeed live up to its meaning for even now, at ninety-three, she had retained a subtle grace and elegance. However, Isabelle was haunted by the thought of living out her final years in some nursing home, patiently waiting to meet death as her faculties crumbled around her. It was perhaps an overly pessimistic view of her future but constant pain soon gnaws away at your optimism. During the last couple of years the arthritis had pushed its barbed hooks deep into her joints; hooks she couldn't get rid of and didn't she have to give a lot of thinking time to what day it was lately? And weren't relatives' names becoming harder to remember?

As she pulled on her coat and made slowly for the car, poor Isabelle had no idea that very shortly her twisted deportment would become more severely impaired quickly followed by a permanent resolution to her fears about the future.

On that morning, Barry was still the buyer for an engineering outfit, been there since leaving school. No highflyer but good at his job, industrious and dependable and he was highly thought of, so much so that the firm supplied him with a company car. In a light mist he was driving that car with his wife beside him and his daughter behind her when he noticed Mrs Beckett's Ford parked at the side of the road. Everyday decisions can have the gravest of consequences and it was Isabelle's spontaneous determination to return to the house for an umbrella that proved this point. Those barbs of arthritis had been digging into her neck more and more lately making head movement painful so on this fateful day she decided to trust to luck and exit the car without looking behind her. All Barry saw was the door swing open, a leg appear and an articulated lorry coming the other way.

He made an immediate judgement; if it was between a leg and a door or head on with a wagon it had to be the former and he tightened his grip on the steering wheel to ensure a straight line and shouted loudly for everyone to hold tight. Although the lorry driver couldn't read Barry's mind he did have over twenty- five years of driving experience to fall back upon and he knew that the outcome of situations such as these was that almost always the driver would take evasive action to avoid the door so anticipating wrongly he swerved to the right, slammed on the air brakes and turned white.

Barry only heard the car door being ripped off, the leg separated without sound and then he saw the lorry. He had a split second to think and that thought screamed back, 'GO RIGHT! GO RIGHT!' The driver was veering into him, go right and save them all and that was precisely what he tried to do but it was too little too late. He'd turned far enough for the lorry to miss his side of the car but it ploughed into the passenger side and his wife suddenly disappeared, thrust backward by the enormous bumper of the wagon. His car slewed to the left and was propelled into the doorless one behind further crushing the passenger side then, seconds later, the lorry caught up and mounted the two vehicles as if performing some horrendous, metallic rape.

Isabelle Beckett was unconscious when she died, Barry's family were not but mercifully only realised their fate for seconds. Miraculously he was completely unscathed other than four scratch marks to the side of his face where his wife's hand had caught him as she vanished; in fact Barry was able to open the door and step out of the car unassisted, oddly remembering that the interior light came on when he did.

As he sat waiting for Cressida the memory of the tragic event was clear but his feelings toward it were blurred. It was like an elderly person casting their mind back to when they were young, seeing themselves as they were but forgetting how they felt. The crash to him was a jerk-less reflex so when Stan awoke and began to talk his mind left that catastrophe with ease.

"Barry," he whispered cautiously staring straight ahead, "you know all that money I've got?"

"I do," he replied.

"Is it safe? I mean can anyone steal it?"

"No one can steal it," he reassured him, "it's in what's called the Post Office and they've given you that book, the one in your shoe to prove only you own it."

"That's good, Barry, that's good," continuing to stare forward, "d'you know why it's good?"

"Tell me."

"Because I know what I'm going to do with that money and it's going to be such a surprise," and Stan rubbed his hands together with glee.

Chapter 3

Bill had spent many hours working out the best way to explain his plan to Angelo, the order it would take, the tone he would use. He had felt confident; after all, like his old dad had said, "practice makes perfect," but sat there, the sudden realisation of what was hanging on this, the removal of the man who controlled him, who had blackmailed him into committing the dirtiest of deeds caused his mind to become momentarily vacant and it was Angelo's voice that succeeded in bringing him back to his senses.

"What is it then?" he said brusquely.

Bill gathered himself and remembered the script.

"How many institutions have you been in, Angelo?" he asked and Angelo shook his head in ignorance.

"Well let me tell you, shall I?" and he removed Angelo's case notes from the drawer and opened them. He flicked through the pages raising his fingers at intervals.

"Including the one you're presently sat in you've been in six, six institutions in your sixteen years on this earth."

He peered across at the young man anticipating a response but he remained silent.

"Do you know why you've been in six homes?"

"Nope," he replied impassively.

"Your upbringing: your lousy, cruel, unnatural upbringing. Instead of having loving parents, or in your case, mother, you ended up with someone who neglected and abandoned you through no fault of your own.

Angelo didn't like the sound of this. Deep down he knew exactly how monstrous his mother had been and from what she'd said, how evil his father must have been, but that unfathomable love a child has for its mother, no matter how terrible her deficiencies, still resided somewhere within him.

"But do you know the funny thing about that?" Bill continued rhetorically. "The real funny thing about that is that your parents almost certainly had disastrous childhoods themselves, maybe just like the one they gave you. Their parents were crap and your parents were just carrying on where they left off."

Angelo started to take notice when he heard that. Bill was giving him a reason for his mother's behaviour and it was pleasing to him.

"Now I know I said it was a funny thing back then but funny it isn't because everyone involved just keeps getting hurt and usually those around them too, even people who don't even know them."

Bill pushed back on his chair so it was balancing on two legs and clasped his hands behind his head and Angelo straightened up even further. He liked to listen to Bill talking away and especially now as this was making perfect sense to him.

"Now I can have sympathy with all of this," he continued, satisfied that his performance was going well and his audience was enthused, "because there's a reason for parents' bad behaviour and it's mostly out of everyone's control but there's a group of people living among us, Angelo, who have an illness, an illness that causes much more harm and it's a terrible illness that can't be cured."

The youth was now sat on the edge of his chair, hanging on to Bill's every word.

"Now I've a pretty good idea of what you went through as a boy and how that's made you behave. I can't imagine everything you had to put up with, how hard it must have been, but I know among other things that you were starved of affection and that's what makes you so terribly bitter towards people, maybe most of all towards your mother and I've set myself a goal to help you with all of this because I believe there's something behind this guard you put up that deserves saving. But like I said, these people I'm going to tell you about are much worse towards children than your parents ever were and I think if you help me to do something about these people, Angelo, it's also going to help you; it's going to give you an aim in life, a goal and you're going to feel much better about yourself; you'll begin forgetting about your past and look at the future as a bright place, full of opportunity." Bill closed his eyes and thought for a second. He felt his little speech was working but he wanted confirmation.

"Are you understanding what I've said so far?"

Angelo didn't answer.

"Listen to me, son, I need to know if you're getting all of this?" he questioned earnestly.

Angelo sat back in his chair, exhaled heavily and began. "She made me look like this. I heard people say that because she drank so much when I was inside her it shrivelled my face." A tear came to his eye. "She would leave me in the house on my own and I was scared. I didn't own up to being scared but I was and then when she came back she would just scream the place down and I would go to the telly to block it all out. I hated her for how she was and I just wanted her to stop being like that." He wiped away the tear. "I knew she blamed my dad for everything so I came up with a plan to kill him so she would stop hating me but it went wrong and they put me in a home and there were men working in those homes that did stuff to me all the time. I knew it was wrong but I couldn't do nothing about it because no one would listen. I tried to be brave but it was hard when you've got no one helping you. Sometimes I would do things to the other kids like what was happening to me so I understand what you say about people copying what they've been taught. I remember a time, a long time I spent with a man called Loveluck." He abruptly closed his eyes and stopped talking, composed himself and continued. "His name was Loveluck and his nickname was Lovefuck and he tried to smother me with a pillow because I wouldn't take my trousers down. It was a horrible feeling, not being able to breathe and I didn't know why he'd do those things and I used to think I must have been the naughtiest boy in the world to get this punishment."

Angelo again stopped talking and as they looked at each other, the silence as loud as it could be, Bill realised there was no need to explain paedophilia any further.

"I want you to meet someone," he said all at once and rose from his chair, "stay there, I'll be one minute," and he almost ran out of the office.

He knew she'd be in needlework and after clearing it with the teacher he returned with Akan. Angelo stared at the scar, Akan stared at the face and they both thought they had something in common. Bill dragged a chair over for her and they sat at the table.

A parley of considerable importance was about to begin.

Chapter 4

"I wouldn't want you to spend any of that money without telling me, Stan, I know it's really none of my business but I am your friend …"

"Best friend!"

"Okay, best friend. I'd just like you to talk it over with me first: so you don't make the wrong decision or something," he concluded, hoping he wasn't sounding too patronising.

"Of course I'd talk it over with you first, Barry, that's what best friends do."

"Well, I'd like to think so, Stan." He tightened the tie he'd found in the room. "I wouldn't want you doing anything you might regret."

"I won't."

"Like buy a motorbike or something, you haven't even passed your test."

"I have, passed it years ago, anyway the bike is just a way of getting us to the surprise," and Cressy walked in.

"Gentlemen," she announced, all full of light and love and enthusiasm, "is the room all right? Have you settled in?" and she sat down, her perfume still as pungent and her outlook still as bright.

"Yes, we've put everything away," Barry replied, then Stan half shouted,

MAYBE

"We don't know what time tea is, that's one. Don't know where we get fresh clothes, that's two. Don't know what time to go to bed, that's three. Don't know how—"

"Stan, Stan," Cressy said soothingly, stopping him going on and Barry, realising that she'd got his name right, was thankful for small mercies.

"It's perfectly natural to be worried about these sort of things after such a long stay in hospital, it really is, but you mustn't get upset, everything will be explained to you."

And it was. She handed them both a folder with explicit details of how the house worked, times for everything, places for everything and she went through it all so precisely that when she'd finished and asked if they had any questions, they hadn't.

"Brilliant," she observed, "so tomorrow the three of us will be going shopping and having a meal, seem like fun?" and Barry's nod emphasised Stan's lack of one.

"Stan," and she pronounced the 'A' in his name for way too long, "please be happy, it'll be great fun," and he caught the steely gaze of his friend from the corner of his eye and decided it would be best to nod too. "Splendid, well I'll meet you in the morning at let's say ..." and for some odd reason she looked at her watch, "ten o'clock. That'll give you both time to have breakfast and make yourselves presentable," and she whisked herself off leaving them both feeling as if they'd been involved with a whirlwind.

They sat quietly for a while and then Barry declared, looking down at the floor. "I don't like surprises."

"You'll like this one," Stan replied, quick as a flash.

Barry looked around, biding his time. He stretched out his arms and yawned then looking away from his friend said, "Tell me what it is, I really don't like surprises."

"Are you sure?"

"I'm sure."

"It won't be a surprise if I tell you what the surprise is."

Barry breathed out loudly. "Stan, just tell me what it is before you burst."

"Well, I can't live here in this town with all the rushing everywhere, all the noise and the crying—"

"Crying?" Barry butted in.

"Yes, crying, I heard someone crying, someone was crying their eyes out," and he looked at his friend defiantly.

"How about the screaming?" Barry asked sardonically.

"Yes, the screaming and the crying and that loud hum, it was driving me crazy." He stopped for breath.

Barry decided to ignore the entrance of the hum, put his head back against the chair and looking at the ceiling said, "Ok, Stan, you've made your point, now what's the surprise?"

"Like I said, I can't stand all that hustle and bustle out on the street and even though you're keeping quiet about it I don't think you can either …"

"What's the bloody surprise, Stan!" Barry said forcefully.

"I'm going to buy us a farm!"

Barry let this sink in for a few seconds then, as he was about to open his mouth to speak, Stan continued. "But first of all I'm going to buy us a motorbike to get there," and he was squirming with excitement as if he were experiencing a thousand tickles.

Barry began rotating his fingers against the side of his forehead. If his wife had still been alive she would have immediately recognised this action. It was something he would do when eager but unsure. Stan asked if he had a headache and Barry motioned no, still massaging his forehead and Stan went on.

"And we're going to have pigs and grow spuds, that's all, pigs and spuds. That's what I think we did when I was a boy and best of all," and he breathed in deeply, "it'll be just me and you, Barry. No big crowds and smelly streets and hums and screams, and do you know what? We'll have no one telling us what to do because we'll make our own rules; you and me will say when to take our tablets and when to get up and when to go to bed and we'll be safe there because the place we're going to have will be miles from everyone, it'll be," and he fished around for the word, "remote, it'll be remote and we'll have guard dogs in case someone does try and get in!"

Barry had stopped the rubbing.

"Listen to me for a moment, Stan," and Stan was all big eyes and ears. "I don't want to put a dampener on things but this Cressy lady knows what she's doing. She comes across as a bit over excited I know but you've been in hospital for a long time and she's the one who's going to get you used to the way things are now, get you back into society. It's not so difficult for me, I haven't been away for so long."

"But we don't need all that if we're going to live on a farm. We don't need to join the society."

Barry thought of rubbing his head again but didn't. "Look, I can understand what you're saying but let me ask you this, Stan, do you care about our friendship?"

"You know I do, Barry."

"Then I want you to do something for me, ok?"

"Okay," he replied without thought.

"Let me have a think about what you're saying, all right? But in the meantime I want you to listen to what I tell you during our stay here, just go along with whatever goes along. It's important, Stan, I've got both our best interests at heart and you have to trust me on this. You don't want to go back up The Nuthatch and spend the rest of your life there now, do you?" and unlike the last time he was posed that question he replied,

"No, indeedy doody!"

Chapter 5

The street was as busy as ever. A few minutes after ten the three of them walked out of the house into a bright but windy day; Barry full of nervous excitement, Stan apprehension and Cressy exuberance. Walking closely together along the packed pavement they reached a newsagent and walked in through the open doors. This was an exercise in product choice and purchase and Barry and Cressy chose different daily papers and approached the counter to pay but as Barry waited his turn he sensed that something was wrong.

Stan wasn't with them.

He looked around anxiously and saw no sign of him until his gaze wandered out to the street and he could just make him out, standing outside, staring at the news stand at the front of the store. He made an excuse to Cressy, gave her his newspaper and walked back along the aisle toward his friend who was looking at the headline printed boldly on the board, large words that Stan could still only just make out.

'KILLER SOUGHT AFTER BODY FOUND.'

"What are you doing? You're supposed to be in there with us buying a paper."

"But what's all this about," he replied, pointing, "it says there's a killer out here somewhere, a murderer."

"Yes, all right, Stan," he said impatiently, "but he's not going to hurt us, the police will find him, you don't have to worry about that sort of thing now come on."

"You seem to be very relaxed about it, Barry," he said, a little displeased.

"It's not that I'm relaxed about it, it's just something that happens. You have to accept it and hope they're caught quickly now come on, please, Cressy's waiting inside for us," and they both walked back in. Stan had recently been buying small items at the hospital shop and had no problem enacting the niceties of the purchase. They exited the newsagent's each with a paper under their arms and once again Stan stopped at the news stand and stared at the headline. This time it was Cressy's turn to say something.

"Is that worrying you, Stan, the fact that someone's been murdered?" she said concernedly as people jostled around them to pass.

"Yes, it does worry me," he replied, "and it scares me."

"Well let me tell you something," Cressy began, aware that his fear needed to be allayed immediately. "It's a sad fact of life that these things happen but thankfully it's not very often, in fact it's a very rare event and in the majority of cases it's not a random occurrence; the victim usually knows the assailant."

She perceived he wasn't convinced.

"What I'm trying to get at, Stan, is that the chance of anything like this happening to one of us, for instance, is so remote that it's simply not worth worrying about."

He continued to glare at the board, however, and when Cressy announced that there was lots to do and they should be making tracks, Stan didn't go anywhere.

"No," he suddenly blurted, loud enough to make passers-by throw questioning glances, "there's something I have to say, something I have to tell you," and he took a handkerchief from his pocket to wipe the beads of sweat that were beginning to form on his forehead.

"I think I know who the murderer is," still looking at the headline, "and I think we'd better go and speak to someone about it."

Barry's jaw dropped and Cressy saw it happen.

"Stan, that's ridiculous," Barry huffed, "of course you don't know who did it. You don't know where it happened, if it was a man or a woman, you don't know anything about it, stop being so…" and he hesitated; searching for a word then said, "ridiculous," again.

"I'm not, Barry," he replied, continuing to mop his brow, "you must believe me, I know who did this and I need to speak to someone in authority."

Barry looked over at Cressy and she shrugged her shoulders. He knew Stan's admission was completely absurd and also knew that their venture into the big wide world would be short lived if Stan didn't shut up.

Barry's reactive depression was one of the relatively few conditions that was generally understood and treatable but although he thought that his friend was reasonably sane and of sound mind he was also acutely aware that he had been resident in a mental institution for a very, very long time and they wouldn't keep him in just for the sake of it, would they? He turned his hands palms up, tilted his head at Cressy and with a shocked expression asked,

"Well what next?"

"Stan, are you absolutely certain, beyond question, that you might know the identity of this person?" she said directly.

"There's no might about it," he said convincingly, "I not only know who the person is I also know where he can be found and I know where he can be found right now."

"In that case," she declared, "we need to find the nearest police station as quickly as possible." She set off at speed beckoning them both to follow and they marched side by side in her wake.

"Stan, what the hell are you playing at?" he hissed, hoping that Cressy wouldn't overhear. "I can't believe you're doing this," but Stan didn't respond, he was concentrating on keeping up and dodging the people coming the other way.

"I'm being serious, Stan," he was having trouble speaking and dodging at the same time. "This could mess up all your plans for a motorbike and the farm you know, I mean, how could you possibly know who the murderer is? We only got here yesterday!" but Stan was just staring ahead, walking as fast as he'd ever walked.

Then Barry suddenly had an awful thought. Since leaving the hospital he'd felt that his friend would be totally reliant upon him and he wasn't sure, truth be told, if he could handle that responsibility. But that awful thought was in fact a brief glimpse into the future, a future where Stan had been returned to hospital and he was in this world alone; and that vision was very unappealing and provoked a realisation that they both needed one another equally, in fact, if anything, he needed Stan a lot more.

Barry was getting increasingly worried, worried and frightened. But there was no way to stop him. Stan had convinced himself and Cressy had to play it by the book. He decided he had to have one more try to stop this madness and he stopped dead in his tracks pulling Stan to a halt with him. He drew himself close to his face.

"There is no way you know who the murderer is Stan or where he is," he said matter of factly but Stan pulled away and carried on with his march. Barry ran and caught up with him again.

"Listen to me!" he pleaded, pulling his arm to stop him as Cressy looked back anxiously, "you've been in the hospital for years and years, not reading a paper or watching the telly, you don't know anything about what's going on," his voice now raised, "it's impossible that you know who this person is!" Stan slowly raised his head and looked deeply and intently into Barry's begging eyes.

"Last night you talked to me about friendship and trust didn't you, Barry?"

"Yes I did," realising that Stan, as he was prone to do, was coming from elsewhere, a place where an insightful Stan lived.

"Then as a friend I'm now asking you to trust me on this," he said assuredly. Cressy began to walk back to them and Stan clasped his friend's upper arms.

"I have information that could prevent another death. Now if you had that information wouldn't you want to tell someone in authority?" though before Barry could reply Cressy had arrived urging them to hurry up as the police station was only fifty yards away and they needed to get there. She set off again but Barry remained, locked up by incredulity, Stan still staring up at him. He didn't know what to say or do so when Stan gently pushed him in Cressy's direction he simply began to walk, like a man who had run out of all options.

It was a small police station for such a large town. The three of them walked into a foyer full of wood and thick paint, a strong smell of bleach hovering in the air and in front of them stood a large officer, his ruddy face like a portrait behind the square glass hatch. Stan walked briskly toward it and placing his elbows down he put his upturned hands under his chin, not a good look if you want to be taken seriously. Barry joined him on the right and Cressy on the left then for a few seconds Stan and the officer scrutinized each other, neither speaking.

It was Stan who broke the silence. "I believe there's a killer on the loose, officer," he began, maintaining the eye contact.

The policeman continued to stare and say nothing, Stan carried on.

"A murder's taken place and I know who did it."

The officer's stare persisted for a moment and then he leant forward slightly and pressed a button on the wall beneath causing the door through which they had entered to remotely lock with an audible click. No one turned around, everyone kept looking at the uniform. Stan then put his face a little closer to the hatch glass to make sure the officer heard.

MAYBE

"You can call the search off, sir," he suddenly exclaimed, "I'm your man, I'm the one who did it!" and he genuinely smiled for the first time since being discharged from the hospital.

His two companions simultaneously bent down and turned their heads to look at him, staring dumbfoundedly, then together looked back at the desk sergeant to await his reaction.

"If you'd all like to walk through that door" and he pointed at a black, heavy door to their left, "and I'll meet you on the other side." Stan stepped to it whilst the other two slowly followed as if dazed.

They were detained for almost seven hours. The two leading investigators of the enquiry having to drive forty miles to conduct the interview. Dr Richards was summoned from the hospital and a duty solicitor from the seventh tee. As mid-afternoon approached, the officers finally concluded that it was simply impossible for him to be responsible. When Stan himself embraced that fact the only excuse he could offer was that he had been so distressed by the presumed effect on everyone involved that he had owned up to it to save everyone a lot of trouble. He would willingly have taken the rap to alleviate the family's pain and prevent any more police time being wasted.

"But the true murderer would still have been at large, Mr Heart," observed one of the officers, loud and impatiently, "free to commit further wickedness and if anyone is to be accused of wasting police time I'm afraid to say it's you."

Stan looked at him like the little puppy lying beside the demolished pillow and whispered that he hadn't realised that and simply thought he was helping. He wasn't charged with any crime; the officers taking the view that his feeble mind had become overwhelmed by the new circumstances it had encountered. But the question of should he have been discharged was asked of the doctor and considering this a gross slur on his non-existent integrity and more importantly a hurdle to his ward closure commitment replied cogently that he knew best and it was for the best.

During a brief meeting with Cressy he instructed her to return with them to the halfway house and continue with their reintegration programme as if this event had never happened and then all involved went their separate ways; the two investigators shaking their heads at the doctor's arrogance as they made for their car, Cressy, Stan and Barry hanging their heads as they re-joined the crowds and Tim Richards looking ahead to his impending interview with the delicious Akan.

They arrived at the house but Cressy didn't go in; her shift had finished hours ago and as the two men entered she made her way home. They were both hungry and the smell of cooking was a welcome one. A few staff and patients were milling around in the reception and as they sat in their now usual seats a tall figure in a coat, as black as his skin, approached them.

"Good God it's … it's …" Barry started.

"Charlie!" Stan finished.

These were the first words the pair had spoken since leaving the station. As he neared Charlie extended his long arms and grabbed their shoulders in a display of affection, surprising them, but Charlie's free spirit was alive on this day and anyhow, he was off duty and feeling less restrained.

"Well look at the two of you," he declared, taking a step backward, but he sensed a tension in the air, something wasn't quite right.

"Tell me how your first day out has been, exciting I bet, yeah?" but neither of them spoke. "Come on fellas, aren't you glad to see me?" he persisted, but they remained statue-like, as if he wasn't there.

"Ok," he said dispassionately, "what's happened? There's something happened, right?" and he looked suspiciously at the two of them making them avert their eyes, Stan looking down and Barry across at the unmanned reception desk.

"I'm going to find out one way or the other so let's have it. I'm a big boy you know, I can take it."

MAYBE

It was Barry who spoke first as he slowly turned his head to face him. "We had a bit of a problem today, Charlie, and I don't know what's going to happen," his voice quiet and tremulous.

"Go on," Charlie prompted.

"I hope Stan doesn't mind me talking for him?"

Stan gave no indication whether he did or didn't so Barry continued. "Ok, well this morning he," pointing at his friend, "read about a murder that's taken place when we were out with Cressy…"

"Cressy?" Charlie questioned.

"She's the lady who's looking after us here," and Charlie nodded, understanding, "and the next thing we were all in a police station and Stan was telling them that he did it," and Barry shook his head as if bewildered.

Charlie waited a second for this to sink in, his mind returning to the recent episode of Stan contacting the police to admit to the murder of some African President.

"I told you this had to stop, didn't I, Stan?" he castigated, his tone serious now and Barry looked at him bemused.

"What d'you mean, Charlie, he's done it before?"

He thought for a moment and decided it best that Barry knew.

"Yes, a couple of weeks ago," and Stan maintained his position of head down, "did a similar thing, thought it would make everyone's life easier if he just owned up."

"Did you tell anyone about it, Charlie?" Barry asked quietly but Charlie remained silent, at the time he hadn't reported it for fear of affecting the discharge.

"Well, anyway," Barry said, breaking the awkward lull, "after a few hours everyone realised that it was sheer madness and it was impossible that Stan had done it then they called in Dr Richards—"

"They called in Dr Richards!" Charlie exclaimed, horrified.

"Yes, they called him in and he was in a mean mood I can tell you, but the thing is, Charlie, I don't know what's going to happen next, whether Stan will have to go back to the hospital or what," and he looked over at his friend whom he thought was bathing in shame though it wasn't that particular emotion that Stan was experiencing; he was just becoming quietly upset that he'd caused his best pal such dismay.

"What d'you think will happen, Charlie?" Barry asked pathetically and it was at that point that Charlie realised the doctor's idea of Barry acting as Stan's crutch was ill conceived. He also realised that the situation was perilous and he had to tread carefully.

"I really don't know what will happen and that's the truth, but I'd like to know from Stan why he did it, like I said it's not the first time."

"How many times has it been, Charlie?" Barry said concernedly.

"A few times, let's leave it at that."

Charlie looked down at Stan and swayed slightly backwards as he watched him shudder, as if his body had abruptly aged by five years and he couldn't cope with it and then he began to weep, quietly and softly like someone who wasn't able to cry hard because it was too painful. A powerful feeling of guilt rushed through Barry. He hadn't been sympathetic to his friend when he should have been and he took him in his arms and held him tight.

Stan continued to weep, Barry continued to squeeze and Charlie didn't really know what to do.

Five minutes later the three of them had moved to a quiet corner of the reception. Stan had composed himself and Barry had dried his own tears. They were sat in a triangle and Charlie spoke first.

"Can you tell me, Stan, as honestly as you can, what makes you do it, what's behind it all?"

"I know what makes me do it, Charlie, I just wish I could stop it. I try to stop people getting hurt but it all goes wrong."

"Well can you enlighten me and Barry here because it's got to stop, man, it really has."

Stan felt their eyes burning into him and he had to stifle an urge to get up and run. "I felt if I owned up it would save a lot of people a lot of trouble. The police could stop looking for the killer, the family would feel better, the newspapers—"

"But Stan," Charlie butted in a little too loudly, "anyone in their right mind could see it wasn't you, didn't you think about that?"

Stan took a deep breath. "Charlie," Stan whispered almost pedantically, "when you're stood in a street with cars flying past at God knows what speed, hundreds of different colours flashing in your eyes," his voice became more voluminous, "loads of people crashing into each other, squirming and screaming and being sick ..."

"Being sick?" Barry asked, that was a new one.

"Well I saw them being sick," Stan admonished, "and screeching and swearing." He paused, staring fiercely at them. "Anyway," and his vehemence subsided with a sigh, "when all that is going on around you, Charlie, you haven't got much time to be thinking of anything else!"

Charlie understood that Stan had scant understanding or insight into the problem and decided not to pursue it any further.

"Look," he began calmly, "it was your first day out of the hospital, a place where you felt safe and secure, but that place was just an existence, you should never have been there. You've an opportunity now to get your life back, experience all the new things that are happening in the world, especially with your mate Barry by your side," and he glanced at Barry who returned his smile.

"But I can't stand all the bustle out here, Charlie, all the rushing and fuss," he complained and then he became a conspirator and a twinkle pinged in his eye.

"So I've come up with a plan," and he rubbed his hands and looked excitedly at him, "because I know we can be safe and secure out here if we stick with the plan, I know we can."

"That's great news," he said, delighted by this revelation, "if you tell me about the plan I'll do everything I can to help you."

Barry sat back, knowing what was coming and Stan cleared his throat.

"You know I've got that post office book?"

"The one you keep in your sock?"

"Yes, the one I keep in my sock, well there's a lot of money in that book and I think it's enough to buy a farm where me and Barry can live; grow spuds and keep pigs, be safe and secure and I can buy us a motorbike to get there when we've bought it and that's my plan, Charlie, and I can't see that there's anything wrong with it," and he waited expectantly for a response but it was a long time coming because for some strange reason the nurse was having little luck in finding any reasons that would dissuade him from this idea. In fact, the more he thought of it the more he liked the sound of it: and then further thoughts tightened his lips. What was the doctor going to do after the day's events? What was Cressy's view? Did Barry think it was a good idea? Stan was fed up with waiting.

"Can you see anything wrong with it, Charlie?" he asked anxiously and he emerged from his thoughts with a sharp intake of breath.

"I'm going to have to think about it, Stan, it's a lot to take in," and he rose from his seat to make an exit. "I'll mull it over and come back to see you both, promise" and he placed his green, pork pie hat on his head, tilting it slightly to the left, "and you need to consider this, Barry," he said sternly, "very seriously."

Though Barry already had, very seriously, and indeed concluded that it was a perfectly good idea, an absolutely and certainly good idea and he was beginning to get the feeling that Charlie was joining him on that wavelength too.

Chapter 6

Bill scanned their faces. The two people who were going to change the course of his miserable existence.

"I would like you to meet Angelo," he began and she offered her hand which he didn't accept.

Bill decided to ignore his bad manners. "Would you mind if I explained to him briefly why you are with us here at the home?"

She shuffled uncomfortably in her seat, put out by his rudeness. "No, I don't mind, Mr Sweet," and Bill explained the tragedy that had befallen Akan leading to her admission.

He sat unmoved by this and when Bill had finished, simply shrugged, giving the impression that it was nothing to do with him.

"Now, Angelo," Bill went on, "would you mind if I explained to Akan why you are here at the moment?" and he performed the same shrug, this time to signify that he didn't care one way or the other.

"Where it appears that you had devoted parents, Akan, who did everything they could to provide a loving environment, Angelo here had the exact opposite. An absent father, abusive, alcoholic mother and whilst in so called care was mistreated and molested; and when I say molested, Akan, and I know that perhaps you are innocent of these matters, I mean grown men would—"

"Please, Mr Sweet," she interjected, "I know what you are about to say and there is no need. I have had long discussions with Ruby don't forget," which Bill acknowledged.

"So why have you brought us here today, Mr Sweet, can I ask?" and now Angelo moved forward showing a little more interest in the proceedings.

Bill knew it was now or never. He recognised the years of his dishonesty and deception could be nearing an end but never in his wildest dreams did he think his fate would rest in the hands of two juveniles, the one of which being a grave liability.

He decided to veer away from her question for the moment.

"Ruby has talked to you about physical abuse, Akan?"

"She has and from personal experience with her parents, things pushed on from simply being made to watch," she replied.

"And if you had the power, what would you do with Ruby's parents?"

"I would kill them both," she said with no emotion.

"Not send them to prison or try to treat them?"

"Children are the reward of life, Mr Sweet. One only shows compassion to those who will benefit from it."

Bill looked at Angelo who in turn was looking at Akan.

"One only shows passion to what?" he said, almost mockingly.

"What I'm saying, Angelo," she said angrily as her head turned rapidly in his direction, still annoyed at his previous impoliteness, "is that all kiddie fuckers should be killed because they don't know the difference between right and wrong. If you're sick enough to bugger kids you're too far gone!"

She really can converse with the prince and the pauper, Bill thought and his estimation of her cranked up yet another notch. Akan's answer to his question was music to Bill's ears. He had never guessed that their views on paedophiles were similar and this was going to make his job a whole lot easier.

"How did you get the scar?" Angelo suddenly enquired becoming more curious about the girl.

She had realised the extent of his mental ability and decided that allegory and imagery, her favoured form of communication, was beyond him and concluded plain speech was far more fitting.

"My papa punched a man who was holding a large knife and it fell from his hand onto me."

He was beginning to like this young lady in exactly the same way he had Bill when they first met.

"What happened then?" he said artlessly.

"I went to hospital and my father to the police station."

Bill felt he should step in.

"Akan's father killed himself in a prison cell, Angelo. He couldn't bear to be without his daughter …"

"And I am finding it hard to be without him so can we change the subject and get to the reason for us all being here."

The reason for their attendance was that he wanted them to form a bond; he wanted them to like each other so when the bombshell was dropped that the doctor had plans for Akan and he had a way to stop him his proposal would be acceptable. Bill felt his strategy was developing well but he needed to push things faster, she was getting impatient.

"Before I explain why we're all here can I ask you, Akan, to reassure Angelo that facial disfigurement does not mean that life comes to an end."

She put her left elbow on the desk and placed her chin in her left palm, squeezed the lids of her eyes together almost shut and stared at Bill as someone would puzzle over a conundrum. Bill felt she was searching into his very soul. After a full half minute of studying him, trying to understand why he should make such a request, she finally retorted.

"Yes, I will try Mr Sweet, if that is what you want," and she removed her chin and turned to the youth.

"I think you are beautiful," she said, openly and sincerely, making him frown, "do you know why I find you beautiful, Angelo?"

Another shrug.

"Because you are liked by Mr Sweet and I find him to be so."

He failed to understand and moved awkwardly in his seat.

"Let me be plain," she went on, sympathetic to his dilemma, "Mr Sweet is obviously your friend, you choose those like yourself to be your friends …"

Angelo began to understand.

"I find him to be beautiful …"

"So you think I'm beautiful too," he said, finishing the sentence for her.

"Exactly, Angelo, and as far as the way one looks, we have no control over that so they are no reflection of us and mean nothing to me nor should they anyone else. For me beauty is what's in your heart not what surrounds your head."

She smiled at him and he smiled back experiencing a warmth toward her that he had never felt for anyone before. Bill abruptly stood up and placed his hands firmly on the desk, his gaze grabbing their attention.

"Thank you, Akan," he began, "I now want to explain why we are all here. You are in …" But Akan raised her hand and asked if she could say something else and when Bill agreed she leaned across the desk and took Angelo's hand in hers.

"I cannot begin to understand how it is to have parents who have no love for you," she said, her husky voice low and sad and full of sympathy. "I see within you a man who has had much taken away from him and little put back," her seriousness made her seem even more beautiful and her two companions sat entranced, "to not know your papa is shameful because he teaches you how to bring strength to a family but to have a mama who has no motherly feelings must fill you with tears as a mama's embrace can place you in paradise, somewhere I have been many times."

She continued to hold his hand and no one moved, the three of them reflecting on her words, then Bill, seeing that Angelo had been mesmerised by her, knew this was the perfect time.

Her outlook on paedophilia mirrored his own, she had empathy towards Angelo, and he was beginning to respect and admire this young woman.

"You are in grave danger, Akan," he suddenly declared and she released Angelo's hand and looked at Bill with a confused expression.

"Do you remember some weeks ago, sitting at the top of the entrance steps and a man walked past you into the home dressed in a way you might remember, shirt and tie, expensive suit, highly polished shoes?"

The last description triggered her memory and she twisted her head upwards casting her mind back.

"And not long afterwards we had that chat about you not leaving the home without me knowing?"

"Yes, of course, I can remember now, I remember him climbing the steps and me thinking he had demon's eyes and shivering because he made me feel cold."

"Well that man wants to hurt you in the way Ruby was hurt and Angelo also. Please don't ask me how I know, you are going to have to take my word for it, just understand that I make it my business to know if any of my children are in danger and I have found out that he wants you."

Akan recoiled in horror and Angelo stood rippling with anger. It was his turn now to grasp her hand.

"No one is going to hurt her, Mr Sweet," he growled and forming a fist with his free hand slammed it down onto the desk. "Do you know how to stop him because I do!"

This is going wonderfully, Bill thought, and he leant forward and covered Angelo's fist with his hand.

"We can stop him, son," Bill said forcefully looking deeply into his eyes, "and it will be as simple as swapping two glasses of orange juice, but I've things to do first, we'll meet here at the same time tomorrow."

Chapter 7

During the seven years that Charlie had been a charge nurse he had gained a reputation for being professional and principled when on duty and a fun companion when not. However, he was also considered to have a free spirit and be occasionally off message and it was these latter traits that had slowed down his promotional path. It had taken fourteen years to attain his present status, the norm for a contemporary being almost half that time. He had returned home via two high street estate agents, picking up their current property magazines and after showering and getting changed he sat down in the cramped living room, propped his feet on the pouffe, lit a cigarette and began to peruse.

He found the men's situation to be truly onerous but a situation that Stan had come to terms with and apparently found an answer to.

He was well aware of the new policy of farming out patients into the community, ostensibly for their own welfare, although he wasn't easily fooled and had guessed it was about money; He was also a good enough judge of character to realise that Tim Richards would be under pressure to fulfil his quotas and that the good doctor would more than likely be trying everything to exceed them; he would consider the re-admittance of a patient such a backward step as to be unthinkable.

Nevertheless, Stan could have gone one step beyond and left him with no other option. Charlie opined that mistakes may have been made in the past over the choice of candidate but he knew that Stan wasn't one of

MAYBE

them. He genuinely felt that over time, Stan would be considerably more happy out than in.

He took a long drag on the last of his cigarette and picked up the first of the magazines then replaced it when the thought came.

If the doctor had been that concerned he would have had them returned to the hospital directly from the police station, perhaps he had decided to leave them where they were and monitor their progress after all but he cut off his thoughts; he couldn't surmise what the doctor was or wasn't going to do and he resolved himself to being in the driving seat and speed was of the essence.

He'd already made his mind up that Stan's idea of a farm was almost brilliant and as he once again picked up the magazine his professionalism lifted the door latch and his free spirit walked through it and he began turning the pages.

At the rear of the magazine was an agricultural section and a large portion if it was taken up by the announcement of a three property auction at a local hotel in two days' time and one of the properties stood out. The particulars described it as a small farm with outbuildings situated at the end of a half mile, single track with passing places. Thirty-three acres surrounding the steading. Guide price £125,000.

Charlie pushed his glasses further up his nose and inspected the picture of the place more carefully. His eyes passed over the stone façade, the small garden fronting it and the solid looking, half glazed, wooden front door. He looked even closer and a strange sensation enveloped him, a feeling that he knew this house and the people who lived there and the people who lived there were Barry and Stan. He was in the grips of an odd portent that told him this farm was meant to be theirs, that all this had been predetermined and a happiness grew in him. His eyes continued their inspection and then abruptly stopped when, at the very bottom in bold capital letters, he focused on an odd proviso, something he found to be curiously unusual.

'A semi derelict mansion is to be found in the wooded area above the property known as Ancoats Farm all of which forms part of the whole.

On completion and only on completion, will the identity of the previous occupant be revealed solely to the successful purchaser.'

Charlie lit another cigarette. How weird is that, he thought? He looked back up to the picture of the farm and imagined Stan and Barry emerging from that ornate door to perhaps greet someone, maybe him. It all seemed so right. Stan wouldn't be panic stricken by the speed of his new life. Their time would be almost blissful and anyway, what else would he want to spend that money on? Okay, there was an old, run down mansion with an enigma attached to it but what the hell, that wasn't going to be a problem.

He closed the magazine and rested his head back on the chair. He could understand the benefits of this move but knew they all had to act fast to achieve it and he put out the cigarette, put on his coat, stuck the particulars under his arm and headed back to the halfway house.

Chapter 8

It was the afternoon following his meeting with Akan and Angelo and Bill was sitting quietly at his desk, going over the plan of dealing with Tim Richards in fine detail. A human being occasionally knows instinctively when something is going to happen and it came as no surprise when, after staring at it for a good thirty seconds, the phone began to ring.

"Hello, Doctor," he said, certain that it was.

"Hello, Bill, how on earth did you know it was me?"

"Intuition," he replied tersely, "prone to it sometimes."

"Interesting," the doctor observed, "does it stretch to you knowing the reason for the call?"

"No, but that's where guesswork comes in, I suppose."

"Go on then, Bill, let's see if your guesswork is as potent as your intuition."

"You want me to bring someone over to you?" he said, resignedly.

"How clever you are, Mr Sweet, and do you know who that person might be?" he asked and Bill could sense a menace in his voice as if the idea of him being clever angered him.

Maybe

"Yes, I'm guessing it's Akan, the young lady you saw recently at the top of the steps."

"Superb, right on every count so far. I'd like you to escort her over in exactly one hour from now and it being her first time, best bring a change of clothes."

Bill's stomach turned over at the thought of what he had in store for her but his planning had been meticulous and he knew he wouldn't be going anywhere that afternoon.

"She's not here I'm afraid, doctor. She's having remedial surgery on the scar, won't arrive back until the day after tomorrow."

It was necessary for Bill to buy time as his accomplices were, as yet, not privy to the plan; a situation he was going to resolve the following day.

Bill heard the banging on the other end of the line almost immediately and if he were able to converse with the statue of Ugo Cerletti he would have been informed that Dr Richards was using the telephone as a kind of punch to make dents in the snakeskin overlay of his desk. Bill kept the earpiece to his head and the banging eventually stopped as his temper subsided.

"This is the second time you've let me down, Bill," he seethed. The doctor had thought of little else during the day and this news had tipped him into a rage. He thrust open his diary and scanned the page for two days hence.

"I want her here at 5 pm. Two days from now—"

"I'm not sure what time she arrives back," Bill butted in.

"You're not fucking listening, Bill, you're going to make it happen. I said I wanted her here at five two days from now and this time there will be no excuses, do you understand?"

"I'll try my—"

"You won't try anything you little fuckwit, get her here at five o'clock the day after tomorrow or I'm going to be very upset, very put out," and Bill decided it was now prudent to go along with his demand because ultimately, it wasn't going to matter.

"I'll have her there, Doctor," and he repeated, "I'll have her there."

"That's better, old boy, I know you enjoy your lifestyle and being in charge of that place; be good to keep the status quo," and then he became more magnanimous, "and by the way, thought you might like to know that your old mate Stan Heart has been discharged. Thought it a good idea to get him away from any memory prompts if you know what I mean, although he can't remember a thing, even after a dose of scopolamine."

"Discharged where?" he replied nervously sitting upright in his chair, the news swiftly focusing his thoughts.

"To the halfway house we have in town. Like I told you before the ECT had to stop, natives were getting restless, but his memory of Mr Wilson has been completely erased, believe me, I know," and the doctor gently replaced the receiver: though Bill wasn't convinced. This was a kick in the guts, an added complication, yet first things first. His eyes went to the containers of formalin he'd purchased using a false name and address and he pushed one of them with his foot making the contents slosh this way and that.

Years ago he had a jigsaw puzzle from a second-hand shop and all the way through its construction he had agonised over it being complete because even if one piece was missing it would ruin the whole thing and as the liquid began to flatten out he was reliving that feeling of uncertainty and doubt and he once again began to rehearse the plan.

Chapter 9

Later that day Cressy sat in the reception and dialled the number then waited for the doctor to pick up. She was feeling out of her depth and in need of guidance.

He answered the phone with an impatient, "Yes?"

"Oh, hello sir," she said apprehensively, her usual exuberance on hold, failing to understand why she felt so intimidated by him. "I hope you didn't mind me ringing but I need to know your thoughts on how we proceed with Mr Heart and Mr Stone." His mind had been on other things and hadn't given the matter much consideration so needing time to think decided to buy some time with a long pass.

"Can I ask you what your take is on the situation?"

The reply, 'well you're supposed to be the bloody doctor' sprang to mind but that comment stayed firmly in her head and instead she took a deep breath, exhaled and ruminated for a second.

"I think it might be a good idea for them both to return to the hospital," she said flatly, "perhaps for a couple of months to assess this disorder of Stan's that's suddenly materialised," and she waited for an answer. When it came it was brief, succinct and caused her a problem.

"Go on," was all it was and it threw her.

She was seeking guidance and all she was getting was a superior asking her for the answers.

"Um, I mean, did he ever display a tendency in the past for owning up to something he didn't do?"

He had no intention of confirming that as to do so would question his judgement over discharging him. No mention of this personality trait had ever been noted and that was the way he liked it. Additionally, he had no intention of allowing these men to return. He was relieved that Stan had been removed from the scene of Wilson's murder, even though the drug fuelled interrogation had proved he'd lost all recollection and hadn't he just, that very morning, discharged another patient and wouldn't another two mean a ward could be mothballed and he was back on target?

He had to get Cressy on side and he didn't really care about the tactics. Her last remark could be construed as questioning his ability and concluded that that was as good a place to start as anywhere, a method he'd had the opportunity to use many times before.

"Am I sensing that you think we just throw these people out of here without thorough preparation?"

Her heart sunk. She'd annoyed him and that was the last thing she wanted to do.

"Of course not, sir, I wasn't suggesting that at all, it's only I find it a little strange that this was the first time anything like this has occurred with him."

She was backpedalling and making it worse.

"I'll repeat myself," he said with horrible condescension, a streak of malice in his voice, "do you think we simply throw them out of here without thorough preparation?" his voice now raised.

"I'm not insinuating that," she cringed and the duty receptionist, who was in earshot, felt it inappropriate to remain and left for the tea trolley.

"I sincerely hope not," he said emphatically.

He'd knocked her down, held her there for a while and now it was time to build her back up and pipe her aboard.

"Cressy, isn't it?" his voice now soft and downy.

"Yes, it is."

"Mr Heart has been a patient of ours for many years, hardly been out of the place in all of that time. His day consisted of sitting on a particular chair, vacantly smiling. A long course of ECT was necessary to treat his condition and then Mr Stone arrived and a transformation took place."

He was talking as if a storyteller to a young child.

"They seemed to click, they were actually mutually helpful because as much as Stan," he began using their first names to give the impression they were well acquainted, "began to emerge from his shell Barry equally began to emerge from his depression. The next obvious step was a move into the community and my team and I are absolutely convinced that discharging them was the right thing to do and I am also absolutely convinced that to reverse that decision would be a serious backward step for them both."

He paused as if he were turning a page.

"I think that Stan's behaviour is down to his sudden immersion in a situation that he couldn't cope with, it was a case of too much too soon."

"It's the standard procedure we use with all our patients, it's tried and tested," she replied defensively.

"I'm sure it is," he said as if he cared, "I'm sure it is, but perhaps a slower approach would be better, especially with Stan." He had now questioned her competency but unlike Tim Richards, she didn't play that game, didn't even know the rules.

"I think you're right," she concurred. "I understand what you're saying and I can moderate the programme though the whole process will obviously take longer."

"The time it takes doesn't matter, Cressy, the important thing is that these men are equipped both mentally and emotionally when they leave you to become worthwhile members of our society," and, liking the sound of that, he glanced across at the mirror opposite and couldn't resist the urge … he put his thumb up and winked at himself.

"I know you have their best interests at heart," she said sincerely, "and please don't think I was doubting you earlier on, Doctor, I've just never experienced anything like this before and I wasn't sure what I should be doing for the best."

"I think we both put our patients first, Cressy, it isn't a case of that," he said reassuringly, "but I believe every patient is an individual and perhaps our methods should take that into consideration," and, once again, his thumb went up and he winked.

"You're right," she said decisively, "I know where I'm going with it now, Dr Richards. Thank you so much and I hope you didn't mind me bothering you?"

"Not at all."

"I'll keep you up to date on their progress."

"Thank you, Cressy," and as she replaced the phone, now believing the doctor to be a compassionate man, he replaced the phone believing that he'd done enough to ensure those pair of bastards never returned.

Chapter 10

It was early evening when he stepped out into the street, the light drizzle prompting him to remove the green pork pie hat from his coat pocket and place it on his head, adjusting it slightly to the left.

It was a little quieter now and as he walked he began to consider the position he found himself in. From the very beginning, when their discharge had been first mooted, he had been told, quite unsubtly, that his participation would not be required. Once in the community they would no longer be his responsibility. The different stages of their reintegration would be dealt with by those trained to do so. Charlie's genuineness resided in the space between the bottom of his boots to the top of his tilted hat. During his time at the hospital, at the forefront of his mind had always been the well-being of those he looked after, but occasionally, his caring ways caused him to collide with the accepted view that you don't let your patient's worries become yours, that you don't take your work home with you. Charlie squared that particular circle by believing he could see a bigger picture and ideas set in stone could still be questioned.

His eyes rose to the halos formed by the drizzle around each streetlight, vanishing as he passed and reappearing as he approached and he stopped for a second to wipe the wetness from his face. Replacing the handkerchief in his trouser pocket he once again lifted his head to the lights and the interesting illusion sparked in him a greater clarity. He knew that getting involved with Stan and Barry like this put him on dangerous ground and he felt an abrupt desire to spin around and go back home, throwing the magazine in a bin on the way, but as the rain began to settle on his face he heard Stan's voice as if he were stood right next to him.

"I can't see anything wrong with it, Charlie, can you see anything wrong with it?"

And it strengthened his resolve because he realised that whereas some might think what he was about to do unorthodox and others simply wrong, he knew that Stan's idea was brimming over with sense and he pushed his hat tighter and continued to walk.

They weren't in the reception area and he eventually found them on the beds in their room, both lying face up observing the ceiling. He sat down next to Barry.

"The big wide world tiring you both out, eh?" he joked but neither man laughed.

"Not really," Barry responded seriously, "we're still worried about what's going to happen to us," and he lifted himself up onto his elbows.

"We haven't seen anyone since you left, Charlie, and my imagination's had room to wander."

A silence descended and they all looked in separate directions. Charlie's doubts resurfaced and he played with the idea of telling them it was unethical to help patients away from the hospital, that it was outside of his responsibility; there were guidelines to be adhered to and he could get into a lot of trouble - or he could stand by his convictions.

There was really no contest.

"How much have you two talked about this farm idea?" he piped up and it was Stan's turn to prop himself up.

"We haven't talked much about it, Charlie, though I've been thinking about it most of the time," Stan replied, "but I can't picture it, I have a problem seeing what the place should look like, though when I come to think about it I've always had a problem seeing pictures in my head," he said forlornly, a look of sadness appearing.

"How about you, Barry, what d'you think about it all?" he was now chairing the meeting.

"I've been thinking a lot about it as well," and he pushed himself further up on the bed, "and I've been thinking that Stan and I have no experience of running a farm but I've also been thinking that it might be fun finding out." Stan looked over at his friend and the sadness left his face. "I don't know if I'm up to finding a place," he continued, "and then helping with buying it; I think it's pretty obvious that Stan hasn't had experience of this sort of thing and a lot of the work would be down to me and if I'm honest, I don't know if I'm ready for all that, Charlie." He paused and caught Stan's eye. "I've also been thinking that I haven't any money and the whole place would be yours and that could cause all sorts of problems."

"It would be both of ours, Barry."

"Well that's the problem, Stan," Barry corrected him, "it wouldn't really, it would be your farm and I can see times where that could make me feel …" and he shook his head until, "awkward," popped out.

A further silence descended as the three of them sat digesting what had been said then suddenly Barry carried on.

"I need to say these things, Stan, get them off my chest, because I think it's only fair on me and you." He then turned his attention to Charlie. "I mean, what would the authorities have to say about it all? The people up at the hospital and the people here? Can we just up and leave like that and don't forget we've only left the hatch for a matter of days, what if one of us throws a wobbly at this farm, that would be interesting wouldn't it?"

Charlie stood up and walked over to the window. It was now night-time but the darkness and drizzle were no deterrent to the town dwellers and a goodly number of cars and pedestrians continued to populate the street. This busy world had changed beyond Stan's imagination and he knew, looking down at the activity, that both of them had problems. The little man was never going to cope with it and Barry would be lost on his own should Stan be recalled. He turned and looked at them individually, convinced more than ever that he was doing the right thing and he returned to Barry's bed and sat down.

"Right," he began, "let's just take stock of the situation for a minute, guys," and he swallowed, nervous of what was to follow. "I completely understand your concerns, Barry, and I also know that, for various reasons, the two of you might have a problem with getting into the swing of things out here so, as far as I can see, there's only two options open to you: the first is to go back to the hospital where, and I'm sorry to be blunt, you, Stan, will probably remain for the rest of your life and you, Barry, run the risk of becoming institutionalised, ie completely dependent on the place," and he paused to let that statement sink in, "or," he went on, "you go ahead with this farm idea."

Neither man responded and Charlie pushed on.

"Now I need to tell you both that I've made a decision, but more of that in a second. Regarding your fears of the authorities stepping in, Barry, well they're groundless; you don't have to worry about it. They would have to invoke something called a section to stop you doing it and there are specific legal guidelines that would have to be met and your situation doesn't justify that. I don't think either of you is going to throw a wobbly as you put it as the environment you're going to find yourselves in will actually be therapeutic and I'll be coming to visit most weeks anyway," and he smiled at the faces watching him intently. "As far as Stan being the sole owner is concerned, that's just something you're going to have to come to terms with Barry, but the rest of the stuff, buying the place and all that, well that's where my decision comes into it because I'm happy, if you both want, to help you buy this farm and get you organised."

He waited for them to say something and it was Barry who put his arms lightly around his shoulder.

"I think that's a decision that you're very brave to make," he said quietly, "and I'd like to thank you," and he removed his arm and they both looked at Stan.

"How you gonna do it, Charlie, how you gonna help us?" and Charlie opened the magazine he'd brought to the agricultural section.

"You know you said you had trouble picturing things, Stan?" he said, passing it over to him, "well what d'you think of that little beauty?" and Stan's eyes lit up as they focused on the image of the farmhouse.

Chapter 11

As Cressy placed the phone upon the cradle, confident now, after speaking with Tim Richards, that she could devise a new way forward, Bill Sweet, Angelo Goodwin and Akan Dotse were meeting once again and all were sat in exactly the same places as the day before.

Bill had been busy that morning and, prior to their arrival, he had been on a shopping trip that necessitated him visiting all three pharmacies in the town as well as a builders' merchants, chandlers and home brew shop. All the items he had purchased were housed in a large holdall under the desk, other than the four-foot length of three-inch square wood with a pulley attached to the centre that was instead propped against the wall.

Angelo had spent the night with murder on his mind; a protective volcano had erupted inside him and no one, but no one, was going to harm a hair on this exceptional young lady's head, whereas the exceptional young lady had spent the night worrying, not about the deed she was anticipating was going to happen, but about the actual guilt of their intended victim.

Bill had been more than vague and it wasn't sitting well with her. She needed to make sure this man was in fact a child abuser beyond any doubt and she knew she couldn't proceed until her fears had been allayed.

"I didn't want to involve either of you in this," he began, his face a mask of sincerity, "but it's something I can't do on my own; if I could, believe me, I would," and he slowly shook his head, feigning regret. "I'm immersed in a crisis and I've spent hours upon hours trying to find the right answer and there's only one. This monster who's posing such a threat to one of my children has to be removed."

Without warning, Angelo jumped to his feet and wrapped Akan in his arms, Bill recoiling when he saw the awful depth of hatred in the boy's face, a visage of pure malevolence.

"Tell me where he is!" he snarled, an animal like sound, frightening in its malice, "tell me now and I'll remove him, good and proper."

Bill thought quickly, he had to curb Angelo's enmity although not quash it.

"Please, son," he said softly, motioning for him to return to his seat. "I understand how you must feel, but something as important as this, as serious as this, needs a great deal of preparation and that's something I've already done and it's so very important that you both act out the parts I have given you in exactly the way I say or everything could go terribly wrong."

He reluctantly released her and returned to his seat, his unworldly face still screaming odium for this man who posed such danger to the girl who was quickly becoming an obsession.

"Believe me," he went on, "I know how you must feel, I know you've met many men like him in the past but you must be guided by me or this menace won't be ended, you have to realise, Angelo, that anger will bring failure," and the young man shuffled further back into his seat, his pique seeming to subside slightly.

Akan, who had been silent thus far and feeling a tad ruffled by the force of Angelo's hold, cleared her throat, diverting Bill's mind from the youth. As their eyes met she smiled pathetically and Bill recognised that all his attention should now be focused on her, Angelo was already in the bag.

"Can I ask you some questions that have been concerning me, Mr Sweet?" and she removed a scrap of paper from the pocket of her white dress. Angelo leaned over to look but the scribblings meant nothing to him, no one had ever bothered to teach him how to read properly.

"How certain are you that this man wants to hurt me, violate me, and how did you find out about it?"

The smile had now left her face and she was observing him ardently. Bill had anticipated this question and had already contrived a response.

"I know the man; I know him very well and he has confided in me, told me his intentions."

"So why don't you go to the police? Surely that would be the right thing to do?"

"He is a very powerful man, Akan, and very persuasive. He has friends in all walks of life, including the police and I would not be listened to, simply not listened to," he reiterated, "and when he'd found out that I'd gone to the police his desire for revenge would be unstoppable. He would do everything in his power to silence me and you would be completely at his mercy. I would be unable to provide any protection, nothing at all."

"I would!" the boy growled.

"You are becoming like a son to me Angelo and I say this to you as a father," he said as his head turned towards him, "your life has been rotten so far and I have no intention of letting that rot continue. This is not something that will be solved without cool thought; you are both in my safekeeping and even though I'm about to place you in danger I can see no other way out of this mess. I have to place you in this danger to get Akan away from it."

He calmly put out his hands towards them and they both reacted reciprocally to his gesture and they stayed like that for a while, a mutual bond growing between them.

"Tomorrow, at four-thirty in the afternoon, I will drive you both across to the hospital," he said, still holding their hands. "You, Angelo, will remain in the car and myself and Akan will go to the man's office. I will introduce you to him and then leave. You will sit opposite him and set down on the desk you will notice two glasses of juice. Not long after sitting down there will be a phone call and the man will go to the far end of the room to look for something; this will be your opportunity to swap the drinks around. It is essential you do this Akan as your drink will have a drug in it and his will not. When he returns he will speak into the phone and replace it, he will then raise his drink to his lips and invite you to copy him and you will both then drain your glasses. Almost immediately you will notice a change in his manner. He will become quiet and dreamlike. You will tell him sternly to stay seated and not move. He will do exactly as you say and then I want you to go to the window, there is only one in the office and you will see me waiting by my car. Don't move until you see me returning the wave then go back to your seat and wait for a knock at the door, it will be Angelo and myself."

Akan studied him feeling convinced that she was indeed safe in this man's care and Angelo studied him feeling that he was in the presence of greatness.

"Have you got all that?" he asked, releasing their hands and sitting back and they both intimated they had.

"Good, but I'll go over it all again and you can repeat it back to me. We have all day to get this right and if that's how long it takes then so be it." and he started from the beginning, knowing that one mistake would spell disaster for them all.

Chapter 12

The day was designed to reintroduce Stan to public transport and Cressy had organised it meticulously. The starting point was a bus journey then lunch followed by a train excursion and a light tea before returning to the house.

Unfortunately her plan was not to be enacted, at least not all of it, as the duty nurse found out when Cressy rang to inform her that the migraine had grown in intensity and she was going to have trouble making it downstairs let alone into work. But bad news for one can be good for another. As Charlie made his way to the house that morning he felt tired after racking his brains all night and failing to come up with a believable explanation for why he wanted to take them out for the day so when the nurse described his idea as a godsend, because Cressy was ill, his feeling of relief almost buckled his knees.

Stan and Barry were in their room both feeling excited and when Charlie walked in they were bubbling like schoolkids. After checking the book was safely in the sock the three of them departed the house and joined the throng in the street; the look of alarm appearing on Stan's face strengthening Charlie's resolve. When they arrived at the post office the teller was reluctant to hand over a blank cheque and called the postmaster but when Charlie explained the reason in detail the request was quickly granted and they left with an envelope securely housed in his inner jacket pocket.

Maybe

The auction began at three that afternoon enabling them to make a lazy journey and stop for lunch at the small welcoming pub near the bus station and they sat in the corner next to the pot-bellied stove.

"We could have a stove like this at the farm," Stan suggested, positioning his glass on the centre of the beer mat, "we could roast chestnuts on top of it," and Barry and Charlie smiled at the idea.

"And spuds," Barry proposed.

"Yes," Stan agreed, "and spuds," and Charlie imagined the cogs of Stan's interesting imagination whirring.

"And pork chops," he continued, his enthusiasm growing, "just think Barry, chestnuts, pork chops and spuds …"

"And a beer!" Barry added.

"Yep, and a beer, who could ask for anything more?" Barry nodded his head in agreement.

Charlie was delighted to see them both in such high spirits but, realising how devastated they would feel should the auction be a failure, decided to explain the rules.

"I bought a house once at auction," he began, "and looking back it seemed pretty straightforward," he took a sip of his pint, "let me tell you what happened," and they looked at him wide eyed, giving their full attention.

"The guide price for the farm, what they think it's more or less worth, is a hundred and twenty-five thousand. Now the winning bidder will have to pay ten per cent of that today which is why we've got this cheque," and he patted his jacket outside of the inner pocket. "The present owner will have set a reserve which is a price that he or she won't sell below and that's going to be around the asking price so if the bidding doesn't go above that reserve the auctioneer may not sell it."

"We'll just give 'em what they want, I'd rather be living in the farm than have a book in my sock."

"I know that, Stan, but we want to get it as cheaply as we can, don't we?"

"I just want to get it," he replied firmly.

"That's right," Charlie agreed, not wanting to labour the point, "and if it doesn't sell there's always the chance we can do a deal after the auction so don't worry too much about it," but Stan was becoming agitated, something that Barry noticed immediately and he thought it best to step in.

"You mustn't worry," he said kindly. "Charlie's looked into everything for us, he'll make sure nothing goes wrong; have a sip of your beer and take some deep breaths," and Stan complied, casting a thankful glance across the table at Charlie, who carried on.

"Okay then, if you're the successful bidder you have four weeks I think it is to pay the balance and then the farm is yours."

"I'll just pay for it today," Stan announced.

"I'm not sure if that can happen, Stan. I think there's legal stuff—"

"It can't be much of a problem, Charlie," he butted in, "as long as we have a piece of paper saying I paid who's selling it, we can buy it today, can't we?"

He thought about this for a while.

"I think a solicitor may have to register the place in your name and set up something called a deed of transfer, but we can ask them about that when we get there," and he finished his pint, "though what's a bit concerning is due to the lack of time we haven't had it surveyed, it could be falling apart and we haven't checked if there's any restrictions in the deeds, you know, whether people can walk through your garden or the neighbours have the right to drive over your land, stuff like that. I don't want us to act in haste and repent at leisure sort of thing."

"I'm not worried about any of that, Charlie, and I don't want you to worry either. If the place is falling apart then the money in the book can put it right and if a driver wants to drive over the land, well we can wave and be friendly."

Charlie looked askance at Barry who met him with a look of resignation as if to say, 'he's going to buy it Charlie no matter what you say'.

He reverted his gaze back to Stan and as their eyes met Stan chuckled, a large grin filling his face.

"It's going to be great!" and another chuckle bubbled up. "I've never been happier, not in my entire life," and right then and there Charlie realised he'd said enough. He'd just have to be as vigilant as he possibly could. He thought of mentioning his reservations over the mysterious former owner of the mansion but Barry's previous look of resignation persuaded him against it and instead he asked them both what they fancied for lunch.

"Is there any pork and spuds we can have?" asked Stan and Barry perused the menu.

"Well there's pork chops, chips and beans," he replied.

"That'll do, if they haven't got any spuds I s'pose we can have chips," and this time it was Barry and Charlie's turn to chuckle.

Chapter 13

As the three of them tucked into their lunch Bill Sweet was busy loading some of the items they would need into the boot of his car.

The anxiety he felt over what was about to happen was only partly diminished by the relief that would arise from its success. There were so many things that could go wrong he was giving little thought to the aftermath.

He had arranged for them to be in his office at three for a final run through and as he was about to re-enter the home his foot stopped on the first step of the flight as his stomach somersaulted in panic.

What if the statue won't take the weight?

The thought pounded on the inside of his skull like some mad thing trying to get out. He screwed his eyes up tightly.

"Think Bill, think," and then the idea rose in his mind like a blossoming flower and he turned around and headed back through the bus station to his car.

He needed to find an agricultural merchants and procure a seven-foot post and a sledgehammer.

Chapter 14

Charlie paid and they left the pub and made their way to his car. The hotel was situated in a small town, thirty miles away in the neighbouring county and after an uneventful journey they arrived in the main square an hour before the start time. He took note of the large number of vehicles parked up and the equally large number of people milling around and suspected this wasn't a usual occurrence for such a small place, the sale was going to be well attended.

They made for the hotel and walked between the two ornate pillars fronting it, up the steps and into the somewhat tired foyer. Heads turned as they made their way through and Charlie realised that three strangers, one being a black man, was provoking uneasy interest. He had become used to dubious glances and unperturbed he led them to the small table and requested a catalogue. The thin man passed him a thick pamphlet along with a paddle number and veiled sneer and Charlie turned and walked away from him without saying a word, Barry and Stan keeping close like pet lambs. Back in the square he spotted an empty bench and made a beeline for it then curiously opened the pamphlet to find details of the three properties along with their individual legal packs. He removed the relevant one and began to read, scrutinizing every line and he was pleased with what he found. No restrictive covenants were mentioned and a deed of transfer was included along with a land registry form necessary to record the new owner; Stan's wish to buy the farm immediately may not be an impossibility, he thought.

But there, in bold type at the end of the report, was the paragraph informing potential buyers that the identity of the mansion's previous owner would not be revealed until the sale had been completed. He scratched his head and eyed his two companions.

"Everything seem in order?" Barry asked, seeing Charlie's quizzical expression.

"Pretty much I think, Barry," he replied and then decided he had to tell them. "Only there's a bit in here about a derelict mansion that belongs to the farm and until it's sold the new owner won't be told who used to live there."

"Strange," Barry commented.

"I know, it's puzzling. It's almost as if they're warning people that they might not like who it was; if you buy it don't blame us 'cos we told you so, sort of thing."

"Does it say if they're alive or dead?" Barry asked.

"No, it doesn't."

"I'm not worried either way," Stan remarked. "They're not there anymore are they, Charlie?"

"No, they wouldn't be, it's just a bit bizarre that's all," and he inserted the pack back into the catalogue. "But if it's not worrying you I suppose it doesn't really matter," and he stood up and they followed suit.

"Might be someone famous," Stan suggested as they began walking back to the hotel, "might be someone on the telly."

"Maybe," Charlie answered, "but why would that stop them telling anyone?" and they re-entered the foyer and made their way to the ballroom to find somewhere to sit.

The huge room was filling fast and they were lucky to find three adjacent seats. There was a prodigious variety of people from farming types wearing wellingtons, dirty overalls and caps to those more gentrified clad in tweed, brogues and trilbies.

Charlie scanned the room and, seeing no other black faces, turned to Barry.

"At least the auctioneer won't be able to miss me," he whispered, looking at him askance.

"Why's that?" he asked, and Charlie lifted his finger up and rotated it around his face. It took Barry a while but he eventually got the point and tittered briefly.

Before long, the seating capacity had been filled and people were beginning to stand. The hubbub created by the crowd was becoming cacophonous and it masked the hiccups that Stan had unexpectedly developed and it wasn't until the appearance of the auctioneer and his staff, causing a halt to the commotion, that Charlie heard his temporary affliction.

"Go and get a glass of water or something, Stan," he said advisedly.

"No time!" he replied and his diaphragm spasmed loudly, "it's going to start."

"Then try and keep your mouth closed, God knows we're creating enough attention as it is," each hiccup ratcheting up his paranoia.

The auctioneer introduced himself then announced the order of the proceedings and placed a ream of papers in front of him; their intended target was to be the last of the three.

Using a splayed hand to draw an unruly mop of hair away from his face he asked the substantial audience to make any bids obvious by either raising their paddles or a copy of the auction catalogue and tension mounted as a freckle faced young man, who was standing in front of the podium, raised a picture of the first lot high above his head.

The absence of a sound system combined with the size of the room resulted in a hushed silence as those present concentrated on hearing. Following a description of the property he invited bids and the arm of a

MAYBE

besuited, middle-aged lady rose, a catalogue held within her attractively manicured hand. They were sat behind and their view was limited but Charlie immediately recognised from the cut of her clothes and intricately coiffured, jet black hair that this woman had money and meant business; although her voice didn't conform to her style and as she called out her bid Charlie had a feeling she'd made it the hard way.

"Two hundred thousand!" a good twenty below the guide price. The auctioneer roamed the room asking for more creating a swathe of paddles to be lifted and in seconds the bids had soared through two hundred and twenty thousand, rapidly approaching a quarter of a million. When two hundred and seventy was reached however, there was only two contenders, one of which being the middle-aged lady who had started the process and currently owned the highest bid.

All eyes were on her competitor; a large, ruddy faced individual who resided behind an expansive beard, his bulk squeezed awkwardly into one of the seats on the raised section overlooking the crowded dance floor. A dropped pin could have been heard as the room waited in noiseless anticipation of his response and Barry, out of the blue, sadly remembered the minute's silence afforded his wife and child on the morning of their funeral.

It was at this most inappropriate of moments that Stan felt something flop deep within him as an unleashed shudder, followed by a voluminous hiccup, erupted from his open mouth, the sound piercing the peace like some enormous dagger. It seemed as if the entire assemblage turned to look at them as one and Charlie, mortified, cringingly leant forward, his hand covering his face in an attempt to hide the embarrassment. Desperate to reintroduce the drama that he knew could result in the contestants overextending themselves, the auctioneer speedily asked the ruddy face for a further bid but the tension had relaxed, the moment had gone and the ruddy face shook his head regrettably.

There being no one else, Georgia became the new owner and as the gavel was dropped she turned to her equally well presented companion and whispered that the first nine holes were bagged, now for the back nine and the clubhouse.

During the long, solitary nights behind bars she had fantasised over one desire, one aim to achieve on her release. If the warders knew of the idea that was bouncing around the head of this most hated of prisoners they would have been sliding down the walls laughing, collapsing with hilarity, but to her it was the epitome of success, the proof of her worth and the antidote to her self-loathing. Georgia wanted to own a golf course and remarkably, on Saturday, 27th April, 1963, she was on the verge of achieving it. With the sound made by the instrument still reverberating in his ears the auctioneer moved closer to the spotter sat by his side.

"There was another five grand there at least if it wasn't for that twerp hiccupping," and he focused reproachfully on the little plump man who had now placed his hand firmly over his guilty mouth.

As that hardwood gavel was striking the softwood block, the door of Bill's office was pulled firmly shut and Akan and Angelo sat down at the table, nervously watching him.

Their youth had prevented them full access to the possible repercussions of what was about to happen and their complete confidence in his leadership had bolstered their resolve, purging any qualms and convincing them that the impending operation was nothing more than an honourable act.

"The gentleman with the unfortunate hiccups," boomed the auctioneer, "would you like my young assistant here to bring you a glass of water?" pointing at the freckle faced youngster.

Stan nodded affirmatively still clasping his hand over his mouth and the youth left the room, reappearing a minute later with a pint of water from the bar.

Charlie remained crouched forward, keeping his face buried in his hands and when he'd sensed the freckled face had arrived, delivered and departed, sat upright and removed them to behind his head, screwing his face in bewilderment.

"I told you to get a glass of water," he derided, vehemently, thankful that the crowd's attention had reverted to the new picture being held high.

"Well I've got one now, haven't I Charlie?" he replied, petulantly, sipping it carefully.

"Yes, I know that," the lingering embarrassment raising his voice too high, "but if you'd got one when I said …" and he paused, realising he was banging his head up against a brick wall.

"Oh, never mind, Stan, just try and control yourself," and he took another sip.

"I can't help it, Charlie," he moaned, ruefully. "I'm excited and these things happen when I get excited," and he looked past him to Barry. "Don't they, Barry? You tell him."

But Barry didn't hear the question for out of nowhere she appeared, the perfectly applied black olive make-up accentuating her handsome features and her suit, stylish and chic.

His eyes enlarged as she bent down beside Stan and pulling his head gently towards her, whispered in his ear.

"You saved me a few quid there darlin,' there's free beers behind the bar for you and your mates after this load of bollocks is over," and she tapped his chubby cheek and returned to her seat.

The auctioneer hurled out the details of the second lot and once again the babble in the room subsided.

As he was about to commence Bill welcomed them and, like the day before, he held out his hands which they eagerly grasped.

He confirmed their continuing willingness to assist in the doctor's removal and he once again began to conduct a dress rehearsal, determined to leave no stone unturned.

"So who will start me at, let's say, two hundred and twenty thousand?" but the players in this game remained motionless; no paddles were raised, no offers were shouted.

This second property consisting of a larger farmhouse, three considerable barns and fifty seven acres was situated to the north of the previous lot but the only two flat fields were small and marshy and the rest of the land harboured swathes of gorse and became increasingly steep negating anything arable and even making stock farming difficult; but everything has its price and the talented auctioneer began to prod and tease, urging someone for a starting value.

"Come on now, ladies and gentlemen," he cajoled. "Don't forget they're not making land anymore, who'll start me at two hundred thousand then?" but he was staring at statues.

"A hundred and eighty, it has to be worth that," he cried plaintively and then ruddy face, who knew the true value of the place, shouted "ninety-five!" A few from the crowd gasped at his brassiness and his bid was ignored, the lot going unsold.

If a lot is sold or not, the gavel still comes down and when, at that exact moment, it met the block, thirty miles away a man and his two young cohorts were leaving a children's home next to a park, carrying the remaining, concealed assortment of implements and apparatus on an assignment that they all now believed to be a mercy killing: For when Angelo, a few minutes before, suggested they should sever the doctor's testicles while they were at it, Bill had reminded him of his previous day's words, that anger would bring failure and this was nothing about revenge or getting even and all about the removal of a monster who could only be neutralised by assassination.

The man was dangerously sick and there was nothing that the medical community, or any curative community come to that, had in their therapeutic arsenal to cure him.

Bill turned the ignition key and they sat back, satisfied in their individual comprehension, that what was about to happen was correct and wholly justifiable.

Georgia dug her elbow gently into the side of her male associate as freckle face held up the picture of the third and final lot.

"Right, Johnny," she said quietly, leaning close as she had with Stan, "now let's go for the full eighteen," and with a deft, almost unseen movement, she brushed her hand over his buttoned fly and the electric charge it generated reminded him of the reason why he was spending all of this money on two farmsteads to create a golf course … it was the siren sat next to him. If the money pit is bottomless and the desire strong enough, no matter what the cost the desire will be dealt with. This wobbly and weakly lord of the realm had fallen head over heels from the moment they were introduced at the somewhat inelegant and bawdy 'Murray's cabaret club' in London's Soho and her £100 a night 'all in' charge seemed a pittance when he considered what it had purchased.

Lord Johnny had visited heaven on that night and continued to do so frequently during their following three-month acquaintance resulting in a belief that should he satisfy her wish to become the part owner of the most prestigious golf course in the South of England she would remain his forever.

Meanwhile, Charlie and the boys straightened up as one. Barry ran his fingers through his hair and centred his tie, Charlie repositioned the paddle in his hand and Stan, using his other foot, made sure the book was safely in the sock.

The crowd had once again hushed as the auctioneer began to read out the details of the final lot.

"Thank you, ladies and gentlemen, we now come to the last property in today's sale, a twenty-three acre holding surrounded by its own predominantly flat pastures. I'm sure those interested have taken note of the mansion type building above the farmhouse and as is highlighted in the brochure, the previous owner of this now derelict edifice will be revealed privately to the successful bidder. Now who will start me at—" then Barry stood up and raised his hand, he had been thinking long and hard and simply couldn't help himself.

"Is that a bid, sir?" the auctioneer enquired, "because if it is there's no need to stand up."

"No," he replied, aware he was suddenly on stage, "it's this mysterious owner you refer to; I'm concerned you're not willing to reveal who it is until it's sold."

Many in the crowd now turned to the podium, after all, Barry was asking a question that the silent majority also wanted answering.

"I know this is an unusual situation, sir, but it is what it is. The owners have asked us to proceed on this basis and the buyer will be purchasing on this basis and if anyone feels uncomfortable then they should refrain from bidding." He let everyone dwell on this for a moment then began again. "Now who will start me at a hundred and twenty-five thousand?" and Charlie tapped Barry's leg as if to say well done and lightly held Stan's hand.

"I don't think you should bid on it, Stan, something doesn't feel right."

"I have to Charlie," he whispered forcefully. "I can't go back to that town and I don't want to go back to the hospital for Barry's sake, he'll get stutionised!"

"But there'll be other sales, Stan," ignoring the mispronunciation, "straightforward ones with no weird strings attached."

Maybe

"Please, Charlie," he pleaded, "please let me buy it," and a full, bulbous teardrop appeared in the corner of his left eye. Charlie was a sucker for two things, spicy curry and lachryma, unable to resist when confronted with either and as ruddy face raised his paddle at a hundred and twenty-five Charlie raised his to increase it to a hundred and thirty and the bidding carried on upwards in increments of five thousand until it reached a hundred and eighty and the ruddy face dropped his paddle, shaking his head in defeat.

Barry looked over at Stan and winked warmly at him; it had to be theirs now even though he would be paying more than anticipated. No other offers were being made and the last of the competition had dropped out.

"Are there any advances on one hundred and eighty thousand?" the auctioneer called, both his and his spotters' eyes darting around the audience. "In that case I have a hundred and eighty once," his eyes continuing to search for further interest, "one hundred and eighty twice," and Charlie felt an excitement stir in his stomach unlike anything he'd experienced before, "one eighty for the third and last time," and Stan slowly slithered, as if poured, from his chair and onto the floor; a physical response to an overwhelming, mental overload, but as the gavel was raised a voice from in front of them, unkind and ungenerous, boomed out,

"Two hundred thousand!"

The auctioneer's gaze now turned to Georgia, her painted face deadly serious and he found himself having to look away as he saw a warped determination in her eyes that for some reason made him feel uneasy. Charlie put his hand on Stan's shoulder, which was now to the right of his knee and leaned downwards.

"Stan, it's two hundred thousand, it's too much, we need to wait for another sale."

"Keep going," he replied steadfastly remaining sat on the floor, "just keep going."

Charlie raised his paddle.

"Two hundred and one," he announced unwillingly.

"Two hundred and fifty!" Georgia almost shouted, causing some present to gasp in disbelief, including the gentleman sat by her side.

Charlie again leaned downwards.

"Stan, she's bid a quarter of a million, it's too much," his voice tremulous, "way too much, we can't bid anymore, it's madness!"

"Keep going," he said authoritatively, a sureness and certainty to his words and Charlie loosened Stan's shoulder and began to shake his head in disbelief.

"I can't, Stan, it's the wrong thing to do, I couldn't live with myself."

"Then pass me the stick," and Stan straightened his legs, raised himself up and sat back on the seat.

"It's my decision, Charlie, I've listened to your advice and it's my decision, you have nothing to blame yourself for," and Charlie reluctantly passed him the paddle.

The spectacle had the crowd enthralled and the man on the podium now realised that this was one of those rare moments where two parties, as desperate as each other to succeed, could drive his commission into the stratosphere … then his common sense made an entrance as he eyed the forlorn figure, odd Stan, the hiccuper. A winning bid meant nothing if it wasn't financially supported.

"I'd just like to remind everyone that there are penalties for unsubstantiated bids and please let me remind you, ladies and gentlemen that ten per cent of the purchase price is payable immediately with the balance in twenty-eight days."

Everyone knew why the warning had been made and to whom it was being directed, other than one.

"What does he mean, Charlie?" that one asked his friend, "all that was written in that book, wasn't it?"

"He doesn't think you've got the money, Stan, he doesn't think you can afford it," he said uneasily.

He thought about this momentarily then smartly stood up and began walking down the central aisle leading toward the podium. As he arrived, he bent down and retrieved the post office book from his sock and gave it to the freckle faced youth, open at the relevant page.

"Could you pass this to him please?" and the youngster placed the picture he was holding on the floor, took the book and handed it up to the auctioneer who, after putting on his reading glasses, flicked through it and passed it back.

He looked at Stan and his face reddened. "Thank you," he said softly.

Stan nodded, reinserted it into his sock, turned and began to walk slowly back up the aisle.

As he neared Georgia he came to a halt and looked deeply into her eyes.

She stared back, her countenance completely altered from when she'd offered the free beer; that venom that always lingered below the surface rising and making her seem fierce.

He grinned at her, an innocent and genuine expression, designed to achieve nothing, then raised his paddle as high as he could, his small frame expanding to the maximum.

"Three hundred thousand!" he roared and some, indeed most of the crowd began to applaud, completely engrossed by the sheer theatre.

"Don't bid another penny, Georgia," Johnny hissed, a wave of financial realism breaking out and overpowering his obsession for her. "I mean it, we'll find some other way, but don't bid another penny."

None of his words registered with her, she was like a hawk fully focused on its prey and nothing was going to get in her way. As Stan arrived at his seat and was about to lower himself into it, again, her voice reverberated around the hall.

"Three hundred and fifty thousand!"

Stan stood rooted to the spot. He felt enclosed in some sort of revolving apparatus that wouldn't let him get off, as if a persistent fly was constantly landing on him no matter how much he swatted and swished it.

Through his increasing despair he could see Charlie and Barry's mouths moving. "Leave it, Stan, let it go, there'll be more, there'll be another farm," but it was this one he wanted because this one represented everything that was missing from his life … happiness. It was within touching distance and he twisted on his feet to face the podium and ignoring the enthralled faces and the pleas from his friends, lifted the paddle once more. But before he could speak a different purposeful voice rang out.

"I want you to dismiss that last bid." The tone was strong and urgent and emanating from the man sat next to Georgia.

"I am financially backing the lady who made it and I am withdrawing my support."

Stan's paddle dropped as Georgia's hand lifted and she struck her benefactor savagely, the ring he had recently bought her drawing blood.

"You fucking worthless shit!" She was seething with anger. "You'll regret this," and she pointed at him menacingly, "mark my words, you'll regret this," and barging into anyone who got in her way she marched out of the room, through the foyer and into the darkening afternoon, methods of revenge already beginning to develop.

The place was now in uproar and the auctioneer banged his gavel ferociously to regain some order. Voices began to quieten and when the noise reached an acceptable level he returned to the proceedings. Although a wily character he was a fair minded individual and like everyone who came into contact with Stan, realised that the little fellow was genuine with a generous spirit and he decided to carry on the sale in an equitable way.

"Ladies and gentlemen, can I apologise for the unusual occurrences and behaviour you have just witnessed, but now that the gentleman," and he looked at where Lord Johnny had been sitting and noticed that he had also departed, "now that the gentleman who was sat in one of those vacant seats there," he composed himself, "now that the gentleman has decided not to proceed I think we should return to where we were before they

Maybe

entered," and there was a murmur of agreement in favour of this reasonable way forward.

"So the bid is one hundred and eighty thousand," then he remembered the name on the post office book, "and it's with Mr Heart there up on my right."

He paused and shuffled some of his papers aimlessly.

"Any advance on a hundred and eighty thousand?" but this time he wasn't scouring the crowd so intently. "In that case it's one eighty once," and a little squeak came from Stan's throat as if he was trying hard to stop something larger escaping. "One hundred and eighty twice," and another little squeak, this time with more volume and intensity as if that something inside was becoming more restless and impatient. "One hundred and eighty for the third and final time," Charlie grabbed him around the shoulders. "Sold to Mr Heart, well done sir!" but he couldn't hold him and Stan ran up and down the aisle, waving the paddle high above his head, squawking like a chicken who'd laid a big one, the people patting him on the back and some managing to shake his hand.

Fifty yards away in the square, Lord Johnny had managed to catch up with her; the financials had been satisfied and the lust was now re-emerging. She'd had a chance to cool down and weigh up the situation and when he called out her name she continued the fast pace although secretly wishing to be caught and as he eventually placed his hand on her shoulder and turned her around she feigned resentment, not looking him in the eye.

The lord was a big player in what was known as the Cyprian set: an informal group of silver spooners and low ranking politicians who had regular soirees in and around Soho. His family were amongst the wealthiest in the home counties although Johnny's personal wealth had been severely diminished by his unfortunate lack of gambling success and general profligate lifestyle. Their first meeting had been regarded as highly amusing by the rest of the members due to his offer of marriage just two hours after being introduced. He was intoxicated by her, adored the streak of menace and dangerous air, but his fixation had wavered back there when he'd refused to buy the second farm, their intended other half of the course and clubhouse and she was very unhappy about that, very unhappy indeed.

"You've let me down, Johnny," she said indignantly, her eyes focused on the floor, "you made promises and you let me down," her voice wavering as she tried to portray contempt.

He thought she looked gorgeous in the glow of the streetlamp and could have ripped off her clothes there and then.

"It was too much money, Georgie," inexplicably, he refused to call her Georgia, "it'll cost a small fortune to develop without paying God knows what for the farms."

She still refused to make eye contact and he was desperate to placate her.

"Look, we've one in the bag, I've paid the deposit on the way out; I'll find another way to get what we want, don't worry, perhaps they'll sell us the land we need, that chap bidding against us didn't seem very bright."

She briefly looked up at him and their eyes met.

"Please Georgie, forgive me," and he lowered his head to the right, " please forgive little Johnny."

He sensed her mood was cooling as she glanced up and held the look a little longer.

"How do you know he bought it, you didn't stay to find out?"

"Well no," he stammered, "but he must have; anyway, I was more concerned with finding you."

"You should have stayed and found out who he was, we could have done some homework."

She ended the charade, after all, she reasoned, no point in killing the golden goose.

"I can find out all about him, Georgie, you know that, I'll know how big his dick is by Friday."

425

Maybe

She now stared him full in the face.

"If it's as big as yours you might have some competition, Johnny, you know I like them big," and he clenched his teeth to stop his jaw dropping.

He loved it when she talked dirty.

Chapter 15

The rain was getting heavier as they drove, the weary wipers only just managing to keep the screen clear. There were several parking areas that served the institution but the only one that was going to serve Bill's purpose was a little used, remote spot at the far end of the hospital, situated directly outside of the doctor's office.

At 4.50 pm Bill steered his car and occupants into a concealed bay, pulled on the handbrake and heaved a deep, uneasy sigh. If all went to plan his years of collusion with a monstrous paedophile would be over along with the fear of being revealed a murderer.

"You need to lie in the footwell, Angelo, and cover yourself with the blanket. Don't move until I get back."

"You've told me a hundred times," he replied irately.

"I just don't want there to be any mistakes," he stated, almost apologetically and then he regarded Akan, the main player and the one most at risk. He was pleased that she seemed at ease and unanxious.

"Are you ready, Akan?" Bill enquired. She nodded her head and they exited the car.

Remaining inconspicuous was a prerequisite for success and, pulling the hoods of their raincoats tight, began making their way to the office. Fortuitously, they were in the quietest section of the hospital, housing only the doctor's wing and laundry and had encountered no one as they reached the door. As usual, Bill knocked three times and while he was waiting for a response felt a small hand tighten around his fingers. He tilted his head and saw the beauty in her face that far outshone the beautiless scar and she was smiling at him, an expression of comfort as if she was aware of his apprehension. Instantly Bill knew that should everything go wrong he was going to kill the doctor anyway and hang the consequences. A paternal instinct had emerged from a great depth, overwhelming that of self-preservation.

Tim Richards opened the door and ushered them in, surreptitiously checking the corridor before closing it behind them.

"Bang on time, Mr Sweet," he announced, then in a whisper. "The one and only one virtue you possess, your punctuality."

Bill's loathing of this man had long ago reached the top rung of the ladder and the taunt went straight over his head.

"And who do we have here?" and he looked down at the child, beaming delightedly.

"This is Akan Dotse, Dr Richards." She raised her hand and he, rather than shake it, kissed it.

"Far more gracious," he propounded, "let me take your coat." As he removed her wet rain coat his eyes lit up at the sight of her attire.

"A fan of white, Akan," he observed and a deviant sneer arose on his face, a look Bill had witnessed many times when introducing a new one. The doctor asked her to sit. He hung the raincoat on the stand, an occasional drip landing on the floor. "Typical, it was full sun this morning, wish I hadn't walked in," he mused. "Anyway, thank you Mr Sweet, your presence is no longer required," he barked harshly sitting opposite her.

"I'd like to have a little more time than usual with this young lady so if you returned in say … two hours?" he said as if asking a question.

"Of course," Bill complied. "I'll come back at seven," and he lifted his hood and turned to leave.

"Oh, before I go, can I quickly check something on the wheelchair, I assume I'll need it?" and before he could answer Bill had walked across to the wheelchair which was parked next to the settee behind the statue.

"Your assumption is correct, what's the problem?" he asked, craning his neck to see.

"I thought I felt it wobbling the last time I used it, just remembered," and he removed his coat, threw it on the settee and began pushing and pulling the contraption pretending to check his apparent suspicion; then bending down he inspected the wheels. "Yes, here it is, this one needs tightening," and he straightened himself, redressed and pushed the wheelchair toward the door. "I'll have it sorted out before I get back." He leant awkwardly across it to open the door to leave, his heart thumping like a piston in the confines of his chest.

His back-up plan appeared to have worked and he shot off as fast as possible to the laundry where the internal phone hung on the wall, just inside the entrance doors, chosen because the likelihood of being overheard was remote. He positioned the chair against the wall outside the doors and pushed the one to the left which refused to move; he quickly tried the other and it too wouldn't open. Bill cupped his hands around his face and peered in through the circular glass panels and the place was in darkness.

The laundry closed at midday on a Wednesday, something that Bill had overlooked. Mistake number one. In panic, he wrapped his head in his hands then suddenly raised them.

"You idiot, you bloody idiot!" he scolded himself, but not for long. Bill grabbed the handles of the wheelchair and set off again; he had to find another phone to provide the diversion, allowing Akan to switch the drinks.

MAYBE

She sat there looking incredulously at the two plastic beakers he had placed on the table, his black hers white.

How was she going to swap the drinks? He would need to be blind not to realise his beaker had changed colour.

Mistake number two.

She concentrated hard, every hitch has a fix. A bud of an idea began to form in her mind but if the phone didn't ring soon it wouldn't matter; the man sat opposite her was pointing at the cup.

"Before we start the interview why don't you have a drink, my dear, there's a small amount of medicine in there that will put you at ease, help you relax," and he smiled at her, a dead smile, one he used from recollection not kindness.

She stretched her arm and grasped the beaker, her mind racing; Mr Sweet had said the phone would ring before he mentioned the drinks. Closing her eyes her memory conjured up a picture of her father, holding her tightly, his comforting words cocooning her in their security.

"You are bound for the stars, Obabaa, and I will always be with you on your quest to reach them."

She squeezed them ever tighter and she was no longer sat on that hard chair but on her papa's soft lap, he was right there with her and when she opened them the doctor had stopped smiling and was glaring at her acerbically.

"Is everything all right, my dear, are you in some sort of pain?"

"No, Dr Richards, I am in no pain," and she drew the beaker towards her. With the perceived arrival of her father came a strengthening of her resolve and although Mr Sweet's description of the man's wickedness was compelling and the mention of a wheelchair suspicious, the powerful sense of justice that had been instilled in her demanded definitive proof of his guilt and she looked down at the beaker then to him.

"Will you need to examine me?" she said coyly, a slight grin beginning to emerge.

"Of course, Akan," he responded, tightening from a jolt of pleasure.

A wave of embarrassment washed over her as she realised her imagined father was going to hear what she was about to say but she knew he would know, knew he would understand what she was trying to do.

"Well perhaps we could examine each other, doctor?" she cooed and that jolt became a thunderbolt and his eyes became windows into his very soul and she could see corruption in there and abnormal immorality and as he stood and walked around the desk, unbuttoning his fly, she had to bite hard to stop herself screaming. The proof was in front of her.

"I think that we can perhaps dispense with the drinks, my dear," he spoke in a lustful tone, as his right hand reached down into his underpants, "I think you might enjoy it as much as me."

Then, like Stan's hiccup, the sound ruined the moment.

Bill's stomach turned over as he thought of what might be happening to her.

He knew of another phone, in the short stay ward at the far end of the block, but unlike the laundry room, it was in the office and he couldn't risk being overheard. There was only one thing for it, he had to enact the back-up plan and leaving the wheelchair where it was, began to retrace his steps to the doctor's office.

The urgent rapping on the door stopped Tim Richards in his tracks and he removed his hand and re-buttoned himself.

Who could that possibly be? He guessed that all of the admin staff would have left some time ago and nursing personnel would have rang rather than turn up in person.

"Excuse me, my dear," he said hesitantly, not looking at her and walked to the door that was still being feverishly knocked. "Wait a minute! Wait a minute!" and he tentatively unlocked the door and pulled it partially open.

"Bill, what the hell do you want?" and Akan, realising that this was maybe her only chance, stretched across, raised his beaker and emptied the contents into her mouth, then in a deft movement, emptied the liquid from her beaker into it and, placing her mouth over the top, refilled hers by simply parting her lips.

"I'm sorry, doctor," Bill replied breathlessly, "my car keys, I can't find them, I must have dropped them in your office somewhere."

"Is it really necessary you have them now?" he asked with annoyance, still holding the door and barring his way, then realising it was the only way to get rid of him, acquiesced and stepped back to let him in.

He now saw the opposing colours of the beakers too and his expression turned to one of horror as he realised the predicament Akan was in, but recognising his alarm, she lifted the white beaker and, for his eyes only, winked and gently sipped and he realised that she must have found a way.

"Hello, Akan, silly me," he shrugged, the look on his face now one of relief, "I think I've left my car keys here," then looking at the doctor but for Akan's ears, "I would have rang to ask you to take a look but I couldn't find a phone," and he walked around the statue to the settee, purposefully looking around, ostensibly searching for the keys.

The doctor remained by the door, more than displeased at the intrusion and Bill turned sideways to them and fell to his knees, his right side out of the doctor's line of sight and as he strained to look underneath Bill eased the keys out of his right coat pocket and, grasping them firmly in his hand, thrust his arm upwards.

"I thought so," he declared, feigning delight, "must have fallen out when I was checking the wheelchair," and he held them up in front of him, admiringly.

"Oh good," the doctor remarked, opening the door, anxious for him to go. "Now perhaps you'll leave us alone, Mr Sweet, this young lady and I have much to attend to," and Bill raised his hand and pocketed the keys.

"I know, I'm sorry to have intruded," and he glanced across at Akan but she was stoically looking forward, seemingly oblivious to the conversation and he felt that oddly, she too wanted him to be out of there.

"I'll be back at seven then," Bill said weakly as he walked past the doctor who, with an angry flourish, slammed the door behind him and turned the key firmly to lock it, brushing the nape of her neck seductively as he returned to his seat.

She hadn't consciously been ignoring Bill but simply taken advantage of the interlude to work out her next move. Her contrived compliance with his perversion was necessary to prove his guilt but it had left her with a problem: he now believed she was agreeable and willing and that the drug was now maybe unnecessary. However, as Bill had walked out of the room she'd heard a faint noise like a breeze through a tree and she recognised that it was her father's voice once again prompting her, helping her in her gravest moment.

"Remember Ruby's words," it whispered, "think deep," and, concentrating hard, Ruby's words had come to her.

"He'd love me to flatter him, every man loves flattery, they'll do anything for you and it makes you feel in charge and that helped until I realised what I was in charge of."

She looked at him sitting there like some twisted emperor, full of pomposity and arrogance and an anger rose up so strong it made her feel mighty and vengeful but another's words, those of Bill Sweet, now rang in her ears.

"Anger will bring failure," and she calmed herself, her hand moving to the beaker and her deep, penetrating voice floated across the desk making the doctor believe they were enveloped in sex.

"It was a pity Mr Sweet came when he did. I think I was about to be pleasantly shocked."

A shiver of lust surged through his loins and he once again moved around the desk and stood in front of her, beginning to unzip himself.

"Let's start again, shall we?" he asked, his voice trembling. "Carry on where we left off?" but she stopped him by raising the palm of her hand.

"Before we do I want you to indulge me, doctor," and she raised the white beaker. "It is a custom of those who came before me to drink a toast before an event that will bring great danger or great pleasure. Let us both drink to the latter," and she looked at his drink and motioned him to raise it. He complied and they simultaneously lifted their cups.

"Woo, woo, *w'ani awu, ollman*," (shame on you, old man) she said under her breath and they drained their drinks in unison, Bill's previous mistakes now reversed.

His heart was racing as he made his way back along the deserted corridor, the dull light from the bulkhead lamps casting long shadows as he passed.

Grabbing the wheelchair, Bill headed out of the hospital toward the car park, his mind focused on the next part of the plan as he walked into the cold evening air. The area was completely unlit, a few lights from within the hospital just enabling him to navigate back to the car and he brought it to a halt, pressed on the brakes and opened the rear passenger door.

"Angelo," he said urgently, "are you ready?" but there was no reply.

"Angelo!" he said more loudly and leaned further into the car but there was no sign, Angelo had gone.

"Jesus Christ," Bill said to himself, "this is all going wrong," and he gently pushed the door shut and began to scan the car park, praying there was a simple explanation for his disappearance.

"I'm here," a voice, stark and severe from out of the darkness and Bill strained to ascertain its direction.

"Angelo, is that you?" he asked, loud enough for the ears of the voice but quiet enough for anyone else's.

"Yeah," came the reply from above. Bill looked into the tree and just managed to make out the shape above him.

"What are you doing up there for God's sake, I told you to wait in the car."

"Needed to go up," he replied in a monotone.

"Well come on down now, we need to wait for the signal."

"I'll wait up here," he said defiantly, "see more," and Bill was so relieved in finding the boy that he decided to leave it at that and knelt down beside the car.

The window of the office was twenty yards or more to the side of them, a glimmer of light barely visible behind the closed blind. When Akan was certain the doctor was under the influence she was to open the blind and wave to them and they both peered hard through the gloom concentrating on the window, waiting for their cue.

He brushed the back of his hand lightly over his mouth as they placed the beakers down on the desk. A curious expression came on his face in response to the high pitched tone that had suddenly become apparent in his left ear. He looked around to try and determine its source but realised the noise was coming from within and he exhaled heavily as the noise departed the left and now appeared in the right. The sound acted like a weight, inducing his head to tilt in the direction of the tone, then it dramatically stopped and he looked straight ahead, wide eyed, his self-awareness diminishing.

An overwhelming desire for liquid now crashed in and he grasped his throat as if choking himself. Bill had told her that a sure sign of the drug working was the victim craving water and she moved toward him.

"Thirsty?" she asked brusquely, having no sympathy for the man.

"Yes, yes," he moaned, "need a drink," and he tried to reach the beaker but was unable to move his arm.

"Stay where you are, I'll do it," she commanded and standing up realised that her father had left her, his help was no longer needed.

Maybe

Akan took the beaker across to the steel sink and before filling it, poured the powder carefully from the sachet that Bill had given her. He hadn't been sure if the dose that the doctor had administered was sufficient for an adult and knowing he'd need more fluid, had prepared in advance.

She returned and held the receptacle to his lips and he drank eagerly then his head lurched forward onto his chest.

Akan slapped his face unnecessarily hard and he groaned, stupefied, then with force she cupped her hand under his chin and lifter his head.

"Can you hear me?" she asked loudly, "can you see me?"

His eyes rolled and she again let his head fall forward. The plan was working. She walked over to the window, squinted her eyes and, just making out the outline, waved her hand then returned to the desk. Akan looked at the figure in front of her, slumped like a dropped puppet and she extended her arm to once again cup her hand under his chin.

"Why do you do it, Dr Richards, tell me, why do you do it?" and she could see in his flickering eyes that there was a grain of comprehension. Through his jumbled thoughts he knew what she was referring to and he opened his mouth slowly as if his jaws were clamped by springs and the reply left his arid mouth like his words were being forced through a ringer.

"Because they like it!" he gasped.

She continued lifting his head although every ounce of her self-preservation was screaming at her, "Run! Run, Akan, get away from the beast!"

"So that's how you've explained it to yourself?" she said, her disbelief turning the sentence into a question, "you've made yourself believe these children, these loneliest of children, enjoy you betraying them? Breaking them? Hurting them for the rest of their lives like my friend Ruby?"

Though as insightful as Akan was, not even her perception came near to understanding the enormity of what resided within him. He was infected by something that had infiltrated the root on which his very being rested, his sole reason for being alive and to rid him of it was impossible. This something had countless tendrils that controlled his every cerebral function. He was as much a slave to it as the drunk was to the sauce.

Then she remembered the way Bill had explained his viewpoint; that the doctor was some sort of messenger and it was the sender of that message who was the culprit; and he'd said that this old saying stated that the messenger shouldn't be hurt because even if you didn't like what he'd delivered the messenger shouldn't be shot. But in the doctor's case and all those like him, you could only do something about that communique if you did indeed shoot the courier, because they themselves were the culprit and the message was too imbedded in their hearts. She released his head and again it dropped.

A deep sadness enveloped her as she imagined what this man must have put innocent children through and she placed her arms over each other, lowered her head onto them and began to whimper. She felt exhausted, as if she was buckling under the strain of carrying a hundred broken hearts and then his eyes began to slowly open and they were almost vampire black, the pupils hugely dilated from the drug, filling all but a thin white border of the socket. Through the fug he could see the top of her head, the tight corn row braid laying limp to the side and a vague apprehension, a cerebration that dwelt below and beneath began howling at him.

"There's peril ahead! You're in jeopardy!" and his eyes focused on the braid and the howling told him what to do.

"Grab it, Mr Richards, she's going to do you, grab it!" and his eyes opened wider still, their thin white circumference now completely covered by the black.

They both recognised the signal and as he wheeled the chair to the rear of the car Angelo descended from the tree and sat squarely in it, pulling his hood tightly up to conceal his face. Bill transferred the paraphernalia in the boot to the underside of the chair and then carried the fence post and sledgehammer briskly across the wet grass and placed them underneath the office window.

He returned, closed the boot lid and released the wheelchair's brake. As they approached the doors leading into the hospital Angelo straightened his legs and Bill pushed him through, going so fast that they had travelled almost halfway up the first corridor before hearing the door slam.

He slowed down, had to remain calm and in control.

Thankfully the place was still deserted but he knew someone may appear at any time and they couldn't raise suspicions.

As they arrived at the doctor's door Bill was becoming exultant. Beyond it was his salvation, his deliverance from years of torment and as he stretched over Angelo and knocked upon it he envisaged the worm that had made that stain in the potato wriggling and squirming as its lifeblood began to drain away.

The knocking further galvanised the doctor and as Akan lifted her head in response to the sound he somehow found the strength to lift his arm and thrust it forward, grabbing the thick braid in his hand. He yanked her head around. She was now staring at him full in the face, his pitch dark eyes sinister and repellent. His mouth slowly opened as the knocking intensified and he took a shallow breath, about to speak, but she caught hold of his hand to counteract the pressure and placed her other hand over his lips.

"Let me go, Dr Richards," she demanded compellingly, "shame is worth than death," and she felt his hand loosen its grip slightly and, taking her chance, pulled away from him and dug her pointed fingers, as hard as she could, into those menacing, inky pools. Instinctively covering his face, she sprang from the chair and dextrously turned the key allowing them both entry.

Angelo exploded from the wheelchair and flung himself at the doctor, bending his right arm around the man's neck and forcing his left hand into his throat stopping the oxygen supply.

Akan rushed over in an attempt to stop the assault but Bill pulled her away.

"You know we have to do this, Akan," he said sternly, then looking at the boy, "as soon as he faints you release him, understood?" but Angelo failed to answer. "I mean it!" he said harshly. "When he goes limp you let him go!" and this time he answered with the merest of head movements.

Bill dramatically dropped to his knees in front of her.

"Akan, I've decided I don't want you to see what we're about to do, I want you to go back to the car and wait for us there," he said pleadingly, but she stayed still, looking down at him.

"I am sorry for trying to stop him, Mr Sweet. I was shocked, it was a reflex," and she moved away from him and stood next to Angelo, pushing her hand hard on top of his to increase the pressure.

"I will help you now," she said quietly, "it is the only way."

Chapter 16

The three of them were in a small room of the hotel with the tousle haired auctioneer, their delight increasing with his every word.

"It's an unusual request but if the legalities fail and you're prepared to sign a disclaimer to forego the ten percent deposit, I see no reason for not giving you the keys today."

Stan clasped his hands gleefully then raised them, shaking his fists as if he wanted rid of them.

"But I must advise you … no," he corrected himself, "I must warn you, that should problems arise that negate the sale then you will vacate the property, return the key and pay the eighteen thousand deposit with no recourse to appeal. I would prefer it if you allowed the sale to proceed in the usual way but you require immediate access and this is the only way we can achieve that."

He realised the whole situation was unorthodox but he knew all bases had been covered and he'd started to become fond of the characters he was dealing with and was going the extra mile.

The freckle faced boy entered the room and passed the contract to his boss who scanned through it then passed it to Charlie. Charlie read it thoroughly and, satisfying himself that all was in order, passed it to Stan.

"Are you happy with it, Charlie?" he asked, ignoring the form.

"Yes I am," he replied and then realising Stan's inability to decipher it, took it back and read through everything out loud. Stan's attention began to waver causing his eyes to wander around the room then Charlie completed the task.

"That sounds good, let's go!" he said eagerly and made to stand up but Barry, who had been listening, fascinated by it all, placed a hand on his leg.

"I think you might have to sign it, Stan," he said kindly and Stan sat back, a little disconcerted.

"Thank you," the auctioneer uttered, a grateful smile appearing as he caught Barry's eye and he passed over a pen, motioning for him to sign.

Stan scrawled his initials where instructed and slid the form back and the man placed it in the desk drawer from whence he grabbed a large skeleton key which he dropped in the little man's hand.

"That fits all the locks," he said, "including the door to the mansion," then all of a sudden he raised his index finger. "The mansion," he repeated and moved the finger to his cheek, "now there's a problem, I can only divulge the identity of the previous owner once the sale has been finalised."

"We don't mind," cried Stan, "we don't care, do we, Barry?" and Barry shrugged non-commitally, "we don't care if we never know," Stan added.

"Well the beneficiaries have instructed me to inform the new owners, so I'll write to you in due course once the sale is completed, yes, that'll solve the problem," and the auctioneer, happy with the resolution, crossed his arms in front of him.

The meeting concluded with Stan handing over a cheque for the full amount and the freckled face holding the door open for them to depart.

"I'm sorry if things went a bit awry in there today," the auctioneer said finally as they prepared to depart. "I've never experienced anything like it before, but I want you to rest assured," and he placed a friendly hand on Stan's shoulder, "you have bought yourself a lovely property, Mr

Heart," he said to him genuinely. "I knew the lady occupant very well and she had many joyful years living there," and they left the hotel and made their way to the car in high spirits, though mildly stunned by the events of the day.

Charlie drove faster than normal as he had to be back at the hospital later that evening to work a nightshift. They were beginning to lose the light and he was keen not to arrive in darkness so the precise directions in the particulars proved invaluable. They stopped for provisions on the way and finally entered the village, drove past the pub and he steered carefully up the long approach with the sun just setting. As they rounded the final bend the farmhouse appeared before them and Stan felt he'd suddenly been reacquainted with a long lost friend. A broad smile replaced a tentative one and he gripped his friend's hand excitedly.

"It looks lovely, doesn't it, Barry?" he said dreamily, "It looks like …" and he paused, thinking of an apt word, "home, it looks just like home."

They pulled up on the large, gravelled space outside and got out of the car, standing in awe as they looked around, captivated by the building and the gardens surrounding it. They remained silent, absorbed by the sheer allure of the place; the stonework façade made virtually invisible by the clinging wisteria, the porch dripping with clematis blooms, two ancient, gnarled apple trees forming an arch over the pathway leading to the front door.

"We've come up trumps, haven't we, Charlie?" Stan whispered in reverence, amazed by what he was seeing, "we've come up flippin' trumps," he repeated and they made their way up the path, Charlie, being the tallest, having to duck under the arch. Stan inserted the skeleton key and opened the door.

They entered apprehensively but any fears instantly evaporated as they realised the place had beauty from within and without. None of the furnishings had been removed and they walked into a home that was ready to live in, even the services were all still connected. Charlie picked the few letters up from the floor inside the door and placed them on the oak sideboard to his left and then he turned the light on.

MAYBE

The broad fireplace that took up most of the far wall housed an interesting bread oven, under which was set a huge basket of logs and kindling wood; a hundred matches were crammed in the indent of an old brick and directly in front of it, standing invitingly, were two club armchairs covered in worn, soft leather.

Charlie knew where the two would be sitting later that night and he clasped his arms around their shoulders and drew them into him.

"This is more than I could ever have imagined," he beamed, "I'm so pleased for you both, it's just like you said, Stan, a home, a great home."

For the next half hour Barry and Stan explored, Charlie chuckling at their squeaks of delight as he lit a roaring fire in the capacious dog grate.

The man never knew and would never know how Tim Richards died, but as that crackling fire began to radiate a welcome warmth into the room, forty miles away, in the place he was about to leave for, the doctor's body was conversely losing heat, its life source having been drained away.

Barry and Stan eventually finished their reconnoitring and joined Charlie by the fire. He had never seen them so happy. He thought of the hardship they had both had to endure and was unable to stop himself from hugging them again, a gesture of pure joy.

"Try out those armchairs, fellas, I can't think of anywhere better to sit in the whole world," and they both did as he said, sinking deep into the soft padding. Stan took another look around the room then focused squarely on Charlie.

"They can't take this away from us, can they?" he said, solemnly. "I mean, none of that legal stuff will go wrong?" and he looked plaintively at him, craving his reassurance.

"You have all the money and a lot more besides, Stan. I can't see that anything can go wrong. That auctioneer took a chance letting you move in today and he struck me as a cautious sort of bloke so he wouldn't have let that happen if he thought anything could go wrong," and Stan puffed his cheeks and blew out, grateful for what Charlie had said.

"Now, I have to love you and leave you, got to get back to the hospital in a couple of hours," and he placed the ornate fireguard in front of the flames and began to put on his coat, "and make sure that stays there, especially when you go to bed tonight, oh, and another thing, what about getting yourselves something to eat?"

"I'll sort that out, Charlie," Barry chipped in and he trundled off to the kitchen.

"I'll be back soon, Stan," he said, buttoning his coat, "make sure you're both settling in," and he walked to the door but Stan jumped up and pulled him back.

"You don't have to go back, you can stay here and live with us, we can all be together like a family," and Charlie's lightness became heavy. He didn't like what he was hearing. Stan seemed worried by his leaving and a spear of doubt pierced his elation, deflating it.

"Come on, man, this is what you want, you and Barry both together, living in this lovely place, no one bothering you," and Charlie lightly punched his shoulder. "I know it's a big step but you're going to be fine, I know you are." Then Stan smiled uneasily, a cautious smile and he drove off into the darkening night having already made his mind up to revisit the following morning, even though he would have worked all night.

There was still a lot of hand holding left to do.

CHAPTER 17

Bill returned to the door and rotated the key, firmly locking it, then moved across to the desk and after committing to memory everything that was upon it, carefully removed each item and placed them on the floor.

Meantime, Akan and Angelo both felt the doctor become limp and, as instructed, released their hold, although Angelo somewhat reluctantly necessitating some physical persuasion from his accomplice.

"Right, let's get him on the desk," and Bill hooked his arms under the limp man's armpits as the other two each took hold of a leg. With some effort they managed to get him on and Bill, with a final heave, positioned the man face upwards.

He removed the flat rope from beneath the wheelchair and after removing the doctor's upper clothing tied it tightly around his left leg and began threading the rope under the desk and over him, Bill using all of his strength to ensure he was firmly trussed.

The young ones looked on as he now removed everything, other than the scalpel, from beneath the chair and set it all down by the desk. He needed to work fast to keep the initial blood loss to a minimum, to curtail the mess and he started prodding the doctor's neck to ascertain the position of both the sternomastoid artery and the jugular vein. Satisfied that he'd found them he made a two inch incision near the base of the clavicle and inserted a cannula into the vein leading towards the heart. He opened the valve and blood began to flow through the tube attached and he placed the end into the collapsible, five gallon wine container.

Akan shielded her eyes as Bill now made another incision, this time into the carotid artery and he introduced a second cannula and clamped off the end.

There was neither movement nor sound from their victim until Bill introduced a large syringe, filled with formaldehyde into the arterial tube and began to pump in the liquid. As he pressed, the blood flow from the vein increased, making a swishing within the wine container. Tim Richards' soot black eyes suddenly opened, a bewildered expression materialising on his face. He was semi-conscious, the drug performing to its fullest, but he was able to vaguely recognise that something dreadful was happening to him and he stared at Bill, desperately trying to organise his thoughts.

"What are you doing to me?" he uttered huskily, his throat bone dry, "what have you got in my neck?"

"Don't worry, Tim," Bill replied. "I'm embalming you," the years of hatred for the man lending his voice a maliciousness, a cold hostility.

"You only embalm dead people," the doctor growled.

"Well, be patient, Tim, that's been arranged. We just thought we'd drain all the badness out of you, you know, clean the cesspool," and he filled the syringe once again with formaldehyde and continued to pump.

"Lie back now and enjoy it," he carried on. "I've read all the books, I know what I'm doing," his tone now completely flippant and uncaring. "I'll be puncturing your organs and cleaning them out too in a minute, you'll be as clean as a whistle," and the doctor's entire body clenched against the restraint but the rope held firm.

Angelo approached him now and lowered his face to the doctor's so their noses were almost touching, peering into the mineshaft blackness of his eyes. Bill tensed, pushed harder, not knowing what Angelo was about to do then the boy violently jerked backwards.

A high pitched squeal hurtled through his thin lips and Akan held back a scream.

"Oh God, Mr Sweet," she groaned, "his eyes have popped out!" and the three of them stared at the sight in horror. The doctor straining against his shackles and Bill's increased pressure on the syringe had combined to cause the repulsive sight before them.

His orbs drooped forward onto the top of his cheeks like dangling, black prunes, connected only by the red, string like optic nerves. Bill stopped momentarily, the hideous spectacle freezing his thoughts. When he'd been researching the procedure, this eventuality had been mentioned but it was a rarity, a one in a thousand, maybe ten thousand and thought it nothing to worry about.

The doctor's breathing was becoming laboured now, short, sharp breaths as he continued struggling against the rope, grunting with frustration and then, attempting to clear his vision, he began rocking his head from side to side, his eyeballs colliding with his nose, flecks of something puss-like scattering from the sockets and suddenly his mouth opened, the words he spoke seeming to emanate from his hard breathing rather than his voice box.

"I can't see you, you cowards," his speech forced and unnatural, "you cowards," he repeated, more quietly, "you devils," now barely audible.

They remained panic stricken, his words hitting hard and then Akan pushed past Angelo and put her hands firmly down upon the doctor's shoulders, her head directly above him.

"Do not talk to us about cowardice, old man," her voice low and hard and serious, "cowards make the brave act and that is what we're doing. You think as the man who digs the hole for the woman to be stoned to death … no angel will ever kiss you."

Her rhetoric galvanised Bill and he bent down and picked up the man's shirt, thrusting it over his now unrecognisable face, the material rising and falling with his breaths.

He began to pump once more and as the fluid went in the blood came out.

And as the fluid went in the breathing began to lessen.

And as the fluid went in the breathing eventually stopped.

Angelo replied, "White," when he was asked the colour of the liquid that was now entering the wine container and Bill removed the cannulas from the artery and vein and clamped the incision.

Dr Richards was bloodless.

He now picked up an instrument resembling a handled, metal pencil and forced the point firmly into the doctor's stomach, just above the umbilicus. He then attached a small, handheld suction pump to it and began aspirating fluid from the thoracic, abdominal and pelvic cavities, a laborious procedure that took more than an hour but essential if he were to prevent the body from stinking. Akan and Angelo busied themselves with keeping the space spotlessly clean, wiping, from the desk and floor, any spills that occurred, eradicating any evidence.

When Bill removed the trocar he reverted back to the syringe and began introducing formaldehyde into the cavities and when satisfied with the amount, sutured the cut. When he had finished, the wine container was almost full and it took all of his and Angelo's strength to manhandle it to the side of the statue.

Panting from exertion he now concentrated his efforts on leak prevention.

He untied the rope and after asking them for continued courage, unzipped the doctor's fly and using a much practiced, square knot, securely tied the penis with two lengths of twine. He then packed the orifices of his face with cotton wool, the absence of the eyes making the procedure far easier and after washing his hands thoroughly at the sink, went to the window and opened the blind slightly, curling his hands around his face to help his view.

Bill looked out for some minutes and when certain there was no sign of life, raised the blind and opened the window, asking Angelo to assist. They brought the sledgehammer and fence post through the window and quickly drew down the blind, although the cold night air was a welcome relief from the fetid odour of the room.

Placing the post and hammer next to the desk, Bill now picked up the socket set and went to the statue. There was a varied array of sizes lined up in ascending order; with his second try he found the right one and after attaching the ratchet speedily removed the six nuts holding the statue onto the floor.

The doctor had once told him that the construction of the effigy, from papier mache and galvanized netting, had made it not only extremely strong but also incredibly light and he had, in fact, carried the thing in unaided during its installation, so Bill wasn't surprised with the little effort required when he bear hugged it and lifted it off the six protruding bolts, finally lowering it down onto its back.

Everything was now going exactly to plan but he knew the most difficult task was still in front of them and he sat down and took a moment to gather himself and make sure his companions were bearing up.

Angelo was washing a large, blood stained rag at the sink and Akan was busy creating another, mopping up more of the stuff from the side of the desk. Then Bill asked them to stop.

"I'm so proud of you," slowly shaking his head in amazement, "you've both been so strong and like you said, Akan, so brave, but I need you to be even more courageous," and he beckoned them. "Come here," and they stopped what they were doing and stood by him.

"The man lying on that desk was a monster, always remember that, keep it at the forefront of your minds whenever you remember this day, and it's taken a monstrous deed to stop him," and he glanced almost pathetically at them. "His eyes coming away like that was terrible and I'm sorry you had to witness it," and this time he shook his head in dismay, "but he had to be stopped and I could think of no other way," and she stepped forward and held his hand, feeling he needed encouragement. "We could never have got him safely out of this office and disposed of his body; I'd racked my brains, so I came up with this solution but there was a problem, I wasn't sure if the statue would take his weight so there's something else we must do, something vile, but it's completely necessary," and he squeezed her hand as a thank you and walked to the body.

"This is the last thing we have to do to him and then this nightmare will be almost over," and he reached out and undid the doctor's trousers, pulling them off in one movement and then did the same with his underpants.

"I'll need your assistance again, Angelo," and he passed the young man the fence post then forced the dead man's legs wide and began to liberally apply petroleum jelly around the last, unplugged orifice.

"Pass me the post," he commanded dispassionately and positioned it so the point was beginning to enter the anus.

"This is going to take the weight off the statue," he said, coldheartedly and gestured for Angelo to hold the stake in place.

And he lifted the sledgehammer.

The post came to a firm halt when it was extending eighteen inches beyond the bottom of his feet, more than adequate he thought, however, what was to come would demand all of their luck.

He laid down the hammer and carried the jar containing the rest of the jelly to the statue and, crawling inside and beginning from the top, he applied the stuff in dollops to the back surface. He then measured the distance between the internal shoulder mouldings and sawed the timber, that had a pulley already attached, to length and positioned it inside, leaving six feet of spare rope. They then wrestled the cadaver to beneath the hollow figure and Bill securely knotted the rope around its neck.

This was the point where he thought things could go badly wrong; the body could get stuck or the statue could possibly crack but with Bill on the pulley and Akan and Angelo easing his way, Tim Richards slid into his statue like a well-oiled suppository and after one more yank, the bottom of the fence post became level with the base of the statue and he tied it off solidly around the limp foot.

"So far, so good," he observed, "but now comes the hard part, we need to be very careful, remember what I told you."

Bill went to the top end and they to the bottom. The figure itself was light but now there was thirteen stone of dead weight inside and this next manoeuvre would test all of their strength.

They lifted together and heaved a sigh of collective relief as they realised the load was manageable and they manhandled it onto the desk so the base was pointing at the plinth. He went to the wine container and heaved the slops in between the bolts then once again reminded them of what they had rehearsed and after signalling their understanding; the three eased the statue from the desk and set it down vertically beside the plinth.

Bill once again bear hugged it and the other two grasped the base between the holes and lifted, directing him this way and that until eventually the holes married up with the threads, the slops were concealed and everything sank onto its housing with a satisfying rigidity. They were exhausted, but not that sapped to stop them clasping shoulders and hugging one another, but it was Akan's grip that was the weakest; it was only she who felt any remorse for taking a life.

After the one sided celebration, Bill instructed them to stash every piece of equipment beneath the wheelchair whilst he set about applying a silicone bead to seal the gap between the base and the floor: He thought it unlikely but it wouldn't do to have any juices dripping out.

Content that they'd removed all of the tools and apparatus he returned the desk furniture and they gave every surface one more wipe. It was now 9 pm. and the entire operation had been completed in less than three hours. Had it been present day, using modern techniques, those who were to investigate the disappearance would have soon understood that he had been murdered and an attempt made to preserve him; but this was 1963, the science was not at their disposal and it was to be nine months before the truth was realised and the trail had long gone cold.

Now they had to get out of there!

Chapter 18

Stan stared out of the window into the gloom, watching the lights of Charlie's car diminish into the distance.

He could hear his friend in the kitchen preparing the meal, could feel the heat from the fire, could relax knowing that the crush of people and cars didn't exist just yards away and yet he felt anxious. The hospital had been the mother ship, the womb, and although fearful events had happened there it had provided security. The asylum had given him asylum, a refuge that protected and gave him certainty and as he closed the curtains he shivered and hoped the night would pass quickly so the morning could bring Charlie back.

Barry was still noisy in the kitchen and the little man, old smiling Stan, walked back to the club armchair with his head down and stared at the patterns as the flames danced.

He raised his hand and inserted his thumb into his mouth, lifted his legs up onto the chair and began to rock and, before long, began to resemble that fellow that Uncle Theo had found all those years ago in that flat that, from a distance, looked like a fist; but this time he wasn't rocking into madness, he was trying to rock away from it.

Chapter 19

Bill purposefully cast his eyes around the office and, certain that everything was as before, went back to the window and peered through the blinds.

Had he lifted the slat five seconds earlier he would have been alarmed to see the headlights of the other vehicle now out there and he was about to realise that not everything was going to go their way after all.

Charlie's journey back had been quicker than anticipated and he'd decided to park up in the neglected area at the far end of the hospital and have a sit for a while; cast his mind back over the events of the day, contemplate his future because, oddly, he was giving some space to Stan's offer. As he drove in he caught a glimpse of another vehicle there and made the decision to park as far away from it as possible, wanting to feel alone.

Seconds after switching off his lights he noticed a thin ray of light appear from the window of the doctor's office and a minute later the blind was raised and the window opened revealing two figures inside.

He leaned forward. It was gone eight o'clock and the doctor should have left hours ago. The two shapes climbed out of the window, the one carrying a large implement made his way across the grass to the car and the other stayed by the window, apparently talking to someone inside. Charlie turned off the interior light and quietly opened the door, leaving it open as to close it might alert them, and began to skirt his way around the periphery of the car park, looking across and trying to understand what these people may be doing.

He'd lost sight of the one who had returned to the car, assuming he must have got in it, and as he reached the building and pressed himself up against the wall he heard the person outside of the window whisper good luck to someone inside and that someone closed the window and drew the blinds.

Although Angelo's eyes were almost concealed behind their overly apparent lids his vision was perfect and he easily made out the dark shape moving around the perimeter of the parking area. He climbed the tree once again and picked up the carving knife he'd hidden up there whilst waiting for Bill.

Angelo had managed to keep this knife from the night he had tried to kill his father and its presence, incredibly, had never been detected. When necessary he had kept it on his person but very rarely. Mostly he'd hidden it in far up places where no one looked or cleaned, or places down below where no one had any reason to look.

His hand tightened around the handle as he watched the vague, creeping form arrive at the wall of the building. He thought of using the sledgehammer but he'd always wanted to use that knife, experience the feeling, and his grip tightened further as he saw the shape approaching Bill.

As Akan grasped the wheelchair and began pushing it through the empty and dimly lit corridor Bill stood outside the window, breathing in the cold night air, a ripple of happiness and relief becoming a swell as he began to apprehend how his life was about to change. No more worry, nor torment, nor lament and then his stomach somersaulted as he heard the voice. He swung around to face it and saw the figure, black and dressed in black and he suddenly knew why he hadn't seen him.

"What's going on?" Charlie asked sternly, his face only inches away from Bill's and then he recognised him.

"Bill!" Charlie gasped, taken aback. "Bill Sweet, what the hell are you up to?" But Bill didn't answer. His attention had been averted to the shadowy outline approaching Charlie from behind and almost instantly Bill knew Charlie was dead when he saw the glinting tip of the blade emerge from just below his chin.

The man in black looked at him in a brief moment of unknowing and then collapsed in a heap, the cruelty from the knife removing his ability to live.

Bill began to pant.

Seconds before he was relishing the thought of a new future and now he could see it all slipping away.

"Jesus fucking Christ, Angelo," he moaned, looking down at the dead man, "what the fuck are we supposed to do now?"

He looked across at a movement in the distance and could just make out Akan emerging backwards between the doors, pulling the wheelchair carefully through.

"Leave him," Angelo hissed and he bent down to withdraw the knife which made a sucking sound, like something being pulled from beach mud, "they'll think old dead doc was to blame," and he began to clean the knife callously, as if sharpening it, on Charlie's black jacket.

Bill's mind was racing and as that idea of Angelo's sank in he began to consider it. What were his options anyway? The disposal of the doctor's body, away from the hospital, had proved impossible for him to resolve so where was the difference? A body was a body. He had to think quickly; someone else could show up and then the shit would really start to fly. In an instant he'd made the decision.

"Ok!" he blurted, "let's get going," and he raced over to Akan who was advancing towards the car.

"What's happening over there, Mr Sweet?" she asked as he grabbed the wheelchair from her and began to push.

MAYBE

"Don't worry about it, I'll explain later," and he ran the short distance to the car where Angelo now stood, Akan effortlessly keeping up with the pace.

"We all need to get out of here as fast as we can!" and he threw all of the equipment from under the seat into the boot, heaved the now collapsed chair on top and drove off, without lights, until they reached the main road.

"Bill was the only one panicking but the farther they got from the scene the lighter his frame of mind became, and before long his mood had returned to how he had felt seconds before Charlie's appearance.

Remarkably, Akan had fallen asleep in the back and as the car hurtled towards Bill's bungalow, where they would deposit the tools of the crime, neither he nor Angelo felt any remorse; even though they had been the judge and jury it didn't matter. That they had left no clues was what mattered to the driver and that he had at last used the knife to kill was what mattered to his passenger. Bill's good spirits bubbled over and he grabbed at Angelo's knee and started shaking it.

"That was brilliant son, brilliant," he repeated.

"Yeah, I dropped him good," he replied, heartlessly.

"No, not that," and he smoothly turned into the driveway, "the blame, blaming the doctor," and he dimmed the lights and pulled on the handbrake.

"I've always liked alliteration, you know," and he turned off the engine, "do you know what alliteration means, Angelo?"

But he didn't answer, just kept looking forward.

"I'll give you an example," Bill said, used to Angelo's reticence, and he cleared his throat.

"The dead doc did the deed, the dead doc did it," then he cackled like a jackal and if a psychiatric panel, taking notes, had replaced Akan in that car they would have had a difficult job in determining which one of them was unhinged and which one demented.

Chapter 20

When Barry entered the room with the tray of food he'd heard Stan rocking before seeing him. The chair was creaking with the movement and he quickly lay the tray down and knelt before his friend.

"Stan, what is it? What's the matter?" he asked concernedly.

"I'm frightened," he whined, his thumb distorting the words. "I know I shouldn't be but I can't help it," and Barry eased himself forward then after gently removing the thumb, held his hand.

"Everything is going to be fine, my friend, you'll see," and he squeezed that hand reassuringly, "a lot's happened, Stan, it's difficult to take it all in but we've come this far, let's give it a try," and he calmed a little as the spiritual warmth from his friend matched the physical warmth of the fire.

Stan removed his hand from the grip and placed it lightly on the side of Barry's face.

"Sometimes, when you get something you have wanted so much you get a bit miserable, like putting the last piece in one of those jigsaw puzzles. It's like you're happy you've done it but sad it's all over. I think that's maybe what is making me feel like this," and Barry understood his description of an anti-climax and knew what to do.

"But our adventure's only just started, Stan," he said, a smile appearing on his face. "We've got to get the pigs and plant the spuds, we've got to get more wood for the fire, we've got a hundred and one things to do so don't think of this as the end, think of it as the beginning," and Barry raised his eyebrows. "D'you think you can do that?"

"Yes, I do," he replied, reacting positively to his friend's support. "Could we get the pigs tomorrow, Barry?" he said hopefully, "I've got the folding money they gave me when we left the hospital."

"Well," and he placed the bowl of soup in his lap and passed him a spoon, "we can take a walk down to that shop tomorrow if you like and make some enquiries."

"Yes, I'd like that, Barry," he replied, not seeing the look of worry that had appeared on his friend's face.

Charlie's non-appearance the following day concerned them both although Barry, not wanting it to unsettle his friend unduly, calmly put it down to him maybe falling ill or perhaps his car malfunctioning. Though when they both heard the rapping on the door an hour later it was Barry who rushed to get there first, jubilant that Charlie had finally arrived.

His jaw dropped as the ruddy faced man from the auction stood before him.

Only having seen him sat he hadn't realised just how large this individual was. His frame seemed to inhabit the entirety of the porch and when he spoke, the magnitude of his voice matched the proportions of his anatomy.

"Welcome to the parish!" he boomed and walked uninvited into the lounge. "Well done on getting this place, you paid too much but that's your business," and he walked across the room in a couple of strides and sat down in one of the chairs, the thing groaning under his weight. "If you want anything you come and see me," he declared as they stood in front of him. "I can see the pair of you ain't pastoral so you'll need all the help you can get," and he laid his hands across his substantial stomach and gazed at them both.

"Is this a dry house or do I get a cup of tea?" and Barry, shocked by the explosive entrance, nodded his head and meekly made for the kitchen leaving Stan to cope with their mysterious guest.

"You're big," Stan suddenly observed, not really knowing what to say.

"And you're little," came the reply, "but you did well back at that sale, putting that stuck up moll in her place, so you're big as well in my eyes, come 'ere," and Stan almost automatically lurched toward the outstretched hand and grasped it, a surprised expression as he felt his fingers delve into something like a bag of sandpaper, the result of years of physical labour.

The man could have been the type who held a grudge, a mean spirited soul who felt aggrieved at not winning at the auction, but nothing could be further from the truth.

Toby 'Jug' Titmuss was an affable human being who gained pleasure from helping others. His huge body cradled a huge heart and when Barry handed him the mug of tea the room seemed a happier place and after a short while he had gained their acceptance and by the time he had left, their affection.

Jug was the owner of the adjacent farm that lay on the opposite side to that purchased by Lord Johnny. Over the years he had carved himself a reputation in the community as the man who could get almost anything and if he couldn't he knew someone who could and when, as he was leaving, they asked him about logs and spuds and pigs he replied that that would be as easy as jumping up and down to procure.

That afternoon he reappeared, a ton bag of logs swaying to and fro on the front end loader of his old Massey tractor. They came out to meet him and he lay the sack down gently outside their front gate.

"It's ash," he shouted, his voice barely audible over the machine's raucous engine, "best you can get, but keep it dry and save the bag for me," and he pushed it into reverse, the cogs grinding, "worth their weight in gold!"

MAYBE

"What about paying you?" Barry shouted, surrounding his mouth with his hands in an attempt to increase the volume.

"Buy me a few pints on Saturday night," he bellowed. "I'm taking you both down the pub," and he headed away, purple grey smoke billowing from the vertical exhaust pipe.

The rest of their afternoon was taken up with stacking logs in the ample woodshed at the far end of the front garden and that night they slept like contented babies.

The following day, the second full day on the farm, their disquiet over Charlie's no show was peaking and when Jug turned up with two hessian sacks of seed potatoes Barry decided to ask him for his help. He explained who Charlie was and where he worked and whether Jug could somehow make some enquiries as to his well-being but he didn't hold out much hope. The hospital was a long way away and he felt a bit awkward about ringing the place from the village payphone to ask about a member of their staff.

"Maybe his car has broken down," Jug suggested.

"I know," Barry replied, "we thought that."

"Or perhaps he just thinks it's best you boys give this a try without him, you know, throw you in at the deep end," but Barry knew that wasn't the case, he wouldn't just leave them without some sort of explanation.

"Could be," Barry mused. "We really need to get a phone installed," he went on.

"Six month waiting list," Jug informed him, "that's what they'll tell you," and he hopped back aboard. "Mrs James over at Glebe waited eighteen months," and he hit the accelerator, the smoke a greyish blue this time.

On the third day they were beginning to come to terms with the idea they might never see Charlie again. It was mid-morning, Barry was washing up in the kitchen and Stan was cleaning out the fire, preparing to lay it for the evening. It was he who heard the noise of the vehicle first, tilting his head to hear more clearly. The sound was increasing as the vehicle came up their drive; this wasn't the cacophony of a tractor engine but the low purr of a car and, without thinking, assumed it must be Charlie.

He called out to Barry as he looked out of the window.

"It's Charlie, Barry, he's got a new car," and Barry entered the room, eagerly drying his hands on a tea cloth.

"It's red and white, he must have had trouble with the other one like we thought."

They opened the door as the Morris 1000 van drew to a halt outside, 'please address clearly and correctly' emblazoned on the side accompanied by a picture of a man holding a letter.

"It's the postman," Barry observed disappointedly as they approached the van, "it's not our Charlie."

The postman remained sat and wound down the window.

"Is one of you a Mr Stan Heart?" a brown envelope in his hand. Stan raised his arm.

"Letter for you," and he passed it out, wound his window up and departed.

"Blimey, he was in a rush," Stan remarked and passed the envelope to his friend, "d'you think it's one of those bills they told us about?" and Barry scrutinised the letter.

"No, it's franked with the name of the auctioneers," and he carried it into the house and began to read through it silently."

"It's a copy of the contract you signed and they've got special clearance on the cheque, looks like the sale has gone through without any hitches." At this point he thought Stan would start whooping and wailing but to his surprise he remained remarkably composed.

"Anyway," he said, continuing to read, "we have to get a form from the post office and send it to the land registry within four weeks," he turned the letter over, "and there's something here about the mansion," and Stan began to get to his feet.

"No, stay there," Barry urged, "I think it's important," and he finished, reading to himself, until the end. He placed the pages down on the side table and looked at Stan seriously. "That mansion, in fact the whole of the farm including this house, used to belong to a family called Moseley."

Stan shrugged his shoulders. "Doesn't matter who it belonged to," he said matter of factly.

"Well, maybe so," Barry replied, "but a member of this family, a man called Oswald, who is still alive, used to lead a group of fascists before the war; had thousands of members, I can remember reading about him and the letter says although we should know about this it would be ... hang on, let me check the letter again," and he read until he found the word, "it would be prudent if we kept the information secret."

"Fascists!" Stan spouted. "What are fascists?"

"They're people who are against democracy. They want a dictatorship so only their views are listened to and no one else's."

"Dictatorship!" Stan exclaimed. "Don't know what you're talking about, Barry."

"Listen, I don't know too much about it either, Stan," he admitted, "but the letter is saying we should keep all this to ourselves. By the seems of it there's a lot of people in our country who still think this Oswald Moseley bloke is some kind of hero so it's best we shut up about it or they might come flocking round after some memento or other."

"Then that's what we'll do," Stan suggested and it was then that Jug turned up with fourteen piglets.

Stan thought he felt the ground shake as the man jumped down from his Massey.

"Where d'you want them, boy?" he shouted, beginning to heave bags of feed from the tractor's link box and stack them in the garden.

"Where are the piglets going, Barry?" Stan asked, passing the buck and Barry held his palms up to the sky.

"Well you need to make your minds up, gentlemen, they're feisty little fellas and they need somewhere to sleep," and he hauled the last of the feed sacks from the box and lifted it onto the stack.

"Can they stay in the garden?" Barry asked innocently.

"If they do you won't have a garden by morning."

"How about one of the fields?"

"Any shelter?" Jug asked, now sitting on the stack he'd made, "and what about the fencing?"

"Um," Barry hesitated.

"You're not ready for these pigs are you lads?" he suggested.

"We didn't know you were bringing them," Stan piped up.

"You asked me to get you some, Stan, I thought you had somewhere for them to stay," he said, a bit miffed.

"The mansion," Barry came to the rescue, "there's straw in the old barn. The place is falling apart I know but they can't get out, the doors are still good," and for the next hour they set about strawing the concrete floor of the largest downstairs room and Jug coupled up an old water trough in the corner. With superb competence he manoeuvred the tractor and trailer around the side of the farmhouse and traversed the narrow lane to the mansion then, utilising a disused gate and some pallets, he created an enclosed walkway from the rear of the trailer to the door. When Jug lowered the ramp they saw the animals for the first time. They were all bunched at the back, stock still, eyes wide and alert. Some were black, some were white, some ginger, others all three. Stan stared through the makeshift walkway and immediately fell in love. They were the cutest creatures he had ever laid eyes on and as Jug climbed the ramp and began herding them out he looked at Barry in amazement, the way he used to look at the trains.

"They're only pigs, Stan," he said, almost chiding him for that look, "they're only pigs."

MAYBE

"They're not only pigs," he replied, censuring his friend and he watched in awe as their little legs moved like pistons as they scurried into the mansion.

"They're our babies, Barry," and he laughed for the first time in a long time.

Jug dismantled the race and swung up the ramp.

"Give 'em half a bag a day for the first week and a full bag for the second week; a bag and a half for the third week and two bags on the fourth and when you reach six keep it there for the duration. Walk over to my place when you've a few left and I'll bring some more, but gimme a few days' notice, I need to get 'em from the supplier," and he made his way to the front of the tractor where Stan moved forward and took hold of his arm.

"Thank you, Jug," he said warmly, "you're a good friend to us, don't know what we'd do without you."

"He's right," Barry affirmed, "you're so helpful, but we need to pay you for all this."

"Like I said, we'll sort it in the pub tomorrow," and climbed into the tractor. "I'll meet you there at seven."

"I wanted to speak to you about that actually, Jug, "he said, feeling embarrassed, "I'm not sure if we're up to going to the pub just yet, you know, meeting lots of new people."

"Has Jug been looking after you?" he asked, sitting his huge body on the metal seat.

"You most certainly have."

"And I'll look after you tomorrow night as well," he said with gusto and turned the key, the engine slowly coming to life.

"See you at seven," he shouted as he gently pressed the accelerator, "and don't get dressed up … the place is a shithouse!" and he was gone in a cloud of diesel fumes.

Chapter 21

Akan and Angelo remained in the car when Bill stashed the equipment in the small garage attached to the bungalow and they set off back to the home. The boy went straight to his room, Bill to the office and Akan, still half asleep, made for the day room.

Angelo removed the knife from his leg sheath, washed it thoroughly, dried every inch of its surface and placed it carefully on top of the tallboy.

Bill explained to the night staff that they had been to the new Wimpy bar in the town and very tasty it was too and Akan sat down next to Ruby who was alone, always the last to go to bed.

As Ruby looked up she noticed her friend was troubled about something, her thoughts elsewhere.

"Hi, Akan," she said tentatively, "where've you been? Had a good time?"

"Oh, we've been to that new burger bar," only just remembering the script. "I think Mr Sweet is going to take all the kids there, as a bit of a treat."

"Fab," Ruby declared, "hope I'm next," she said cheerfully, "did that weirdo Angelo go with you?" and she said he had.

"Bet he scared the living daylights out of them, didn't he?"

"He's not that bad," she said thoughtfully, "had it rough like you," and she stood up, "tripped when the starter's gun fired," and she gave her friend a weak smile.

"I need to borrow some clothes from you, Ruby," her face vacant, "in the morning," she added and Ruby nodded her agreement.

"Thank you," and she turned and began walking to the door. "I'm going to bed now, I'll see you tomorrow," and she left leaving Ruby feeling that she'd never seen her friend so preoccupied.

Chapter 22

"I was last here eighteen years ago, almost to the day," the inspector said to his colleague as they made their way through the grounds. "I was a young PC like yourself and I was with Henry Cadogan, did you ever come across him?"

"I've heard talk of him, sir," the constable replied, "but never met him, I think he retired a few years before I joined," and walking around a corner, noticed a pale blue, Ford Anglia in the otherwise deserted car park, the driver's door curiously wide open.

"Presumably that's the dead man's car," and they carried on.

"Yes," the inspector continued, "old Henry and I had been called to investigate a suicide," and at the far end of the car park they could now see the murder scene.

"Young chap, what was his name?" and he looked above him for guidance, "same surname as that chap who's just become the labour party leader … Wilson! That's it, William Wilson," and the officer, who was ostensibly guarding the scene, saluted him as he ducked under the tape.

"Pop over and have a look at that car, son," he said, looking back at his young colleague, "see if there's anything out of place," and the constable began walking, "and try not to touch anything," he said loudly, "might be something important over there," and his focus turned to the body slumped on the floor.

MAYBE

"Mr Charles Bello, sir," one of the two officers inside of the tape informed him. "Charge nurse, thirty-nine years old, single. Knife wound, in at the back of the neck and out through the front, the duty doctor left a few minutes ago and is preparing a report for you, sir, should be available by midday. Apparently he would have died almost instantly; looking at the exit and entry the doctor reckons the spinal cord's severed."

"Witnesses?" the inspector asked solemnly.

"We've officers interviewing staff, but up 'til now, nothing."

"Fingerprints?"

"Nothing found."

"Time of death?"

"Late yesterday evening, give or take a couple of hours."

"Black," he stated, "racially motivated, maybe?"

"Possibly," the officer replied.

"Which part of the hospital is this?" he asked, looking around.

"It's the quietest part, sir," the other officer now speaking, "it houses the laundry and the superintendent's office, a Dr Tim Richards. Behind there's his office," and he pointed to the window directly in front of them.

"We don't actually know why Mr Bello was in the vicinity, sir," the first officer announced. "His nightshift was on the ward at the very front of the hospital, a long way from here. He should have parked up in the main car park and entered for work through the principal entrance; this area is hardly ever frequented by all accounts, even Dr Richards parks out front and walks through the hospital to his office."

"Have you interviewed the doctor yet?" the inspector enquired.

"We can't locate him," the second officer replied, "his car isn't here, although his office is unlocked, but, as yet, we haven't been able to find him."

This news intrigued the inspector. The doctor had made quite an impression on him all those years ago; the memory of his arrogant and commanding presence and the fawning attitude adopted by his former boss, had stayed with him and he instinctively knew the man needed to be found quickly. You didn't get what you saw with this Dr Richards and he was sure the man held the key to the mystery.

"I want you to put all your efforts into finding the superintendent," he said forthrightly, "and as soon as you do I want to be informed, is that understood?" and they both acknowledged him, "and I want a hundred yard search from this wall to the far edge of the car park and I want it to be meticulous. Anything found, no matter what, I want bagged and labelled and I want one of you to organise and conduct it, is that also understood?" and they acknowledged him again.

"Can we remove the body to the mortuary, sir?" the first officer asked. "We've photographed everything and the medic's completed his examination."

"I've no objection but double check with the doctor first … by the way, who identified him?"

The second officer removed a small pad from his inside pocket and stared into it. "A Mr John Turvey," he said, reading through his notes, "also a charge nurse here."

"Ok, I'd like one of you to contact this Mr Turvey and have him meet me in half an hour at the main reception," lifting the tape again and stepping out, "and remember, concentrate your efforts on finding Dr Richards, make it a priority," and he left the men with their orders and walked across to the constable and the car.

"Anything of interest?" he asked, his estimation of him growing as he noticed his gloved hands.

"The interior light switch has been turned off so it wouldn't be activated with the door open."

The inspector was impressed.

MAYBE

"And there's a brochure of some sort on the passenger seat but I wasn't sure if I should touch it, sir."

The inspector walked around to the other side of the car and embarrassingly having no gloves of his own, asked his colleague to open the door and retrieve it.

"Looks like Mr Bello was looking to buy a farm, constable," he observed, reading through the thing. "Take it over to the investigating officers and have them bag it, you never know," and as the constable quickly stepped through the grass the inspector slowly walked back to the main entrance.

He ambled through and found a place to sit in the large foyer. A police officer had been stationed beside the receptionist's desk, attracting quizzical glances from those oblivious to the events and he bowed his head to him resulting in a salute. Ten minutes had passed when John Turvey appeared and approached the inspector who immediately stood up and offered his hand.

"Thank you for coming to see me, Mr Turvey, I appreciate your time. My name is Inspector Burnes, I'm heading up the enquiry."

"Only too pleased to help, inspector," a sadness in his voice. "I knew Charlie well, he was a good nurse and a good person ... I can't believe this has happened," and the inspector noticed his chin begin to quiver and placed a steadying hand on his shoulder.

"I've only a few questions to ask you, it won't take long," and the two men sat down next to each other.

"Do you have any thoughts on what might have happened?" he began. "Had Mr Bello fallen out with anyone recently, did he have any enemies that you're aware of?"

The charge nurse shook his head. "Charlie was just a lovely, easy going bloke; he was very popular with everyone working here."

"Was he married?"

"No, he never married, confirmed bachelor."

"Anyone here didn't like the colour of his skin?"

"Good God no," he replied, somewhat indignantly, "in a place like this, inspector, minds are very broad, they have to be."

"What d'you think he was doing around the far end of the hospital, Mr Turvey, wouldn't he have parked near to this main entrance?"

"Yes, he would, it's a bit odd that, I've been trying to work it out but I've no idea what he was doing around there."

The inspector remained silent for a short while. His colleague then walked into the foyer and noticing his boss was with someone, nodded to him understandingly and joined the officer at the desk.

"I believe Mr Bello was attacked directly outside of Dr Richards' office," the inspector mused.

"Yes, that's right, but the doctor would have left around five o'clock yesterday and Charlie would have arrived hours later so I don't think their paths would have crossed."

"I was simply making an observation, Mr Turvey."

"I'm sorry, inspector, I shouldn't make assumptions."

"Make as many as you like, we've very little to go on at the moment."

He now put his chin into the palm of his hand and looked intently at the nurse.

"Would Dr Richards, the superintendent of the hospital, have known Charlie?" he asked purposefully.

"Yes, indeed," he replied without hesitation, "they knew each other very well."

"Did they get on?" and this time the charge nurse did hesitate.

"What's the matter, Mr Turvey?" he asked earnestly. "Did they have a problem with each other?"

"Well sort of," he said reluctantly, "you see," and he moved a little closer to the inspector and lowered his voice. "Over the years Charlie had disagreed with some of the doctor's methods and I think they had an unwritten agreement to steer clear of one another," and the charge nurse screwed up his face, hoping he hadn't said the wrong thing.

"Do you know where the doctor is now, Mr Turvey?"

"Probably in his office, although …" and he pondered for a moment, "having said that, if there's a murder enquiry being convened just outside, then probably not. He's possibly in one of the ward offices preparing a statement for the staff; but surely you've spoken to him this morning, inspector? He'd be the first person you'd speak to, wouldn't he?"

But instead of answering him he stood up and thanked him, said he appreciated his time again and as the inspector called the constable and departed, John Turvey's mind sagged from the weight of questions developing, questions to which he had no answers.

Chapter 23

When Jug left, Stan spent the rest of the evening with the piglets. He laid in the straw and let them clamber all over him, unperturbed by their inquisitive wet snouts prodding and poking him. One of them, the smallest, he took a special liking to and Stan was cradling it tightly in his arms when Barry shouted from behind the door that it was gone midnight and he wanted to lock up.

Stan slept well though Barry sporadically; the nightmare of the crash invading his dreams, causing him to constantly wake, sweating and shaking and it wasn't until dawn that he managed to clear his head of those vagaries and sleep deeply, accompanied by a loud snoring that unfortunately woke his friend in the adjacent bedroom.

But Stan was glad to be awake. After quickly dressing, he descended the stairs and, in the semi-light, went outside to the store, the sun, a sparkling thin arc, just emerging from under the horizon and he tipped half of a feed sack into a bucket and made his way to the mansion, his little legs almost buckling under the load. He opened the door and quickly entered, slamming it shut behind him and it was then that the piglets, having sensed food, charged, knocking him backwards into the straw, the feed flying every which way as they dove in, their heads flicking away the stalks as they searched greedily for the nuts.

Stan arched his back and propped himself up, astounded by the feeding frenzy and then he saw his favourite, right in the middle of them, staring

Maybe

at him, and he put out his arms and the piglet barged past them all and jumped into his lap squeaking and snorting with delight. Stan squeezed him as tight as he might and the ECT and panic attacks and the worry of Charlie's desertion were as far away as that rising sun and today, nowhere near as bright in his mind.

It was mid-morning when Barry surfaced and went in search of his friend. He had an inkling of his whereabouts and when he opened the mansion door he stepped in, as Stan had hours before and the sight he met tickled him pink. There in the corner lay Stan, fast asleep, his back propped up against the wall and the piglets, every single one of them, including a tiny thing astride his stomach, were also fast asleep: some straddled over his legs, some snuggled under them and a few lying on top of those beneath.

He took in the scene for some minutes, happy to see his friend so contented. Their anxiety over Charlie's non-appearance had been difficult to accept but the arrival of these piglets had brought a diversion … and spring was in the air! They would soon be preparing the ground, planting some spuds and he returned to the farmhouse, a spark of excitement growing over the prospect of what lay ahead.

It was mid-afternoon when Stan finally put in an appearance and the day being a cold one had prompted Barry to light the fire. He felt its warmth as he sidled in to find Barry in the kitchen, preparing the evening meal and when he yawned, Barry thought it was the worst piece of acting he'd ever seen.

"Do we have to go out tonight?" he moaned. "I'm so tired I can hardly stay awake," and when he feigned another yawn Barry realised he was opening his mouth without inhaling.

"We do, Stan, we owe it to Jug," and he removed a steel from one of the kitchen drawers and began sharpening a large utility knife.

"He's been a real friend, you said so yourself, we shouldn't let him down," and he began to carve a small ham, "and we need to get going soon; we're running out of food and we'll have to pop in the shop first," making Stan heave a frustrated sigh.

"But who'll look after Gruntlet?"

"Grunt what?" he questioned with a half laugh.

"Oh, never mind," he said annoyed. "I'll go and have a bath," and as he walked out of the kitchen Barry thought that was one of his better ideas.

Chapter 24

Cressy was at her wits' end. Her patients had gone missing and she didn't know what to do. She had been thinking of phoning the doctor all day and when she eventually plucked up the courage and got through to reception alarm bells rang when she was told of the terrible incident and his disappearance.

Realising there was no other alternative she made her way through the early evening crowds to the police station where, just days before, Stan had made his ridiculous confession.

When she entered the building, still racked with embarrassment following the event, the same desk sergeant was stood behind the partition and his attention focused on her as she approached the glass.

Chapter 25

Walking together down the lane, the cloudless night allowed the moon to illuminate their way and Barry left the torch in the bag.

The lady shopkeeper was packing away for the day but she was grateful for their custom and they left the store with heartfelt thanks as well as two laden shopping bags.

The Wheatsheaf was fifty yards away at the other end of the village and as they wrestled the bags through the swing door, the heads of the dozen or so already there turned in their direction. It was an awkward moment until a voice boomed from the far end of the bar and Jug stood up, the customers' heads now turning to him and Barry felt relieved that they had ceased being on display.

"Over here, boys!" his deep voice reverberating around the place and now the suspicious customers, on hearing the greeting, became friendly new pals smiling at them warmly as they walked by, one even bidding them good evening.

Toby Titmuss was sat on a wall bench, his enormous frame filling it and Stan realised that Jug, even sat down, was taller than him.

They offloaded their cargo, relieved as each other to lose the weight and sat on the chairs opposite. On the table were two, half-drunk pints of beer, one a luscious black and the other golden.

MAYBE

"Right boys, what ya goin' to have? The beer's a bit pissy but it'll get ya drunk!"

"No," Barry said forcefully, standing up. "We're buying, Jug, we agreed, now what are you having and before that what do we owe you?"

"I only want the money for the feed, everything else was favours."

"Jug, come on now …"

"I mean it, money couldn't buy that entertainment you gave me at the auction," and he wrapped his spade-like hands around each glass, completely enveloping them, his right around the black, left around the golden and draining each pint one after the other, slammed the empties down with a bang and belched as if his life depended on it.

"Cheers, Barry boy, Floss knows what I like," and he leerily looked across at the barmaid who returned his glance with a coy grin.

Barry approached the counter and waited his turn, surveying the tired old bar room, thinking that it could do with a big lick of paint though, before that, a full blown scrub; the years of cigarette smoke had discoloured the walls, curtains, ceiling, even most of the regulars. The smoke was so ingrained he thought whoever took on the task was going to need a long holiday afterwards. Then Floss was suddenly stood in front of him, big hair, big bosoms, big grin. He put his hand across the bar and opened it revealing a five pound note.

"This is for a tab," he said to her quietly. "I don't want Mr Titmuss to put his hand in his pocket this evening so whatever we have, please just take it out of this," and she winked at him and he ordered Jug's two drinks and a couple of pints of Watney's pale ale, delivering it all back to the table in two trips.

Jug lifted the black and lowered it, half full, a few seconds later.

"How you getting on with the porcine?" he said, still holding the glass. "Have they got out yet?"

"You've got to be quick with the door," Stan answered, sipping his beer, "and with the feed," he added, making Jug laugh.

"You keeping those logs dry, tar up the chimney wet," he asserted, "and those seed spuds, keep 'em dark," and a tall thin man with a pencil moustache walked into the bar and he raised his glass to him.

"Mr Titmuss," the tall man said and gave him a half wave, half salute then propped his elbows on the bar.

"Richard," Jug replied, returning the wave.

"That's Richard Thompson," he said in a whisper after leaning closer to them, "big noise round here, owns the local rag among other things. Only comes here once in a blue moon, I used to go to school with him," and he gulped the golden and sat back.

The room was beginning to fill and Jug seemed to know them all, raising his glass to every new entrant.

The landlord had now joined Flossie behind the bar and they were just managing to keep up with the orders. The beer was flowing and the volume was rising but Barry and Stan were sat seemingly apart from it, sipping their drinks, overpowered by the increasing intensity of the room and then Jug's hands were on their shoulders, his arms easily spanning the table, his bright blue eyes commanding their attention.

"Now listen, boys," he said artfully, "I've got you here tonight to make a few acquaintances, meet a few of the parishioners. Round here everyone helps each other out and it's important, believe me," and his eyes dropped to their almost full glasses. "Now I can see you're a couple of shy ones so what I suggest is that you drink up and have another. Conversation flows with the beer and anyway, we've got to make sure those hard working brewery lads up at Watney's have something to do, now don't we?"

He sat up, ramrod stiff, his broad back flat against the wall then lifted his hands and pointed at their drinks.

"Come on, fellas, you know Jug'll look after you," and he tilted his hand in a drinking action.

They looked at each other simultaneously and then, sensing the others' thoughts, raised up their glasses and with some difficulty and gurgling, managed to quaff the lot.

"That's better," the big man beamed, "that'll unblock the stoppage," and he raised his arm to get attention.

"Another round please, Floss," he shouted, "and chuck in a dozen cheese and onion, love, feeling a bit peckish," and he comically rubbed his bulge of a belly.

Their evening took off after that.

They were presented to the local characters, their host introducing them both as the 'learners'. The alcohol was having an effect and he was gladdened by the way it had transformed them from cold to convivial, it was good to see them laughing but he knew they weren't boozers and, having their best interests at heart, it wasn't long before he was asking Flossie to put mostly lemonade in their glasses.

Stan was the first to succumb to a demanding bladder and as he made his way to the gents his spirits were further uplifted by the warmth he felt radiating from his new acquaintances. He felt at ease with these people, accepted by them.

He was happily humming as he stood at the urinal, his aim a little precarious, when the hubbub from the bar rose as the door was opened. The tall man with the pencil moustache entered and stood by his side, a little too close for comfort and Stan stepped away slightly. The noise abated as the doors spring contracted and they both stood there quietly for a moment and Stan stopped peeing in mid flow, an involuntary action, then the tall man spoke.

"It's good to have new faces in the community," his voice clear and cultured. "I'd like to welcome you both, I'm sure you'll be very happy, especially with Toby looking out for you, he's a good man."

Stan suddenly relaxed and began going again. "Thank you, we've got pigs," he said randomly, making the tall man laugh.

"Well that's a good start, old chap, animals put the heart into a farm. My name is Richard and you are ...?"

"Stan," he replied, "and there was a heart in the farm before those little pigs arrived."

"Really, how's that?" he asked, puzzled.

"Well you see, my name's Stan Heart and ..." but he stopped speaking as the tall man erupted into laughter again.

"I like your style, Stan, I like your style; you're going to fit in well around here," and he shook his old boy and folded it back into his pants.

"Do you know, I was a friend of the fellow who used to live in that old mansion you have up there, used to keep himself to himself, no one knew who he really was, I think you bought it off his mother" and he hesitated for a second. "Good grief!" he declared, fabricating surprise, "I've forgotten his name, how odd?"

"Oswald," Stan piped up, buttoning his fly.

"Oswald, of course, Oswald ..." and he hesitated again, hanging on the name.

"Moseley," Stan assisted, lulled into forgetting the need for secrecy.

"Oswald Moseley, that's right," the tall man confirmed as if overjoyed, "strange I couldn't remember his name must be my age," then after a second, "or the gin," and he opened the door ushering his prey to go first.

"Oh, Stan, one last thing, can I take a quick snap? I'll put a piece in the paper, do a little write-up about newcomers, be interesting for people," and before Stan knew it, Richard Thompson had taken a photograph and his image was securely in the camera.

"Well it's good to meet you and again, welcome aboard," and the tall man left the pub, his mission accomplished.

As Stan returned to his seat Barry stood up.

"My turn, I'm bursting!" he announced and as he turned his head and watched his friend walk off, he noticed them, sat in the small alcove looking at him, a strained friendliness on their faces; the woman's black make-up and jet black hair making her instantly recognisable and he turned around quickly and looked at Jug.

"Those people are here, the ones who wanted to buy our farm," he said worriedly. "I don't think they like me and Barry very much," and he raised his glass then replaced it, untouched.

"D'you think I should go and say hello?" he asked innocently but Jug shook his head.

"Leave it, Stan," his words laboured now, he was getting tired. "I think they're the taking sort not the giving," and he went to pick up his drink but failed to raise it, just held it, his eyelids seeming to get heavy and then they closed and Jug's head fell softly forward onto the table where he relaxed into sleep and then, out of nowhere, she was sat in Barry's vacated seat, her perfume swirling, dark eyes staring into him and he felt afraid and excited by her all at the same time.

"Hello again," she said seductively. "I wanted to congratulate you on your success," and she held his hand gently and he sat as if set in concrete.

"My friend and I wondered if we could call over sometime, pay you a visit?" but all Stan could do was stare at the whiteness of her teeth, the black lipstick making them glitter and shine, "you see, we're all newcomers aren't we? You and your friend, me and mine. I think it could be interesting if we spent an evening together, perhaps one night next week?" and she waited expectantly for an answer though not anticipating the one she received.

"All right," he nodded, "we've got pigs."

"Riveting," she replied, patronisingly and took a long suck on her cigarette and tapped the ash into Jug's curly hair.

"His head is concealing the bloody ash tray," she said defensively, responding to his disapproving glance and she took another puff.

"We'll see you next week then," Georgia repeated and she returned to her partner who picked up his coat and followed her out of the door.

The breathalyser was four years away and anyway, Richard Thompson felt perfectly all right to drive even after consuming three large gins. He knew it would be an embarrassment to his two sons' godfather and bridge partner, should he be pulled over by some fresh faced bobby and taken into custody, charged with 'the ability to drive properly was, for the time being, impaired,' but he also knew that his Bridge partner, the chief constable of the county, would also have him out of there in no time and he stamped hard on the accelerator, the urgent call he had to make being the excuse. His wife was in bed and, after pouring himself another gin, he lifted the phone, made the call and his night editor answered.

"Eric, when's the deadline for Monday's copy?"

"One, possibly two o'clock tomorrow."

"Brilliant, I have a new front page, I'll be there in the morning," and he replaced the phone and sat at the kitchen table, removing a notebook and pen that could always be found in his jacket pocket.

'Mystery of mansion owner revealed,' he printed boldly then drew the pen through it. He knew the story would be easy but it was the headline that he had to get right. The headline would suck them in and he thought harder.

'Newcomers reveal mystery mansion owner,' but he drew through the words again.

He was going to mention the name in the accompanying article but then realised the name had to be part of the headline.

'Oswald Moseley revealed as owner of mystery mansion.'

He looked at it and liked it. Moseley was still a big draw and combined with the word mystery, even more so. He sketched lines around each of the words and inked in the spaces, making the sentence appear as it would in the paper. The regional press would fall over themselves, he thought, maybe even the nationals and he was right.

By the Tuesday most regionals and by the Wednesday every national paper carried his story in their first editions; *The Daily Express* actually making it the lead headline.

Richard Thompson used his years of experience to control the story and made enough money to keep him in gin for the rest of his life but a bigger story was about to unfold on his patch; one that would enable him to buy the distillery.

When he lifted his head from the table and realised where he was Jug was more or less sober. The pub was still full of people and noise and his vision gradually focused on the two men in front of him, staring across anxiously.

Stan bent his head down and looked up at him.

"Hi, Jug," waving his hand and the big man waved back and then Barry spoke.

"It's been a wonderful night," he said genuinely, "but we need to be getting back, Stan wants to …"

"Feed Gruntlet," he interrupted.

"Feed the pigs," Barry explained, "and it's getting a bit late."

"I'll come with you," he announced.

"No, please," Barry said, raising his hand, "we'll be fine, you stay here with your friends; you've done enough for us."

"Gentlemen," he said assertively, rising to his feet, "I don't want you getting lost," and he picked up their bags effortlessly. "Few years back an out of towner went astray from this very pub and we found him next morning, half dead, under my trailer … so come on, I'm taking you home," and the three of them trundled out of the place to a hearty farewell from the clientele, making their way through the village and past the shop, on and on until they turned into the narrow farm lane.

Jug was walking strongly and purposefully and they were having difficulty in keeping up, both staggered at the ease with which he was carrying the bags.

"We're lucky to have Jug," Barry said breathlessly, half running.

"I know," Stan answered, his short legs stepping four to Jug's two, "did you hear what he said in the pub when we left?"

"What, about that out of towner?"

"No, about taking us home," he replied with emotion in his voice and Stan began to swing his arms as if it would make him go faster, "he said he was taking us HOME!" and Barry began to swing his arms also and from a distance they resembled two happy windmills behind a lighthouse.

Chapter 26

On Tuesday, the 30th of April, 1963, a series of events occurred that were to play a significant part in an unavoidable tragedy.

During the morning, the desk sergeant had taken the statement from Cressy and deposited it on top of the inspector's in-tray.

The investigation was taking up most of his time and manpower but, nevertheless, some hours later, he read it thoroughly; but ignorant of its significance had re-filed it in an ever growing pile of unfinished business.

That afternoon, Georgia and Johnny were the only two people sat in the lounge of the Wheatsheaf. He was enthusiastically swallowing his way through a bottle of Hirondelle, the landlord having specifically ordered a crate on his behalf and she was indifferently sipping a lime and lemonade. They were racking their brains as to how they could beg or steal the land they needed from Stan and getting nowhere.

Johnny had been astounded when Georgia, just weeks after meeting him, had suggested they invest in some land to create, of all things, a golf course. He knew little of her deplorable past and just how much a share in such a prestigious development meant to her, but if that's what it took to secure her favours then so be it.

He also knew little, in fact nothing at all, of her intention to marry him as soon as possible then divorce him equally as fast once the eighteenth hole had been completed, the course being her settlement. He was a silly, spoilt man with no moral compass and no idea of the Machiavellian individual with whom he had become involved. Seduction was her forte but she had realised, after her brief chat with Stan four days before, that that particular ploy would be useless. The man was a half-sized, halfwit who would prefer to stroke a pig's arse than hers.

After finishing her drink she explained to her now unsteady companion that the only thing for it was to pay them a visit. She'd already done the groundwork and they needed to quietly find out all about them, not go at it like a bull at a gate but 'slowly slowly catchy monkey'. Befriend them, find the Achilles heel and then make their move and she thought the approaching Friday evening was as good a time as any.

Later that afternoon, it came to Bill that he had only seen Akan fleetingly since the murderous night and decided to find her and make sure nothing was untoward.

He'd been told about the feverish police activity over at the hospital, the searches and the interviews and he thought it only a matter of time before the police spread their net. He needed to ensure that she was fully committed and fully conversant with the alibi he'd concocted though he didn't have to look that far.

Pulling open the door he was taken aback to find her standing there. Small black bows in the crossovers of her braid, a loose fitting white blouse under thin white cardigan and tight, black denim dungarees. He had never before seen her dressed in any colour other than white and his jaw dropped. When she saw his reaction she unconsciously raised her hand and covered the scar, an automatic movement she adopted whenever she sensed alarm in a face.

"I'm sorry, Akan," he said, ushering her in, "it's not your ..." and he stopped himself, "it's your clothes, they're not all white, I was surprised," but she said nothing; just walked in and sat down as if she had a weight of worry on her small shoulders. "You look tired," he said, concernedly, sitting down, "you need to be strong, what we did was the right thing you know, I've no doubt in my mind."

"We took the law into our own hands," she replied quietly, a tone of regret in her deep voice, "and I am finding it difficult to come to terms with."

"The chief constable of the county was in his circle of friends, like I told you, no one would have listened to me."

"Looking back, I think that maybe we should have tried." Akan wasn't making eye contact; she was talking whilst looking down, something that Bill had never seen her do before.

"There's another thing, Mr Sweet," she continued, "in addition to the doctor, someone else's life was taken, wasn't it?"

For the first time in their relationship Bill was becoming angry with her and taking a deep breath to calm himself …

"What were we to do?" he asked in a low voice.

"You could have explained to whoever it was like you did with us, justified what we were doing, reasoned with them."

"I didn't have a chance, Akan," and he paused before casting the blame. "Angelo had used the knife before I could stop him."

Her head slowly rose and she looked at him for the first time.

"A man who uses force is afraid of reasoning, Mr Sweet," and her face remained expressionless.

He stared back at her, his anger growing, and decided it best not to mention anything more about the second killing of that night.

"The doctor was going to abuse you for God's sake, like he had many children; the man was depraved, evil," his voice now elevated, "you knew all this, you knew the man was a monster."

She lowered her head once more.

"I know, and when you left me in the room with him I knew for certain, but I didn't know how I was going to feel after …" and, sounding in pain, she gasped suddenly, "after we had murdered him," the words shooting out as if she was glad to be rid of them. "I own my feelings but have little control over them," and he noticed the anguish in her face and his anger receded.

He focused on the scar, like a rip in silk and thought of the pain she had suffered in her short life. Bill's ability for compassion was elusive but she always made it reachable and he stretched his arm and took her hand.

"You're wise, Akan, but you're still young. Your parents raised you with great care, I know that, but I have taken their role now and I couldn't allow that devil to harm you, you must understand that," he said seriously although knowing it to be a half truth.

She looked at him and smiled and then, abruptly, she frowned. "I think Angelo is mad," she announced unexpectedly, seeming to ignore what he'd said, "he is like no one I've ever met. He scares me, Mr Sweet, not because of his looks, he can't help those, it's because I can guess what he's thinking and it's always awful, like they're putrid and rotten and I hate feeling like that about him."

"Akan," he said sternly, releasing her hand, "without him we could never have stopped the doctor. If I could have come up with another way and not involved you both I would have but the deed's done and the three of must stick together."

He was defending the boy now, putting him above her.

"Never forget why we did it and never forget that Angelo played a huge part in keeping you safe," and Bill began getting concerned about her commitment to their secret, understood her misgivings, began to worry her guilty feelings could result in confession and then she said something else that heightened his uncertainty.

"I know I should be grateful, but …" and she paused and clasped her hands together, "when you told me about this man and what he intended I had been with Ruby for much of the time and she had been so upset describing her suffering that I agreed with your plan at once, I thought it was the right thing to do, but now it's done," and she began to nervously rub them together, "now it's done," she repeated, "I can't help thinking there could have been another way and that idea is pulling me this way and that and they've made me change the way I dress, it's made me wear black with the white," and she pulled the dungarees away from her leg to emphasise the point. "And there's something else that I need to understand," her gaze now burrowing into him, "how did he find all these children he was abusing? How did he get them to his office? Could he have done that all on his own?"

Bill swallowed. He felt his heart speed up and he averted his eyes.

He wished she hadn't been so inquisitive because those questions had caused a very bad notion to materialise, an awareness that no one was indispensable no matter how much he respected them.

Their eyes met once again.

"That is something I've been asking myself," he said softly then she frowned as he oddly put his hand to his face, gently rubbing the side of his right eye.

Bill had felt a long forgotten tingling, a thin prickle in his cheek, the sensation that occurred before, the tug the tic, and he was trying to knead it away, press it aside.

"Are you all right, Mr Sweet?" she asked worriedly, "should I leave?"

"No, no, Akan," he replied, his rubbing hand now raised, the palm pointing at her in a gesture to stay, "it's nothing, just an itch," and he gave it one last scratch," It's been shocking for the three of us, we're all under a lot of pressure," but her frown remained; there was now something false about him, something deceitful.

"Perhaps he did have an accomplice, I don't know," he went on. "I only found out about all of this the day he saw you sat out there at the entrance," and Bill, knowing this had to be believable, placed his elbows on the desk and in a dramatic gesture, sunk his head into them.

"He just barged in here, saying he had to see you, demanding I bring you to his office saying he needed to examine you."

She noticed he had closed his eyes, screwing them up as if he was thinking hard.

"And when I asked him why he seemed to change and although he was calm there was wildness in his eyes and then he told me everything. How he'd been defiling children for years and you were next." Bill was shaking his head now, getting into the part. "And then he began threatening me, I can see his face now being just inches away from mine, his hot breath on me," he exhaled loudly. "I can't remember everything he said but I know he made me feel like my life wouldn't be worth living if I breathed a word about it," and he opened his eyes and looked at her harshly, "and it was then I knew I had to protect you, Akan, and there was only one way to do it."

They continued to look at each other for a long time, both evaluating the situation in silence. Bill was an accomplished liar and thought his story believable, a certainty that was about to be underpinned.

The frown slowly disappeared from Akan's face and as she had with the doctor, felt the presence of her father in the room and he was telling her to be wary, be careful. She now knew that Bill Sweet's story was concocted. She could see it in his eyes, hear it in his voice and perceive it in his body language … but she knew to stop pressing. Living within him was a guilt of huge proportions, a secret that had to be kept and she remembered sitting on her papa's knee a long time ago, immersed in his devotion, listening intently to his words of advice and wisdom.

"Words are like spears, my darling; once they leave your lips they can never come back," and she thought deeply before she spoke.

"I want to thank you for everything you have done for me, Mr Sweet," and it was now her turn to hold his hand.

Bill simply shook his head, forcing a pathetically forlorn look upon his face.

"And I know you will understand the way I feel because you are a man who can see others' pain," and he modestly shrugged his shoulders although not really understanding her. "I will never tell a soul what happened for as long as I live, but I never again want to be involved in such a thing ever again. I sense that you have almost been broken, but you have remained kind to others and that deserves admiration as high as the sky," and she released his hand and stood up.

"Now I must go and change, I need to wear white again," and she left the office, them both knowing that nothing more should be said.

Chapter 27

The next morning, on his way into work, Bill stopped at the newsagent's to pick up the local paper. Every day the murder and disappearance of the doctor was front page news and Bill had developed a macabre fascination with the increasingly bizarre speculation, the latest theory being a patient had killed Charlie and had imprisoned Tim Richards in some remote building. He was waiting for things to die down and then his old mate George would be getting a call because George knew where they went on release.

He found the two night staff sat in the office finishing the last of their drinks that they hoped would keep them awake on the drive home. He greeted them with a happy grin and dropped the paper onto the desk, moving briskly to the recently installed coffee machine.

"Another one, ladies?" but they both declined and the one picked up the rag.

Bill flicked the switch on the device and placed his hand flat on the wall calendar, holding it steady as he ripped off yesterday's page.

"First of the month," he declared, looking at the new page he'd revealed. "Wednesday the first of May, nineteen sixty-three, doesn't time fly?" and he took the tab off a plastic capsule of milk and poured the contents into the cup.

Maybe

"Blimey! A new story for once," the night nurse commented, holding the newspaper high and Bill stood behind her, craning his neck to see what it was.

"Oswald Moseley's mystery mansion," she announced loudly, "hardly warrants front page news, where's the latest on the murder?" she said a little ghoulishly turning the page over. "Ah, here we are," and she folded the page and began to read.

"Wait a minute," Bill said irately, he'd bought the thing after all.

"What was that about Moseley?" and he went to take the newspaper from her.

"Oh, come on now, Bill," she moaned, playfully scolding him, "you've got all day to read this, we'll be gone in a few minutes," and she shook the paper and continued to read.

"For Christ's sake give the thing to me!" he shouted, reaching over and snatching it from her grasp. "You can buy your own newspaper!" and the two women immediately jumped up, both equally startled by his outburst.

"Crikey, Bill," the reader complained, astonished, "there's no need to lose your temper," and she picked up her bag. "I can't believe you acted like that over a stupid bloody newspaper," and she made for the door.

"I'm sorry," finding it hard to believe he'd overreacted so badly and throwing the paper back onto the desk, "I didn't mean it," desperately backtracking. "I've a lot on my mind at the moment," and he looked at them pleadingly for forgiveness.

The reader was a big hearted sort who had a lot of time for him and she immediately responded to his apology in a selfless way.

"Don't be sorry, Bill, I'm just engrossed with what's happened over at the hospital; I shouldn't just pick up your paper."

"Please," he talked over her, "please stop." He was angry with himself and desperate to remedy the situation, not wanting them to get a sniff of his interest in Moseley.

"I can't believe I shouted like that," and he turned around and bent over.

"Kick me up the arse, Mabel, go on, kick me up the arse."

"Don't be daft, Bill, I'm not going to—"

"Kick me up the arse," he repeated more forcefully and she stepped forward, steadied herself against the desk, raised her leg and gently connected with his rear end.

"Harder, Mabel!" he urged and after a sideways glance at her friend, who gave an encouraging flick of her head, she raised her leg again and with a little more force, booted him up the backside.

"There," he said, swivelling around, "I'm an idiot, it won't happen again," and the giggling women left only to remember the kick and not the reason for it.

As the door swung shut he made a grab for the paper, exposing the front page.

'OSWALD MOSELEY REVEALED AS OWNER OF MYSTERY MANSION.'

Ignoring the 'ready now' ping from the coffee machine he began to eagerly read the accompanying article, his excitement making it hard for him to take it all in.

A Mr Stan Heart, along with a companion, had purchased a small estate upon which a derelict mansion stood, a mansion whose previous owner's identity had, until now, been a mystery; and the piece posed a question.

Why had the owners allowed the mansion to fall into disrepair?

Finally the readership were being asked to get in touch with the news desk if they had any explanation and a contact address and telephone number appeared at the bottom in bold print. Bill began to re-read the story, the name of Stan Heart not registering with him until he noticed a grainy picture alongside the narrative - a black and white close up of a man's face. He moved his head closer to the page, angling it to allow the overhead light to sharpen the image and his eyes widened in instant recognition. It was Stan the smiling man, Stan the cuddly nutcase, Stan,

MAYBE

the only person left in the world who knew the truth behind the death of Mr William Wilson!

He dropped the paper onto the desk and stared straight ahead. Desperately trying to slow his whirlpool of thoughts, he stood and walked to the coffee machine and robotically fixed the drink, his mind beginning to focus, the whirlpool winding down and as he began to overload the cup with sugar, a dot of a scheme turned into a big picture and he instantly knew what had to be done.

Hot, sweet coffee splashed onto the back of his hand as he dropped the spoon into the cup but he didn't flinch, his mind was on the goal.

A call to George was further away now … he had to speak to his boy.

Chapter 28

Thursday, 2nd May, 1963.

It was late in the afternoon of a windswept day and the light from the single window had taken on a greyness, a reflection of their moods.

Inspector Burnes and the constable were in the doctor's office, the former holding Bertie, the toy used as a soother, although neither of the policemen knew his name, nor indeed Bertie himself but many young children did and hated the sound of it.

Their enquiry had ground to a halt. Every member of staff, including those recently retired, had been interviewed and no one had seen nor heard a thing. No worthwhile fingerprints had been lifted and searches of the hospital grounds, along with the homes of both Charlie and the doctor, had unearthed nothing; even the countywide poster campaign failed to produce a response. But the inspector was an optimistic sort and, coupled with his perseverance, knew that something would be found or be said, some snippet would surface to break the deadlock. When he began to pontificate he was looking up at the Cerletti statue.

"Why would Mr Bello have turned the interior light off, constable?" he mused, as if he were putting the question to the figure.

"I suppose he didn't want to be seen, sir, or recognised."

"Ok, so he didn't want to be recognised, so can we also assume he didn't want to be heard and that's why the door was left open or did he maybe, for some reason, not have time to close it?"

"I think they're all reasonable assumptions, sir."

"But if you'd arranged to, let's say, meet someone, you wouldn't care if you were seen or heard, would you?"

"Dare say I wouldn't, sir."

"Although, if you wanted to surprise someone, catch 'em unawares, being inconspicuous would be important, yes?"

"Very important, sir," he concurred.

"So Mr Bello parks up in an area of the hospital that ordinarily he would never use for a reason, a very good reason and he doesn't want anyone to know he's there because maybe he wants to ambush someone and maybe that person discovers him and reacts violently."

"But that someone, sir, would have to be armed with a knife, so he—"

"Or she," the inspector interjected.

"Of course, or she," he corrected himself, "must have already known that the situation could be dangerous."

The inspector returned to looking at the effigy. His colleague was a worthwhile sounding board and he was pleased with his interaction.

"So whatever Mr Bello saw, or whoever he wanted to meet or possibly confront, was making him act invisibly."

"Seems that way, inspector," pleased with the way he was being involved with this train of thought.

"You know, son, I don't think Mr Bello was an innocent party in all of this, I think he had something worrying him, maybe even tormenting him and he was there to sort it all out."

"So where does the doctor's disappearance fit in?"

"I know, I could be miles away from the truth," he looked up for inspiration, "but the murder and the disappearance have to be linked, you don't get two events like that happening at the same time and place without some sort of connection; perhaps he was there to have it out with him and the doctor committed murder?"

"That's a possibility, sir," and then he paused because he was about to say something above his station, "but I think there's many explanations for what's happened and until we have definite evidence …"

"I know that, constable!" he responded loudly then heaved a sigh. "I'm sorry, son, I didn't mean to shout," and he rubbed the back of his neck, annoyed with himself, "sometimes it's theories that can actually point you to the evidence." He walked across to the window and looked out. "I've been trying to come up with a feasible answer but, I don't know," and he placed Bertie on the window ledge and sat down. "I've been turning it over and over in my mind but nothing makes much sense. The doctor has obviously gone home after work because his car's parked in his driveway. For my theory to work he would have had to walk back to the hospital and there's no way he could have done that without being seen."

He stood back up and leant against the statue. "You're right, constable, there's probably a dozen or more explanations. I'm just clutching at straws, trying to guess, but I bet this old boy knows what happened," and he patted the figure. "And that little fella on the window."

But if Bertie could talk he wouldn't be able to speak, the trauma of his experiences would prevent him.

The inspector's oversight of not considering the doctor could have walked to work suddenly didn't matter.

"Maybe the farmhouse can throw some light on things?" the constable said, out of the blue.

"The farmhouse?"

"Yes, the farmhouse."

The inspector stared at his companion vacantly.

MAYBE

"You've got me there, son, the farmhouse?"

"You know, sir, the details we found on the car seat, Mr Bello's car seat," he added helpfully.

"Good God, constable, I'd completely forgotten about that!"

He'd become respectful of his boss's honesty and candour from the beginning of the investigation and the inspector's memory loss, rather than exasperating him, further enhanced his admiration.

"Where are they?"

"Back at the station, they were bagged and labelled."

Inspector Burnes glanced at his watch, it was almost 6 pm.

"You've got little one's haven't you, constable?"

"Two girls, sir," he replied.

"Get on home, son, I'll see you at the nick in the morning, nine o'clock sharp. I think we'll go on a little journey tomorrow," and then added, "a little Friday road trip."

Bill Sweet hurriedly left his office and made his way to room three. There was no reply from his knock so after an impatient pause he eased open the door. The curtains had been drawn and the room was in semi darkness. He stepped in and closed the door behind him, waiting for his eyes to adjust to the gloom. The appearing scene was so bizarre that he needed to step further into the dimness for clarification.

Angelo was completely naked, his back tortuously arched allowing him to submerge the hind part of his head in the overflowing sink, his face seeming to float on the surface of the water, his scarred arms grasping the sides to hold him in that precarious position.

Bill eased a little closer and discerned that Angelo's cheeks were bloated and distended like some amphibian, a dribble of water leaking from the corner of his shrivelled mouth. He cautiously moved closer and stood over the youth, peering down at his deviant features that appeared all the more grotesque in this shadowy half-light. He could see no signs of breathing and he lowered his face even further in an attempt to listen when he saw the slit eyes suddenly part and felt a wave of warm fluid cascade over him as Angelo spurted out the contents of his mouth.

Bill jumped back in shock, wiping the slimy water from his eyes as the boy pushed with his arms and straightened his back, emerging from the sink and standing upright, water splashing to the floor. Bill was speechless and Angelo barged passed him and sat on the bed, grabbing a towel from the side table as he went. He began drying his hair and as Bill recovered his composure, drew open the curtains and sat by his side.

"You scared me there, son, I thought you might have been dead."

But he didn't reply, just continued to dry himself.

"What were you doing with your head in the sink like that?"

He stood up and began dressing himself, still unresponsive.

Bill continued. "There's something big we need to talk about, I need you to listen to—"

"What I need," Angelo said dramatically, "is to do it again."

"Do what again?" he asked, relieved that the boy had at last spoken.

"Use the knife," he said matter of factly, "or my head is going to ..." and he thrust his hands upwards to imitate an explosion.

A wide grin appeared on Bill's face and he relaxed. He loved this boy, his anger and his weirdness.

"My head was getting hotter and hotter like what was inside was beginning to boil," and he stepped into his trousers. "I had to cool it down, make it colder," and he zipped up his fly and put his hands on his hips.

"I've been practicing for hours, Mr Sweet," he went on, "don't matter where somebody is, above me, by the side of me or behind me. I can stick 'em easy by using one of the moves," and he lifted a chair and placed it in front of the wardrobe, stood on it and groped on the top for the knife.

"And this," he announced, jumping down from the chair and revealing it to Bill, "this is so sharp it can cut through paper," and he ripped a page from the bible by the bed, flung it into the air, swiped and the page magically became two, both halves floating together to the floor like a butterfly dying in flight.

"I've been sharpening it and sharpening it. Nicked one of those steel things from the kitchen," he said proudly and then he lightly passed it over his forearm, a line of blood appearing in its wake.

"Look at that," he said, astonished, "and I hardly pressed!"

Bill carefully took the knife and placed it on the bed, then using his handkerchief, pushed hard on the cut to staunch the flow. He was close to Angelo now and even though the youth was thin and pinched he could feel a firmness within him, a sinewy strength about him and he shuddered at the thought of the force the boy could muster when using the knife.

"I'm glad you haven't been wasting your time, son," he whispered into his ear. "I'm glad you've been practicing because I do need you to use that knife again, Angelo," and he felt the boy's body clench as if it was readying itself. "There's another monster out there who needs killing," and still pressing his arm he manoeuvred Angelo onto the bed and sat beside him.

"Come to my office tomorrow at two, it's a quiet time, I'll explain it to you and we'll go over everything like we did with Dr Richards, ok?" and he nodded his head, eagerly. "But remember this, son," and he was happy that the blood had stopped flowing when he removed the handkerchief, "this man I'm going to tell you about is ten times worse than that bastard doctor, no, a hundred times," he said fiercely, "this one kills them first!" and Angelo, without warning, leaned across Bill and grabbed the knife, jumped up from the bed and began to wildly swing the blade this way and that, deftly passing it from one hand to the other, stabbing to the left and the right, to the side and the back, silently, surely and murderously.

Bill got to his feet and, edging around the activity, began walking out.

"Good boy, Angelo, you keep practicing," he said, opening the door, but he wasn't heard, the boy was too immersed in the role play.

"Friday's a good day for murdering," he whispered, grinning and he closed the door behind him, a very good day indeed; the words, this time, a thought.

Chapter 29

Just as the door closed, sixty miles away in a tree-lined field with a pretty stream meandering along its bottom border, Jug was struggling to release the exaggerated bolt that secured the long blade of the pasture topper. He had been clearing the field of thistles when the frightening jerk shuddered through the Massey, combined with an ear splitting clash of metal as one half of the shank fragmented, confined, mercifully, by the topper's surround.

As he engaged the tractor's rear arm and raised the huge device he could see, underneath, the broken blade lying on top of the rock that had caused its demise. However, long ago, due to Jug's foresight and anticipation of such an event, he had attached a replacement blade to the body of the topper though hadn't bargained for the obstinacy of the retaining bolt which, no matter how much he heaved and pulled, remained tight. He dropped the spanner and crawled out from beneath the contraption for a breather.

He was at the highest point of the field and there being scant foliage on the trees, had a clear line of sight to Ancoats Farm.

Jug was a righteous man who made friends easily and cared for them deeply and as he looked through the trees he thought of Stan and Barry, doing their best to adapt to a life that was totally alien to them. He knew little of their past or why they'd wanted to buy the place but he was impressed by the way Stan had conducted himself at the auction, how they had both knuckled down to their new way of life and he particularly liked the appreciation they showed for his help.

He moved his gaze to the capacious mansion just fifty yards away from the farmhouse, the chimney pots visible above the surrounding trees.

"Bloody hell!" he cried out loud, remembering the piglets, "they'll be running short on feed," and went to get up but then he eyed the broken topper, glanced around at all those thistles, worked out how long it would take him to corral the sheep in the barn later, ready for market in the morning. Then he recalled telling them to come over and let him know when they were going low and he hadn't seen them.

His panic subsided.

He would get the stock to the sale in the morning, meet up with old friends, make a few quid and call into the agricultural merchants on the way back. From there to the Wheatsheaf; Thursday was darts and the captain had to put in an appearance, then the next day, the Friday, he'd call round to his new friends and drop off the bags. Pleased with this arrangement, he crawled back under the topper and offered up the spanner. It fitted snuggly over the bolt and he pressed his feet firmly against the machine's side, tightened his grip, took a deep breath and heaved.

Chapter 30

Bill was in bed early that night. He needed the solitude of the bedroom to concentrate on concocting the fiction and it wasn't until the early hours of the morning that he finally stopped concocting and sank into sleep, happy that he had fabricated a believable story.

This Mr Stan Heart was a prolific paedophile who had taken advantage of the chaotic situation during the war to commit the most despicable and sordid debasement of children imaginable. He had falsified his employment and educational history to obtain a position with the National Camps Corporation, a body formed to build residential camps for young people, mostly evacuees, using the status of his position to satisfy his perversion. He was finally apprehended when a young boy was found with a slit throat and anus. Miraculously, he was also found to be alive and when he had eventually recovered sufficiently to identify his attacker this Mr Stan Heart was arrested and charged with attempted murder and buggery. He pleaded diminished responsibility due to insanity and was detained in Rampton high security psychiatric hospital.

As often occurs when a sexual offender is taken into custody, many more of their victims feel empowered to come forward, since the threat had been removed along with potential reprisals. Twenty-six children made statements, (the number of Bill's bungalow) and the police suspected there were many more that didn't.

MAYBE

This Stan Heart was a devious and conniving individual who over time was able to persuade the authorities that he'd been able to cleanse his deviance by identifying with a new reality ... God. He had stared his wickedness full in the face and converted to pietism thereby freeing himself from the unbearable guilt of his sin to walk a different path.

He arrived at The Nuthatch three years ago, on probation from Rampton, having been deemed a reformed character and after the thirty months he spent there, before being reintroduced into the community, he was a trusted and liked patient.

"But these bastards never change, Angelo!" Bill said forcefully.

It was the afternoon of Thursday, the second of May, 1963 and, as arranged, they were sat in the office.

"It's like a birthmark, you're born with it and it never goes away," and the young man nodded in agreement.

Bill lifted the newspaper and pointed at the headline.

"I know you can't read this, son, but it says this Stan Heart has set up residence in some old farmhouse with another ex-patient and right by the place is a mansion that was once owned by a man called Oswald Moseley, someone who could make the world a much better place, a much safer place," and he thrust the paper angrily down on the desk.

"But what it doesn't say is that just a fortnight ago, a young eight-year-old boy was found murdered a mile away from that farmhouse and in the last two days another young lad has been reported missing," and from the corner of his eye, a few inches above his lying mouth, he could see that Angelo had clenched his fists.

"It's this Stan Heart," the boy said coldly.

"I think you're right," Bill agreed, furtively fanning the flames. "My friend in the police force, who told me all of this, won't listen to me ... thinks that the hospital would never of let him out if he was still a danger, but these people are cunning, that Dr Richards would still be doing it if we hadn't stopped him."

"Well we can stop him," and Angelo bent down and lifted the leg of his trousers, carefully removing the blade. "This can stop him good," a glint emanating from the knife and his eyes.

"You're a good boy, Angelo, a very good boy," and he opened the small desk drawer and removed an Argus C3 camera and passed it to him. "Tomorrow I'm going to drive you up to this farmhouse and you're going to have this camera round your neck. If you're spotted, that's going to be the excuse for being there, to take pictures of the Moseley mansion that you saw in the paper. You're going to have to be crafty though, craftier than this Stan Heart, get him on his own, away from anyone and then," he pointed at the knife, "and then you can use one of your moves," and he smiled shiftily at him, "get rid of the stink."

"Don't you want to be with me? See it all happen?" he asked.

"I'd like nothing more, son, but there's a bigger chance of someone seeing two of us, best if you're on your own."

"You gonna wait?" he said, re-sheathing the knife.

"D'you want me to?"

Angelo thought about this for a moment. "Need to get back here somehow," hooking the camera round his neck.

Bill's planning had stopped at dropping him off thinking the boy would use public transport thereafter, an idea he now felt absurd and quickly thought of a solution.

"We'll find the nearest phone box then I'll drive you up close to the farm. When it's done, make your way back to it then ring me here. I'll be waiting to come and get you," and Angelo nodded his head, satisfied with the idea and began to leave. "And if you can get a few snaps of that mansion I'd be interested in seeing them," Bill suggested and although he had difficulty in deciphering any expression on the young man's unfortunate face, the current unclear one spelt 'fuck that' loud and clear.

MAYBE

As he left, Bill was feeling good and reclined in his chair. The matron was gone, the doctor was gone and by tomorrow night the last one privy to his secret would be also. He breathed in deeply and relaxed.

Friday would be the day he could pop the cork and finally say amen.

Chapter 31

Friday, 3rd May, 1963.

Jug felt worse for wear when he woke that morning. The dart team's first success in months had resulted in far too much celebration and his mouth was dry and his head in a clamp.

As he rolled to get out of the bed his back cramped in pain and his memory shot back to the previous day; that bolt unexpectedly snapping causing a wrench as he twisted.

With a groan accompanying each step he lumbered to the sink, turned the tap and filled a pint glass, drinking the contents with one mighty gulp, then repeated the process and stumbled back. He'd intended taking the pig feed to the boys that morning but it would have to wait. Jug had more sleeping to do.

As he pulled the eiderdown over his aching head, Georgia squeezed into the parking space and squeezed out of the Frogeye Sprite. She was late for an important solicitor's appointment and even her five inch heels weren't impeding her progress. She was ushered straight in, her seductive presence causing the man's hand to quiver as he gave her the sealed envelope.

MAYBE

He required a signature on the contract therein along with a cheque for the agreed price to enable the transfer of fifteen acres of Mr Heart's land, the amount she needed for the second nine holes.

He admired the ebony black nail varnish as Georgia offered him her hand and then she left, not five minutes after entering.

While she was cautiously positioning herself into the low seat of the sports car, the two policemen were stood over a desk studying the sale details, their mugs of steaming tea untouched.

Without saying a word the inspector lifted the phone out of its cradle and dialled the number for the auctioneers.

The secretary explained that the person he needed to speak to wouldn't be in the office until after lunch due to a family funeral and he replaced the phone moderately bothered but decided to postpone the drive until that conversation had taken place, a decision the inspector would live to regret.

Chapter 32

There was a hint of rain in the air as they set off on their journey. Angelo had had a bad night and was in a darker place than usual. After listening to Bill's dishonest description, his loathing of Stan Heart had built into a capstone of malice. All through the night his sleep was interrupted by memories of Loveluck Jones; he felt his touch as the man lustfully removed his clothing, tasted the acid tang as his tongue wormed into his mouth, smelt the clinging, feculent odour after the man had finally finished defiling him.

Sitting in the car those feelings were still strong and his contempt for Mr Loveluck Jones had now been transferred to Mr Stan Heart and all Angelo could subscribe to was murder. He sat silent and seething and Bill was getting worried that perhaps he was having second thoughts but when he asked his passenger what was wrong the answer allayed any concern.

"I just wanna stick him, Mr Sweet, I just wanna stick him."

The journey took over an hour and no further words were spoken until they reached a red telephone box that Bill guessed was a walkable distance from the farm. It was stood in a layby and he pulled in, opened the heavy door and checked that the thing was in working order. Satisfied that it was, he called for Angelo to join him and after explaining the procedure of making a call, gave him an envelope containing three sixpence pieces and the phone number of his office. Angelo placed it securely in a zipped, inner pocket of his parka and they continued on. The previous night Bill had studied the ordnance survey of the area and after a half mile they drove into the village that was local to the farm, passed the Wheatsheaf, then the shop and just as they were leaving the fabric of the village he began slowing down and pointed at an open entrance to a lane.

"That's the way into the place, son, it's about a quarter mile up that track," and he carried on, driving slowly. "I'll drop you off further on, somewhere quiet," and after a short distance he noticed a rough pull in beside a gate and brought the car to a halt, the engine still running.

"Good luck, Angelo," and the boy opened the door, "and be crafty, not angry, you make mistakes if you're angry," but Angelo was beyond angry and he leaped over the gate and, hugging the hedgerow, began to make his way to the farm.

The ground was flat, easy to traverse, and before long he was lying on a small rise overlooking the farm, the camera firmly around his neck.

It was enormous, the mansion seemed six times larger or more than the farmhouse like a father and small son; fifty yards separating the two with a mountainous, ancient ash towering over the divide and he stealthily made his way to beneath it and started to climb.

He needed to understand the place, get the geography, take note of the ins and outs and he reached a wide, horizontal bough and waited and watched, content that no one would see him because he had learnt from hiding the knife that nobody ever looks up.

Chapter 33

She parked up the Frogeye, barged through the unlocked door, set the full kettle down on the flames of the gas stove then went upstairs to change. Off came the display and on went the practical and she returned to the kitchen in walking boots, loose jeans and a thick roll neck sweater. She sat down with the cup of tea and when Johnny entered and enquired how the appointment had gone she simply held up the envelope and winked.

"Use all of your cunning, my darling," he said, lighting a thin cheroot, "if you pull this one off it'll be champagne tonight," and he winked back at her beguilingly.

Thirty minutes later Georgia left and began the walk to her neighbours and as she swung open the gate that led onto the fields she so desperately wanted to acquire, Jug, a mile away, slept the sleep of the innocent and the policeman, a lot further away, was again ringing the number of the sale room.

"Hello there," the auctioneer replied. "I'm sorry I wasn't available earlier."

The line was poor and the inspector could only just make out what was being said.

"That's quite all right, sir, I completely understand. The line is bad so I'll get straight to the point. I have particulars in front of me of a farmhouse your company recently sold and I'd like to ask you a few questions."

"Which property would that be, inspector, there were three?"

He winced as he strained to hear. The room was full of police officers and voices and rustling paper and the reply wasn't quite what the auctioneer was expecting.

"Would you hold the line one second, sir?" and he placed his hand over the mouthpiece, looked around, then bellowed over the din.

"Everyone, can I have your attention please?" and the room fell silent.

He held up the phone, "important call, bad line, could I have some hush for a minute?" He waited for a moment. "Thank you," and removed his hand.

"Sorry about that, sir, you were saying?"

"There were three properties in the sale," he continued, "which one was of interest?"

"The farmhouse that included the mansion, the dilapidated mansion."

The room was quiet now and everyone couldn't help but listen to the inspector's side of the conversation.

"Oh, good grief," came the reply, accompanied by a laugh. "I don't think I'll ever forget that particular sale, stands out as one of my strangest. What was it you wanted to know exactly?"

"Can you remember a man, a coloured man by the name of Charlie Bello ever making enquiries about it?"

"I'm not sure of the name … wait a minute, thinking back I'm sure they called him Charlie."

"They?"

"The two men who bought it, they were accompanied by a coloured gentleman and I'm certain they called him Charlie."

The inspector sat down. This was the first substantive lead in the case and he needed to focus his attention.

"Would you have the names of the two gentlemen, sir?" he asked, tentatively.

"It's actually been in the newspapers, haven't you seen it?"

The inspector ignored his remark. Newspapers were for reading when he had time on his hands.

"I said do you have their names, sir?" he repeated firmly.

"Of course," becoming flustered by the inspector's sudden change of tone. "I'll get the file," and during the delay he looked up at the constable and gave him a thumbs up.

"Right, I have it in front of me. There was only one purchaser, a Mr Stanley Heart, a very interesting character if I might say."

"Mr Stan Heart you say, sir?" he replied loudly and the inspector pointed at the constable and then at the file on his desk, remembering the desk sergeant's memo and the name.

"In what way was the sale strange, sir?" and two officers walked into the room animatedly discussing a case and the inspector raised his hand to quieten them.

"Well the sale itself was quite dramatic as Mr Heart and another potential buyer, a lady, both desperately wanted it but when the bidding reached a ridiculous figure her backer pulled the rug and she stormed out. But what was strange happened after the sale more than during it. You see, they wanted to move in immediately and I had to have a special document drawn up to safeguard ourselves and the seller should the money not be forthcoming."

"And that's unusual?"

"Very unusual, in fact it's never happened before."

The constable found what he was looking for and handed it to his boss who, once again, asked the auctioneer to hold the line as he read through it. Passing it back, he repeated the thumbs up and returned to his conversation.

"And had the money been forthcoming?"

"Every penny of it."

"And are the men in residence now?"

"As far as I know; they wanted it so much I suppose they're bound to be."

"Can you cast your mind back to Mr Bello for a second, sir? What seemed to be his relationship to the two men?"

"Well, if I had to describe it, inspector, I'd say it was a chaperone. He seemed to be guiding them, watching out for them almost."

"Was there any arguing? Any animosity?"

"On the contrary, they all appeared to be very close, especially Mr Heart and his companion, whose name escapes me I'm afraid."

"Does Barry sound right?"

"Yes, Barry, that's it," then he paused for a second, "perhaps I shouldn't be asking this, inspector, but is there something I'm not aware of here, have these men committed some sort of crime?"

"I've no reason to believe they've committed a crime but I will need to interview them. You see, Mr Bello was recently found murdered and there's a possibility they could have information that could lead to an arrest." He wanted the conversation to end now, needed to get to the farm.

"Good God that's unbelievable!" his voice quivering.

"Quite, now are the directions on the particulars accurate?"

"Very," he replied, the shock still in his voice.

"Then thank you for your time, you've been extremely helpful. I'll be in touch if I need to speak to you again."

"Of course," and the line went dead.

The inspector jumped to his feet.

"I want two other cars with four officers in each," he shouted, heading for the door, "full sirens until we're a mile away and limit the radio use."

A sergeant barked out names and the officers began to run to the carpool.

It was just after one thirty when the three panda cars sped off, two uniformed officers stopping the traffic and waving them through and Jug had finally got out of bed and as he walked into the utility room to put on his boots, Georgia walked up the path to the farmhouse, the once misty rain getting heavier.

Chapter 34

For more than an hour Angelo hadn't seen a soul, the only movement being the thin trickle of smoke from the farmhouse chimney and the fluttering of leaves. He'd had no intention of using the camera but when he noticed any insect or grub, couldn't help photographing it.

Angelo enjoyed being in a tree, felt protected by it, felt it was looking after him. He liked trees more than human beings; maybe Bill and Akan were exceptions, but only maybe.

He'd heard the unusual noises coming from the mansion and was curious to know what was in there. They weren't noises he recognised. There were squeals now and then and occasional squeaks as if whatever was in there was happy and excited.

The rain was getting heavier and the wind was picking up and, satisfied he'd memorised the lay of the land, he decided to check out the mansion, see what was in there. He repositioned himself to climb down when he heard a faint knocking coming from the front of the house. Angelo was beginning to think the place was deserted and he cupped his hands over his ears and listened hard, just making out muffled voices and a door closing.

They were home! And a smile appeared. Though, whereas a smile would normally brighten a face, for Angelo it had the effect of distorting even more his already deformed features, causing the abnormal to be even more so. Last night's memory of Loveluck Jones reappeared in his mind and he felt the anger inflate something inside him; it rose through him in waves and his right hand slid down and felt the bulge of the knife, his left slid down and felt another. He'd brought a spare, stolen from the kitchen, not as good but good enough. A successful murderer comes prepared and as he caressed the blades he knew that soon his anger would subside.

He skilfully descended the tree, landed gracefully on the ground and crouching low, zigzagged to the mansion's front door. He unhooked the string from a metal device that resembled a question mark and cautiously entered the building. Angelo had never before seen a piglet and the sight of them made him jump backwards, his shoulder blades banging solidly against the door. The creatures were equally as startled and as pigs in these situations do, they all suspended whatever they were about and stared at him statue-like, as if every joint in their small bodies had locked.

The ensuing silence was suddenly broken by a low groan, that began to almost vibrate as it came from between his thin lips, he realised he was looking at a dozen images or more of what he saw in the mirror. He groaned even louder as, in unison, the piglet's bodies relaxed and they began slowly walking towards him and, with corresponding slowness, his hands dropped down and rested on the knives.

And then he felt the jolt.

Chapter 35

She apologised for turning up unannounced but explained there was no way of contacting them and what she had to say was very important.

Barry made her feel welcome by offering a cup of tea and taking her wet coat for which she graciously thanked him. Turning around to aid its removal she noticed a form on the side table with Stan's childlike signature and her eyes lit up; if all else fails, she thought.

He went into the kitchen and Georgia stood in front of the fireplace to warm herself. Stan felt awkward in her company and as he recognised that she was about to speak informed her that the piglets needed feeding and excused himself, apologising profusely as he went. Georgia wasn't perturbed by this as she had an inkling that it was Barry who pulled the strings anyway and she rubbed her backside that the fire was warming and waited for him to return.

The last bag of feed was propped in the corner of the small shed and the sight of it actually lifted his spirits. Here was a perfect excuse to further avoid the lady as it meant he'd have to go over and see Jug about further supplies. With some effort he hoisted the bag onto his shoulder and walked around the farmhouse, bypassing the lane, and went the quicker way to the mansion over a rough section of ground. He had no desire to find out what was so important to her and he took his time, watching his step as he plodded through the sodden ground.

When he arrived at the door, a little unsteady from his raised centre of gravity, he looked at the dangling string with unease. He knew absolutely that he was the last one to be in there and he was equally as sure that he had fastened the string properly when he'd left. He further knew that the door was inclined to open inwards if it wasn't fastened so what was keeping it shut. Stan turned and pushed his hip against it and Angelo let out a startled grunt as he felt it. His mind raced as he thought of what to do and then he remembered the excuse that Bill had come up with and he grabbed the camera to his chest and, leaping over the pigs, ran to the hay bales that were stacked at the far end and squatted.

The door now gently swung inwards and one, then two, piglets came into sight and although the dangling string remained unexplained he thought they were the reason for the sticking door and then Stan saw the figure. He shook his head when, at first, he ridiculously thought it was some sort of misshapen animal then he peered forward and screwed his eyes to get a clearer look and more detail appeared and Stan recoiled in horror as it stood up, the features of the young man becoming apparent. He took a step back and dropped the sack, a bolt of disgust forcing his face to skew.

The piglets were motionless as if his shock were infectious and in the fearful silence Stan could feel his heart pounding like some wild thing frantically trying to free itself, banging against its cage.

The figure's small face dwelt within a large hood and it seemed out of shape as if it were being pulled forcibly back and then the arms of the form began rising and the piglets suddenly screamed in concert, a deafening, cacophonous squeal and scrambled to a corner as in an instant the mansion blasted into light, its intensity almost tangible causing Stan to fall to the floor.

He lay there, dazzled, and could inexplicably hear the guttural hum of aeroplanes and explosions, shivered as if his skin were being sprayed with freezing water and he passed his fingers over his eyes and as they opened he could see the figure stood over him, its frightful face looming above like a hovering, twisted mask and its hands were holding a camera and for some reason, he thought he was going to die.

The tranquillity of Jug's world was in stark contrast to that of the inspector's.

As he hummed an old tune and methodically moved the feed sacks from his vehicle onto the flat bed, the inspector and his men were on heightened alert: their cars wailing and speeding precariously as they journeyed, careering passed stopped traffic and gawping pedestrians.

Jug's head was still pounding and he wished he were back in bed but knew that was impossible, shit always needed shovelling and mouths always needed feeding and he gritted his teeth and finished the job.

But he didn't set off.

After his exertions Jug's fluid reserves had dropped and, rubbing his sore back, returned to the kitchen and turned on the tap.

"Saw it in the paper," Angelo said quietly.

He knew there were two of them living in the farmhouse and wasn't sure if this was the one he was after. However, he did know he was looking at a scared little runt and that gave him much pleasure.

"Wanted some pictures," he continued, "didn't know it would light the whole place up," he remarked, looking perplexed at the camera that had produced the brilliant flash.

Stan was frightened by the youth's appearance and manner but he was on home ground and a seed of courage began growing.

"You shouldn't be in here, you left the door open, they could have all got out," and he began getting to his feet.

Angelo stepped back a pace to enable him to get up and the small man brushed the straw and dust off and finger combed his hair back into place.

Due to Stan's rebuke, Angelo was having trouble subduing his temper and his hands clenched into fists making Stan's knees tremble when he noticed.

Maybe

"All right, you can take some pictures," he said, backtracking, "but I have to feed these little piglets," though the boy ignored him as he focused intently, his piercing stare making Stan almost quake in his boots, the only movement in the mansion now being the opening and closing of Angelo's fists.

Stan could virtually smell the exuding menace and he closed his eyes as if in some way, not being able to see him would remove the danger. He squeezed them tightly shut and then heard something moving. His bladder seemed to enlarge and he moved his legs slightly together and clamped to prevent any embarrassment.

He heard it again and he compressed his eyes even more, tightened his lips then curled his arms around his chest, readying himself for something awful and then he felt it. A rhythmic warmth on his face and within that warmth was a tainted and fetid odour and when he nervously opened his right lid he was looking into a fissure, the eye within barely evident, the face it was on no more than two inches from his. He held his breath and swallowed and suddenly he could hear speech but it was garbled and indistinct.

Angelo spoke again in a low tone and this time Stan was able to understand.

"I said, what they call ya, mate?" irritation embroidering the words.

He opened his other eye. The malodorous breath continuing to envelop him, the fear preventing him from making sense of what was being asked of him.

He repeated the question in his mind.

"What they call your mate?" and he withdrew his head a little and mumbled, "Barry," knowing that he was the only person in the world he could refer to as being his mate.

But Angelo was, in fact, asking Stan for his name and he heaved a sigh; this was the wrong one and he began rubbing his forehead in thought. Stan didn't want to be alone with this youth any longer, he wanted to be down there with the friend he'd just mentioned and when the second question was asked his ability to concentrate was all but gone.

"So Stan?" and Angelo pointed in the direction of the farmhouse but instead of comprehending the meaning behind the query assumed he was being asked if they could go to the house so he replied "Yes," further cementing Angelo's belief that his prey was elsewhere.

"We can go for a cup of tea down there if you like," and Stan relaxed a little the fact that the youth knew his name not registering with him, while Angelo couldn't believe his luck.

This man would take him to his intended victim and no further planning was going to be necessary. He eagerly nodded his agreement.

"But first these little fellas need to be fed," and he returned to the dropped bag and pulled firmly at the drawstring, the noise reanimating the animals who rushed towards them.

Angelo appeared to jump into the centre of the room away from them and Stan scooped the feed nuts onto the floor, the piglets greedily tossing the straw away with their snouts.

"They won't hurt you," he declared and his fear marginally abated when he recognised Angelo's vulnerability, a feeling of pity replacing his anxiety as he considered the way he looked and what his experience in life must be.

"Don't worry, they like people," then added, "animals only hate nasty people," and, as if to emphasise the point, he reached out and stroked little Gruntlet who was always the closest to hand.

Angelo could have easily slit the throats of the lot of them and their keeper but he held himself in check.

He had an assignment and this man he had mistook for another was oiling the wheels.

Chapter 36

Georgia was explaining to Barry why they were drinking tea together and was only slightly distracted by the faraway noise of a tractor bursting into life, a sound that, since her move to the sticks, she had become familiar with.

Jug released the key as the machine erupted with force and fumes, the noise making him grimace and he dug around in his pockets and found the soft, orange ear plugs and pressed them in, breathing with relief as the discord decreased and he gently eased the gear stick forward and set off. When he reached the bottom of his lane, that led onto the main road, he paused to check the way was clear then, lightly lifting the accelerator stalk, drove on passed the Wheatsheaf and the shop towards Ancoats' entrance.

He wouldn't have heard the sirens even if the ear plugs were still in his pocket and the tractor coasting in neutral as the panda cars had come in sight of the telephone box and the inspector had ordered silence.

"Thousand yards up on the right should be a pub," he barked over the speeding commotion, quoting from the sale details, "and then another thousand to an entrance on the left," and the constable nodded, concentrating on the road.

The pub came and went and the driver took his foot off the throttle, aware they would soon be having to make a left and then they saw it. A battered, red old tractor pulling an equally battered old trailer turning slowly into the entrance of the lane and the constable raised his eyebrows when he hears his boss, for the first and only time, swear.

"Bollocks!" he thundered and slammed his hands down onto the dashboard.

Stan emptied the last of the contents into the hay then threw the bag into the room knowing the piglets would have hours of enjoyment from pushing and pulling at it. He hated the forced intrusion into what he now considered to be his home but the youth standing there, who had initially scared the living daylights out of him, had somehow stirred his paternalism and he called across to him.

"All done, let's go and have a cuppa," and Angelo warily skirted around the room to avoid the pigs and joined him by the door.

Stan tugged it open and the youth was now stood directly behind him, summoning all of his ugly strength in an attempt to stop himself from stabbing him there and then because he must know what his friend Stanley Heart gets up to, now, mustn't he? Probably a party to it ... but sort the big fish first, he theorised simplistically and the hand that had descended to the knife rose and Stan, ignorant to any of this, hooked the string to secure the door and began to walk to the farmhouse.

"He's got no lights, no mirrors and he's just come off a main road!" the inspector gasped. "And that load looks unsafe; he's breaking every rule in the book," he added for good measure as the three police cars proceeded at a snail's pace behind the tractor, the driver of which being completely oblivious to their presence.

"No way of getting past him, sir," the constable said to his increasingly fretful boss, "about a foot to spare either side," causing the inspector to crane his neck and fifty yards up ahead noticed the hedgerow veer into a field fronted by a gate.

"There's a passing place or something up on the right," he announced thankfully, "when I say, give a short blast of the siren," and the constable's hand hovered above the button in readiness.

Barry and Georgia were sat on the chairs in front of the fire, sipping their tea; although hers was hardly touched … she was doing all the talking. Georgia thought it best to present herself as prim and proper and from the off referred to Lord Johnny as her hubby.

"And that's why my hubby, you see, stopped me bidding on the whole of this place; it's only the land between you and us that we need, Barry, not everything. I was upset at the time, I know, but I want this golf course so much, it'll give jobs to so many local people and, as I say, we're willing to pay you twice the current market value and we'll even throw in life membership of the golf course for the two of you, a lovely golf course right on your doorstep."

And then something happened that he had heard of but never before witnessed.

When the back door of the farmhouse was opened he believed it was only Stan returning and didn't bother to look around, but Georgia had and as he kept looking at her face it seemed to drain of all life and colour, as if she had aged ten years in as many seconds.

His jaw dropped in astonishment as he became aware he was watching somebody turn white and he jerked his head in the direction of her stare and thought he understood why.

When he saw Angelo he thought she'd become petrified with fright but he had no way of knowing that this abnormal person was in fact her son and she was agog. Then Barry imperceptibly tilted his head and gulped in alarm. He'd seen this person before and he honed in on the youth's face. He was in the car, by the side of the road, when they were leaving the hospital and on their way to the halfway house and he remembered that frightful face and the effect it had on him and he was feeling that sense of dread once again.

Barry's eyes reverted to his friend, who he sensed was in great danger, a desperate and questioning expression on his face.

"He wants to take some pictures that's all, seen it in the paper," Stan said, matter of factly responding to the look and then he suddenly cowered as Georgia powerfully pushed against the chair and stood up, a shriek emerging from her as she ascended.

And then nothing … no motion, no sound until, a few seconds later, with her hands in front of her she began to walk toward her son.

"Angelo, darling, why are you here? I don't understand," she stammered, totally mystified, her face now an unearthly grey.

"Don't touch me!" speaking for the first time, slanting his head to get a better look at her features, "if you're her you mustn't touch me!" and he rushed forward and pushed with all of his might causing her to fall heavily to the floor.

Barry quickly stood and Angelo's head clicked sideways, his eyes red hot pokers and Barry thought he could feel their heat.

"Where you goin' you brown cocked fucker?" the words growled and snarled out and Barry stepped back a pace as he felt the enormity of the boy's hate.

"Now!" the inspector shouted and the piercing siren wailed as the constable's hand pushed the button.

They were good earplugs but not that good and as Jug arched around he could see the inspector's flailing arms, urging him to pull over.

He began to panic and yanked at the stalk, the tractor putting on a sudden burst of speed causing the feed bags to shunt backwards though mercifully stay on board and he steered the machine a further few yards on and into the pull in, the tubular guard at the front of the Massey coming to rest against the padlocked gate.

But all to no avail.

The rear of the trailer still jutted back into the lane preventing them passing and Inspector Burnes abruptly shouted another command.

"Switch the engine off, son," pulling the lever to open the door. "I don't know why but something's telling me we've got to get up there fast," and motioning for the other officers to follow he began to run; steadily and fixedly, pushed on by an unknowing sense of urgency.

Barry was now terror stricken, the siren blast magnifying his fear and he dropped the half full cup and shouted at Stan to run but his friend was bewildered and remained rooted to the spot. He made a dash for him and Angelo crouched then sprang forward, blocking the way so he turned and headed for the exit. The youth grabbed his shoulder and pulled him around and he staggered backwards, his back against the door, spreading his arms wide, preparing for something dreadful and then he saw the boy crouch low again, maybe four feet away and when he stood there was something pointed and gleaming in his hand and as Barry Stone took his last breath Angelo executed one of his moves, a pirouette, the blade gathering momentum as it flew full circle and then a dull thump as the knife sliced into his unprotected neck, slid through and embedded itself in the door, forcibly skewering him to it.

Georgia and Stan watched in horror as Barry began performing a ghastly death act.

With his last few heart beats, pumping bright crimson blood from the wound, his arms bobbed up in front of him and his fingers started to wiggle and jerk as if he was playing an imaginary piano.

The inspector heard the scream and increased his pace.

Something bad was happening up there. His intuition had been right.

It was more of a howl than a scream; a spine chilling, blood curdling howl and as it erupted from her it caused Stan to pull out of his shock and run to his friend in a vain attempt to save him. He grabbed the protruding handle of the knife and pulled with all of his might but it wasn't moving, it was as if a sledgehammer had driven it home and all the while Barry's nerves were conducting him, his dancing fingers scrawling over Stan's chest and face like wriggling spiders smearing the blood.

And then he mustered all of his strength and with one final effort, powerfully pulled down, finally freeing the knife along with his friend and as Barry slumped off the door, thudding onto the floor, Stan lurched backwards against the wall, the knife in his hands, covered in the blood of his only friend.

Angelo looked impassively on, his anger diminishing like the pulse of his victim and then his mother was with him, grabbing at him and he recoiled as if her touch were lava hot but she persisted, holding his wrists tightly.

"You've got to run, Angelo, for God's sake the coppers are here!" and she pulled him into the passage leading to the back door.

"I need my knife," he groaned, trying to free himself.

"For fuck's sake, son," attempting to keep pushing, "that thing is the last thing you need, believe me!"

Then Stan abruptly uprooted himself and began walking.

"Don't worry about all of that," he said as if in a trance, his calm voice stopping them in his tracks.

He was stood right by them now, the knife still in his hand.

"If anyone asks I'll just tell them I did it, it'll save a lot of trouble if I do," and he began to grin, an open and innocent grin and they stopped struggling with each other, trying to make sense of what he was saying and she looked him up and down, observed the knife and the blood and a grin began to appear on her face too.

"I don't know why you're here or what this is all about," she began, totally bemused, looking at Stan but speaking to her son, "but the way I see it, I'd say this is your lucky day." She turned and pushed him fiercely again.

"Now for fuck's sake go!" and this time he capitulated and barged through the rear door and out into the mist and the rain.

There was no time for any more words as seconds later, the inspector and his men were barging in through the front. Barry's body began to slide and was squashed against the wall as the burly officers forced open the door and squeezed their way in, then they parted as their boss eased past, his eyes darting around the room trying to make sense of it all.

Georgia was panting from her exertions but turned her gasps into sobs in an attempt at distress and Stan simply stood there smiling, knife in hand and bloodied, looking guilty as the sin he hadn't committed. The inspector coolly took out his handkerchief which he unfurled and placed over his open hand, offering it to Stan.

"Put the knife in here, Mr Heart," his voice calm and controlled although his breathing was laboured from the running and Stan dropped the blade gently onto the cloth and he passed it back to the constable. The action lessened the tension and they all visibly relaxed.

He asked the officer nearest the body to check for signs of life and he bent down and placed his fingers on various pulse points, his shrug confirming the worst.

"I don't mind which one of you wants to start," he said, his eyes flicking between the two of them, "but I want to know exactly what has happened here today and I want to know now."

Georgia's sobs were decreasing and she inhaled loudly as if to speak but it was Stan who responded first, his words jejune and babyish.

"It's an open and shut case," he said copying the phrase of the doctor when William Wilson died, "he told me I couldn't have the pigs so I killed him," his smile now wide and bright.

Inspector Burnes eyed him seriously, not sure if the little man was going or had already gone, mad.

"I can remember many years ago, Mr Heart, in a hospital a long way away from here," he said softly, "you admitting to a murder that everyone at the time thought it impossible for you to have committed, can you recollect that?"

Stan frowned, his mind trying to revive the memory but the years of electricity had created an impenetrable barrier.

"No, but I expect it was me," he replied, head down, his tone now ever more childlike.

"And what about Charlie, Mr Heart, was his death your fault?"

"Charlie's death?" but his urge to confess overcame even this most terrible bolt from the blue and he clung on to his composure.

"Yep, that was me too."

Inspector Burnes was starting to think the situation wasn't quite ringing true, his sideways glance at the constable confirming it, but Georgia, although reeling from the events and mystified by the conversation being had, was steered by an overwhelming desire to protect her son and she knew she had to intervene.

"Were there any witnesses back then?" she said abruptly and all eyes turned to her.

"And you are?" the inspector asked.

"My name is Georgia Goodwin, I'm a neighbour, I only came over …" and all of a sudden she stopped and began to cry, a performance that came easily to her, "I only came over to see how they were, if I could be of any help," and she raised her hands to her cheeks and rolled her head back and forth; then breathing out deliberately, appeared to control herself.

"Were there any witnesses that time at the hospital?" she asked again, her black mascara smudging her face.

"I don't believe so," he answered.

"Well there is today," she said deceitfully and stepped back a pace, pointing at Stan, "there is today," she repeated, more loudly and maliciously, "because I have just witnessed that man," her voice now trembling, "that monster, stab poor Barry to death and I can't believe what

I've just seen," and she continued stumbling backwards until the chair was reached which she dramatically collapsed upon.

Two of the officers rushed forward and Stan put up no resistance as they grabbed his arms; just letting it all happen as his mind reversed into a shell, a place where no one could find him or hurt him. Inspector Burnes instructed them to fit handcuffs and get him into the car, then knelt by Georgia and explained compassionately that she would also be required to accompany them but he would make it as painless as possible.

As he carefully helped her up the bellow, heavy and booming, made his stomach turn over.

Jug had appeared, his bulk filling the doorway, his face contorted and full of dismay.

"Where you taking Stan?" he roared. "Stan's a good man, you can't …" and then he saw the lifeless body of Barry, the swamp of congealing blood and the realisation of what must have happened replaced the dismay with astonishment.

"Calm down, sir," the constable said forcefully, gripping his arm and forcing him outside, "there's been a tragedy, a murder, and the less people that go in there the better," and Jug, stunned and open mouthed, shook his head incredulously.

Those remaining left the room; none of them seeing Georgia deftly lift the sale contract and slip it into her bag. She knew she'd be home in a couple of hours and after a further couple of hours of practice, she also knew she would be able to adroitly copy it onto her own.

She sat in the rear seat made vacant by the officer who was now guarding the scene awaiting forensics, another policeman separating her from Stan with the inspector and constable up front.

Although the cuddly nutcase was a long way in time and space from that apartment and the blitz, his mind was right back there and as they sped away he began to melodiously hum an, as yet, unwritten song, with the policeman looking on disgustedly as his bloodied left thumb found its way into his mouth and right hand tightened firmly around his crotch.

CHAPTER 37

The wailing of the sirens finally faded in the distance and the officer on guard looked through the apple arch at Jug who was sat in the tractor, motionless, a large head cradled in large hands; and then he felt his heart rate rise and breathing increase as the giant of a man gracefully dismounted and, with long purposeful strides, began to walk toward him. He'd been charged with protecting the scene of the crime, an order he intended to obey and as Jug approached he steadied himself, his hand unobtrusively dropping to his truncheon.

"Can I go round and feed the pigs? I know Barry's dead and everything," and Jug gulped as if to swallow his sadness, "but they still need checking and feeding, none of this is their fault."

The officer, relieved, looked up at the sorrow in the big man's face and nodded sympathetically.

"Of course," he said with kindness in his voice, "I'd help you but I can't leave …"

"I know," Jug butted in. "It's good of you to offer but I'll be okay on my own," and he trudged back up the path and effortlessly threw a bag of feed over his shoulder.

The light was beginning to fade and the mist was increasing and as Jug walked around the side of the farmhouse, treading carefully on the slippery surface, he ducked under a low branch jutting out from the enormous trunk of the ash tree; but not low enough and the bag snagged and became weightless as it disgorged its contents onto the wet ground. He squeezed his eyes shut as Stan had done just an hour before, making the blackness hide his mistake and then he felt his energy drain, like fingers had loosened on the neck of a balloon and he dropped to his knees, his weight pushing them deep into the sodden ground. The shock of it all surged through him like the electricity that had once enfeebled Stan and as his left leg gave way he tumbled and turned as though in slow motion, his back coming to rest on the thousand, soggy feed pellets. Jug straightened his arms and widened his legs and lay there spread-eagled, the rain like pins on his skin.

He stayed like that for some minutes, trying to understand why Stan would have done it, allowing himself to become drenched and then something odd occurred to him.

Piglets were lively and loud and he hadn't heard a sound since the rip of the bag. With difficulty, he slowly got to his feet, the effects of the previous night's celebrations still with him.

The small streams of blood flowing under the door was the first indication of the horror, the pools of the stuff behind the door the confirmation.

They lay there, stacked in a heap, some missing legs others without heads, and all of them dead. The second knife having done its job.

He turned away from the sight.

"Oh Stan, why this? Why did you have to do this as well!"

Jug forced himself to look again and he moved closer to the pile and began pulling each piglet away in the forlorn hope there may be a survivor.

He carefully lay them down, childishly not wanting to hurt them anymore when, almost at the bottom, he removed what he thought to be the last two remaining and Gruntlet came into sight, motionless but definitely breathing.

To his amazement, of all the strong and well grown, healthy pigs, the runt, the smallest and weakest of the litter had been the only one to survive.

With great care he picked the little thing up and carried it to the water trough, Gruntlet being so traumatised that even his immersion in the cold water failed to produce any movement.

Jug washed him clean and dried the piglet in his thick jumper, placing him in the deep pocket of his great coat for warmth.

Walking out of the mansion with a bleakness in his soul he again paused under the ash and turned his head up to the heavens, his eyes tightly shut against the rain.

But had they not been, had they been open and gaping and wide he might have noticed through the branches two deformed eyes peering down, the eyes of a human runt that could barely be seen through the thin slits on its distorted face, a phiz that had been cruelly misshapen, like its mind, when it was heartlessly passed The Baton.

THE END

Printed in Great Britain
by Amazon